BISON
BOOKS

BEYOND ARMAGEDDON

TOMORROW!

by

PHILIP WYLIE

University of Nebraska Press
Lincoln and London

Library of Congress Cataloging-in-Publication Data
Wylie, Philip, 1902–1971.
Tomorrow! / Philip Wylie.
p. cm. — (Beyond Armageddon)
ISBN 978-0-8032-2662-3 (pbk.: alk. paper)
1. Middle West—Fiction. I. Title.
PS3545.Y46T66 2009
813'.52—dc22
2009026791

Dedicated
to the gallant men and women
of the Federal Civil Defense Administration
and to those other true patriots,
the volunteers,
who are doing their best
to save the sum of things

TOMORROW!

X-Day Minus Ninety

1

When the pioneers came across the plains to the place where the Little Bird River flowed into the Abanakas, they halted. The tributary was clear and potable. In the muddy main stream, an island served them as a moated campground. It was called Swan Island owing to a shape which, it later proved, changed radically with the floods. They renamed the Abanakas the Green Prairie. The Little Bird, as a town crept south along its banks, became Slossen's Run—thanks to a trapper who, in the early part of the nineteenth century, set his lines in the headwaters of that creek.

The Abanakas, or Green Prairie, flowed generally east through a flat and fertile land. But below Swan Island it made a wide turn toward the south and sank between low sandstone bluffs. The water deepened there and a shingle beach served for a towpath. Above the bluffs, the river shallowed; they marked the most westerly local point to which barges could be drawn by mules in the seasons of deep water. This conjunction of navigability, good fresh water, game-filled woods and fertile prairie made an inevitable site for habitation.

Fort Abanakas, the first settlement, was often attacked by hard-riding Sioux. The Indian Trading Post was next —on the north bank, since it had a more gradual slope which made for easier unloading of the towboats. Farmers followed the trappers, and merchants came to deal with both. Long before a shot was fired at Fort Sumter, two sizable towns had come into being on the opposite banks. Their certain rivalry was soon redoubled. For when the territory was carved into states, the Green Prairie River became a boundary over a considerable stretch. Thus "Green Prairie," the southern town, and "River City" on the north bank, were loyal to different states though connected even then by bridges a few hundred feet long. The loyalty, and rivalry, grew after Sumter: River City's state was free, Green Prairie's, slave.

After the Civil War, lead and zinc were discovered beneath the prairie sod. In distant hills, at the century's turn, a dam heaped up the river's energy. Hydroelectric plants followed. Oil was found in Bugle County and good coking coal in Tead. Smoke covered the prairies from then on. And the immigrants arrived.

They unpacked their carpetbags. They sold skills learned in the mills and mines of Europe. They created lichenlike slums, went to school, entered politics, became the gangsters of the twenties and some, the heroes of the Second World War.

By then the combined population of River City and Green Prairie approached a million. Where the sullen, sweating mules had brought the barges to rest, where Sioux arrows had fired cottonwood logs in the fort, skyscrapers stood.

By then, there were families who could look back to four or five generations of unbroken residence in the region. Some of these "natives" were rich and powerful; some were poor; but most were ordinary people—prospering modestly, loving freedom, hating interference, intelligent by the lights of their society, fair citizens and superb neighbors. The Conner family in Green Prairie was such.

Their white frame house had been built in 1910, set back in a big lawn on Walnut Street in the "residential south section," then a long trolley ride from the busy downtown district. The houses around were like the Conner house in atmosphere even though some were frame, some brick and some stucco. The people, too, were like the Conners: indistinguishable from millions in the nation, at first glance—yet, like the millions, on any second look more individualist than most other people of the earth. At the end of the Second War, during the great expansion, the Conners had thrived. But like all their fellow citizens, and more keenly than many, they shared the doubts and anxieties of the new age.

Its very voice influenced their lives, even their domestic lives, as the years chased each other swiftly, rewardingly, after the century's mid-point. Green Prairie and River City were halves of a happy, urban world, separated by a river and a political boundary but united by bridges both actual and spiritual. Typically American, content, constructive, the Conners, too, were happy. And yet. . . .

The sound came through the open windows of the dining room. Each of the five members of the Conner family was differently affected. Henry, the father, stopped all movement to listen. The gravy spoon, which he had been about to plunge into his mashed potatoes, dripped midway between the bowl and his plate. His wife, Beth, looked out through the screened windows, frowning, as if she wished she had never heard a siren in her life.

Nora, who was eleven, exclaimed, *"Brother!* You can hear it *this* time, all right, all right!"

Ted Conner pushed back his chair, stood, started to go, and snatched a fresh roll, already buttered and spread with homemade jam, before his feet took the stairs with the noisy incoherence of a male high school student in a hurry.

Charles, the older son, smiled faintly. This was the first evening of his leave and the first time he'd worn home the proud silver bar of a first lieutenant. The dinner—especially the roast beef which had filled the kitchen with a hunger-begetting aroma all afternoon—was a celebration for him. Now the sound surging over the city would interfere with that homely ceremony. Charles's smile expressed his regret. "Can I help?" he asked his father, who had risen.

"Guess not. This is a civilian party!" Henry Conner took the stairs in the wake of his younger son, but more deliberately.

"It's a shame it had to be this evening," Mrs. Conner said. "Still, Nora and you and I can at least eat."

"Aren't you in it?" Charles asked.

"I'm in the First Aid Group, yes. But we don't have to answer this call."

Nora, always ready to amplify any subject, her mobile mouth apparently unembarrassed by potatoes, said informatively, "This is just for air-raid-warden practice, and the rescue teams, and cops and firemen, and like that."

"Nora! Don't talk with your mouth full. And don't say, 'and like that!' It's bad grammar."

Charles Conner, Lieutenant Conner, laughed a little.

It was good to be home, good to listen to the gentle reprimands that spelled home and were nothing like military correction. After dinner he would get out of uniform, enjoy the comfort of slacks and a sports coat. He would go next door and see if Lenore Bailey would like to take in a movie.

The siren gathered strength and volume. Its initial growl and its first crescendo had seemed far away; soon its slow rise and fall became pervasive and penetrating; when it slurred into each high warble, the human head was invaded not just by noise, but by what seemed a tangible substance. Nora reflected the fact. "This new one," she yelled above it, "sure is a lulu!"

"They must have hung it on a tree in our back yard," Charles replied loudly.

His mother shook her head. "It's on the new TV tower, out on Sunset Parkway by the reservoir."

Henry Conner came down the stairs two at a time. "Where the hell are my car keys, Beth?"

"Right on your dresser."

"I *looked* there——!"

"Behind Charles's photograph."

"Oh!" He bounded up the stairs, hurried back, opened the front door and yelled from the porch, "Ted, that moron, has left his jalopy in the drive! How many times do I have to . . . ?"

"I'll move it." Charles pushed back his chair to go to the third floor, where his brother would be tuning in his ham radio as his part in the drill.

Beth stopped him. "Don't bother. Your dad's forgotten he's sector warden, now. Ed McWade's supposed to drive him."

She hurried out on the porch and repeated the fact to her husband.

"Just as well Ed is coming," Mr. Conner said. "That monstrosity probably wouldn't start."

The automobile—without fenders, with a homemade engine hood—did not look operable. It had been repaired with wire and sticks and painted by hand in half a dozen different colors. These hues were superscribed with initials, emblems, symbols, slogans and wisecracks, so that it resembled a tourist attraction rather than a vehicle.

"Here comes Ed," Mr. Conner cried, and raced down his driveway, waving. The effort caused his crimson arm band, on which the word "Warden" was stenciled in white, to slide off his unused arm. When he bent to retrieve it, his World War I helmet clattered on the sidewalk. At the same time, Mrs. Conner called, "You forgot your whistle!" and ran indoors to get it. The lieutenant hastened down the walk to help his father reassemble his gear.

At the dinner table, alone in the presence of a feast, Nora made a hasty survey and passed herself the jam. She piled an incredible amount on half a slice of bread, tossed her two braids clear for action, and contrived to crowd the mass into her mouth. She was still masticating when her mother and older brother, having dispatched the paterfamilias, returned to the table.

"Everything's cold," Mrs. Conner said ruefully.

"Far from it," her son answered. "Best meal I've looked at in six months." He sliced a square of thick and juicy beef. "Best I've *ever* tasted!"

Her rewarded look was warm, but it vanished as she noticed the diminished aspect of the jelly dish. "*Nora . . . !*"

In the car as he sped down Walnut Street beside Ed, Henry Conner was thinking about the wild-strawberry jam and the roast beef, too. His companion had identical sentiments: "Caught me," he said, as he slowed to cross Lakeview Road, "just as we were sitting down to dinner."

"Me, too. Guess they figured everybody would be doing the same. Ought to be a good turnout, on account of it."

Ed slammed on the brakes in time to avoid the chemical engine of Hook and Ladder Company Number 17. It pounded across the intersection, its lights on in spite of the fact that the sun still shone, its clanging bell drowned by a whoop of the siren. "Something *else* to think about," Henry yelled, letting his nerves down easy. "When those sirens are going, you can't hear car horns or even fire-truck bells!"

Ed wiped a little diamond dust of sweat from his forehead. "Could have been closer, Hank."

"Oh, sure."

The sedan turned into South Hobson Street and slowed. The school was only four blocks distant and converging Civil Defense cars were piling up, even though volunteer "police" were blowing whistles urgently and urgently waving their arms, and even though Hobson Street was "one way" during this surprise drill. They could see, now, hundreds of cars parked and being parked in the playgrounds of the South High School. They could see the "wrecked" corner of the gymnasium where, later in the evening, the fire fighters and rescue squads would rehearse under conditions of simulated disaster, including real flames and chemical smoke. The very numbers of the congregating people stimulated them. That stimulus, added to a certain civic pride and the comparative verisimilitude of the occasion, helped Hank Conner and Ed McWade to forget they were middle-aged businessmen, middle-class householders, who for weary years had periodically and stubbornly pretended that their city in the middle of America was the target of an enemy air raid.

Before Ed parked the car, Henry leaped out and went to his post to assemble his block wardens. One of them, Jim Ellis, proprietor of the Maple Street Pharmacy, was incensed. "You know what, Hank? This is my druggist's night off. I had to shut down the prescription department since I can't be there to roll pills myself! Probably cost me twenty, twenty-five bucks. Maybe customers, even. People don't like to come in a drugstore and not get a prescription filled on the dot. Next time we have one of these fool rehearsals——"

"You shouldn't be here, anyway, Jim. How come?"

"I said that. I phoned headquarters when the letter about this new drill came. They told me whenever the sirens went to report here at the school——"

"Well, I'll be responsible for that. You get your car and go back to the pharmacy. All the pharmacists in *my* area, by God, are going to stay in the stores. What zigzag chump ordered you here? In a *real* raid you'd be indispensable at the store."

"That makes *sense!*"

Hank nodded and his easy voice rose to a pitch of command: "Sykes! Evans! Maretti! Get Jim's car cleared and see him around to Baker Avenue! Hold everything up till he's out of the parking yard!"

A woman wearing a warden's arm band rushed up from a knot of people gathered around a placard that said, "Station Forty-two." She cried anxiously, "Mr. Collins! I left rolls in the oven!"

Henry drew a breath, expelled it. "How often do we have to go through the routine, Mrs. Dace? You're supposed to check all those things before you jump in a car and start for your post. You'll have to get a phone priority slip and tell your neighbors to turn off the gas——"

"It's a coal range."

"All *right!* To turn down the drafts and haul out the pans." Hank began searching the school grounds for some-body connected with telephone priorities. He wondered with a kind of good-humored annoyance how in hell the citizens of Green Prairie would learn to save lives when they couldn't remember to salvage biscuits.

In that segment of the attic which had long ago been converted into "the boys' room," Ted Conner worked fever-ishly amidst a junklike jumble of wires, dimly glowing tubes, switches, dials, condensers, transformers and other parapher-nalia with which gifted young men—specialists at the age of sixteen or so—are able to communicate with one another, often over distances of hundreds of miles. Ted Conner was a member in good standing of the American Radio Ama-teurs' Society. He was also a volunteer member of Civil Defense, Communications Division.

To Ted, more than to any other person in the family (and partly because his function was the most realistic), the rise and fall of the siren spelled excitement. It was his instant duty to rush to his post, which meant his radio set. It was his assignment to get the set going and tune in headquarters. It was his additional assignment, every five minutes on the second, to listen for thirty seconds to his opposite number in Green Prairie's "Sister City," directly across the river.

Ted was going to be big like his grandfather Oakley, a blacksmith. He had his mother's light-brown hair—as did Nora—and his father's clear, blue eyes, as also did his sis-

ter. Only Chuck had the Oakley brown eyes; but Chuck
hadn't inherited the size, the big bones and the stature;
Chuck was slender. Ted sat now with one leg hooked over
the arm of a reconstructed swivel chair, his blue eyes shining, his usually clumsy hands turning the radio dials with
delicacy. He was oblivious to everything in his environment: the pennants and banners on the wall; the stolen
signs that said, "Danger," and "Do Not Disturb," and
"Men"; the battered dresser and its slightly spotted mirror
framed in snapshots—snapshots of girls in bathing suits and
girls with ukuleles and a burning B-29.

He did not see any of it. Not the rafters over his head.
Not the end-of-summer leaves on the treetops outside the
window, where a setting sun cast ruddy light. Not the moraine of mixed garments which lay, contrary to familial
orders, on his bed—not made up, contrary to the same rules.
To Ted Conner, who was sixteen, a hideous danger now
menaced Green Prairie and its sister metropolis, River City.
To Ted, the theoretical enemy bombers were near. To him,
brave men like his brother Chuck (though Chuck, actually,
was a Ground Force officer) were even now climbing from
near-by Hink Field into the stratosphere to engage atom-
bomb-bearing planes that winged toward Green Prairie.

This stage setting was necessary to accompany the rest
of the dream he had, every time there was a drill:

One enemy bomber was getting through. Man after man
was trying for it and missing. Its bomb-bay doors were
opening. The horrendous missile was falling. There was an
earth-shaking explosion. Half of Green Prairie and even
more of River City were blotted out. Now, Ted Conner
was alone—alone at his post in the attic. His family had
been evacuated. The place was a shambles and on fire. But
there he sat, ice calm, sending and giving messages which

were saving uncounted lives—to the last. They would put up a monument for him later—when they found his high school class ring, miraculously unmelted in the ashes of the Conner home.

His earphones spoke. "Headquarters. Condition Red! Condition Red! Stand by, all stations."

Ted felt gooseflesh cascade down his back.

He stood by.

Headquarters had been saying that off and on for twenty minutes. And not much else.

Downstairs, Nora asked if she could have another piece of pumpkin pie and whipped cream. Mrs. Conner said, "Absolutely not."

"Then I'll go out and play till it's dark."

"You'll do your homework, that's what you'll do! It'll be dark in a quarter of an hour, anyhow."

"*Mother!* It's *ridiculous* to ask anybody to study during an *air raid*."

"It is ridiculous," her mother replied, "to think you can use a drill for an alibi. You go in the living room, Nora, and do your arithmetic."

"I hate it!"

"Exactly. So—the sooner you do it . . ."

Chuck grinned reminiscently and excused himself. He went through the kitchen to the back door. Queenie, the Conner tomcat, was meowing to be admitted. The lieutenant let him in, marveling briefly over the mistake in gender which had led to the original name and his young sister's defense, which had permitted the misnomer to stick. "A cat," Nora had said long ago, "can look at a queen. So, he'll *stay* Queenie, even if he has got a man sex."

He had stayed Queenie for five years though, Chuck thought fleetingly, and after a glance, the scars on the aging tom suggested he had overcompensated for what he must have considered a libel.

Dusk was gathering in the yard. On the high clouds there remained signs of where the sun had gone—purplish shadows, glints of orange. But the Olds was already hidden in the darkness of the open garage and the soldier could smell rather than see that his brother had recently mowed the lawn. He could see, however, that Ted hadn't trimmed the grass along the privet hedge which separated the Conners' yard from the Baileys'. Chuck reflected that in his boyhood he had been a precise trimmer and clipper. But then, he'd always wanted to be what he would be now, were it not for his uniform: an architect. And Ted was different: he wanted to be an inventor—at least right now. Inventors were probably not much interested in even lawns, while architects definitely were.

Chuck stood in the drive and looked uncertainly at the Bailey house. Time was when his family's house and the residence next door had been quite similar—ordinary American homes—two-story-and-attic frame houses, white, with front porches and back porches, clapboard sides, scrollwork around the eaves, and big lawns. Both had been planted with spirea and forsythia, with tulips for spring, random crocuses, and, for fall, dahlias. Both had had vegetable gardens in the back and both had long ago lost barns and acquired garages.

But the Baileys had "modernized" their place in the years just after World War II. The sprangly shrubbery had been replaced by neat evergreens. The front porch had been carted away and the front façade remade with imitation adobe bricks and a picture window instead of the old comfortable curved bay. The vegetable garden had vanished

entirely and in its place were a summerhouse and a barbecue pit where, wearing a chef's hat and an apron with
jokes printed on it, Beau Bailey, Lenore's father, sometimes
ruined good beefsteak while his guests drank martinis in
the gloaming.

As a man with a degree in architecture (who had gone
into uniform from the ROTC before he had professionally
designed so much as a woodshed), Chuck now skirted the
Bailey property, critically surveying the *moderne* effect and
looking for any recent changes. The house didn't seem right
any more, he thought. Its proportions were wrong. There
was nothing in Green Prairie to warrant the use of imitation adobe either. It might be "modernistic," but it was
suitable for the desert, not for a region where winter came
in November and went away in May. All in all, Howard
Bailey (who was called "Beau" even by the president of
the bank where he worked as cashier) had spent a lot of
money for his remodeling job, and failed to fool anybody.
Such was Chuck's professional opinion—and his human opinion was similar. Putting on "side" characterized not only Beau,
but his wife.

Lenore was different.

At least, Chuck hoped she was different, still.

For Chuck could hardly recall a day in his life when he
had not been in love with the Baileys' only child. Propinquity might have explained that: there was no day when
Chuck had not lived next door to Lenore. But propinquity
was not needed to explain the attachment.

Lenore long ago had won a "Prettiest Grade School Girl"
contest that had included River City as well as Green
Prairie. At eighteen she had been May Princess at the
South High School, which meant she was the most attractive

girl in her senior class. And she had been voted the "Most Beautiful Coed" when she had graduated from State University.

Beauty, then, could have explained Chuck's fealty—the simple fact that he had grown up next door to a girl who became one of the loveliest women in the city. But the matter of Lenore's desirability involved more than the impelling forces set going by loveliness. She happened to be bright, and in addition she had been sweet and gracious, democratic and sincere.

Now, Chuck wasn't so sure. Where Lenore was concerned, he'd had no lasting assurance anyhow.

They had always been "friends." As "friends" they had enjoyed an intimacy of a particular sort. Chuck was sure, for example, that he was the first boy who had ever kissed Lenore; but it was not very impressive assurance. He had kissed her when they were both six years old. In fact, he had then carried a mixture of ardor and curiosity, which she had shared, considerably beyond mere kissing. The Baileys and the Conners were one day appalled to discover that their two six-year-olds were not merely kissing but that—in the elderberry thicket which had then existed in a then-vacant lot behind the Bailey premises—they were both stark naked, their small shoes, socks, overalls and underwear commingled in an untidy heap. Such findings perennially stun nearly all parents, and Lenore and Chuck had suffered the shocked, conventional punishments. But though Chuck recalled the episode with warmth and savor, his close amity with Lenore at six did little to bolster his confidence at twenty-four.

He hadn't written her that he was coming home for his thirty days because, until the last moment at the base in Texas, he hadn't been sure of the date on which his leave would begin. He'd reached the house, by cab from the air-port, just in time for dinner. He had wanted then to phone Lenore of his arrival. But he had felt it would slight his family, his mother especially, if he immediately sought out someone else. He had hoped all during the meal (which the siren had spoiled as a family reunion anyhow) that Lenore might step across for some reason or another and find him there. Maybe the Bailey phone would be out of order—or they'd need to borrow coffee—or something. He had known the hope was preposterous. He had also re-flected during the meal (while he told his mother that life in the Air Force "wasn't bad at all" and while he had watched with incredulity the amount of food Nora con-sumed) that in years past he had run over to the Bailey house freely, casually, while now he felt a definite con-straint.

He still felt it as he walked along on the mowed grass between his driveway and the privet hedge, examining the Bailey house. There was a Buick parked at the curb—"a Buick," his father often said, "trying to look like a Cadil-lac"—and a Ford in the back yard. That meant all three Baileys were probably at home: Beau, Netta and Lenore. But it didn't mean Lenore had no date that evening or that Chuck, at twenty-four, could simply enter without even knocking as he'd done when he and Lenore had studied algebra together.

He had about decided to go back in the house and phone formally when a door opened and somebody came out.

At first he couldn't tell who the person was.

Not Mrs. Bailey: too tall. But it wasn't Beau: no sign of his expanded waistline. It was somebody, he could see, in a kind of plastic jumper, yellow, with a hood that covered the head. The person was carrying a box with wires attached to it and a silvery gadget dangling from the wires. This figure turned toward the open door and called in a husky, pleasant voice, "Don't wait up for me. I've got a date—after."

It was Lenore's voice. Chuck, completely bewildered, shouted, "Hey!"

The box with its attached gadgetry was set on the lawn. The voice now floated toward him. *"Chuck!* When did you get back?" Lenore ran toward him.

Had Charles Conner been more experienced in the behavior of women, had he even been of that temperament which is given to shrewd scrutiny of others, he would have noticed the impulsiveness with which the girl started toward him. It was emphasized by the fact that she remembered the outlandishness of her costume only later, when she had skirted a neat bed of tea roses, come up to him, held out both her hands and exclaimed, "What a wonderful surprise! Why didn't you let me know?"

He was not such a person. He was a gentle and dreaming kind of young man, somewhat introverted, modest, in his opinion far from handsome. His head was long and narrow, his features somewhat ascetic; his hair had retreated a little way: he would soon be half-bald like his father; meantime, the effect was to make his forehead seem extraordinarily high. Lenore's good looks invariably brought out his diffidence.

In addition, her regalia (astounding for any woman and all but unthinkable for Lenore) put him off. She was dressed as if she were going to crawl under the Buick and fix it—a chore of which she was capable; but it was not for that, he knew. He knew it if for no other reason than that neither her mother, whose social ambitions were limitless, nor her father, who had matching financial desires, would let their daughter play mechanic in the street.

It was only when they touched hands there in the gathering twilight, with a subconscious pulling—when they felt warmth and strength each in the other—that Chuck associated the girl's costume and recent events. "Ye gods!" he cried, letting go of her, "a *Geigerman!*"

She nodded serenely, a little impishly. "Isn't it becoming?" She pirouetted like a model. "Yellow," she went on, "is the fall color. The material is simply amazing. Not only weatherproof and mothproof, but fire-resistant too. Absolutely dustproof. No common chemicals can damage it. The hood"—she pulled it farther over her face and drew down a green, transparent visor which sealed her from view—"provides adequate protection from the elements, *all* the elements, including their radioactive isotopes!" She broke off, pulled down the hood, disclosed blue eyes, tumbling dark hair, raised, crimson lips. "Oh, *Chuck!* I'm *so* glad to see you! Kiss me."

He tried to kiss her cheek and she made that impossible. She held the kiss, besides, for a long moment and when she settled on her heels she whispered, "Welcome home."

He dissembled his feelings, pointed. "How come?"

"This?" she looked down at the radiation safety garment. "Spite."

"Spite?"

"I'll explain. I've got to take off in a sec—South High. Want to drive me there?"

" 'Whither . . .' and so forth," he answered.

She stared at him, shook her head as if she couldn't quite believe him real. "Come on, then. We'll take my Ford."

"Just a mo!" Chuck reverted to a bygone period. He ran back toward the open kitchen window and shouted, "Hey, Mom!"

Beth Conner's voice floated back from above the dishpan. "Yes, Charles? No need to yell so."

"I'm going to run Lenore down to the school."

"All right." Mrs. Conner wiped a copper-bottomed pan and hung it up with her set, one of her many small sources of pride and joy. It was just like Charles, though now a man grown, to let her know where he was going. Teddy had reached an age when he preferred never to say, or else forgot. And Nora had never known a time, never would know one, probably, when she considered her private destinations any affair of her mother.

Chuck carried the Geiger counter to the car, climbed in, and backed down the driveway. He switched on the headlights and started slowly along Walnut Street. The girl beside him began to turn the knobs on the radiation counter. "Let's see if you're radioactive," she said. She held up the wandlike detector and frowned down at the dials. "Nope. Just overheated."

"Warm day—for September."

"Since *when* wasn't September warm?"

"How are things?" he asked.

"Just the same." She shrugged one shoulder somewhere under the coverall. "But absolutely, painfully the same. Possibly a shade worse. Dad seems to be drinking a little too much, a little too often, if you know what I mean. And Mother keeps crowding me a little harder all the time."

"Why don't you go away?"

"Away like where?" she asked. "Didn't we kick that around till it got lost, the last time you were home on leave?"

"I kept thinking about it—at the base."

"I didn't need to. The family didn't let me study what I wanted. Couldn't afford graduate courses. You know that. They hate the very thought that their darling daughter has a knack for science instead of a knack for rich men. So why should I go away, to New York even, and work at something I'd detest, myself? Being a secretary. Or a model. Phooie!"

"Anyhow," he said, not happily, "you'll make a damned good Geigerman."

She ignored the hurt tone. "Won't I? And doesn't it burn mother to the core!"

"Does it?" He could understand her relish. Lenore's parents frightened him, in a sense: they were able to influence Lenore.

"About six weeks ago the Civil Defense people called at our house," she began. "They gave Mother and Dad a long spiel about how this state is high up on the national list in preparedness and how everybody in Greek Prairie who could, ought to be in the organization. You can imagine the fascination Mom and Dad had for *that!* The defense people didn't stay long; they could see that the senior Baileys were a dry hole as far as public spirit and atomic war are concerned. But they left some pamphlets. And I got reading them one evening when Mother was chewing me out for refusing to go to some beastly Junior League thing, and I saw in the pamphlet that Green Prairie badly needed people who could handle electronic equipment. So I phoned up to see if they'd take women. Well, there *is* one other woman Geigerman, a schoolteacher, a Mrs. Phollen. So I signed for it."

"*Great.* And now instead of going to beastly Junior League parties, you're out playing air raid——"

"To the infinite annoyance of my parents! And they really can't say anything about it. When they try to, I just hang my pretty head and tell them the Baileys have to do something . . ." She broke off with an abrupt mood change familiar to him. "Oh, all right, Chuck. You always do see through me. I got into this absurd Civil Defense thing on one of my impulses, and now I'm plenty sore because it takes a night a week. We've been briefed and briefed and briefed; some of the people have been at it for years—and the whole business is simply fantastic anyhow! Tell me about life in the army."

He relaxed a little. "That's even duller. *You* know. I'm not in the glamour department of the Air Force. I'd be, even in the highly unlikely event of a war, at some base probably, far from peril—attached to a Colonel who was attached to a good dugout—keeping track of the lubrication stock for B-47's."

She said, "You do think there's no chance of a war, don't you?"

"Are you asking me as a person? Or as a military man? Because, as the latter, I'm supposed to say we can't afford to drop Uncle Sam's big guard."

"As *you*, Chuck."

"I think the Reds want peace—need it—and mean to have it. They've conceded about everything lately, except letting the free world come in and inspect them. But I'd trust sharks quicker. I'm kind of glad you're in something."

He swung into South Hobson Street. It was solid with cars. From time to time they moved up a few inches. In the distance, the playgrounds of South High, floodlighted now, were swarming with people, most of whom wore brassards and helmets. Whistles blew. Teams of various sorts formed and marched together toward a place where flames licked around a huge heap of broken boxes, barrels, old lumber. Hoses played. The thrumming of a fire-engine pump could be heard. A searchlight snapped on somewhere and threw so much light on the simulated burning wreckage that the flames became invisible and only the smoke showed.

Chuck fixed an eye, half-humorous, half-melancholy, on the scene. It was just a little like basic training, when you crawled along under live bullets from real machine guns and when you ran through actual poison gas, wearing a mask. But, he thought, it was nothing whatever like a real city after the detonation of a real bomb—even a high-explosive bomb. "Terrific," he said.

Lenore raised her eyebrows. "Ridiculous, too?"

"Just what do you do?"

"We form," she answered, "exactly one hour after the siren. I'm late, but everybody in my section will be because they can't get their counters working right, or can't find where they put them, or took them over to the lab for repair. Then we approach the 'simulated radioactive site.' Tonight, they told us, they will actually have a small chunk of radiating metal somewhere. We're supposed to probe around till we find it."

He shook his head, inched the car up, braked again and watched as she opened the door. "Carry on!" he said, saluting her with mock solemnity.

She laughed a little. "I've got myself in this, and a date later, when all I want to do is go down with you to our spot by the river and neck."

"I'll be home," he answered, "any evening for the next thirty."

"And as soon as Mother knows it," she answered, grimly

picking up her instrument, "she'll raise heaven and earth to make it as nearly impossible as she can for me to see you at all."

"Still—you being twenty-four——"

"But jobless and dependent." She slammed the door. "I can't fight them to the point where I'm really kicked out."

He wanted to ask why she couldn't. He wanted to say, as he had said before, that there were young women, lovely ones, who managed to live on a lieutenant's pay. But he knew what would follow any such suggestion. It began with the reminder that, when he ceased being a lieutenant in one more year, he wouldn't have an income at all. When he was settled in civilian life, it would at first be on the minute income of a draftsman in some small architectural office in River City or Green Prairie. "Barely enough," Lenore had said once in a bitter moment, "to pay my dry-cleaning bills."

"Do I call back?" he asked.

"I'll get a ride. This monkeyshine won't break up till around eleven. Then we go to somebody's house for what the older veterans of Civil Defense call refreshments and jollification."

"Ducky."

She swore and stalked down South Hobson Street, making better time than the traffic.

He parked her car beside her house and saw, through the picture window, Beau Bailey sitting in a deep chair with the evening paper, a highball, and the top buttons of his trousers undone. Hurriedly he crossed the lawn to his own yard.

Nora and Ted were studying.

"I thought," Chuck said to his brother, "you were supposed to be at the switch. One of the minute men?"

"Oh, heck. I am! But they just repeated the same old baloney over and over and it got sickening." His imagination, vivid when the "attack" had begun, was now a faded thing.

Mrs. Conner had come from the hall with her darning basket. She smiled at her straight, thin son and sat down with a murmur of relief. "Ted's been very faithful, really, Charles. And it *is* tiresome. This is your father's fourth year. I don't see how on earth he keeps up his enthusiasm."

Ted said with scorn, "He's enthusiastic about *everything!*" His voice cracked on the last word and he repeated it with dignity: "*Everything.* Besides, afterward they have beers and they bowl. Also it's political. He's getting to be such a big shot in this part of town, the next thing you know, he'll be elected dogcatcher. Then he'll be away from home every night, looking for old ladies' lost poodles." He yacked mightily at that sally.

His mother laughed a little too.

Charles picked up the evening paper and took his father's chair under the green-shaded drop-lamp. He reflected somberly that it was odd how homesick one could get at an Air Force base in Texas and how soon the feeling evaporated when one actually got home.

Nostalgia for home had been changed by some unwanted trick to nostalgia for the past. He was thinking about Lenore, in a wordless stream of pictures.

Lenore in the days when he'd been younger than Ted, when he'd been given his own first jalopy by his father and learned to take care of it; Lenore, fifteen, half-tomboy and half-woman, more fascinated by machinery than he, adept, helping him, summer afternoons, when they sprawled together in overalls in the drive, under the car with wrenches, tightening bolts and swapping kisses that tasted faintly of engine oil, Lenore, taking the high school chemistry prize in her junior year, the physics award the year after, a pretty kid with a man's aptitude for the sciences, encouraged by the teachers, who said she'd "go a long way."

The times, the times that went back as far as he could remember, when usually at her instigation, they "collected"— birds' eggs, moths and butterflies, insects, stamps, coins, and shells from the distant ocean that neither one had ever seen, then . . .

And—Lenore when she'd won the first beauty contest— slender but mature-bodied, proud but vaguely ashamed, walking a runway at the Swan Island Amusement Park Beach, head high, breasts high, her dark, almost black hair perfectly curled down her back between tan shoulder blades, her blue eyes straight ahead, her smile too fixed— winning the cup and beginning to move away from him, not meaning or wanting to . . .

Her college years. She knew a little about the trouble with herself, by then; nobody, no intent professor or research graduate, expected to look up from some glass maze and see a dream girl working at the bench opposite; nobody could quite believe glamour and brains could live together. And her family: a mother openly outraged that she'd birthed a brainy daughter, publicly maintaining that beauty, by which she meant a body, was a woman's one useful asset and brains were the certain road to inconspicuous poverty; Beau, the indulgent father, scared of his wife, happily awed by his child—scared and awed first by his own mother—indulging Lenore when he could but never making any assertion of family values, never leading, always either following Netta or pursuing Lenore like a nervous secretary . . .

It was a dilemma all right, and Chuck was accustomed to it. He didn't exactly blame Lenore for reaching no decision, for drifting along, a lovely college girl, "back at home," awaiting events, like myriads of other girls. Maybe she was spoiled. Maybe she was really lacking in initiative like her dad. Maybe she shared, deep beneath the intelligent mind, the realism and pert but warm aliveness that appeared to be her whole self, some taint of her mother's infinite cupidity; perhaps she had caught some contagion from her mother's striving to escape an inferior background. Maybe Lenore wasn't the woman the girl had been. But maybe she was.

"I think she still loves you," Chuck's mother murmured across her sewing.

His brown eyes gleamed. "Wish I thought so."

"If you'd only . . ." Beth Conner broke off. No use telling Charles to take any "bull by the horns," any "bit in his teeth"; it wasn't his way. He went at life, even when everything he valued was involved, slowly, quietly, in his steady fashion.

"If I'd only *what?*"

She bit a thread. "Lenore hasn't changed a particle—so far," she said. "But she's getting worried about herself. Restless."

"Keep *quiet!*" Nora expostulated. "I'm *studying!*" She sank her teeth into an apple, glued her eyes to a geography. Concealed behind its brown covers was a paper-backed novel with a near-naked, huge-bosomed young woman printed on its sleek exterior and the title *Sins in Seven Streets*. A period of perhaps five minutes passed while Nora "studied,"

Ted completed a math problem and Mrs. Conner read. Charles turned the pages of the paper unseeingly, his mind steadfast on Lenore. But even he was startled when the alarm went off.

"What's *that?*" he exclaimed.

Mrs. Conner glanced swiftly at her two younger children, Nora first. Then she said drily, "What *is* it, Ted?"

"You'll see." Pride was commingled with misgiving in his tone. The room was suddenly flooded with hollow-sounding din as the TV set switched itself on. "Invention," Ted explained modestly. "So we wouldn't miss *Tootlin' Tim.*"

Tootlin' Tim was apparently on the air, for a studio audience laughed and the Conner household was filled with the lunging, sepulchral explosion which represents the combined efforts of hundreds of persons, with nothing to do and no sense of humor, to express what they regard as amusement.

The same sound from the same source—radio laughter— was surging through millions of Middle Western homes at the same instant. It is an utterly savage sound, mirthless and cruel, usually inspired by the sadisms which constitute most popular humor. It is a sound that would stun to silence the predatory night noises of the wildest jungle, a sound of madness, more frightful than screaming.

2

The same sound from the same TV program intermittently belched through the Bailey living room where Beau, the evening paper in his lap, now slept. He snored lightly and he stirred from time to time. But whenever the TV set gave forth its collective guffaw, its mechanical replica of the mechanical mirth of morons who opened their mouths and chortled every time the emcee made sucking motions with his hands (and who slammed their mouths shut when the same all-pimple showed them his palms), whenever this rock-slide cacophony struck his ears, Beau's belly jiggled in cadence, his snoring ceased and a miniature replica of the audience noise escaped him.

Indeed, in many homes and public places, where people had no idea what program was on the air or what jest occasioned the brickbat risibility of the unseen audience, the mere sound elicted that response—a chuckle, cackle or snort. For they were so slavishly conditioned to this style of diversion, so inertly used to the inanities which push-buttoned their sport, that the mere noise of other nitwits being tickled elicited the reflex. They laughed without knowing why, or even that they laughed. They laughed while drying dishes and emptying garbage and adding columns of figures and shaving and defecating and picking their noses and reading Sunday-school lessons and swallowing pork pies and custards and beer. They chortled.

Beau, among them, though asleep and patently troubled in his slumber, nonetheless snored and snickered, tittered, nickered, nasalized and woke up with a start because Netta had spoken to him—yelled, rather, since her first words had been overridden by a fresh, oblong block of guffaw, and she detested above all else to be outshouted. All Beau heard, or needed to hear, was *"Telephone!"*

He got out of his chair and buttoned the top of his fly as if the telephone were going to be able to see. Then, as if it had the additional power to do harm to him, he snatched up his highball and gulped it down protectively.

He picked up the instrument and cleared his throat. His

tone was suddenly buoyant and friendly, "Howard Bailey speaking."

"This is Jake."

If Netta had been in the hall she would have seen that Beau's face lost all its color. The whisky, too, went out of his brain. Nothing was left but a pallid and wobbling man's body, frantic eyes—but the voice intact, for Beau knew his wife would be listening though she could not look. She always listened.

He said, after a pause, "Oh, yes. How are you?"

A businessman, Netta decided upstairs. Somebody of whom Beau was slightly afraid, which didn't mean much, since he was somewhat afraid of everybody. She looked down bitterly at the bedroom floor as if she could see through it and watch her husband standing below. She would have liked to listen in on an upstairs phone but Beau, six months before, with a remarkable show of determination had had the second-floor extension removed. It was an "economy measure" he had said, but she had known his true motive: to prevent her from eavesdropping on his calls.

The voice that reached Beau was level, a little too level and, though not foreign, it used English in a fashion alien to Green Prairie—in a way which anyone familiar with American dialects would have identified as related to Chicago, to the South Side, to the period of 1920-1930. "Shallcot Rove ran fifth today, Mr. Bailey."

"Yes, I know. Of course."

"It puts the total up to five thousand, even."

Beau gave a little laugh. "As much as that, eh? I wouldn't worry. I expect the market will take a turn for the better——"

"No more 'market,' Mr. Bailey, until you pay up."

"I'll come down and have a conference in a day or two . . ." Beau could feel the sweat forming and he could hear Netta on the stairs.

"Yes," the voice of Jake said flatly. "You come down to The Block tomorrow, to the horse room, Mr. Bailey. And I think you better bring the five thousand. If not all, then at least half. And half later—but soon. And no more bets. Frankly, I told the Bun not to take bets from you last week, till you paid. I was sore at the boys for doing it against orders. He is home sick now because I was so sore. I made him sick."

Jake hung up.

So did Beau. He hung up fast and found, by listening to his wife's tread, there was time to get back through the archway into the living room (sunken two steps since the remodeling) with the appearance of casualness. The wall then hid him long enough so that he was able to whip out his handkerchief and wipe his face. He contracted his abdomen in an effort to flush up a little blood, for he could see in the mirror wall around the fireplace that he was pale. He tipped the Scotch bottle over his highball glass, with his free hand—and when Netta came through the archway he was apparently imbibing the weak dregs of a drink, prior to pouring a fresh one. Even she did not realize he had just gulped four fingers of straight liquor.

Netta was forty-eight and, though she had never had the coloring which made Lenore so peculiarly beautiful, she had once possessed the same perfect features and the same unusual, slightly slanted shape of eye. Netta was a River City girl, the daughter of a railroad brakeman who had seven other children. As a child, she had learned all there is to know about the flea-bitten ways of life. Her world had been a mean street seen through second-hand lace curtains darned not to show. She had worked her way through normal school in near-by Lummus Center and taught second grade for two years. But she had never entertained an intention of making a career of teaching. Normal school had been her only feasible way of acquiring something resembling education. She had not even wanted real erudition—general or specific—merely its sufficient facsimile.

Netta was pretty as a young woman; she was also durable and indomitable. Her personality was identical with her ambition which had been formed, delineated and defined to the utmost detail by American advertising. It is true, as advertising exponents hold, that advertising is educational and brings to millions a numberless bounty of cultivated benefits. It is also true, although the advertising exponents dislike to be reminded of the fact, that while their art creates a demand, often where demand did not thitherto exist, this same demand, in the case of multitudes, is greater than the fiscal capacity for its satisfaction or the cultural control for its employment. A struggle for additional revenue to satisfy cravings both synthetic and inordinate ensues everywhere in the land. Among persons whose morals are weak, the struggle becomes, *ipso facto,* unscrupulous.

Had she been reared in a strict, Presbyterian family, Netta's ethics would have been mighty indeed: she would have become a moral Midas. Unfortunately, her father, the brakeman, had been nominally a Methodist but actually merely an alcoholic. Her mother, though sporadically pious, by a kind of heritage from a backslid Baptist grandparent, was a woman of negligent libido with a chronic weakness for receiving and returning affection due, perhaps, to the small amount she ever received from or gave to her husband.

The result was that Netta's brothers and sisters, all younger, were in some hidden doubt concerning their true and probably several sires. Such circumstances obtain widely among the impoverished; they obtain at least quite often amongst the well-born and the well-heeled, too, though here they are differently regarded. In such latter circles, drunkenness may be known as "temperament" or "sensitivity" and loose sex manners in a mother may be designated as anything from "feminist pioneering" to what the country-club set does for fun. Poverty is deprived of such pretty tissues to put between human pretensions, and the almost universally rejected fact that people are, after all, animals.

So Netta passed through childhood and into her early teens with one determination: to have nice things someday. The method was always apparent: marriage. In the Sister Cities it was easy for Netta to meet young men with money: they came to the dance halls, the saloons, the places of even more flagrant disrepute. They even came cruising in River City, through the gaslit district, driving large cars and looking for precisely what Netta was at sixteen.

She learned much from them—though at seventeen she barely escaped marrying a drummer of forty who had what she thought of at the time as "money." She learned gradually that her end could be achieved only if she had adequate formal schooling, which was why she trained as a teacher. Tuition was free. She had found out, by the time she got her degree, that the style of man she wanted— rich, of course, important, social, urbane and worldly— would also have to be (if he were to marry her) weak and vain and somewhat gullible.

She marked down Howard Bailey within ten minutes of their first meeting, at a picnic on the banks of the Green Prairie River in 1928. They were married—rather hastily and to the infinite puzzlement of Beau—and there Netta's luck failed. In 1929 Beau's father (who had owned an automobile agency in River City) shot himself to death, two weeks after the historic Black Friday, which wiped out other thousands of millionaires. Beau was left with nothing but his job in the Sloan Mercantile Trust Company. Curiously enough, Netta discovered that, though the self-evident thing to do was to get divorced and find a new spouse whose bonds and stocks had not been touched by the market collapse, she was by then attached to Beau in a way she could not fathom. His very weakness, his dependency, made her postpone repeatedly even talk of divorce.

Those were home-brew days, bathtub-gin days. Lenore was a result of the overpowering quality of such anodynes, in the waning epoch of prohibition and jazz.

Years passed. Beau, the handsomest senior in his high school (where the nickname had attached), started to shed, one by one, the attributes of male beauty. His dark hair silvered, lost its curl, began to vanish. His skin reddened and his face became puffy. He skirmished with reducing for years and gave up. His mustache and eyebrows turned gray and he was obliged at first to touch them up. Later, dye and a toupee restored a sort of ghostly caricature of the "handsome Dan" he had been. He had flat feet, which exaggerated the out-toeing, ducklike walk he developed as a fattening man with no more musculature than that of a youth whose only sport had been the Charleston. At the same time, he was still full of a kind of eager and boyish affection; a willing listener, he was also popular at parties for having the largest fund of dirty jokes of any man in the two juxtaposed states. In addition, Beau was extremely good at figures. Had he not been lazy, he might have been a mathematical prodigy. Lenore's scientific aptitude came that way.

Emmet Sloan, board chairman of the Sloan Mercantile Trust, a far-seer and expert conniver, the richest man in the Sister Cities, had been Beau's boss. When Mr. Sloan died in 1935, "of Roosevelt," they said, his widow, Minerva, became the head not only of the bank but of the sundry factories, newspapers, mines, railroads and other interests her late spouse had collected, created and purloined.

Minerva Sloan, a size forty-four daughter of one of River City's oldest and best families, was even shrewder and tougher than her husband. She knew Beau Bailey's weaknesses the first time she saw him. But he had always been amiable, sedulous and amusing: Minerva liked rough jokes. She saw to it that he rose steadily in the bank, for his mathematical skill was exploitable. She saw to it that men were put where they could watch his more important acts. She realized that he was useful for his brain and also might (someday in a pinch, and owing to his feeble sense of ethos) be made even more useful as the patsy before an embarrassing investigating committee, or on the occasion of a shaky lawsuit.

It did not occur to her, however, that he was stupid enough, as cashier of her largest bank, to bet on horses. The idea had never crossed Netta's mind, either. She had not questioned the occasional "bonuses" and "little bonanzas" he had fetched home recently. (For at first, Beau had been extremely lucky.) Netta was used to taking cash unquestioningly; it was only its dearth that aroused her to sharp attention. . . .

As Lenore entered her teens, as the Baileys struggled up the complex social ladders of River City and Green Prairie,

Netta saw that her luck had potentially taken a swing for the better, after many hard years which she regarded, not without a sort of reason, as loyal and sacrificing. Lenore was going to be beautiful. Soon she *was* beautiful. To Netta, who had herself parlayed prettiness into a marriage that provided some, if not all, of the products recommended by class advertising, beauty could be stage-managed so as to open the grand cornucopia.

Unfortunately, Lenore proved to be a person in her own right. She early developed an interest in the boy next door, the Conner kid, which Netta regarded as mawkish and entirely inappropriate. This youngster wanted, even as a mere boy, to become nothing more remunerative than an architect. In addition, Lenore had inherited her father's mathematical ability and in high school became greatly interested in science, especially physics. Netta felt that perhaps the most difficult operation of her life had been the one by which she had managed to hinder her daughter from becoming a teacher, a professor, a laboratory worker or a technician. The struggle involved had become a kind of stalemate. Lenore had gone to college and come dutifully back home. She had not taken the job the du Ponts offered her and had in fact allowed her science to rust; but she had not married a rich man either—and she was twenty-four.

There was one rich man, especially, whose name adorned Netta's mind year after year. The fact that Lenore had once attracted and then rejected him was, quite possibly, the largest thorn in Netta's thorny life. He was eminently eligible, extremely handsome, socially so impeccable that his in-laws would automatically be lifted to the top strata, and destined to be very rich; he was Minerva's son, Kittridge Sloan.

If Beau's family background was average, Netta's had been far below the American norm; hence, in a real sense, she had improved herself far more than he. Furthermore, though both had skeletons in their private closets, though indeed Netta's young womanhood (a closed book from the day she saw Beau) was the kind which reformers wrongly imagine leads invariably to a wretched end in some such place as Buenos Aires, the Baileys had attained a complete "respectability." They found pleasure in that estate.

They were, according to their lights, good to their one child and they furnished her with what they truly believed to be a splendid home environment. They were worthy members of the River City Episcopal Church and rose early every Sunday morning, often in spite of painful hangovers, to drive across the Central Avenue Bridge to services. Netta taught a Sunday-school class and Beau, who had a fair tenor voice, led the hymns in Sunday school. Minerva Sloan was the Sunday-school superintendent. But even that fact, which explained why they traveled so far to attend church when there were many handier places of worship in Green Prairie, did not mean their faith was entirely opportunistic. They did believe in God, childishly, as the source of pleasures and gifts and undue punishments.

One afternoon a week Netta sewed with the colored women at the Mildred Tatum Infirmary. It was, to be sure, a Sloan charity. But Netta enjoyed that afternoon sincerely: she liked colored people and felt, in a sense, completely at home with them. Moreover, Beau not only led Sunday-school singing but he contributed generously to the River City Boys Club, which was not a Sloan charitable concern, and he gave a certain amount of time to that rather sad American enterprise of "leading" boys. Beau was also a member of the Elks, Kiwanis, and the Society of

Green Prairie Giraffes. He served as the perennial treasurer of all three. He was also an active Republican and had been a leading and early Eisenhower protagonist, after finding—surreptitiously and owing to his acquaintance with the accounts—that Minerva had made a large contribution to the Eisenhower campaign fund. The measure of Beau's stance in such matters was this: that if he had discovered Minerva was backing Stevenson, he too would have paid lip service to the Democratic Party, but without enthusiasm, and he would doubtless have voted for Ike secretly, denying it afterward.

The Baileys, in sum, were not intentionally evil people. Like many, they were engaged in striving toward that place in life where their hypocrisies, small dishonesties, speculations and shady deals would become *"unnecessary."* To them, as to millions of other American families, not only "keeping up" but "getting ahead" have priority over conscience; honor is a luxury they conceive of as desirable, even ideal, but possible only to those lucky few who somehow have run all the gantlets, crossed all the goals, and bought all the nationally advertised essentials, including airplane trips abroad, summer homes, large annuities and permanent vaults.

Theirs were the vices of ambition, which has come to be identified with progress, thus obscuring its other name —greed.

They were superficially much like their neighbors, the Conners, and only underneath unlike in certain ways. Neither Henry nor Beth Conner was greatly afflicted by the desire for things. Henry was content to stay forever the head of the accounting department of the J. Morse Company, the second largest hardware store chain in the state; Beth was not particularly interested in clothes, in country-club living, in "society," in concerts or plays or lectures (doings regularly patronized by the Baileys), or even in modernizing her house or relandscaping her yard.

"She seems," Beau once said perplexedly, "to *like* kind of beat-up housewares and sprangly bushes outdoors and old duds."

In money contributed and time devoted, the good works of the Conners far outweighed the somewhat opportunistic benevolences of the Baileys. Henry Conner belonged to even more organizations—charitable, fraternal or merely sportive. Henry, indeed, was known to thousands of his fellow citizens, and his warmth and down-to-earth wisdom endeared him to them all. His younger son's joke about his election to the office of dogcatcher was warranted: if he had desired office, Henry could have been elected to any of dozens. For that very reason he had been appointed a sector warden. Beau Bailey, on the other hand, while known to hundreds of the most prosperous citizens of his region, was not known to thousands—save perhaps as a dimly recalled face at a teller's window, in the days before he had a desk and his own office.

Yet it was Beau who regarded himself as "important" in the community, a figurehead and social pillar. Netta shared that belief. Both Beth and Henry Conner would have deemed silly the suggestion that their family was "important."

Such, in outline, was the background of Netta Bailey, *née* Meddes; such therefore was the etiology of her emotion when she came downstairs while her husband was on the telephone, occupied by nothing more than a marriage-long habit of anxious inquisitiveness and a very slight feeling, not that the phone call was of a serious nature but that her husband had been a little quieter, a little more obsequious than usual. She saw now that Beau was frantically afraid. His swift effort to dissemble went to no purpose. She said, "What's wrong?"

"Nothing. Nothing whatever."

"*Beau.* You can't fool me."

"I'm not trying to!"

Netta walked around the bleached mahogany table in the room's center. Her eyes needled. She was somehow made more ominous, where it would have rendered most women ineffective, by the fact that she had been "experimenting" after supper with creams and lotions: her rusty-musty hair overtopped a towel and dangled from it and her face gleamed greasily. "Okay," she said steadily. *"Who was it?"*

"Netta, for God's sake! It was a *business* call."

"Your business, though. Not the *bank's."*

Beau made a tactical error. "How can you tell?"

The question allowed her to pretend the reality of a mere assumption. "So it *was* personal. *Beau!* What have you been up to?"

"Nothing, I tell you. Nothing."

Netta sat down on the arm of the huge, flower-print-covered divan the decorator had chosen for them. "You can tell me now or you can argue awhile. Either way, Beau, I'll find out from you."

His voice suddenly filled the room, taut, shrill, surprising him even more than Netta. "None of your goddamned business!"

"It's really bad trouble, isn't it?"

"Who said it was trouble?" His face had puckered like the face of a baby trying to decide whether to produce a tantrum or a spell of pitiable tears.

"How much is it going to cost us?"

"Netta—stop jumping to such crazy conclusions!"

She could tell, to a decibel, a hairbreadth, when he was lying and when he was not. She went on implacably, "If you've just hocked something—or borrowed on the cars . . ."

"What have we got to hock that isn't already hocked, *including* the cars?" He stared at her with momentary self-righteousness.

She said, "Then it *is* money?" Her arms were folded now on the back of the divan and her uncorseted body sagged between the two supports of rump and elbows.

"Quit hounding me." He reached for the bottle.

"No more drink until you explain."

He put the bottle down. Another man might have continued the defense for hours, even for days. Beau himself might have gone on fencing for a time, in spite of an inner awareness of inevitable capitulation, save for the fact that he was now far more afraid of another person than of Netta. It was the first time in his life such a thing had happened to him. He took a chair. He lighted a cigarette. He looked at his intent wife and said, "Okay. You brought it on yourself. This time we really are in a jam."

"*I* brought it on myself! *We* are in a jam! Speak for yourself, bright boy!"

"I'll tell you," he said, "just how bad a jam it is. If I hadn't borrowed up to the full value on my insurance . . . !" He pointed his forefinger at his temple, cocked his thumb in a pantomime of shooting himself.

"How *much* money?" she asked again, unimpressed by his drama.

"Five thousand dollars."

Netta moaned softly, sagged, slid from the arm of the divan onto the cushions. "Five—thousand—dollars." She murmured the words, wept them. "Even one thousand the way we're fixed . . . !" Then she screamed, "How in God's earth do you owe that?"

Tears filled Beau's eyes. "All my life," he recited, "I've done just one thing and one thing only, scrimped and sweat and slaved and hit the old ball, so you and Lenore could have a fine life. I have no pleasures of my own, no vices, no indulgences——"

She was looking at him, white-faced, oblivious to his stale stock of good providing. "Those—'bonuses,' you called them! The 'little windfalls,' *you said!* The fur coat you got Lenore! The new deep-freeze you made a little killing just in time to pay for! All *that?*"

"A man," he responded in a ghastly tone, "can get so devoted to his family he'll stop at nothing for their sake——"

Netta said a word she had learned in her childhood environs, monosyllabic and succulent-sounding. It was one of the first words she had ever known. She sat up. "You've been *gambling!*"

"How do you know?"

"*Horses!*"

"And I did *all right.*" Her guess seemed to release him. "And if I had some *real* dough to lay on the line, I could get back what I'm down——!"

"Where? What bookie. *Jake!* That was *Jake* on the phone!"

Now, for the first time, Netta was more frightened than angry. "Beau, do you really owe Jake Tanetti five thousand dollars?"

"I didn't think it was that much. I thought—around three. But *he* says five."

"Then it's five." Netta sat silent for a moment, her chest

heaving. Once or twice she looked speculatively at Beau. Finally she smiled at him wanly. "Come over here. Sit beside me."

"Net, I don't want to. I'm too ashamed."

She beckoned. Heavily, he rose and cautiously approached. He seated himself as gingerly as if the divan had been an electric chair. But Netta didn't swat him or even yell at him. She just took his hand and held it in her own and stared at it and finally said, softly, "Beau, my boy, you've done some dumb things in your day, but this is really Grade-A trouble. I'm not sore. I'm sorry."

She meant it. Meant the compassion she displayed, the calm. Intellectually Netta knew that the only way to manage Beau now would be with gentleness. Anything harsh might easily snap the thin threads of his remaining pride and cause him to do something still more rash. Not suicide. But he might confess to Minerva Sloan and throw himself (and her and Lenore, as incidentals) on the mercy of the old woman. There was no such thing as mercy in Minerva, Netta knew; she'd had a good deal of experience in the absence of mercy. So there was reason for her to hold her tongue and to treat Beau with restraint.

But something much deeper also moved Netta, something she did not understand. It was pity. She realized that she had never pitied Beau before; she had always, in fact, felt slightly inferior to him because of her background. Now, however, she suddenly felt equal. His descent to this level, his victimization by the bookmaker, even his gambling per se, as his way of trying to clamber from his eternally sticky finances, touched Netta in a familiar spot. Her mother, father, brothers and sisters, aunts and uncles had *lived* in this place, owing what they could not pay, guilty of merely taking a chance and losing, and faced in sudden consequence with the malignity of forces vastly mightier than themselves: rackets, unions, the law, the church, street gangs, hoods, noble powers that became suddenly evil and evil powers that were ceaselessly opposed to everybody, to life itself and letting live.

Netta came closer to loving Beau then than ever before.

"You're the cashier of a big bank," she said carefully, "so you *can't* gamble. That means this business *must not come out.*"

"If I don't pay Jake——"

"Sure. If you don't—it will. That's Jake." She said it as if "Jake" were a force of nature, not a person. "So he has to get paid."

"How?"

"That's what we've got to figure. He'll probably take something down. . . ."

Beau brightened a little. "He said he would. Half now. Half later."

"So, okay. All you need right off is two grand and a half."

He shrugged. "Might as well be two million."

"I've heard you say, Beau, you could lay your hands on fortunes, and nobody would be wiser for years."

He pulled away from her. *"The bank?"*

"You said . . . ?" she gestured casually.

"My *God,* Net! I *said* so, sure. Portfolios full of negotiable stuff that I check, sometimes. You could slip out millions and borrow on it—cash it in—and nobody would know till somebody looked. Maybe six months, maybe a year, maybe longer. But that's *out!"*

"You got any different inspirations? Or better ones?"

"That one isn't even an idea. Look, Net. I appreciate the

way you're taking this. I—I—I guess I thought you'd just kick
me out on the street if you got the facts. But I'm not borrowing
from the bank without notice. No embezzlement. Defalcation.
No. *That* would be strictly criminal. I could go to jail!"

"Have you thought just where you stand now, and what
could happen if you didn't pay up Jake?"

"I could lose my job——"

"Lose your job, my eye! Jake has put men in the Green
Prairie River in a barrel of cement for less. That's the only
way he can keep his books in the black: making his col-
lections tough."

"Maybe Hank Conner . . . ?"

"Look, Beau. You borrowed five hundred from Hank last
year. Remember? And eight hundred, two . . . three years
before that."

"Sure. But——"

"But *what?* Hank's generous. He's a damned good neighbor in a lot of ways. He's come to your rescue five or
six times. And you never paid him back a cent."

"Sure, but he knows I'm good for it. Someday I'll——"

"Someday you'll—nothing! You don't even know how
much you've borrowed, over the years. Okay, go to Hank.
If you get the twenty-five hundred, I'll really think he's
crazy. If you don't . . ." She broke off. She had already
said enough about his access to inactive portfolios. Enough
for the moment. To Netta, raised in the wrongest part of
that wretched territory on the wrong side of every track,
being in trouble with Jake Tanetti was far more dangerous than lifting a few bonds from a bank—especially when
one way or another you would make sure to get the bonds
back before their absence was checked.

Beau drew a long breath, exhaled, picked up the bottle,
saw that Netta was not going to forbid him, and poured

a highball. He breathed again and said relievedly, casting the whole burden away from himself and toward the woman, "Brother! Are *we* in a mess!"

In the hall, the front door closed with a click. Lenore came in, tiredly, her coverall over her arm. She set down the Geiger counter. "Is there anything unusual about the Baileys being in a mess?"

"This time," her mother said, "it's a real one. Beau . . . !"

His eyes implored. *"Don't*—Mother! *Not to Len!"*

Netta brought to an end her state of uncompromising sympathy. Beau deserved to be punished. And so, for that matter, did Lenore. Just for being intractable. Just for passing up her opportunities. Just for refusing to do what a daughter should in behalf of parents who had sacrificed everything. Netta thought that if Lenore had any sense of obligation they wouldn't be sweating now over any measly five thousand dollars.

She said, "Your father, Lenore, has at last succeeded in making the priceless kind of horse's behind of himself I always expected."

The girl dropped on the end of the divan near her parents and ran her fingers into her hair, pulling out pins, letting it fall. "Now what?"

Netta told her in a few flat sentences.

Lenore said nothing. Her eyes filled and overflowed. She didn't look at her mother or her father. She just sat still, crying silently. Her anguish was a source of satisfaction to her mother, an intolerable spectacle for her father.

"Don't baby." he kept saying. *"Don't* cry. Net and I will find a way out of it. We always have."

But she kept on crying. After a while she rose and went to her room and left her parents sitting together, not talking.

Beau had a drink.

3

The Green Prairie Civil Defense "practice alert" had repercussions.

These repercussions had long heralded their approach, in complaints and criticisms, gripes and threatened suits. To be sure, Green Prairie took pride in its Civil Defense outfit for the reason that its state was one of the "top-ranking five" in the "National Ready Contest"—and the Green Prairie organization was the best in the state. The perpetual competition between the Sister Cities, like every eternal war between siblings, furnished a further motive for local pride and support: for the six hundred thousand inhabitants of River City, being citizens of another state, shared the views of its thrice-elected governor, Joseph Barston, that Civil Defense was "a waste of money, a squandering of public energy, a meddlesome civil intrusion into military spheres and, all in all, just one more Washington-spawned interference with the rights of common man."

Governor Barston had made the statement at a private banquet and off the record years before. Somehow it had found its way into print and it keyed a near-universal attitude in his bailiwick. Gentlemen in the state legislature, loath to enter into the costly, intricate affairs of Civil Defense, had been only too glad to follow the governor's lead and table as many bills referring to "CD" as possible.

As for the politicians of River City, though it was obviously the only worthy "enemy target" in the state, and though a hit across the river would damage them, their feeling was that for once they were off the hook. Competition with Green Prairie was a standing plank in the platform of every one of them. Here was a chance to compete by doing nothing. Instead of laboring mightily to construct a CD outfit equal or superior to that in Green Prairie, they had only to relax—and make jokes about the earnestly rehearsing citizens across the river.

The truth was that after a number of years (and even though Green Prairie had rescue teams, hordes of auxiliary fire-fighters and police, tons of medical supplies and the like) almost nobody believed there was any danger. Few had believed it to begin with. The passage of many years of "cold war," "border war," satellite seizure, international tension, international relaxation, deals made and broken, peace offers, peace hopes, peace arrangements—along with the corresponding variations in American sentiment, national economy, draft laws and a thousand other domestic matters—had convinced most people everywhere that Russia and China were without the technical means to wage a large scale war, would never undertake one, relied wholly on prickly politicking and small grabs to exhibit power, and did not warrant the anxiety of those few citizens who continued to predict that Armageddon was forever around the corner.

Long before, Harry Truman, speaking as if still in the White House, had said that in his opinion the Soviet probably did not have even one real atomic bomb. The Sister Cities thought that kind of information, passed on to the people at the close of his Administration and thus having the sound of a "last-word" confidence, represented "one of the few good things Truman had done." They were, after all, inland Americans. They had been "neutral" in spirit before the First World War and isolationist until the hour of Pearl Harbor. With the opening years of the Atomic Age, they returned to their habitual attitude.

People for the most part have little imagination and less will to use it. The prairie cities were far away from the border of the sea; its level suggestion of distance and otherness beyond was not present before their landlocked minds. The air ocean over their heads they regarded as a kind of property; they thought, indeed, it differed wherever they were, so that a special blueness canopied the Sister Cities and their sovereign states. Everyone in the region felt that same way and talked about "Missouri skies" and "Kansas skies" as if the atmosphere had taken cognizance of political boundaries.

Every day, many times over, planes left the local airports to fly nonstop hops longer than the distance from the Sister Cities to the closest potential "enemy" air bases. But such facts, determined by the simple shape of the planet, were dismissed with a single popular word: *globaloney*. It may be that people who live on flatlands retain the Biblical belief that the earth is flat. Or perhaps people who live between great mountain ranges feel specially secure. At any rate, the River City citizens eschewed Civil Defense and the people of Green Prairie embraced it out of pride and for fun.

Both groups felt that the "domestic Communists," interminably quizzed by Congressional committees, were more a menace than all the Communists in Russia together with with their weapons and intentions—an attitude which possibly had its basis in the unconscious fears of Americans during that long period. It was a time when Americans once again refused to face certain realities that glared at them with an ever-increasing balefulness.

What actually precipitated the "Civil Defense scandal" was a trifle. When the snow's right, however, a cap pistol can bring down an avalanche.

Minerva Sloan, on the afternoon of the practice alert, attended a directors meeting in the Mercantile Trust

Company which lasted until six o'clock. When she left the bank, she could not immediately find her limousine. A large, a very large woman—tall and fleshy, imposing, heavy-jowled and bemoled—an English bulldog of a woman—she paced the wide sidewalk angrily and at length. Because dinner at her home would not begin until eight-thirty (when ten guests would sit down to one of her famed repasts, followed by a musicale), Minerva went into the near-by White Elephant Restaurant and took a table at the windows, to watch for her delinquent chauffeur.

Outside, heavy traffic poured south on Central Avenue between the towering skyscrapers of downtown Green Prairie, south toward the residential sections: during afternoon rush hour, Central Avenue was a one-way thoroughfare. Minerva ordered coffee and a doughnut and kept watching. Traffic—four lanes wide wherever trucks were not parked to unload goods, wherever buses were not loading people and wherever other chauffeurs, double-parked, were not waiting for homing businessmen—moved slowly and clamorously. Minerva scowled at this stasis of the big artery and thought poorly of Green Prairie's city fathers, though traffic in her own city across the river was at least as loud, as slow, as frustrate. She dunked her doughnut angrily and not furtively because, being Minerva Sloan, she could do as she damn pleased.

Finally, she saw her car and ran out peremptorily—also because she was Minerva Sloan and the waitress knew it and would collect from the bank. She held up her pocketbook to bring traffic to a stop and took her time about getting into her car.

She sat back, unrelaxed. "Willis," she said, "where were you?"

"The police," he answered, "made me move from Adams Avenue."

"Didn't you tell them *whose* car . . . ?"

"They were very apologetic, ma'am." Willis's gray head faced forward and his outspread ears reddened. His corded hands tightened a little on the wheel. He had expected her indignation but, even after thirty years, its majesty alarmed him.

"Then, why did you move?" This inquiry was interrupted, suddenly, by the beginning growl of sirens. The limousine had gone less than a block meanwhile. One of the largest sirens was on top of the Sloan Building, which Minerva owned. It was a double-horn, revolving type, with a ten-horsepower motor. This was its first test. Officials hoped it would serve for the entire skyscraper section, penetrating every ferroconcrete tower in the municipal thicket, thrusting its noisy way through them to the warehouses on the bluffs above the river, and perhaps even traversing Simmons Park, to serve in the same harsh breath as a warning for the dwellers in hotels, apartments and apartment hotels along Wickley Heights Boulevard, which was the "gold coast" of Green Prairie. It subsequently proved that the horns were inadequate: they could be heard better in parts of River City than in Wickley Heights and not in the warehouse district at all. But their effect on Central Avenue was astonishing.

As the beginning growl of the siren intensified, traffic stopped dead. Minerva had time to say, "What on earth is that?"

Willis had time to shout back, "Air-raid practice."

Minerva's infuriated rejoinder was lost in a crescendo of pitch and volume that yodeled through the streets, the vertical valleys, the stone labyrinths. Car doors, truck doors popped open. People ran toward the vaulted entries of the tall buildings, following instructions printed in the papers bidding them, if caught in their cars by the surprise alert, to pull to the curb, park and take cover. It was, of course, impossible to pull to the curb in the rush hour on Central Avenue: the whole street was a solid flux of molasses-slow vehicles. So people just stopped where they were, piled out, and entered those doors and arches marked "Shelter Area"—a designation which included virtually all the buildings and arcades for some blocks in every direction.

The first sound-apex of the siren was not its best effort. Even so, Minerva was obliged to wait till the head-splitting scream diminished before she could make herself audible. "Willis," she bawled, "get us out of this!"

He seemed ready to oblige. "I'll find an officer," he said and jumped out with alacrity, considering his age.

Minerva leaned back on the cushions of the car. The siren went up again and this time the noise, surging through the canyons of the city, was literally painful. Her ears ached. One of her fillings seemed to vibrate, hurting her tooth. She snatched the hand tassel and hung on as if she were bucking the sound while riding at a fast pace.

The scream held until she thought she could not bear it and then descended the scale. Around her, now, was a sea of cars and trucks and buses, all untenanted. For a moment, she couldn't see a soul. Then she caught sight of two men approaching, men with brassards and helmets.

"Wardens," she said with the utmost disdain. "Oh, the idiots! The meddlesome fools!"

The wardens were looking into the cars. They spotted Minerva and swung through the stalled cars toward her—young fellows, strangers. They opened the door politely enough, if it could be called polite when rank invasion of privacy was involved. "Madam," one of them said, "you'll have to take cover."

Minerva sat like a she-Buddha. "I will not."

They were obliged to wait—wardens and the obdurate woman—for another crescendo of the siren. "Rules," the spokesman of the paired youths then said. "If you'll step into the Farm Industries Building here, it'll all be over in twenty minutes."

"Twenty minutes! I haven't got twenty minutes. I'm Minerva Sloan."

They looked blank. She supposed there were people in Green Prairie, newcomers and illiterates, who didn't know her name. She waved brightly at the thirty-five-story stone edifice on the corner behind the limousine. *"Sloan Building,"* she bellowed. And then, because the tearing sound was rising again, she pointed at herself—at the center of her full-rounded bosom where a bunch of violets reposed between the much-lifted lapels of her beige gabardine suit.

It didn't mean anything to them. They in turn pointed to the entry of the Farm Industries Building, which was newer—and loftier—than her own structure. She shook her head and covered her ears with gloved hands. It helped. The pressure of sound finally waned.

"We'll have to call the police, if you refuse," the warden said.

"I wish to God you would!" she answered.

They went away.

The siren didn't stop.

Stopping it became a sort of willed goal for Minerva. She was shaken by it, physically, and emotionally also. If a thing like that went on very long, she thought, it would drive a person mad.

It went on and on, and she sat alternately raging and cowering, growing desperate at first with the thought that she might be late for her dinner party, and soon becoming a little hysterical with the thought of nothing but the siren and its interminable, buzz-saw effect on her nerves.

Willis, her chauffeur, seeking police, was approached by two burly air-raid wardens who promptly thrust him into a shelter, paying not the slightest attention to his protests. They then took up guarding positions among the late shoppers, early diners, truck drivers and motorists who were by and large enjoying this change from regular habits.

The paired wardens, who Minerva was later to claim had "forcibly restrained" her, found two policemen sitting in a squad car, smoking, gazing with rapt amazement at a city jam-packed with cars in which there was nobody at all. "Big fat woman in a limousine up the line won't take shelter."

The cops eyed the wardens. "Carry her into a building," one cop suggested.

"Says she's Minerva Sloan."

The cops both lost their grins. "Let her sit," one said.

The warden protested in an eager-beaver tone, "We're supposed to get *everybody*—but *everybody!*—off the streets. And the police are supposed to *help*—if people refuse. . . ."

The older cop batted his cap back on his head and blew smoke. "Look, bud. In this territory, if Mrs. Sloan says she won't co-operate, there will be no co-operation, believe me."

The two young men wearing brassards went slowly away from the squad car, their confidence in the law's majesty somewhat shaken.

Fuming impotence ill suited Minerva—unless it *did* suit

her; unless, that is, it had an object or an objective. Now it could not. She was alone.

The fact gradually engraved itself through the levels of her mind until she noticed it in a new, abnormal way. And she was immediately discomfited. In her life, solitude occurred only while one slept. For the rest, there were people to bid and to do—or, at least, people available at a bell-touch. Now there was nobody. Nobody she could summon, nobody she could even observe. The streets, packed with still traffic, held no human form; even the wardens had rounded some corner or other. The police were out of sight. Bending, looking up the infinite-windowed façades of the skyscrapers, she saw no one. Nothing moved, except high birds, the flags on the building summits, and the somehow unnerving rise and drop of the red and green traffic lights. Her discomfiture became anxiety.

Anxiety redoubled as she thought how awful, how truly awful it would be to enter a totally untenanted city. Then she thought how much more frightful to succumb to any such idea—to scream hysterically, for example, when one knew all the screaming in time wouldn't summon a servant or a policeman or anybody. For perhaps ten seconds, incipient panic held her heart still and slacked away the brick red of her broad cheeks. Then she brought to bear her tremendous will. By sheer inward violence, she banished dread and its accompanying fantasy. Her kindled rage flowed back to fill the vacuum. Someone would pay for this infamous trick. She sat back firmly, snugly, in the limousine, studying out possible victims and suitable means, with her vivid, rapid brain.

Minerva was obliged to wait the full twenty minutes. The sirens stopped, but nobody came. Then the hideous horns tootled at broken intervals and people swarmed back, including Willis.

But it was forty minutes before the stream of traffic downtown moved at all. It took forty minutes on Central Avenue to get stalled cars going blocks ahead, ·a mile ahead, two miles ahead, and to get the drivers of cars back behind the wheels. On some other streets, it took longer to restore traffic flow. Mothers were caught with young children in toilets by the "All Clear." They took their time about returning to their cars. Two or three stolen cars were abandoned by culprits afraid to return to them. Half a hundred people, startled by the alarm, had failed to take note of precisely where they stopped; after the "All Clear" they were unable to locate their cars. Several people couldn't identify their own models in an arrested parade of vehicles that suddenly all looked alike.

Willis listened to one of the longest and most vituperative tirades he could remember until finally traffic moved. He drove cautiously south on Central, swung over Washington, and on down James Street, creeping along the edge of Simmons Park toward the bridge. Traffic was fouled again, four blocks short of the bridge.

"Go investigate!" Minerva bellowed.

It was now nearing eight o'clock and darkness had fallen. She would definitely be too late to dress for dinner but with luck she would be at home in time to greet her arriving guests. When Willis returned, that hope expired.

"The bridge," he said deferentially, opening the rear door, "is destroyed."

"Whatever . . . ? Oh! For heaven's *sake!* You mean this— this moronic *game* is still going on?"

Willis peered through the car and across the eastern edge of Simmons Park to the curving façade of the "gold coast" hotels which glittered above the silhouettes of park trees. "The whole area is supposed to be totally destroyed, ma'am. *Vaporized.*"

Minerva abruptly perceived that her aging chauffeur was not altogether sympathetic with her plight and mood. That awareness might have sent a lesser woman into a new spasm of invective; Minerva had scant tolerance for life's negative experiences, less for impudence and none at all for frustration. Now, however, she saw that she faced total, if temporary, defeat. The next bridge over to River City was at Willowgrove Road which became Route 401 to Kansas City. At the rate traffic was moving, it would take an hour to get there, to cross, and to come back through the slums of her city to her residence on Pearson Square. For all she knew, Route 401 might also be in the area of imagined total destruction and they would have to proceed east to the Ferndale Street Bridge.

So she did not rant or upbraid any longer. She thought.

"Willis," she said presently, using the speaking tube, as the car budged along in fifty-foot starts and stops, "we won't *go* home. Instead, I'll phone. My guests will have to make the best of it with Kit for host. Drive to the Ritz-Hadley."

Around and beyond Simmons Park, tall and resplendent on the proudest stretch of Wickley Heights Boulevard stood the Ritz-Hadley. Traffic along the boulevard was already becoming normal. The hotel doorman greeted Mrs. Sloan with a soothing word. She swept under the modernistic marquee, up the marble steps, across the red-carpeted foyer and into a phone booth. She had to come out again for dimes.

She dialed her home, grimly relieved to find the phone system had not been "vaporized." She told Jeffrey Fahlstead, her butler, to do the best he could with her guests, the dinner, the musicale. "After all," she said, "they've been coming to my place for years. Maybe they'll enjoy it once without me!"

"They'll be greatly disappointed, ma'am. Very unfortunate mishap——"

"The unfortunate part," she shouted back, "hasn't begun!"

She spoke briefly with her son.

She then dialed the offices of the Green Prairie *Transcript*, in which she was a majority stockholder. She asked for Coley Borden, the managing editor, and soon heard his crisp, "Yes, Minerva? How's things?"

"Things," he learned, even before she finished a preliminary clearing of her throat, were not good. "This business has got to stop, at once," she began.

"What business?"

"This Civil Defense nonsense!" She began to talk.

She was angry. She was very angry. It was not unusual.

He argued, but to less than no avail. He pointed out that it was *Transcript* policy to back up CD in Green Prairie, that she had her River City paper in which to condemn it.

Minerva was not moved, not moved at all.

He had never heard her more furious, more determined, or more irrational:

"Two of the biggest cities in America," she thundered, "blocked up for hours!" Green Prairie and River City, together, added up to one of the largest twenty or thirty American municipal areas. Minerva always spoke of them, however, as if they were aligned just behind New York, Chicago, Los Angeles and Philadelphia. "You know what it is, Coley? It amounts to *sabotage*! Sabotage left over from the imbecilities of Harry Truman's Administration! It wastes millions. It squanders billions of man-hours. For *what?* Absolutely nothing whatsoever! Do you know what I suspect about Civil Defense, actually?"

"No, Minerva." His tone was wary.

"That it's *Communist-inspired.* All it does is *frighten* people." She warmed to the idea. "Terrorize them by making them react to weapons the Reds probably don't even own. Meanwhile they are completely diverted and weakened in their attempt to wipe out dangerous radicals at home. The last thing a *sane* government would do would be to get its citizens playing war games in the streets . . . !"

Coley said, "Hey! *Wait up!*" because he was extremely well acquainted with the old lady. "Doesn't it go the other way around? Doesn't the failure of the American people to get ready for atomic warfare reflect *lack* of realism and guts? Isn't Green Prairie rather exceptional—because it *is* sort of ready, after all these years? If *you* were the Soviets, wouldn't you rather America *neglected* atomic defense and wasted its muscle chasing college professors and persecuting a few writers? You *bet* you would!"

There was quite a long pause. Minerva's voice came again, as quiet but as taut as a muted fiddlestring. "Coley. Am I going to have to replace you?"

Sitting in his office, high above Green Prairie, sitting in the new Transcript Tower which he'd help build by building up the newspaper, Coley felt the familiar whip. "No," he said. "No, Minerva."

"All *right,* then! Stop arguing—and get to work on the kind of job you know how to do!"

She swept from the phone booth into the main dining room of the Ritz-Hadley and ordered a meal of banquet proportions.

Coley Borden hung up and dropped his head onto the desk blotter. He struggled with his rage. After a few minutes, he sent out the night boy for a ham sandwich and a carton of coffee.

Coley was, simply, a good man—with all the strengths inherent in the two words. He had weaknesses, also; his capitulation to Minerva exhibited weakness. But his courage and love of humanity outweighed lesser qualities. He had, in his life, deeply loved four persons: his mother, his wife, his son and his elder brother. His mother had died at forty-eight after a long agony of cancer. His wife had been killed by a hit-and-run driver in 1952. His son had died in the polio epidemic of 1954. And his brother had become a hopeless alcoholic who (though Coley had tried everything to save him) had disappeared in the skid rows of unknown cities.

In spite of that, Coley maintained unaltered a snappish yet tenderhearted steadfastness. Every year, his shoulders had stooped a bit more, his retreating hair had moved farther from his arched, inquisitive brows, and his hands had trembled more as he smoked his incessant cigarettes. But his smile never slackened; the directness of his eyes never wavered and his newspaper acumen seemed to increase. The Green Prairie *Transcript* was read everywhere in its home city, and almost everywhere in the city across the river; it had an immense circulation in the state and a fairly large one throughout the Middle West.

Coley was the man responsible. A liberal, an agnostic, a lover of mankind, a great editor.

He looked out now, through the evening, at the other skyscrapers—some glittering from top to bottom, others splashed with the bingo-board patterns of offices being cleaned at night. To the north, half a mile away beyond the bluffs and the river, rose a second thicket of ferroconcrete, of sandstone, brick and steel: the lofty architecture of the River City downtown section. He went to the window and looked out. Traffic torrents were flowing freshet-fast again, paced by the red-green lights. All four lanes on the Central Avenue Bridge (the "Market Street Bridge" at its River City end) were crowded, tail lamps crimson on one side, white headlights like advancing fireflies on the other. Between, in uncertain shafts of light, were the roofs and escarpments of ten- and fifteen-story buildings.

At all this he looked fondly and he looked out across the flat, winking expanses of residential areas, across the night-hooded hulks of the warehouses, up and down the river where he could see the running beads of traffic on many other bridges and out toward the dark, toward the rich reach of the plains. Gradually his whimsical mouth drew tight and two sharp wrinkles appeared, running from his big nose to the resolved lips like anchor lines. He turned from the spectacular view of the double metropolis and walked into the city room.

Most of the leg men were out on assignments having to do with the air-raid drill. Some were at dinner. Around the horseshoe of the rewrite desk a half-dozen men worked, separated by twice the number of empty chairs. They were in shirt sleeves; some wore green visors. Coley Borden walked toward them, beckoning to others, who looked up from their typewriters. He sat on the end of the horseshoe. "How's the drill going?"

The night city editor grinned. "Dandy! About an eighty per cent turnout. That means, over thirty-five thousand volunteers actually participated."

"We're going to crap on it."

For a moment, no one spoke. Then the city editor said, "Why?"

"Minerva's mad."

"You can't do it!" Grieg, a reporter, a man of forty with graying red hair, made the assertion flatly. "The whole town's proud—except for the usual naysayers. It's the best CD blowout ever staged in the middle west. About the *least* popular thing you could do would be crap on it."

"Civil Defense," Coley answered, with nothing but intonation to indicate his scorn, "is Communist-inspired."

"*What!*"

"So Mrs. Sloan claims."

"I always predicted," Grieg moodily murmured, "they'd come for that moneybag with nets someday. Men in white."

Payton, the city editor, said, "Just what do you want, Coley?"

The managing editor sighed. "I merely want to undo the work of about forty thousand damned good citizens—not to mention a like number of school kids—over the last years." He considered. "Every day in Green Prairie, people get hurt in car crashes. All people hurt this afternoon will be victims of our crazed Civil Defense policies. Any dogs run over will be run over because of the air-raid rehearsal. Any fires started. All people delayed will be delayed unnecessarily. If anybody died in the hospitals, it will be— because the traffic jam held up some doctor."

Grieg whistled. "The works, eh? *Jesus!* She *must* be mad!"

"She didn't get home for dinner," Coley answered quietly, "and she had guests."

"Has she got a fiddle?" the reporter enquired.

"Fiddle?" someone echoed.

"—in case Rome burns?"

Coley looked out over the big room. "I was thinking that. Now look, you guys. Payton, spread this. No clowning. You could overdo CD criticism in such a way as to make everybody realize it was orders, and that the staff disagreed. I don't want it! When we obey orders of that kind, we really obey 'em. Run only stuff that actually seems to indict CD."

"A lot of pretty devoted people are going to hate it. Have you considered mutiny?" Payton asked.

Coley said, "Yes."

Grieg muttered, "Sometimes, boss, even I get the old lady's feeling. Why the hell drive yourself nuts getting set for a thing that probobly never will happen and a thing you can't do much about, if it does."

"I know. It's just the alternative that annoys you: do nothing; lie down; quit; take a cockeyed chance. *That*, in my opinion, is totally un-American. However . . ." His head shook. "A lot of Americans these days, a lot I used to respect, are doing and saying things I call un-American. Anyway, gentlemen, as of tonight the *Transcript* is anti-CD."

Coley Borden went back to his office, back to the windows, back to staring silently at the area, beautiful in its garment of colored electric lights.

Later he approved the morning lead:

SIXTEEN HURT IN CD ALERT
Sister Cities Paralyzed
"Outrageous and Unnecessary"
—Says Mayor

GREEN PRAIRIE. September 21: Air-raid sirens, sending the population of this great metropolis cowering

into "shelters," keynoted at six P.M. yesterday the on-
set of a great fiasco in which sixteen persons were injured and large but unestimated damage was sustained
by property.

He was still standing at the window, still staring at the
same scene and thinking thoughts grown familiar over the
years, thoughts he usually kept to himself, strange, grim
and yet honest thoughts, when the early editions hit the
streets and angry citizens began to set the *Transcript*
phones jangling.

4

Nora Conner was a wonderful child. Unfortunately, she
knew it. She was blessed with a remarkable intelligence;
the blessing was accompanied by an overweening desire to
put it to premature uses. The matter of studies was an example. The geography period had covered "Our Country,"
and "Our State," and was immersed in "Our Town." There
had been a homework assignment the day before. "Our
own industries!" Mrs. Brock had breathed with enthusiasm. "Just think, class! We've studied the imports and ex-
ports of dozens of foreign lands and of the nation and
we've learned the principal industries of our state and *now*
we're going to memorize all we do right here in Green
Prairie!"

"All we do in Green Prairie," Nora had murmured,
thinking of an overheard parental discussion of gambling,
"won't be in any musty old geography book."

Mrs. Brock had diminished her smile—perfunctory, per-

haps, from its long use in connection with local industry—
and said with slight sharpness, "Nora. Did you speak?"

"Possibly," Nora answered.

"What did you say, Nora?"

"I wasn't aware," Nora responded thoughtfully, "of saying it aloud. Pardon me."

Mrs. Brock meditated, and pursued the matter no further. The last time she had persisted in probing Nora's
murmurings, Nora had reluctantly vouchsafed their subject: certain frank facts of natural history gleaned from
idle reading in a book on pig breeding. Mrs. Brock re-
sumed the mien of good will related to home industries—
and myriad other subjects.

She would like, Nora thought judiciously, to teach us
something; it's just that the poor woman doesn't know
anything worth teaching.

It has been noted that Nora had evaded the study of
geography on the previous evening. She had, very honor-
ably, opened the book. But she had pored over other matters than home industries and resources: matters contained
in a hidden, paper-back volume entitled *Sin in Seven
Streets.* This item, borrowed from a classmate in return
for the use of one of Nora's mother's necklaces at a party,
purported to be "a frank and factual account of the shocking international traffic in womanhood, written by a team
of world-renowned journalists."

So it happened the next day (which was sunny and very
hot) that Nora found herself ill prepared for geography
recitation. Bells, which regiment the lives of children, rang
loudly. Arithmetics had been put away and thirty-nine sixth
graders had taken out geographies, setting them on their
desks, closed. Blackboards were erased.

"Now, class," Mrs. Brock began, "we have memorized the industries of Green Prairie *and*, though it's not in 'Our State,' of River City, also. I'm going to call on one of you to start the list and when he—or she—thinks it's complete, I'll ask for hands. Nora Conner. How many—and what—industries did you memorize last night?"

Nora stood. It was her opinion that she was being picked on. Inasmuch as she had done no memorizing whatsoever, she could only regard her predicament in that light. It would not have occurred to her (under these circumstances) that very little in this wide world bored Mrs. Brock more than the lists of what nations and cities made and shipped to each other. Nora was incapable of imagining—for all the yeastiness of her brain—that teachers even had such feelings, or to guess that Mrs. Brock had singled her out in the hope that her voluble memory would complete the dull circuit faster than any other pupil's.

In her dilemma, however, Nora was not without resources. She had, to begin with, lived in Green Prairie for eleven years, the sum total of her life. She was observant. Her family was a lively one. She had also perceived early in her school career that where a long list is asked for—or a complex matter is to be discussed—and where the victim of such inquiry is unprepared, a very thorough exposition of some recollected or guessed-at *portion* of the unknown whole will satisfy a teacher, even fool one, and often lead to a good mark when flat failure threatened.

"Green Prairie," Nora therefore began, taking her time, "has a vast metals industry. Early settlers in the area noticed the peculiar color of some of the rocks. These rocks, occurring in sandstone hills, are much older than most of the Missouri Basin. They were pushed up by volcanoes before the dinosaurs came on the earth. They are called igneous intrusions. They contained lead and zinc and other ores——"

"Just the *list*," Mrs. Brock murmured. "The *geology* is something from last week's lesson we got from *Life* magazine. Now. Our industries. Metals smelting is one, of course."

"Petroleum . . ."

Mrs. Brock nodded. "Green Prairie has a cracking plant."

". . . and, of course, agriculture and all that cities do with it. Sugar beets grow all around, wheat and corn, oats and barley. Green Prairie refines beet sugar and makes oatmeal. It——"

"Nora. Did you study last night?"

"Yes, Mrs. Brock." Nora would have been happy to oblige with a detailed résumé of harlotry in Buenos Aires, as noted by two American journalists who had made a three-day survey of the city. But she was not, she realized, on the beam in the matter of "industries." Hands flew all around her.

Mrs. Brock sighed. "Sit down, Nora. Charles Williams."

Charles stood. His small, marblelike eyes squinted, and his freckled face tipped back, his stomach mightily protruding. His voice shrilled and its every syllable was a wound to Nora's self-esteem: "Steel, limestone, coking ovens, brick, brine, sulphuric acid, light metals including a large aluminum plant, airplane frames, farm machinery—this is the biggest business in the area—dairy products, furniture, pumps, hardware of all sorts, tools, dies, wool and flax fabrics, beet sugar"—his slitted eye rolled on Nora—"one of the *least* important industries—and also paint, dyes, wallpaper, plastics, patent medicines and varnish. Linoleum, soap, industrial resins and greases and potash. Doll carriages, cement—" his memory gave out.

"Very good—very good, indeed, Charles! Evelyn?"

A solemn child with a pale face, bangs and a surprisingly animated, even sassy voice said, "He forgot—toothpaste, synthetic flavorings, canned vegetables and a small but promising garment industry."

"Excellent! Now, what does River City make and do *besides* these?"

Hands fluttered again, like confetti.

Roy Rich filled in: "River City has many of those industries, also." His eyes did not squint, but shut, as he consulted memory and ripped off in a staccato: "World's biggest built-in, tractor-plow factory, huge ceramics industry, lead and zinc smelters, electric-furnace reduction plants, nation's eighth largest surgical aid and pros- pros- something——"

"Prosthetics."

"Pros-thetics-whatever-that-is-plant, high-grade special oils, tungsten wire, nuts, bolts, screws and automatic screw machines, chicken and fence wire, and that's all I remember."

Mrs. Brock sighed. It hadn't taken half the period, after all, to pull from her class the various items of the Sister Cities' endless business and, she thought irrelevantly, the attendant smoke, fumes, slums, labor troubles and traffic congestion. She brightened. "Now, class, you've pretty well covered the lists in the book. We'll turn to a more *creative* project. What industries can you *yourselves* list that are *not* in our geography book?"

Fewer hands rose.

Nora thought poutily, She's a sucker for *anything* she thinks is *creative!*

It was not far from the truth, though Nora's momentarily low opinion of Mrs. Brock's educational penchant was unjustified.

"Halleck?" Mrs. Brock beamed.

"Candy," said Halleck Watrous, hardly rising and dropping back in his seat at once.

"Well—yes," the teacher murmured dubiously.

"Mr. Papandrocopulis makes the best nougat in the West," Halleck said defensively.

"It's a small local business. Who else?" She looked. "Mary?"

A sleek, prettied-up sixth grader with very blonde hair said, "My own father is superintendent of the Acme Rubber Products Company."

"Very good," Mrs. Brock nodded. Then, catching a subdued snicker in the male section, she flushed faintly and hurried on. *"I can think of dozens of things! John?"*

"Slaughterhouses and sawmills."

"Excellent! Manda?"

"Lace. Old ladies tat it."

"Marvin?"

"The Teen-James Company makes police whistles."

"I suppose they do—very good—novelty products, we should call it."

Nora had an idea and put up her hand, thinking to recoup. Mrs. Brock, surprised, said, "Yes, Nora?"

"Amusement rides—Swan Island's the biggest amusement park in the whole area."

Mrs. Brock's reaction was less than delighted and the class giggled.

"It isn't *play*—for the people that make money out of it!" Nora said defensively. "It's a *business*. I bet they make *more* money than the *banks!*"

The teacher nodded happily. *"Banks!* Now there *is* a *big* Sister City business. Finance, market trading, clearing houses, banks."

Horse dust, Nora thought to herself, with no clear image

of a substance, but a sense that the phrase was appropriate.

Mrs. Brock went on. "Well, let me *hint*. What's big, and mostly glass, that you see in the suburbs and the country . . . ?"

They guessed it. Greenhouses, nurseries and a new hydroponics experiment in winter-vegetable raising.

It was not a good day for Nora. She was unable to define "commission government" in civics, and she got three dates wrong in the history test. Moreover, when she stopped beside the school fence to argue with Judy Martin on the meaning of "morphodite," Billy Westcott crept up behind her, tied her two long pigtails together and hung them over an iron picket. The result was that, finding herself overwhelmed by Judy's superiority in esoteric information and being told there was "no such word," Nora decided to run—and did not. Instead, her head jerked back nastily, her neck-hair was painfully pulled, she bumped the iron fence, and only a fast, reflex scuffling of her feet saved her from falling, and from hanging ignominiously by her braids. She unhooked herself speedily. The same thing had already happened twice before that year: once on the iron cleat of a phone pole and once on a fire extinguisher. She threw four futile rocks at the hilarious, rapidly retreating Billy.

Her journey back to her home did little to improve things.

The way from Public School 44 led out Dumond Avenue and over Walnut—a matter of some twelve blocks, or about a mile. Nora preferred, however, to come by less direct routes. She had several favorites, depending on the season. One, involving a long detour, took her past Restland Cemetery and a good third of the distance into town. Another followed Hickory—the school being on the corner of that street and Dumond Avenue—diagonally across Hobart Park, which placid preserve had been a bequest to

Green Prairie by the long-deceased founder of Hobart Metal Products. The park, once the Hobart estate, contained a pond; Nora enjoyed ponds—ducks came to them, fish lived in them, rowboats tipped over in them, and you could wade, if the cop was trifling with some nursemaid. She also liked, when in the humor, to go clear over to Cold Spring Street, which was beyond her home, and watch trains go by on the Kansas and Southern Railroad.

This day, however, she went along Hickory merely to River Avenue and turned south. River Avenue crossed Plum Street, Oak, Spruce, Pine and Maple, before reaching Walnut. It was a broad thoroughfare, much used by buses and trucks and, in this district, a minor shopping street besides. Now, however, River Avenue was dug up and new sewers were being laid. This enterprise involved noise, fire and big machinery, men, moraines of Green Prairie's underlying clay, dynamite explosions and other interesting features.

Nora's tour, however, was unlucky. She met two boys she'd never seen before who said they lived over Schneider's Delicatessen, challenged her to penny-pitching and won eight cents, all she had on her at the time. Furthermore, a bus hit a puddle at the Spruce Street intersection and spattered her dress.

Her inner condition was mediocre when she reached home. She was about to open the front door and enter, which was her right, when her father drove into the yard with a sound of brakes that meant either he was mad or he had to go to the bathroom in haste. She looked and saw that he was mad. Very mad.

"Nora," he said, "I want you to stay *out*doors this afternoon! I'm having a meeting."

"It's impossible," Nora responded.

Thus challenged, he took closer cognizance. "You *sick?* It's a perfectly swell, hot day!"

"My dress is filthy—through the fault of the Green Prairie Street Transportation Company."

"Well, go round the back way then. I expect a lot of people here shortly."

"Where's Mom?"

He went in. "How do I know? I just got here, too! Making sandwiches, I hope."

"What's the meeting for?"

"Civil Defense indignation meeting. My section. We may decide to cancel all our subscriptions to the *Transcript.*"

"*That* old stuff!" Nora murmured. She brightened. "Anyhow—if it ever *did* happen—it would probably be a hydrogen bomb and there wouldn't even be a stone standing in the uttermost corners of the County."

He stared at her. "Sometimes," he said gently, "I feel that would be best."

He slammed the door. His daughter shrugged several times and tittered. Inasmuch as her mother was putatively making sandwiches, Nora went dutifully around back. She was given a cheese-and-jelly and a cold meat.

These she took into the yard, eating one and then the other, like Alice with the mushroom edges. She thought of climbing on the trunk and scrutinizing the objects her father kept in a locked garage closet. From the trunk, a dusty window gave a good view. But that had lost its shock. She saw Queenie, the cat, move furtively through the hedge into the Bailey yard. Queenie then bounded forward a number of times and flattened out again. Sneaking.

Nora went through the hedge also, skirted the summerhouse and came to rest, kneeling, behind the chimney of the Bailey barbecue pit. What Queenie was after was a bird, Nora told herself interestedly—a small one with red on it. The cat looked at the girl with hate in his eyes until he saw Nora was positively rather than negatively engrossed in his stalking. Then, showing off a little perhaps, he made a pitch for the bird. He moved inchmeal, all but invisibly; when the bird moved he froze. The bird didn't notice Nora, who ate thoughtfully, taking care to make no sudden movement. It was a fairly fascinating thing to see, and she hoped old Queenie would get the bird because she had never seen a cat eat up a bird and never even really got a good look at a bird's insides.

Thus Nora was *where* she was with reason. She was not engaged in eavesdropping, hiding in bushes, or any other such furtive occupation. She was merely watching her own cat hunt, while she ate her own sandwiches. The fact that she was concealed had to do with the cat's quarry, and nothing whatever to do with the descent upon the summerhouse of Lenore and Kittridge Sloan.

Lenore came jouncing and hurrying and laughing in a sweater and a skirt but no bra, Nora observed. The man— Nora at that time did not know who he was—had a mustache, black, small, twisty. She failed to observe that he was more than six feet tall, about thirty years old, built like a first baseman and dressed in sports clothes. She did notice that he wore three gold rings, looked like a "Mexican movie actor," and got out a little leather thing that had a file in it and dug his nails, when angry.

"I haven't got long," Lenore said, "so let's sit here——"

"The Jaguar would take us some place a lot better in about five minutes."

"I told you, Kit, I have to go to a meeting . . ."

He looked across the lawn at the Conner house and said, "You really mean you intend to *go?*"

"Certainly. I'm in Henry Conner's sector."

He laughed a long time. "And I've invited you to the club!"

"I know. But this is important. The *Transcript* was perfectly *beastly*, this morning and . . ." she broke off. There was a pause and she said, "I'm sorry."

That made him laugh even more, and Nora could see the dark young woman was relieved. The man said, "That's Mother's doing. She was trapped downtown last night. *Brother!* Did she ever boil, simmer, curdle and take fire!"

"She has a right to her opinion, but I don't agree——"

The man took Lenore by the shoulder and shook her gently, so that her dark hair swung and her worried expression faded. "I certainly am glad I went shopping today. Ye gods! Imagine you being around town—and me not knowing it! How long . . . ?"

"I graduated over a year ago, Kit," she said.

From behind the barbecue pit and sundry rose bushes Nora reflected that his name, anyhow, was Kit, like First Aid Kit.

"And I didn't know!" He peered at her with what the adventitious but fascinated onlooker regarded as an *oozy* look. "You realize, don't you, that you've turned into the most beautiful piece of stuff in two states?"

Lenore moved away from him and sat down. She said, "Nonsense!" She paused and went on, "Besides, you *have* seen me, or *could* have, when you were in town last winter— at the Semophore Hill Club Christmas party. *Several* places. Only—you were busy."

That made him laugh, too. "Blondes?"

"Various shades," Lenore answered.

Nora began to wonder what would *not* make him laugh or, at least, titter. He sat down very close to Lenore, offered her a cigarette, and put one, for himself, in some kind of holder. A gold one, extremely sissified. "I gave you up," he said, "three years back because——"

"Because I wouldn't—give."

"Still the same old Lenore."

She nodded. "You bet. Untarnished. But with a gradually souring disposition perhaps."

He shook his head in mock sorrow. "*Naturellement,*" he said, which Nora knew was French for "naturally." Otherwise she didn't know what he meant when he went on, "The end product of spinsterdom."

"Are you going to be in River City long?"

"Living with Muzz," he nodded. "For how long? Search me! You know, Lenore, *you* could have something to do with that!"

"I doubt it. Maybe a day or two's difference."

"I was pretty crazy about you."

"You were pretty crazy, period."

"That's really not up to your usual acid rejoinder, dear."

"No." She gazed at him, not happily. "Look, Kit. I was one more of the college girls back then who thought you were a young female's dream, answered prayer—all that."

"But I am!" His bright smile gleamed, his amused laugh sounded.

"Oh, sure. *Every* young girl's——"

"Just a sign of broad taste." He chortled. "*And* the curse of wealth. Let me ask you something."

"All right."

"Is your health good?"

"Why? Of course it is."

"Grandparents long-lived? Have many children?"

"Just what . . . ?"

He grinned. "Tell me."

"One had five and Dad's family has four and they're *all* living. Why?"

He leaned back, blew smoke. "Mother is getting *very* insistent these days. *You* know. The family line must be continued. I must find somebody steady, intelligent, *healthy,* good family, sound stock—you'd really fit the whole catalogue."

"Did she say anything about the girl being willing?"

"Nope. Mother rarely does. Just that she be found by me. The presumption is that the rest can be managed. By her, I suppose, if not by me." He sighed ever so slightly and Nora thought it was not an especially interesting change of mood from his mirth. "Seeing you this P.M. at the handkerchief counter did more than bring back memories, Lenore. It brought to mind Mother's bill of particulars."

"You didn't have to pick up a display umbrella and open it over me and kiss me, in front of all those shoppers and clerks!"

Upon hearing that news, Nora peered at Kit with the first sign of any reaction save disdain.

"Ah, but I did!" he said. "Only kiss I ever got with no fear of reprisal. You didn't dare—in the store."

"Not true."

He took her hand. "That's what I mean, Lenore. Remember?"

"I remember our last date. I wished I had a Colt automatic."

"I'll send you one, and then phone you for a new date."

Lenore nodded. "I really have to go." She looked across toward the Conner house where cars were parked.

"What do you do in Civil Defense?"

"Radiation safety."

"And what would that be?"

"You know. Monitoring. Seeing if it's safe to go in places."

"That's my girl!" Kit Sloan was amused again. "Checking with instruments, for *safety!* All right. I'll take a chance. Phone you tomorrow."

She thought about it and nodded. They got up.

Kit grabbed her and gave her a long and large kiss. Nora edged up a little higher on her knees to evaluate it. You could tell, she felt, that Lenore wasn't particularly keen about the kiss. But it went on for so long that Lenore seemed to weaken a little. People do, Nora had observed. Anyhow, Lenore sagged and when he let her go she just looked at him with a very odd expression and wiped her mouth with the back of her hand. He said, "See you!" and ran away. . . . Then his car started. Lenore just sat down.

By and large, Nora had nothing against the beautiful girl next door. In fact, Nora thought, she was one of the best types of grown-up people. She paid some attention to others. She could tell when a person was discouraged or being put upon and, if she wasn't busy (the curse of maturity), she would do something about it. Buy you a sundae, maybe, or even take you to the movies. Right now, for instance, Lenore was on Nora's side against Nora's mother on the matter of braids. Lenore argued, sensibly, that braids were a bother to kids and hair would grow back when you wanted it.

On the other hand, this business in the summerhouse, Nora felt, was definitely on the two-timing side. Lenore was Charles Conner's girl and always had been and they would be married someday and, in Nora's opinion, Lenore was about as good as her brother could be expected to do—

though she had occasionally wondered why neither Charles nor Ted ever expressed any interest in exotic types. Nora thought if she were a man she would probably marry either a Polynesian or a gypsy, and there was some idea in her mind of adding Latin-American women, in general, to the list.

Letting herself be kissed limp by this Kit-Whoever was not Fair in Love. But Nora thought it might be Exotic. The man had a handsome-stranger look, though she had apparently known him for umpteen years. Nora felt she herself would like, someday, the type who put open umbrellas over you in stores and began osculation without caring about onlookers. She didn't believe Charles would do a thing like that.

All in all, she decided to reserve judgment. A woman, she thought, who was soon going to settle down and marry her brother certainly had a right to a few harmless flirtations. Without them, according to Nora's information from books, taken with her observation of her older brother, a handsome woman like Lenore would probably soon turn into a desiccated shrew with dishpan hands. But such things, Nora realized, shouldn't go too far.

She wondered what would happen if they did, and it was quite an exciting thing to wonder about.

She was sitting in the grass, merely wondering, when Lenore lighted another cigarette and drifted away into the house. Nora kept trying to visualize the extremities involved in going "too far"—trying to associate the imaginary behavior of Lenore with the rather nebulously described activities of the ladies in Sin on Seven Streets, until Queenie made his pounce at the bird, and missed.

The bird merely gave a little squeak and flew away.

Queenie sat down and groomed his tail, glancing once at

Nora with the look of a cat who was fooling anyhow and merely enjoyed scaring hell out of birds.

Nora went home. She stopped at the dining-room doors, but they were drawn together. She listened to voices.

"Henry, you're the leader here! I say we need help from Washington and you ought to phone."

"I say, let's start a campaign to boycott all advertisers in the *Transcript*. We've given years, here, to this organization. It's intended to save Green Prairie in case of an emergency. We cannot allow a newspaper to ridicule us, censure, blame . . . !"

Newspapers, Nora thought loftily, going away, do what they please.

She went upstairs slowly. Music drifted from Ted's radio in the attic. The day, all of it, had blanked from Nora's mind, save for one thing: her braids. She felt she was a neglected child and would have to take care of herself. She went to her mother's sewing basket, found the big shears, and cut off both braids, hastily lest she change her mind.

They did not cut easily. She had to hack them off, one strand at a time. When she finished—when she held in her two hands the light-brown pigtails, still beribboned at the ends, tinged here and there with a slightly greenish cast from their contact with grubby hands—an expression of purest delight set Nora's light-blue eyes dancing. *She had done it. They were done for.* She had done it by herself, because it was her hair and it was unbearable, and nobody else but herself cared particularly *what* happened to her. She ran skipping to see the effect in the long mirror in her mother's room.

And when she saw, she was devastated. In her mind's eye, she had overlooked the present phase—the ragged, wrong-length hacked locks that were not a recognizable bob of any kind but merely the plain evidence of devastation. A long, low wail escaped Nora and rose to a penetrating wail of dismay.

Downstairs, Henry sat with some thirty men and women, block wardens, section heads, neighbors, old friends, most of them his own age, many of them people with whom he'd gone through grammar and high school in Green Prairie. They were angry, intent people, who felt themselves grossly abused and made ridiculous before their own community. Now, as they talked, they valiantly uttered what they had thitherto felt only a little, or fractionally, or not at all: that their work in Civil Defense was of critical importance because of its purpose.

Most of the men were employed in good positions, like Henry Conner; most of the women were housewives. But Ed Pratt, sitting in a kitchen chair (hastily transported for the meeting by Ted) with his hat still on the back of his head and a toothpick in his teeth, was a house painter. Joe Dennison, his broad backside propped on the window sill and his blue shirt open, owned and ran a bulldozer, contracting privately for its use. Ed and Joe were joint heads of the section's demolition squad.

To nearly all these people, to nearly all other Civil Defense volunteers, the destruction of Green Prairie had not actually been thinkable. Good will, community spirit, conformity and a readiness to serve were far more responsible for their efforts than any acceptance of the reality of the booklets sent by the Federal Civil Defense Administration from Washington. Their special organization had long since became a proper enterprise in their town—just as it was an enterprise to scorn, in River City.

There was one further factor which abetted their association: a private pride in private occupations. Until Civil Defense had been established, each lived in a partial vacuum about the occupation of others. Now, rather surprisingly, everyone had learned much concerning the special skills of the community.

Thus Whedon Coles, a lean, lank, preoccupied man who was a Baptist deacon and had five daughters, was able to reveal to his fellow citizens that being "new lines superintendent of Sister Cities Consolidated Gas and Electric" meant he knew about what lay beneath the streets of Green Prairie and where the overhead wire mazes ran and what to do about a hundred hitherto bewildering household dilemmas involving leaks and short circuits. Thus it developed that Ed Pratt did not just *paint* houses; he was able to explain their construction. Joe Dennison could tell all about walls—brick, rock, cement—and what underlay everybody's lawns and gardens. In the same way, Henry, who had come up through retail hardware to accounting, could show his community how to use all sorts of tools and small machines.

Civil Defense had been an interesting way to learn unknown things concerning a city, how it is put together, and what makes it run; it had been at the same time that humanly more valuable thing: an opportunity to demonstrate private skills and special knowledge.

These people, angry, studying what steps to take to express their wrath and to revenge themselves upon the sudden "disloyalty" of the morning paper, were gradually interrupted, silenced, by a penetrating wail coming from somewhere in the house.

Beth Conner heard it first and hoped it would subside.

Henry heard it and went on for a moment: ". . . it's my feeling that we shouldn't appeal to Washington. Civil Defense, for better or for worse, is principally a state matter. We therefore ought to handle our problems at home. People always kicking about too much central government, I mean, hadn't ought to yell for Federal help the minute anybody tramps on their toes. . . ."

He stopped and smiled at his wife. "It's Nora," he said. "I guess you better go up." He went on, "So I think we ought first to get hold of Coley Borden and ask him what in hell he's doing. After all, there isn't one of us here but knows and loves Coley Borden. . . ."

Beth hurried up the stairs, following the steam-engine wail. She found Nora lying on the double bed, on her back, a braid in each hand.

For a moment, Beth nearly burst into laughter. She had liked the child's long hair, but she had been on the verge of conceding to Nora's demands that it be cut. Insistence that it not be had expressed mere sentiment on Beth's part. But now, seeing the shaggy locks against the bedspread, hearing the agony in the voice, Beth lost her smile. She did not conceal it; a genuine, deep sympathy banished amusement. She picked up the girl bodily and hugged her. "Nora. You mustn't cry. You're just upset because it looks so funny at first. I'll take you right straight over to Nellie's. If she's closed up, we'll make her open the beauty parlor and we'll have your hair fixed to look *lovely!*"

Hope and wonderment stirred in Nora. She checked her grief. "It'll *never* look lovely!"

"Come along. My! Your dress is a mess. Never mind . . ."

Beth beckoned her husband to the front-hall door. "I've got to take Nora on an errand," she said.

"Is she sick?"

"No. But——"

"Ye gods, Beth! This is an important meeting. And somebody has to serve the refreshments afterward."

Beth shook her head. "Nora's important, too! Lenore can serve. She knows where everything is, Henry. Tell her the refrigerator—and the plates are all stacked in the pantry. Oh, *she'll know* . . . !"

5

Charles Conner, Lieutenant Conner, had always liked his mother's sister and her family. Perhaps it was the kids he had particularly liked, for the father, Jim Williams, wasn't actually much: an archetypal nobody, a draftsman, a little gray chap who would get lost in a crowd of two. And Beth's sister Ruth, though she had been very blonde and very pretty at twenty, was careworn now. No wonder, with so small a salary and six kids.

Still he boarded the Central Avenue bus reluctantly. He'd been home for a week now, and he'd had only one real date with Lenore. The rest of the time she'd been busy—or had merely dropped in for an hour, or permitted him the same privilege. But there was a tension in the Bailey house he didn't understand, though the Baileys had always been tense. And there was a kind of—distance—about Lenore: an attitude he'd never before seen in her. It made him feel with increased anxiety that growing up, entering the service, getting an architectural degree and a commission—doing the things men do—was steadily alienating him from the loyalties, affections and intimacies of his youth.

His mother had repeatedly reminded him he would have to pay a call on his aunt's family while he was at home on leave. He had at first agreed gladly. But, now that he was on the way, he felt forlorn about the journey and the visit.

He caught the Central Avenue bus and sat on the back seat while it wormed its way north through the residential area, the business perimeter and the shops and tall buildings of the downtown section. He got out in front of the Olympic Theatre, already alight, with an early queue of moviegoers under its marquee. He walked to the terminal and caught a Ferndale bus.

It started across the river. On the way over, Charles observed how low the water was, September-shallow, with boulders showing and dry sandbanks. It forked around Swan Island to the west. Late bathers still dotted the waist-deep water. The Fun House was already bright for evening though roller-coaster cars caught the sun as they heaved up on the latticed curves and slowed before plunging. To his right, he saw the river going away east, the ruddy bluffs crossed by other bridges, the warehouses on the Green Prairie side and the disused, rotting docks below. Across the way, slums where colored people lived, and Italians, Greeks, Jews and Poles.

The lieutenant thought about the river a little, and perhaps only as men can think of rivers, remembering boyhood.

He remembered fishing in its muddy waters for suckers and catfish, and finally, one day, catching a big bass. He remembered camping with a scoutmaster, out where the airport was now. The river then, and at that point, was gouged deeply into the level plains; there were miniature canyons where cottonwoods and willows grew, where deer lived, where tents could be pitched in summer and where in winter an ardent boy could trap a few muskrats, a skunk or two and maybe, once in a lifetime, an ermine or a mink.

It was gone now; the mills had killed the fish and the airport was so close to the gorges (which once had been mysterious and remote-seeming) that nobody in his right mind would pitch a tent there. He reflected that no good places were left where boys on rafts could play Lewis and Clark, or Mark Twain steamboating. Subdivisions had replaced those primordial pockets on the river—or factories, or golf courses, or parallel highways, or airports. Something.

The bus plugged for half a mile, noisily, through a rundown section, competing with trolley cars, trucks, jalopies driven by Negroes and hordes of pedestrians. At last, turning on Willowgrove from Mechanic Street, it made better time and soon covered the distance between the slums and Ferndale, River City's oldest suburb. Charles walked the short way to his aunt's house.

He was sighted in the distance by twelve-year-old Marie. In a moment, four of the young Williamses came down the sidewalk under the catalpas, yelling, he thought affectionately, like Indians. (He found out presently, however, that they were yelling like inhabitants of Venus.) As the youngsters caught his hands and poured forth questions about his family, about the armed forces, about life on other planets as he walked toward the too-small frame house where they lived, Charles lost some of his feeling of forlornness.

He loved kids. He had liked being one, through all the wonderful epochs of childhood from the day of his first sled to the day his father had given him a fly-casting rod and thence to the magical evening when his dad had said, "Well, Chuck, looks like the ducks might be coming in around dawn tomorrow. Sam Phelps has that sprained ankle, and if you look in the broom closet, you may discover something resembling a brand-new, sixteen-gauge, over-and-under . . ."

What in the hell, Chuck thought, turning into the Williams's walk, was life all for—if not this: kids to pass on kinship to?

When dinner was over, the plenteous dinner his aunt provided, in part from the big vegetable garden in the empty lot behind the house, they "relaxed in the parlor." He had played with Irma, the new baby, blonder than the others, he'd said, practically silver-haired. He had thrilled the youngsters and their parents with an eyewitness account of the take-off of a guided missile. He'd shown Don the right way to hold his bow and arrow—and shot a hole through a diaper on the clothesline, accidentally. He'd arbitrated a quarrel between Marie and Tom and admired Sarah's kindergarten art work.

Now, with a tumbler of elderberry wine, he sat with Ruth and Jim. Fireflies winked above the lawn and sounds of play told where the older kids were. The young ones already slept. It was peaceful.

His aunt and uncle asked, diffidently, about service. Did he hate it? Was it really rugged? Jim, who had been deferred in the Second War because of his family, seemed to hide under the question a mixture of guilt and romantic expectation.

"It's just dull," Charles said. "Lord, the kids are growing! Marie's really a young woman!"

Jim hitched a suspender and rubbed his Adam's apple. "That's what she tells us daily," he laughed. "She's a year and a half older than Nora."

"Nora," said Charles, "is getting the same idea. She cut her own hair the other day. . . ." They laughed at the story.

"We haven't seen much of Beth and Henry." Ruth sounded apologetic. "Time was when Ferndale seemed practically next door to Walnut Street. But now"—she sighed— "by the time I get the kids organized, or a few hours of an afternoon, it seems a million miles off."

"I know," Chuck nodded. "Took me an hour and a quarter to get over here."

"Mercy!"

"Both cities," Jim said, speaking with professional assurance, "were horse-and-buggy designed. I read the other day in my drafting magazine that cities are strangling themselves. Green Prairie and River City *sure* are!" Jim suddenly realized that, although his nephew was the younger man, he had a degree in architecture. "What do *you* think?" he asked, yielding his moment of pontification.

"You'd believe so, if you could hear Dad and his wardens talk! They jammed up Green Prairie, but good, last week."

Ruth said, "I wish Hank Conner would get out of that thing!"

Charles lit a cigarette. "Why? He loves it. Dad's a kind of natural leader of folks."

"Think of the effect on Nora, though—and Ted——"

"*What* effect?"

Jim put in anxiously, "You see, Chuck, we're not allowed to mention atom bombs or anything having to do with them in this household."

"It's emotionally destructive," Ruth Williams said emphatically.

Charles realized his aunt was serious. A stiffness had come into her comfortable, plump body. He laughed. "You mean harmful to the kids? I don't know. They were having a war on Venus when I arrived. The carnage was fabulous, they told me. I don't believe hearing a few useful facts about what to do in case of enemy aggression——"

"It's the school," Jim said.

"It is not merely the school," Ruth said heatedly. "It's scientific information."

Charles grinned, yet frowned a little, too. "I don't get it."

"She always goes to the P.T.A." Jim yawned a little in spite of himself. He covered up by taking a sip of elderberry wine.

Ruth appealed to her soldier-nephew. "I can show you the *facts,* in the *Bulletin!* Every time they run off a series of atomic tests anywhere, the kids of the United States show a marked rise of nervousness, of nightmares, of delinquency. The Rorschach Tests prove it!" she shuffled in a stack of papers, schoolbooks, bills, checkbooks, women's magazines on the top of a radiator. The heap made a bulge in the lace curtains.

"I suppose kids do," Charles agreed. "They react to things. Nevertheless, we have to run the weapons tests, don't we?"

"*Why?*" Ruth turned, hot-eyed, from her search. Papers and magazines cascaded to the floor. She reminded Chuck of his mother when his mother was on the verge of administering "righteous" punishment. "*Why* do they have to go on forever scaring the daylights out of people? You tell *me* why!"

"Just to try to keep ahead of the Reds," he answered.

"I thought we were making *peace* with the Reds!"

"We've been 'about to' ever since I was in high school and maybe before that, for all I can remember."

"Peace, peace, peace!" she said heatedly. "Why don't we accept this last offer? The one they made in August?"

"We're trying to, Mother." Jim was obviously endeavoring to divert his wife. "The United Nations is trying."

"Maybe *they're right,*" she said. "Maybe our people—the military men and the big steel manufacturers—don't really *want* peace."

"It isn't that, Aunt Ruth." Charles tried to be lucid.

"Every time, every *single* time, we've thought we were on the verge of an understanding with the Kremlin—*whammo!* They broke loose somewhere else. Stop them there—get a deal set—and bingo! They hit in China again. Burma, the Balkans——"

"*So what?* Are *those* people worth dying for? Worth trillions of dollars? Worth making permanent nervous wrecks of all the children in America and a lot of grownups, besides, like your father?"

Charles considered the idea of his father as a "nervous wreck"; it was such an unfamiliar thought that it fascinated him. He chuckled. "I know how you feel, Aunt Ruth. After all, it's why I have to spend time in service. But look. There's one thing the Soviets have *never* offered—offered and *meant* it. That's to let the world come in and inspect them and make sure they aren't stockpiling mass-destruction weapons. Right?"

"They've offered, time and again, to inspect *themselves!* I don't see why, for the sake of ending all this crazy strain, we can't try having just that much confidence in them."

"You've shown a marked lack of confidence in the American citizens who have turned out to *be* Communists."

"That's *different!*"

"Why?"

"When an American citizen goes Communist, it shows that person is a moral leper and utterly untrustworthy, through and through."

"But the Kremlin, with the *same* beliefs, *can* be trusted?" Charles had felt a twinge of anger at his aunt and met it with vehemence.

"Oh, hell, let's not argue," Jim said unhappily. "Have some more wine, Chuck."

"What would you feel," Ruth asked, ignoring her husband, "if you were a whole government, and another government flatly refused to take your treaty oath and your word?"

"The Soviet Government," Charles replied, "goes on the *principle* that its own word is no damned good whatsoever. That's why we can't trust their mere promise to disarm. That's why we have to test A-bombs and keep up a draft army and remain powerful, until and unless Russia permits the world to see for itself that it is doing what it has promised to do. There's *no* other way! Our Government would have found it long ago if there had been."

"You're wrong!" Ruth was shaking with anger.

Marie came in the front door and stood in the hall, holding the hand of six-year-old Don. She looked very mature for not-yet-fourteen——and very pretty.

"See here," Charles said, trying to restore the tone of good will, "suppose we *do* accept world peace under Soviet terms? Okay. We disarm. We destroy all our atomic weapons, as per the terms. We cut our army and air force and navy down to the bone. *Do we feel better?* That's what you *say* you want, Aunt Ruth. But suppose you got it? Would you then quit worrying? Would you then feel safe, knowing the Soviets had made a big promise, and knowing, at the same time, you didn't have the faintest idea of what they were *really* doing behind an Iron Curtain that would *still* be down?" Charles shrugged. "I think you'd find yourself, in exactly no time at all, so terribly much more worried about A-bombs, you would *really* be a nervous wreck. And you'd have a right good reason for being afraid, too. Because then you'd know the Russians could fly over us any time, and we *couldn't even hit back!*"

At the doorway, Don began to whine. "Stop talking about atomic bombs."

"Why?" Charles asked calmly.

The little boy's face twisted. "It scares me. I don't want to hear about it. I hate talking about cities blowing up."

"You *see?*" Ruth said.

She said it as if every point she had brought up had been proven beyond further debate. Her job was the protection of her children. Whatever assailed them was evil and wrong; worry over world conditions and the dreadful advances of science upset the young; ergo: the world should be altered. Ruth obviously could not reason beyond that— to the theoretical possibilities, to the absolute need of protecting her young from something fantastically worse than nervousness.

This narrowness, this ingrained sense that River City would always be there because it had always been there, the emotional identification with the *immediate here* and the refusal even to look at the hard and horrible face of *tomorrow yonder*, annoyed Charles more than such things usually did. He did not realize that his private irritability was colored by the private disappointment in his leave. He would even have denied stoutly that his visit to his favorite relatives had been a second-choice manner of spending the evening.

He took up the challenge again. "I *don't* see, Aunt Ruth. What I see—*all* I see—is the one fact we must *never* lose sight of! So long as even the potential threat of A-bombs on America exists, nothing we can do in the way of arming ourselves, of testing weapons, of civil defense, is too much. I think little Don here is jittery because *you've made him jittery.* I think——"

Jim said, firmly, "Cut it, son! Mother's mad."

She was "mad." She controlled her temper long enough however, to order the wide-eyed, very blonde Marie to take her towheaded brother upstairs and put him in bed. Then she whirled on her nephew. "I know you're a soldier. That's no excuse for your coming to a quiet, peaceable, domestic scene and scaring hell out of mere children!"

"Somebody *ought* to be scared," he answered.

"*You* should be! People *like* you! People like your crazy father! Yes. People like my sister, stringing along with that everlasting play acting about sudden death! A *fine* way to bring up a whole generation, watching grown men and women make like they are dead and dying. I tell you, Charles Conner . . ."

". . . and I tell *you*, Aunt Ruth, you ought to go get those ancient newspapers out, where they announced Russia had exploded an H-bomb, and sit on your broad backside and reflect what that means to your kids——"

" 'Bout time," Jim Williams said, mildly still, "for you to be running along, isn't it, Chuck?"

He went.

He had walked a mile down Willowgrove Avenue before his vexation abated. Then he laughed a little. Most people took it the way Ruth did. They were frantic inside themselves and trying, somehow, to fight off the feeling, simply because they couldn't, or wouldn't, nerve themselves to look squarely at the cause. Hysterical, that was the word. Hysteria was the thing that knocked out the brain when it refused to face fact and pretended something unreal was true instead. Ruth had got plenty mad and plenty active and mighty effective in the bargain—two years ago when she discovered the fourth-grade teacher once had belonged to a subversive organization. That teacher hadn't lasted three days.

The trouble was, she couldn't carry her fear of Communism into the realm of war. War wasn't her department. She felt it wasn't any civilian's department. Most civilians couldn't imagine that war might suddenly become their whole concern. Not American civilians: Europeans, maybe. So Ruth was living in a dream world, trying to compel the real world to match her dream, where there could be no civilian war. Trying to make a special peace—for her kids, she thought, but actually to assuage her own deep guilt for turning away from the big picture of a nation, her nation, in trouble.

Twelve blocks of walking took Charles well into River City. He decided he might as well walk the rest of the distance. It was only nine fifteen. He cut over to James Street and up the steep bank around the reservoir. The moon had come up, a harvest-sized moon, and the water in the reservoir was so clear he could see the brick-lined bottom— as well as pop and beer bottles, cartons, Kleenexes and picnic residue people had tossed in, despite the signs all along the fence saying, "You Drink It, Keep It Clean—River City Water Supply."

The reservoir was in an old section of town, one much like the Pearson Square section to the west. Along one side were large mansions which had long ago been divided into small apartments and the one-room niches of boardinghouses. On the side opposite, the north, old families who had kept their money and refused to move still maintained their mansions and grounds, mansions behind iron gates and brick walls, with apple trees and grape arbors in back, mansions where often the only relict would be one old lady, with aging memories and trunks full of vintage clothes, albums full of dated photographs.

To the west, the sky line of River City sharp and high,

picket-thick, glittered against the aurora of the Amusement Park beyond on Swan Island. South were the lights of River City's colored town—the streaming radiance of Mechanic Street—and beyond, the darkling shadows of Water Street, the river itself, and the less-visible thrust of Green Prairie's business district.

He went around the reservoir and down to Mechanic Street, taking pleasure from the full-throated aliveness there—markets still open—kids still wide awake and playing on the street—fat colored women talking from window to tenement window in voices like velvet—radios shooting band music over the nocturnal streetscape—fruits, vegetables, hucksters, hock shops, saloons—a pretty, thin girl who walked toward him and enquired huskily, "Busy, good looking?"

He followed Mechanic Street. Its last four blocks led across back alleys and alongside commercial buildings that stepped up to Market's tall structures. Here, trucks and cars went individually and people, too, hurrying alone under the spitting arc lights on errands connected with belated shipping orders, or other, less legitimate errands. For here, in small, brick-fronted buildings that once had been homes, the nefarious part of River City's life was conducted. Charles knew Pol Taylor's place was somewhere here— and here was Jake's.

It was here he saw Beau Bailey.

Chuck Conner did not know the precise location of Jake's, any more than he knew which of the many grimed brick houses contained Pol Taylor's high-class bordello. He knew only that some businessmen of the Sister Cities referred to this area as "The Block" and that it contained numerous centers of diversion frowned on by churches and right-thinking people. He saw Beau because Beau stumbled down three steps to the sidewalk, nearly fell—a man in conspicuous trouble. ‾

Charles hurried. Beau, looking wildly up and down the street, rushed away, not recognizing Charles. He went totteringly, and the younger man stopped. Several things had become plain to him in that instant. Beau's eye was cut and bleeding and his nose was bloody. But he had not been looking for help. His face, in the arc light, had been tormented by fear; he had been furtive. The chance that the man he noted, in the shadows, but near enough to recognize him, would be somebody able to identify him did not even enter Beau's head: most people he knew didn't frequent The Block. Beau rushed on, lurching a little, toward Market Street, and Charles decided he had better not follow: Beau had probably been in a fight; the less said about which, the better.

When Charles reached the river he walked across the bridge slowly. But he was not thinking, this time, of his boyhood. He was thinking of a young woman whose father got in fights in River City hellholes. He was wondering if such a girl, after all, would make a mother for half a dozen kids like his nieces and nephews. Then he began wondering if *their* mother was any better for them than Lenore would be. Lenore, after all, was a realist. Even a Geigerman. And not guiltily scared of any weapons—Russian, male, human or animal. A not-scarable girl.

He caught an Edgeplains bus, which meant he'd have to let himself out while a red light somewhere up toward Walnut Street stopped it. The company franchise didn't allow conductors to drop passengers short of Windmere Parkway, except in rush hour—which showed, he thought, nodding into a half-sleep, that everybody was nuts.

He came over Walnut Street and saw a Jaguar parked in

front of the Bailey house. He slowed to admire the red-leather upholstery, the complex controls panel. He wondered whose it was and saw the monogram: KLS.

Kit Sloan.

When Charles entered his house and his mother called, "You're back pretty early!" he concealed an emptiness. "Yeah. Got in a bicker with Ruth about the world situation. Jim politely threw me out. Remind me to phone and make up in the morning."

He started upstairs.

His mother, in the second-floor sitting room, spread a gingham dress on the sofa. "Poor Ruth! As if she didn't have worries enough, with six kids and only thirty-two hundred!"

"Guess I'll turn in."

But not to dream, he thought; not even to sleep. Kit Sloan.

Across the lawns, on the second floor of the Bailey house, Beau was daubing cotton soaked in ice water on his cuts and talking to his wife, who sat fully dressed, as if she expected a cocktail party to begin any minute, on the toilet seat, holding a basin.

"That's what happened," Beau repeated shakily. "I asked Jake for thirty days more and he told Toledo to 'impress' me with the situation." He didn't seem even aggrieved, merely resigned.

"I—I don't understand, Beau." She did—only too well.

"Look at me, then you will. Toledo slugged me. I tried to hold myself together, Netta, I really did. I told him nobody could assault an officer of the Sloan Bank and get away with it——"

"What'd he say?" Netta had to know every detail.

"He said he only wanted his five thousand. He said I

wouldn't *be* a bank officer—any day he wanted to lift a finger!"

"Don't talk so loud, Beau! Kit might hear you."

"I feel like going down and telling him—and be damned."

"Telling Kit!" The horror of that overpowered Netta for a moment. "Don't you realize . . .?"

"Oh, sure! *Sure,*" Beau said, spitting a little blood. "I also realize I can't go on being beaten up by hoods forever."

"I thought you had *plans,* Beau. I thought you were going to speak to Henry Conner——"

"I did." Beau spat more scarlet in the porcelain washbowl. "Yesterday. That's why I saw Jake tonight. I thought old Hank would come through."

"What happened?"

Beau's face, pale save where blood reddened it, turned toward her piteously. "He offered me five *hundred.* Said, with taxes the way they are, it was all he could spare."

"Skinflint!"

"Maybe it was the truth."

"Henry Conner," Netta said, with more rage than veracity, "probably still has the first dollar he ever made! Look at the cheap way they live. I bet he has a tidy sum stashed away."

"Well—*we* haven't. And Hank's not parting with it. And I went to ask Jake for more time—and——" He shuddered. "Look at me! What'll I say at the bank?"

Netta was bitter. "Oh, *heavens.* Say you fell down the cellar stairs. Say a mouse pushed you. We've got to *plan,* Beau!"

"How in hell can *planning* materialize five thousand?"

"Shhhh!" she whispered. "He'll hear you!" She changed moods briefly. Her eyes became exultant. "They're together on the big divan looking at TV—and necking. I peeked." Her mood shifted back. "Go lie down in your bed. Take a towel, so you won't stain anything. I'll get you a drink. Thank God, you had the sense to sneak home the back way! If Kit Sloan had caught sight of the mess you've made of yourself——"

"*I've* made—of *my*self?"

"You lost the money, didn't you?"

It was not that he had *bet*.

It was that he had *lost*.

When she entered the beige and scarlet bedroom, the *moderne* creation of the best interior decorator in both cities, she carried a strong highball and a weak one. Beau was handed the latter. He at once noticed the marked difference in color and, as his wife had anticipated, was too broken to protest. He flopped back on the pillow, spattering a little new blood on the leather bed-head.

"Now *look!*" Netta began, and he knew it was the peroration of something that would go on half the night, "we're at the point where everything depends on playing our cards right. I couldn't believe our luck when I learned Kit was interested in Lenore again."

"He's just interested in pretty girls. Some of the guys at the bank that play around with him tell tales that'd make your eyes stick out."

She waved that fact away. "Lenore won't be able to accomplish anything fast enough to help you in this Jake business——"

"She doesn't even much *like* the guy."

"That's neither here nor there!" Mrs. Bailey talked on, persuasively. "A woman *learns* to like a man, Beau. Most women at first hate the men they marry, for a while. Though for a girl with all her looks and education to remain so innocent is something I don't get!"

"You shouldn't judge everybody by——"

"My background," she cut in, "is something we do not discuss. Now, Beau—you've got—you've absolutely *got* to do something *yourself* about this gambling debt. We can't possibly afford to have Lenore's chances—with Kit Sloan, for Lord's sake—*ruined*, because some petty racketeer disgraces you! All you need to do is something *temporary*. Something that would hold the fort, until Lenore could get——"

"Get *what* exactly? Disgraced herself?"

"Now, *Beau*. This is the *twentieth century*, not the Victorian Age. You've got to be *realistic*."

"Listen, Net. I'm not going to let my daughter haul me out of this by making herself into a tramp."

"What I'm asking is, are you going to *stand in her way* of making what might be a brilliant—*and* happy—marriage? A marriage that would move you into a real house in, maybe, the Cold Spring section, with *five* cars and half a dozen *servants,* able"—she was perfectly aware of his desires and weaknesses—"to run down to Miami in the winter, to take in the New Orleans Mardi Gras, to join the boys at every good convention, instead of going once in five years——"

"Fat chance!" he replied peevishly. "The last time I came home from a convention and you found that lipstick on my—That was my last convention!"

"Why, Beau? Ask yourself *why?* Because, we can't *afford* that sort of thing. We can't *afford* luxury living. You can't *afford* to date blondes! Your social position can't *stand* it! Your *job* is endangered by it. Don't you realize *everything* would be utterly different, if the Sloans and the Baileys had a hyphen between the two names, owing to Lenore?"

He was smiling a little. "Maybe it would at that!"

"I'll get you another highball."

"Yeah," he said, absently. He returned from his day-dream. "Oh. Yes. Please do. My face hurts like hell." He called after her, "And make it stronger than iced tea."

It was going to go on all night.

But Beau began to think, began for the first time to let himself think, that life might not forever be a round of hard work, of figures and facts and statements, of miles of tape from adding machines, of coming and going in traffic that kept you on the verge of insanity, of the aching anxiety of home finance and stretched funds, of eternal self-sacrifice for a wife and daughter three hundred and sixty-five days a year, with only an hour snatched here and there for personal pleasures or recreation—a redhead kissed in the dim Cyclone Bar, a bet made on a pay telephone.

Things could be better. He deserved them better.

And a man, a self-respecting man, couldn't take a slugging lying down.

X-Day Minus Sixty

1

It was a peculiar farewell. Chuck thought it was probably like thousands of farewells said by soldiers.

He had been raking leaves, the day before. . . .

He raked and thought, Ted ought to be doing this. I'm going back to the base. Back to Texas. Tomorrow I'm *going*. I ought not to be raking up the yard. Officers don't rake leaves.

It was a cold day—October. The wind came all the way from Canada, from Saskatchewan or Manitoba or Alberta, with polar cold and the raw smell of muskeg, of permafrost, of something arctic. He'd heard the Alaska-based people talk about that weather. And it came down from the north to U.S.A., making the prairie states chilly in October.

He wondered why he pushed up the pungent leaf-heaps with the wooden rake and shoved them to the gutter, and he knew. To burn them. To make a sweet-smelling pile and add to the good ozone of Green Prairie his own private incense, his somber contribution. Maybe, also, as a symbol. Burning autumn leaves, like burning bridges.

He fished in a pocket of his slacks, thinking how unfamiliar some pockets became when you wore mufti, how unfamiliar the uniform would feel for a day or so. He lit a match and it blew out, so he found a piece of paper, cupped his hands, got the newsprint going, watched words about "strike threatened in River City plant" blacken and vanish. He thrust the paper into the middle of the breast-high pile, on the windward side, and there was streaming smoke, then a bright blaze and soon a soul-satisfying conflagration. It ate gray holes in the leaf pile and sent a soft-looking, slanted fountain of smoke down Walnut Street. Cars had to slow but the people in them came through the smoke laughing and they waved because they, too, would soon be burning their leaves, stopping cars—mulching roses, getting out storm windows, nailing weather stripping around doors, taking coal into their cellars.

She came.

Wearing an orange-red knitted suit. With her large beautiful eyes and with her black hair done up under a knitted hat. He could see her hips move and her breasts and the immobile "V" in front of her and feel his nerves jump.

"You're going tomorrow, aren't you, Chuck?"

"So Uncle says."

She looked at the fire as if it were a work of art like a sand castle on a beach. "Nice and warm," she said. "I've been over in Coverton, watching State play Wesleyan."

"Who won?"

"We didn't stay to see the end. State was ahead—thirty points—at the half. And Kit wanted a drink."

"He didn't bring you home," Chuck said.

"We had a fight." She kicked a spruce cone into the fire. "About you."

"Me?" He leaned on the rake, slender, dark, smiling.

"I said—you and I had a date for tonight."

"Do we?"

"Heck, Charles! You're going *back* tomorrow. I sort of assumed we'd spend the evening together. Or with your family."

"Swell."

"And, anyhow, he doesn't *own* me."

The fight, then, had been a mere declaration of independence, not of special loyalty. "I'll borrow Dad's car."

"Don't bother! I've got my Ford. And your old man needs his these days. Running around . . ."

Chuck nodded. "He's working hard. And to darn little purpose. People are deserting his organization like . . ."

"I know. Well, what time shall I call for you?" She laughed.

"Say, eight? Mother's made a special dinner. Maybe . . . ?"

She knew she was going to be invited. She didn't want to be exposed to the calm, collective scrutiny of the Conners during a long meal. "Eight. I'll be there."

They drove down to Lee's Chinese Inn and danced a while. But the place, in spite of the gloom in the booths, the oriental lighting, the orchestra and the waitresses in Chinese costumes, didn't have the necromancy that had invested it when they had been high school kids, and then undergraduates. They were both restless.

"Let's go," she suggested, in the middle of a fox trot, "on out the river, the way we used to, and park in that spot where the mill used to be."

It was crisp and cool out there and bright with moonlight. The heater had warmed the car. They pointed its nose
so they could see the water shimmering in the ruined flume.

"Remember when we came here after the basketball game?"
she asked.

He said, "Remember the night you and I—and Wally
and Sylvia—went swimming?"

"If Dad had seen us down there, skinny, he'd have
skinned me alive!"

The recollections bubbled up, glimmered, broke.

"How long will you be gone this time?" she asked.

His shoulders shrugged a little; she felt it, on the seat.
"No telling. Six more months—but I'll be out, all things
equal, in eight more."

"It seems a long time!" She picked up his hand. "A long,
long time. Chuck. It *is* a long time, don't you think?"

"Yeah."

"I wish you weren't going away."

"See any beggars riding, these days?"

"If wishes were horses?" Lenore shook her head. "You
know what I'm thinking about."

"Guess I usually do, Lenore."

"I guess you do. It's Kit—of course. Partly."

"And partly you?"

Her head shook, and the small motion seemed to diffuse
in the night an additional quantity of the perfume she
wore. It came from her hair, he thought, her midnight, wavy
hair. "Not me, exactly," she said in a speculative tone, and
added defensively, "Kit's a lot of fun."

"Why not? He's never had experience in much else."

"He has so! He was a star in lots of sports——"

"That isn't fun?"

"I mean, he does plenty of difficult things. Climbs mountains. Flies. He was a war pilot. He has a pound of medals."

"Shall I try to get wounded?"

"No," she smiled, uninjured by his sarcasm, familiar with it. "Not even—emotionally, Chuck. What I wanted to do, hoped to do, what I suggested we leave that Chink spot to do, was talk."

"So okay. Talk."

"Do you think you could put yourself in my place for a few minutes?"

Charles laughed. "I could come mighty close!"

"You sit still. I mean—look. *You* tell *me* what the score is. I'm twenty-four. Right?"

"Practically senile. Right."

"You're the same. You've got nearly another army year. Then, some architectural office, and maybe—maybe in ten years—you'd have enough to——"

"To what? I've got Dad and Mom. In a year, Lenore, I could have a house in Edgeplains, maybe, and enough money for a kid or two. And if I didn't, the folks would see to things till I got started."

"Would I like it?"

He said soberly, "Don't think I haven't wondered. *Some* parts, you'd surely like."

She murmured, "Let's skip those parts, Chuck. I *know* about them. Like the poem. There is some corner of Lenore Bailey that is forever Chuck. The part of me that grew up with you. Skip that."

"I don't know about the rest of it, from your angle," he said. "Being married, making your way in the world, having kids is one hell of a hard assignment, it looks like, from the visible record. Even my folks have had rugged periods—Dad walked out twice on Mom when they were younger—and Mom went three times to Ruth's home. Once

for a week. Taking me with her, though I was too little to
recall it."

"I can tell you." Lenore listened to the ghostly, tinkling
waterfall a moment. "For six months, maybe a year, I'd
love it. We'd get the Edgeplains cottage. I'd fancy it all
up. I'd make do with the clothes I have—plenty, God knows,
for a long while. Then it would rain and snow and I'd catch
colds and somebody would patronize me at church and so
on. Next I'd see our cottage was just a lousy little bungalow,
in a row, with dozens like it—and dozens of young women
imprisoned there like me—breeding, probably—as I'd be.
Then I'd start to hate it. Mother and Dad, of course, would
be completely off me, drinking too much, taking my marriage
to you as their final, personal disaster."

"It might—just might—serve them right," he said grimly.

"Perhaps. Still, they are my father and mother. Mother's
unscrupulous, but I sometimes think it's because she never
had a chance to be anything better. And Dad's weak. His
mother spoiled him before he had a chance."

"Is that any reason why you . . . ?"

"No. It isn't. But look at it another way. They spoiled
me. They saw to it, all my life, I had absolutely everything
a girl could want to look luxurious, feel luxurious, be luxurious——"

"You were going to throw it overboard in college to be a
scientific research worker . . ."

"I *talked* about it. But I didn't *do* it, did I, Chuck?"

"No. Marriage is important, too, though. Love is."

"Look at it the other way. Suppose, just suppose, I married Kit."

"Has he asked you?"

"No. He hasn't."

Chuck felt relieved—then alarmed. "Just what, then, has he asked for, all the time you've been spending with him?"

Lenore smiled a little. "That? He asked that immediately."

He straightened. "The no-good, God-damned——"

"You stop, dope! Kit's the kind of person who *always* asks that right off, of any girl. It's just like manners with him. If she says 'No,' he accepts it."

"I'll bet!"

"I'm trying to tell you. You want to try to see how I feel? Or shall we go home?"

"I'll listen," he answered sullenly.

"All right. Then try to hear what I'm trying to say. Maybe my parents aren't as sweet and loving and noble as yours. Maybe they're climbers and kind of crumby at times. They *are*. But they are still *my parents*. Now, if Kit ever proposed and I said 'Yes,' a whole lot of very important and terrifying and real problems would come to an end forever. I wouldn't love him—no. We wouldn't have as many things in common as—other men I know. One other anyhow. But at least I'd never be in a spot where I'd wilt at the sight of my own house and hate myself for working so hard and despise never getting ahead fast enough to keep up with the bills. Don't you see, Chuck, either way it wouldn't be a perfect deal?"

"Not if you keep it on a dollars-and-cents basis. No."

"It keeps *itself* on that basis. Where might I be, *either* way, in ten more years? On one hand, with a lot of kids— probably bad-tempered, embittered, envious, and ready to slip out and have fun on the side if I got the chance. On the other hand, I'd have everything in the world, and so would my folks, and I wouldn't be a physical wreck——"

"This is all a lot of nonsense," he said.

"Women," she answered, "shouldn't ever try to tell men what they really think! What they have to *consider*—when men won't!"

"Some men consider other matters are more important than living-room drapes."

"Don't you think I do, too!" Her voice was urgent. "What in hell, Charles Conner, do you think I've gotten to be twenty-four years old without marrying for? I'll tell you. *You.* I've had hundreds of offers and chances to enlarge a friendship into a gold hoop. Rich men, bright men, men in college, men from Kansas City, New York—even. Only first you had to take another year for architecture. Architecture, of all the hard-to-learn, hard-to-rise-in things! Then, two years for the army. And now, who knows? What if they start a new little war someplace? Maybe I'll be *fifty* when you can afford a wife." She stopped very suddenly, caught her breath and stared in the dimness. "Charley," she whispered, "you're crying."

He blew his nose. "Maybe I was," he said unevenly. "It's a little hard to take it—like that. Brick by lousy brick. Maybe, Lenore, you *better* give up the marathon. Maybe you *are* right. It's so damned hard for a guy to separate how he feels and what he wants—from the facts."

She came close to him, familiarly, because she'd been close to him often before, in cars, on hayrides, on warm pine needles at picnics, in movie theaters. "It's a rotten time for young people."

"For *people*," he agreed, putting back his handkerchief.

"Charles?"

"Right here." He kissed her forehead.

"Tomorrow, you'll be gone."

"Don't remind we."

"Charles. Why do we have to do like this all our lives?"

"For freedom," he said ironically. "For God, for Country, and for Yale."

"Can I ask you something?"

"You always do, Lenore."

"Have you made love to other girls?"

"Some," he admitted.

"I mean—really. Actually."

"No."

She hesitated. "Me—either."

"I know," he nodded, his head moving against her dark hair. "That, I always knew."

"With things like this, and you going away . . ."

He said, "Nix."

"I always felt," her voice faltered and went on, "I mean, if anybody else but you, Chuck—was—the first one—I'd *hate* that."

"I'm agin it, myself." She could feel his jaw set.

"Then . . ."

He let go of her. He leaned forward and started the engine.

This, he said to himself, is the hardest goddam thing I hope I'll ever have to do in this world!

"We could go," he said in a strained voice, "to one of the many pretty motels and spend the next few hours. And then Lenore would belong—spiritually—to Chuck. They call it spiritual when they mean anything but. I love you, gal. I always may. But if I start showing you how much, dear, it won't be in some motel, and it won't be a sample. Okay?"

"That's okay, Chuck." She exhaled a tremulous, relieved sigh. "I just wanted to be sure, Chuck."

He swung around suddenly and kissed her harshly on the lips. "Shut up, now, baby. I know what you wanted to be sure of! That's one of the reasons I care for you. You're a *game* dame."

"I—I—wouldn't want you to think I—cheated on you—I mean—held out—because of any reason you disagreed with."

"Must I shout?" He managed to grin. "I *know* what you mean. And now, I'm taking you back home—before I forget what *I* mean."

2

More and more, Coley Borden had taken to standing by the window, especially at night, or on dark afternoons, when the big buildings were lighted. Sometimes when he looked for a long while, he'd sit on the sill—twenty-seven stories above the street, above the people-ants, the car-beetles—watching the last thunderstorm of summer, for instance. When his secretary came into his office, to announce a visitor or to bring copy for the *Transcript*, he'd be there, while black clouds tumbled behind the silhouette of the two cities, while the dull light flattened them so they resembled cardboard cutouts of skyscrapers, and until shafts of storm-stabbing sun restored dimension to the soaring cityscape.

He'd be sitting there, or standing, when fog rolled in or when the wind picked up dry earth from between the myriad acre-miles of corn stubble and plunged the cities into the darkness of a duster.

He'd watch rain there.

Sometimes the men at the city desk would say, "Coley's getting a bit odd." Then, thinking how his family had perished one by one in ways which, to the lucky, are merely statistical, they'd add a kindly, "No wonder."

Mrs. Berwyn, his secretary, would always say, "You're crazy—not the boss. He's just taken to doing his thinking looking out the window. Maybe some of you dumb journalists would improve your work by staring at something more than city-room walls."

Coley was, one night, looking at the moon and its effect upon the spires and minarets of his homeland. A powdery light sifted over the region and picked out not just the loftiest buildings but lesser structures, objects that did not usually draw his daytime attention. Thus the tarred roof of the block-square produce market stood revealed across River Avenue. Out toward Rocky Glen, near the Country Club, he could see the glister of a greenhouse and guessed it was the Thomas Nursery. Slossen's Run, a muddy tributary of the river, indistinguishable by day from a dusty road, now glinted to the west wherever the buildings left a space for it to show—a proper water course by night, however much the day defiled it. He saw, too, the distant spires of River City's Roman Catholic Cathedral newly finished, up on the corner of Market and, appropriately, St. Paul.

He was thinking that there had been a time in America, not long before even by the brief calendar of human lives, when church spires had been the loftiest landmarks. Now, the steeples of commerce towered above, dwarfing and belittling man's homage to God. It was not, Coley reflected, an accidental phenomenon. When men turned from inner values to those outside, to "getting and spending," their tabernacles dwindled while trade places grew majestic.

He heard his door open and sighed, looking away from the moon-lacquered panorama.

"Mr. Conner's here to see you," his secretary said. "And it's almost ten o'clock."

"Conner?"

"Henry Conner."

Borden smiled. "Oh. Hank. Tell him to come right in."

"You haven't had supper yet, Mr. Borden. Would you like . . . ?"

"Later. Later." He snapped on lights and sat down at his desk.

Coley Borden could tell, nine times out of ten, about how a man felt, just from a glance. Seven times out of ten, with the same quick look he could guess what a man was thinking. With women, he wasn't so sure. In the case of Hank Conner, Coley knew even without the seeing what his thoughts would be. He was astonished, however, when Hank came in. Hank was "dragging his shoulders." His hair wasn't iron-gray, any more; it was just plain gray, curly still, but he was getting bald. His homely, solid face was still good-humored, but in a patient way, not with his old exuberance. He looked like a man who would have a quiet chuckle ready for an ironic joke, not like a man who would yell louder than a Sioux and do a war dance in a bowling alley after six strikes in a row.

"Hello, Hank."

And there was also a new, unwelcome diffidence about Henry Conner. He sat down uncomfortably in the walnut-armed, leather-upholstered chair beside the desk. "Good evening, Coley." He didn't add, "You old type-chewer," or anything.

"Like a cigar?"

Hank's head shook. "Brought my pipe. Mind?"

"This place has been perfumed by some of the vilest furnaces in the Middle West. Fire it up!"

Hank did. "Came to talk about Civil Defense, Coley."

"I know."

"Kind of hate to. Always liked the *Transcript*. Respected

it." His big mouth spread with something like his old-time smile and when he rubbed his cheek, Coley could hear the bristles that had grown since morning. "You know, first time my name was in the paper, or my picture, it was the *Transcript*. High school graduation."

Coley said, "Sure."

"Tried to get you at your home. Mrs. Slant said you were still down here. So I hopped in the car."

Coley didn't say anything. Hank's diffidence was real; so was the determination underneath. The best thing was to let Hank go about it in his own way. The editor felt sad. His instincts—and every syllable of his logic—were on the other man's side.

"Of course," Hank went on, after a sip of smoke, "I know Minerva Sloan was responsible for your policy change."

"Yeah."

"But it's doing us bad harm. Real bad." Hank mused a while, got up and lumbered across the room to the big map on the west wall. It was a street map of the two cities, their suburbs and the surrounding villages; there was a duplicate at CD headquarters. Hank used his pipestem for a pointer. "My district, Coley, is here—from West Broad on the north to Windmere Parkway. And from Bigelow to Chase Drive. Takes in a lot of territory—about four square miles, give you a few acres." He smiled again. "It isn't so full of folks as you'd think, on account of Crystal Lake and Hobart Park—about eleven thousand people is all. A little over three thousand homes and buildings. Stores in three small shopping centers. Libraries and schools and churches and hospitals and so on. You know it, about as well as I do."

"Sure, Hank."

"Out of my area, we had darn near a thousand volunteers, all told." His eyes, clear and blue like Nora's eyes, sparkled a little. "Three quarters of 'em roughly were just plain people, working people, running from masons and carpenters and delicatessen owners to the middle category, folks like us Conners. I wouldn't say more than a quarter— if that, quite—came from the big places around Crystal Lake or up in the chichi district toward Cold Spring. Just a cross section of ordinary city people, you might say. And I'm tolerably sure that out of the thousand not every man- jack—or woman-jill—would show up set and ready, if my outfit ever got asked to do what it's here for.

"The point is, Coley, these people are the backbone of not just Green Prairie or the Sister Cities, or a couple of states, but the whole doggoned country. Les Brown may just be a handyman. But if you were cast on a desert island for a few years, you'd be smart to take Les—for company *and* comforts. Alton Bowers may own ten acres of lawn and landscaped gardens and a big mansion, and he may own a pile of grain elevators, but he's as close to Christian as Baptists ever get!" Hank, a Presbyterian, let the joke linger for a moment. Then the brightness left his eyes, he came back and sat down. "Called a meeting of the whole gang at the South High yesterday, Coley." Hank looked at his pipe. "Forty-three people showed up."

"Good Lord!"

Henry sighed. "We usually turned out around five, six hundred."

"What do you want me to do, Henry?"

The bulky man stirred in his chair, frowned, rubbed his thorny cheek and said, "Talk, first of all. Get out from be- hind Minerva Sloan's skirts and talk!" He reached around his neck and wrestled, one-handedly, with his vertebrae, disarranging his neat blue suit. "I've always had a good deal of respect for you. You've been right about things in this man's town—sometimes when I was wrong. You've got a good mind, Coley. You've read a lot of history. You know a lot about this science stuff. Your paper's been wide awake. Now, all of a sudden, because we jam up traffic—and it's not the first time we've done it but maybe the tenth—you change tack on us."

Coley Borden's face wrinkled with intensity, glowed with a burning expression, like helpless sympathy. It was a brownish face, as if perennially suntanned; and the eyes were too big for it. Time, not very much time at that, for Borden was contemporary with Henry Conner, had bent and gnarled the editor. "I can imagine how you feel, Henry."

"The point is—why I came here, is—what do *you* really think? I've talked to lots of people, last few weeks. People in CD and even people from River City who think the whole show is some kind of boondoggle. Those folks haven't even got enough organization on paper. I talked to Reverend Bayson, he's a fire fighter in my outfit. I talked to a couple of professors. I kept asking, 'Should we go on? Is it worth it? Are we doing anything valuable? Or are we what they call us—'a bunch of Boy Scouts'? I decided to put you on my list of people to talk to."

"Thinking of quitting, yourself?"

Henry Conner looked squarely at the editor. "That's it." He recrossed his legs as if his body dissatisfied him. "Not right off. I don't mind looking ridiculous to other people, so long as I don't feel that way myself. Well. What about it?"

"If I were you," Coley said, "I wouldn't quit if hell itself froze over."

Henry stared for a moment. "Be damned," he breathed. "Why?"

"Because men like you, Hank, are the only life insurance left to the people of U.S.A. The other policies have all run out. First, Soviet friendship; then, our lead on the bombs; next, our superiority and our H-bomb. All gone."

"They're talking peace, hard. They made those deals and kept their word, so far." It was almost a question.

"How many times have they jockeyed our politicians into a peace mood? Fifty? Then snatched something. It's got so the people of the United States are scared to say or do anything that sounds hostile, even disagree, for fear they'll spoil some new 'chance' at 'world peace.' Makes a man sick! Can you imagine, twenty years ago, Senators pussyfooting around, trying to stop free men from freely saying what they think for fear *Russia* would be 'antagonized' or made 'suspicious'? I say—the more suspicious they are the better, and the more antagonized the better."

"Then why print in the *Transcript* that Civil Defense preparations in America discourage honest peace desires in the Kremlin?"

"Minerva Sloan."

"Who does she think she is," Hank asked enragedly, "Mrs. God?"

"You've hit it. Yes. Mrs. God."

"If I could only be *sure*," Hank murmured. He got up, went to the window, saw the moonlight and murmured, "Pretty view."

"I like it," the editor said and switched out the fluorescent lamps in the office. That allowed Henry Conner to absorb, as his eyes grew accustomed to the soft silver outdoors, the same panorama that so frequently held Coley fixed at his window.

"Be a shame," Henry said at last, in a quiet tone, "to wreck it."

"Lot of lives. Lot of work."

"You think they'll ever try?"

"That," Coley answered, coming around his desk in the dark and standing beside Hank, "is not the question. The question is, *Could* they *if* they tried. And the answer is, They *could*. So long as that's the answer, Hank, we need you where you are."

"That's your opinion?" Henry stared. "It's darn beautiful out there."

"Darned congested, too, Hank. And darned inflammable, if you want to think of that."

The square, firm head of the chief accountant of a chain of hardware stores, the head of a father of a family, a husband, a citizen and a good neighbor was fixed for a while so its eyes could drink in the view; then a hand scratched its grizzled hair. "I know. I know all that stuff. I know it so well it sounds sometimes like jibberish. As if the meaning had gone out. Blast, heat, radiation, fire storm—all that. *Nuts.*"

"Nuts is the perfect word. Insane. Completely mad."

"You mean people?"

"I mean people."

Henry hardly knew how to say all that was on his mind. His deep respect for Coley Borden made him prefer to appear the easy-going, almost "folksy" kind of individual for whom he was generally taken. Lacking much formal education, he hesitated even to display the insights he had gained through reading and observation. Finally he put a question. "Know much about psychology, Coley?"

"Read a lot of books. Seems the psychologists don't know too much themselves! Keep arguing . . ."

Henry nodded, smiled a little. "Sure. You read much about the unconscious mind? Subconscious? Whatever they call it?"

"Some, Henry. Why?"

"You believe in it?"

The editor laughed. "Have to. Can't explain a single thing otherwise. Take you and Alton Bowers. You agree on every solitary fact taught in school. Comes to religion—you're a Presbyterian, Alt's a Baptist. *Why?* Something unconscious, something not faced fair and square by you both, right there."

"Never thought of it that way," Henry admitted. "I was only thinking about Civil Defense. Atom bombs. I get a lot of what the Government calls 'Material.' Even psychology stuff. It's all about how people will act. It's all based on studies of how they did act in other disasters. But if people have unconscious minds, how in Sam Hill can any psychologist figure *what* they'd do, facing utterly new terrors?"

"Some psychologists know a lot about how even the unconscious mind works—and why."

"Not the ones the Government hires! All *their* birds are mighty chirky about the American people. Think they'd do fine if it rained brimstone. I'm not so sure. I'm *far* from sure! I suspect the *worst* thing you can do, sometimes, is to keep patting people's backs. Keep promising them they're okay because they'll do okay in a crisis. Makes 'em that much more liable to skittishness, to loss of confidence, if the crisis rolls around and they find they're *not* doing letter perfect."

Coley nodded. "I'll buy that. It's like the armed forces. Always calculating what's going to happen on the basis of what happened before. Trying to convince themselves, even now, that an atom bomb is just another explosion— when it's that, times a million, plus an infinite number of side effects, and not counting the human factor. The factor you call 'unconscious'—and rightly." The editor nodded. "They ought to look back over the military panics that have followed novel weapons. Next, they ought to reckon on how much less a civilian is set for uproar than troops. People go nuts, easy."

"And then," Henry went on slowly, "what about the people that *are* nuts? Seems to me I've read someplace that about a third of all the folks think they're sick are merely upset in their heads. That's a powerful lot of people, to begin with. Then, a tenth of us *are* more or less cracked. Neurotic, alcoholic, dope-takers, emotionally unstable, psycopaths, all that sort. Plus the fact that half the folks in hospital beds this very day are *out-and-out* nuts!"

"What's your procedure with them?"

Henry shook his head. "What can it be? They're uneducatable. Can't teach 'em to behave properly in normal situations. How'n hell you teach 'em to face atom bombing? A tenth of the whole population is worse than a dead loss. It's a dangerous handicap, come real trouble."

The editor smiled. "*Only* a tenth, Henry? More likely a third of the people are neurotic. Already over-anxious, fearful, insecure. What about the have-not people? People with hate in their hearts? People who never were free, who never had an even and equal chance? What would *they* do, if things blew sky-high? Stand firm and co-operate? Like hell!"

"I know," Henry murmured.

"And the merely poor people! With a feeling they've been gypped. And look! Five per cent of the total population of River City and Green Prairie, like the people in *every* city, are folks with criminal records. Not just unpredictable. You can predict that—sure—a *few* will become noble in a disaster. Just as sure, you know the most of 'em will keep on being criminal and take advantage of every chance. Loot, for instance. Kill, if they're that type. Rape, if they're in that sex-offense category. *Everything!* What's procedure there?"

"Green Prairie has a lot of volunteer auxiliary police and the cops train 'em. River City? You tell me how they'd handle things. They've got nothing."

"What's Federal policy?" Coley persisted. "After all, the Government must realize that somewhere between a quarter and a half of your big-city people aren't what could be called at all emotionally stable. They're pushovers for panic and naturals for improper reaction."

"No policy," the other replied. "Except force. Police effort. How can there be?"

"And psychological contagion?"

"Meaning what?"

"If the nuts, the near-nuts, the neurotic, the criminal, the have-not people and the repressed minorities go haywire—why, how many of the rest will *catch* it? What's *more* catching than panic?"

"You got me," Henry said. He sighed and stood. "All I believe is, the more people face what might happen, ahead of time, without being deluded about how 'firm' they are, the fewer'll go wild." He glanced around the office as if it symbolized something he cherished and had reluctantly hurt. "I'm sorry to come up here with all this on my mind, Coley. . . ."

"I know."

"Guess you do. Well . . . !"

They shook hands warmly.

When the lights had been turned on, when Henry Conner had gone, saying it was past his bedtime, chuckling, walk-

ing out with square shoulders, Coley Borden sat a while
and then buzzed for Mrs. Berwyn. She came in—red hair
piled high, greenish eyes mapped out as usual with mas-
cara, all her brains and kindness and unanchored tender-
ness concealed in the outlandish aspect of her homely face
and big body. (After Nan died, he thought, I should have
married Beatrice; she'd be terrific—you'd only have to have it
dark.)

"Get your book, Bea," he said over his shoulder. He was
standing again, looking along shelves for a volume which,
presently, he took down. When he turned, she was sitting;
she had brought her pencils and stenographic notebook with
the first buzz.

"How old are you, Bea?" he asked, opening the book
and looking from page to page.

"You never asked me that." Her voice was clear and
rather high.

"Asking now."

"Fifty-three."

"I'll be damned!"

"Why? Didn't a woman ever tell you her right age before?"

He gazed at her and his lips twitched. "Sure. Once. I
thought it was going to land me in prison, too. She was
seventeen."

"Your dissolute ways!" the green eyes flickered.

"I was kind of surprised," he said quietly, "because you're
a year older than me. That's all."

"Oh." She looked at the floor. "From you, that's a com-
pliment."

"Right. We're going to do some work. An editorial."

"For morning? The page is in."

"Yeah. If it comes out right, it'll be for morning. I'm kind of rusty, Bea. But I'll take a crack at it and maybe I'll run it. Ready?"

She nodded.

He began to walk in front of his desk and to dictate:

"Ten years ago and more, this nation hurled upon its Jap foe a new weapon, a weapon cunningly contrived from the secrets of the sun. Since that day the world has lived in terror.

"Every year, every month, every hour, terror has grown. It is terror compounded of every fear. Fear of War. Fear of Defeat. Fear of Slavery. These fears are great, but they are common to humanity. Man in his sorrow has sustained them hitherto. But there are other fears in the composition of man's present terror. These are fears that his cities may be reduced to rubble, his civilization destroyed, humanity itself wiped out; in sum, fear that man's world will end. And this last fear has been augmented through the long, hideous years by hints from the laboratories that, indeed, the death of life is possible—and even the incineration of the planet may soon be achievable, by scientific design or by careless accident.

"Fears of mortal aggression and human crimes are tolerable, however dreadsome. But men have never borne with sanity a fear that their world will end. To all who accept as likely that special idea, reason becomes inaccessible; their minds collapse; madness invades their sensibilities. What they then do no longer bears reasonably upon their peril, however apt they deem their crazed courses. They are then puppets of their terror. And it is as such puppets that we Americans have acted for ten years, and more."

Coley paused. Bea looked up and nodded appreciatively at his rhetoric. But when he did not immediately continue, she said, "I think, if you asked the first hundred people on the street if they were terrified, they'd laugh."

"That's a fact," he answered. "Good suggestion." He went on:

"Man has always reacted with universal panic to notions of the world's end. Time and again in the Dark Ages, some planetary conjunction, the appearance of a comet, or an eclipse led to general convulsion. Business stopped. Mobs fled the cities. Cathedrals were thronged. Hideous sacrifices, repulsive persecutions, stake burnings and massacres were hysterically performed in efforts to stay the catastrophe. Futile efforts. Yet, whenever the people were thus frightened, they turned to violence, sadism and every evil folly. Time and again, multitudes on hilltops, awaiting to ascend to heaven, trampled each other to death while sparring for the best position from which to be sucked up by a demented Jehovah.

"The end of the Dark Ages did not alter this sinister trait. Through the eighteenth and nineteenth centuries our American hills have seen the scramble of the doomed as they awaited Judgment. At the beginning of this very century, the country was stricken by awe when it learned Earth would pass through the tail of Halley's Comet. By that day, to be sure, science had so prospered in a climate of liberty that many millions stood steadfast in the presence of the celestial visitation. These restrained the rest. Blood did not flow on the altars of our churches; infants were not dashed against cathedral walls in atonement for presumed guilt; mobs of True Believers did not loot their own institutions and rape their own relatives in a last ecstasy of zealous horror. But today it is *not* the priest, *not* the self-appointed prophet with his crackpot interpretation of Daniel or the Book of Revelation, who says, 'The earth may end.' It is that very group of reasonable, orderly, unhysterical men upon whom society has learned, a little, to lean for comfort and truth: *the scientists themselves!*"

Mrs. Berwyn interrupted. "Two hundred thousand church-going subscribers of the *Transcript* are going to view that dimly."

"True, isn't it?"

She reflected, tapping her lush lips with a pencil. "Yes. I suppose it's all perfectly true. But . . ."

A muscle tensed visibly in his jaw. He paced away from her, swung around, came jauntily back:

"The more civilized a man may be, or a woman, or child, the less readily he, or she, or the child will admit panic. That is what 'civilized' means: understanding, self-control, knowledge, discipline, individual responsibility. What happens, then, if a civilized society finds itself confronted with a reasonable fear, yet one of such a magnitude and nature that it cannot be tolerated by the combined efforts of reason and the common will? Such luckless multitudes, faced with that dilemma, will have but one solution. Feeling a gigantic fear they cannot (or they will not) face, they must pretend they have no fear. They must say aloud repeatedly, 'There is no reason to be afraid.' They must ridicule those who show fear's symptoms. Especially, they must pit themselves, for the sake of a protective illusion, against all persons who endeavor to take the measure of the common dread and respond sensibly to its scope. To act otherwise would be to admit the inadmissible, the fact of their repressed panic.

"Thus a condition is set up in which a vast majority of the citizens, unable to acknowledge with their minds the dread that eats at their blind hearts, loses all contact with reality. The sensible steps are not taken. The useful slogans are outlawed. The proper attitudes are deemed improper. Appropriate responses to the universal peril dwindle, diminish and at last disappear.

"All the while, the primordial alarms are kept kindled in the darkness of self-shuttered souls. Within them, in mortal quaking, march the impulses that set Inquisitions going, threw over liberty, brought down truth screaming, and assembled men repeatedly for bloody rites. Men's 'leaders,' most of them, take up the suicidal expressions of the mob. For leadership, alas, is of two sorts: one, that courageous chieftainship which administers according to high principle, whatever the mob's view at the moment; the other, specious and chimerical, a 'leadership' which merely rides upon the wave of mob emotion, capitalizing it for private aggrandizement, and no more truly leads than a man 'leads' the sea as it dashes him toward death on a rock. Such leaders—Hitler is an example—are in the end engulfed by that which sustained them. The other sort, true leaders—Lincoln was one—conduct the people by truth and reason through their panic to security, oftentimes *against* its stream.

"There are no Lincolns among us today."

"That," said Mrs. Berwyn, "will get you some dirty wires from Washington."

Coley sat down on the edge of his desk and dictated more quietly, sometimes kicking his heels against the bleached mahogany:

"We, the people of the United States of America, have refused for more than a decade to face our real fear. We know our world could end. Every month, every year, several nations are discovering the fabricating instruments which make that ultimate doom more likely. The antagonism between a free way of life and a totalitarian way is absolute. And it appears to be unresolvable owing to the expressed, permanent irreconcilability of Communism.

"What have we done about all this? The answer is shocking. We have failed to meet the challenge. We have shirked the duty of free men. We have evaded every central fact. We have relied on ancient instruments of security without examining the new risks—reinforcing military strength while we left relatively undefended and unarmed the targets of another war: our cities, our homes.

"Many of us, intellectual men, liberals, humanistic in our beliefs, had stood about for upward of a decade muttering, 'There must be no next war.' That is childish; it is mad. Wars are generally made by unilateral decision: they are the aggressions of one nation. Not a single man among those who has insisted we get along, henceforward, 'without war'—since war may spell the earth's end—has offered a solitary idea or performed a solitary act that has lessened war's likelihood. How could such people, who call their wishful thoughts 'ideals,' be anything but soothsayers? War, if it is to be avoided, must be quenched in the Kremlin and in the broad confines of Russia, taken with its captive states. But these people who say there *must be* no war are all in Illinois, or Arizona, or New York State—not Russia.

"Others, feeling appalled and thus compelled to do *something*, however ineffectual, to assuage the pain of their anxieties, have limited their hostility to the here and the now, to the known—and so somewhat evaded, by the delusion, the real, external source of terror. These persons—and they number scores of millions of self-satisfied good Americans—have been content to launch a long and heated crusade against Communism at home, its dupes, its puppets and its sinister agents.

"Conspiracy to destroy this Government by violence is treason. The mere desire to see liberty abolished in order that a compulsive, Communist state may replace it, seems vicious to every person who loves freedom. There is no doubt that domestic Communists are dangerous to liberty. But is it sensible to convert a true dread of the world's end to a chase of putative traitors and minor spies, giving freedom, the while, no other service and no sacrifice at all? It is not.

"Yet in that one process, multitudes of the people of America and many of their leaders in the Congress have also set aside the concept of freedom itself! They have seized the instruments and ideologies of their foe—with the notion of 'fighting fire with fire.' Every private right has been violated, under the Capitol's dome. The innocent have been condemned without trial. Envy, spite, lies and malicious gossip have been brought to bear on solid citizens, destroying them. So the medieval lust of men cowering before holocaust has been exploited, to make little men look big. We have emulated the tricks of Hitler and Stalin. Today, when some of us pronounce the word 'un-American,' what we mean belies the significance of Americanism as every great citizen conceived it from the Founding Fathers until this day. A love of liberty, fair play, justice now is widely held synonymous with 'un-Americanism!' Today, a man who defends all we have ever stood for is liable to abuse as a 'potential traitor.' All liberty is being turned about: conformity, slavishness, sedulous sycophancy, these are being held true evidences of patriotism. Such traitor-hunting methodology is a sickness of the American mind, a cancer in the frightened soul of a formerly great people. 'Set a thief to catch a thief,' says a cynic's proverb; even the cynic does not admonish, 'To catch a thief, become one.'

"Even religion, even the holy name of God, is used to restrict the rights of a people dedicated to religious freedom."

Mrs. Berwyn whistled. "There you go again!"

His answering grin was bleak. "Then grab your hat, Bea. Because I'm telling the truth, for once." He went on:

"A few years ago a new President of these United States made several loosely considered assertions about God and America. Americanism, he indicated, is founded in a belief in God; atheism, he suggested, is synonymous with the alien doctrines of the Soviet. This was an exultant discovery—for churchgoers, however evil their private conduct, narrow their views, or sleazy their religious tenets. For now, all atheists, agnostics and all the religiously unconforming could be looked upon by millions with suspicion, as Communists, or near to Communism. Special Faith was made to seem an American imperative—and Freedom died a new death.

"The attitude was a desecration of the principle upon which our nation is founded: religious freedom, tolerance, deliverance from persecution on any, and every, philosophical ground. For if we are a free people, we are *not* bound to conform to anybody's belief, but only to let others believe and practice as they will, so long as they do not interfere with the general rights. It matters nothing what Presidents say; they come and go. We cannot, in simple fact, conform religiously. Any overt effort to do so would split and wreck this nation without recourse to arms and bombs. It is liberty that permits us to exist and grow strong, not conformity to one God, one cult, or any other beliefs save a belief in the freedom of the conscience of every citizen. Religious freedom means we are responsible as a people to freedom itself, not to any God. Responsibility even to

God—if it were mandatory in this land, as so many have begun to imagine—would merely raise the question: Whose God?

"It is a terrible question to ask in such an hour, a question more destructive and divisive among free men than enemy assault. For we Americans have come our long way in harmony simply because it is 'un-American' to insist on belief in aught but liberty. If we do, then shall it be more or less 'American' to believe in the Presbyterian Trinity? Or is the Baptist Faith correct and does every individual have to decide for himself about God, acknowledging only certain holy names in baptism. What of the Jews? Is their Jehovah the suitable God of Americans and their Law proper for all? And the Catholics! Is every American obliged to venerate the Virgin in order to show, as all Catholics believe, a true reverence? Suppose a Hindu becomes a citizen here? Are his many 'gods' also to be our God? Is Vishnu? And what of a Confucianist who truly believes 'God' to be good manners and perfect ethics? Then, let us ask, do Christian Scientists believe in God at all? According to millions of Protestants and others, they are rank heretics, the deluded followers of a woman from Boston. What of Ralph Waldo Emerson's Unitarians?

"You can see here why we cannot accept the President's implications that Americanism connotes belief in God: Americans have too many diverse ideas concerning God to attempt conformity. And besides, they have, or once had, freedom in the matter.

"This last leads to a greater irony. For those Americans who are of most value in this terrible age—the men of science, the technicians, the sociologists and psychologists—the only persons who offer America *any* practical hope of deliverance from present panic—do not, by and large, believe in God at all, according to the conventional descriptions of organized Faiths. These men and women are in one sense *opposed* to 'faith.' They have accepted, in their heads and hearts, a search for truth and an inquiry into reality, in place of all creedal statement. Yet they are no less honest, honorable, pure and true than other men. On the contrary, because their minds are not suborned by the intellectual despotism of this outworn creed or yonder debunked dogma, they are, as a group, *more* honest, *more* honorable, *more* truthful and *more* reliable than the conventionally religious. *They are the people who have made most of humanity's advances;* the rest are followers, often reluctant, sometimes sadistic and destructive.

"If, by pretending 'Americanism' is synonymous with religious faith, we alarm these people in our midst—the discoverers, pioneers, leaders of thought, inventors, scientists, educators—then we shall truly have beheaded the nation in the name of Godliness. It is one more symptom of our hidden panic.

"There are many others besides. If the McCarthys should remove from U.S.A. every single Communist and Communist suspect, the present danger to us all—so clear, so terrible——*would not be measurably alleviated.*" Coley cleared his throat. "Underline the last phrase twice, Bea." He continued, "America would be Communist-free, spy-free, to be sure. But half a billion people elsewhere in the world, Communists all or slaves of Communists, would *still* be undeterred and laboring day and night to destroy liberty on earth and the United States in particular. We would have killed a few gnats and let fatal hemorrhage run unchecked. That is the measure of the cosmic *unimportance* of the Senator from our sister state. And that is the measure of the foolishness of those who hold the credulous notion that the Mc-

Carthys are accomplishing work of primary importance in the matter of our imminent doom."

"I never thought of it quite that way." Mrs. Berwyn stretched, sank long fingers in her rust-red hair and yawned.

"That's what I'm getting at. The people in River City, the folks in Green Prairie, don't think of it that way either. But that's the way it is. It's like anti-Semitism. You wipe out the Jews, and what have you got? The same old problems, sins, poverties, wars, troubles and evils as always. Plus a guilt-ridden population, a bunch of executioners who have learned to fear each other. You wipe out every Commie in U.S.A., and what would you have? Russia to deal with, unchanged. And a bunch of Americans who had violated their own trustworthiness and so become scared of one another, for dam' good cause!—without solving their problem *at all!*"

Mrs. Berwyn demurred. "Still, I hate to think of any Commies sneaking around in Government, in the Pentagon, anywhere . . ."

"Me, too. Catching them, though, isn't an amateur sport. It's a hard job for the FBI and the intelligence and counter-intelligence people." He whipped out a pocket handkerchief and wiped his damp face. "Do you realize how nutty we've become? Getting professors to sign oaths? Making a lot out of whether or not people refuse to admit party membership? Your real, dangerous, hard-core Commie will sign *any* oath. He'll swear to *any* lie. He belongs to a church. He maybe even works as an investigator for a Senate committee. His Communism is hidden under careful coats of everything that looks 'American' to the most brassy patriot, the biggest oaf. These Senators have 'exposed' a number of Commies—sure. How many *dangerous* ones have they unearthed? Put it the other way. Why don't they turn up some people who were unsuspected even of liberalism? Get my point? Let a Senator and his posse of meddlers expose one three-star general in the pay of the Kremlin, or a bishop or a nun—and I'll have some respect for this empty game of sifting miscellaneous fools, skeptics and dissenters through a mesh of senatorial bigotry, prejudice, empty-headedness and personal ambition. Show the people the enemies of freedom and you are really a great man, I say. Play on their fears, feed them straw men and whipping boys, and Huey Long's your name!" Coley shrugged.

"Is that all?" she asked.

"All?" He stared uncomprehendingly. "No. Not quite all." He walked across the room and gazed over the moon-ghosted cities as he talked on:

"Some of us, nowadays, take refuge in such medieval and panicky hiding places as these, undoing our own liberty in false hope of saving our skins. Some are sillier still. They look to people, imaginary people not unlike God, to come from 'outer space' and save them. They see Flying Saucers on every breeze and in every night sky and console themselves with the idea that beings 'higher' than themselves will soon come and save mankind from man and his bombs. This is escapism, too, fantasy, exactly such superstitious stuff as was the foundation for many medieval tenets.

"Others take their qualms back to the churches—the churches they abandoned years back for golf on Sunday, bridge, pleasure riding, and TV. There are millions. They are praying for peace, now, and protection against holocaust. Such prayer, uttered ardently by billions to every major diety man's been able to invent, has never yet been answered! The wars have gone on. Those historic devotees who exhausted themselves, their time and energy in such incantations were merely easier prey for foes they would not prepare for. This indeed may be the American fate—the price of doing away with intellectual freedom and putting a compulsion on belief. *Yet, in all the other provinces of peril, we stay sane."*

His eyes focused on the far phosphors of the night. "On our prairies," he dictated, "farmers, fearing the onslaught of the wind, dig cyclone cellars. They rod their barns and ground their aerials, lest the lightning strike. If the autumn is dry, their ploughs make circuits around their homes and livestock pens so prairie fire cannot consume what they hold dear." He looked far away, to his right. "Downstream on the Green Prairie River, and below on the Missouri, men have erected great dams, constructed lakes, set up levees, against flood. In our cities, lest fire break out, we maintain engines and men to save us from burning. And against all crimes, police patrol our streets, in cars these days, vigilant with every electronic device. We have appraised many dangers and prepared against them in these and a hundred other fashions. *What of the peril of world's end?*

"Today in Washington, men who do not, who cannot, understand what it is they are talking about argue interminably concerning how doomsday may be resisted or put off. Since, in their technical ignorance, they cannot appraise recent perils, their thoughts concerning the perils to come are useless. We maintain a navy—against what may never move by sea. We levy vast armies and hold them the final arbiter of every battle even though, just the other year, an empire called Japan fell to us with never a foot soldier on its main islands. We believe our airplanes can deliver stroke for stroke, and better, but we will not count the effect of strokes upon ourselves. We admit our radar screen is leaky. We have dreamed up—and left largely on drawing boards— such weapons as might adequately defend a sky-beleaguered metropolis. In sum, we face the rage of radioactivity, the blast of neutrons, the killing solar fires, with peashooters and squirt guns.

"Indeed, if the findings of our local schoolmarms are accepted, we soon may taboo even the *mention* of such dangers. It upsets the pupils, they say; Rorschach Tests reveal this remarkable perturbation. All hell may be winging toward us in the sky but, in the name of American education, let us not permit it to ruffle a single second-grader!"

Mrs. Berwyn snorted.

His answering grin was bleak. "It's the truth! Minerva just sent us some bloody pedagogical bulletin full of 'data' about 'anxiety-curve-rise' with every set of atom tests in Nevada. Minerva feels, and she's backed up by nervous parents and whole school boards, that the radio, TV and press should, perhaps, stop publishing any reference *whatever* to mass-destruction weapons, atomic-energy tests, or anything connected with the subject."

"The ostrich principle?"

"Yeah. That got us, unready, into two big wars lately and several small ones."

"Anything else?" she asked.

"Just a paragraph or two." His desk chair received him, squeaked a little as he tipped it back, boosted his feet onto his blotter and spoke:

"America had—and missed—its only golden chance. If, in 1945, or 1946, or even 1947, the American people had seen the clear meaning of liberty, there would have been no war and there would be no danger now. The proposition is exquisitely simple. Our nation is founded on the theory that the majority of the people, if informed, will make appropriate decisions. That, in turn, implies—it necessitates—

the one freedom that underlies all others: freedom to know, intellectual liberty, the open access of all men to all truth. That—*that alone*—is the cornerstone of liberty and democracy. When the Soviets showed the first signs of enclosing, in Soviet secrecy, mere scientific principles like those of the bomb, we Americans could and should have seen that Russian secrecy would instantly compel American secrecy. We should have seen that an America thus suddenly made secret, in the realm of science where knowledge had thitherto been open, would no longer be free, and its democratic people could no longer be informed. Hence Russia's Iron Curtain would have been seen as what it was and is and always will be: a posture of intolerable aggression against American freedom.

"If that had been seen at the time, the Iron Curtain could have been dissolved by a mere ultimatum: America then was the earth's most powerful nation, Russia was devastated. But we were powerful only in arms and trusted them. We were feeble-minded in ideals and ideology: our vision of freedom was myopic. We, too, clamped down on abstract knowledge a new, un-American curtain called 'security,' and every kind of freedom commenced inevitably to dwindle in a geometric progression. That was our chance. Our peril today, our ever-growing and ever-more-horrible peril in the visible future, is the cost of saying we were free and acting otherwise. We flubbed the greatest chance for liberty in human history and hardly even noted our blunder, our betrayal.

"Ten years have gone by. We could, at vast expense, have decentralized our cities. We didn't. We could, at lesser expense, have ringed our continent with adequate warning devices and learned to empty our cities in a few hours. We didn't. The cost, still, was too great; the dislocation of human beings, the drills and inconveniences, beyond our bearing. We had cause, in a struggle to regain landsliding liberties, we have always had the cause, to challenge Soviet power earlier, in the name of liberty, brotherhood, justice, human integrity and decency. All we did was to make a few peripheral challenges, as in Korea. We didn't face the issue when the Kremlin's bombs were scarce and weak. We are not even good opportunists.

"Now, the sands of a decade and more have run out. We cannot challenge without venturing the world's end. Quite possibly our death notice is written, a few months or years farther along on the track of this wretched planet. Then, perhaps, our flight from freedom will get the globe rent into hot flinders, atomized gas. But the only question before you, citizens of Green Prairie, of River City, of the wide prairie region, of this momentarily fair nation and the lovely world, is this, apparently:

"What new idiocy can you dream up, with your coffee, your porridge, your first cigarette, *to keep yourself awhile longer from facing these truths?*"

Coley fell silent. He wiped his brow again.

"What do we do with it?" Mrs. Berwyn asked, a little stunned by the blunt finale.

"Eh?" He was paying no attention.

"I said, what shall I do? Tear it up? Do you want it transscribed? Is it for the archives, so you can whip it out someday in case it's justified?"

He was looking at her, then, perplexedly. "I said. It's tomorrow's editorial."

"You're kidding."

"Why?"

She glanced apprehensively at her wrist watch and back at the smallish man in the chair. "It would fill the whole page.

There's hardly time to set it up, anyhow, to make the home-delivery edition. Bulldog's almost out . . ."

"Shoot it right to composing," he said, yawning.

She stood up and came to the side of his desk. "You quitting the *Transcript,* Coley, after you spent your life to build it?"

"Maybe."

"What do you mean—*maybe?* This thing rubs salt in every sore in town! It kicks every private idol to smithereens!"

"Yeah. And may wake up a sleepwalking nation."

"It violates what people *believe.* Even some of what *I* believe."

"Does it?"

"I think it does," she answered, suddenly doubtful. She was close to unprecedented tears. "You *can't* do it, Coley. You can't kick apart the town you love!"

"I'm trying to keep it from *being* kicked apart!"

"Do me a favor. Do us all a favor. Do the *Transcript* a favor. Wait till tomorrow. Let everybody mull it over———"

"Remember, Bea, back in nineteen forty-three. When I went abroad?"

"What's *that* got to do———"

"To England," he said, musingly. "The whole Middle West refused to believe in the blitz. The folks were deluded then, the same way. They wouldn't face the fury of Hitler's *Luftwaffe*—and they wouldn't admit the British had the guts to take such a beating. I went over, just so they could read the stories of a typical Middle Western editor—written from London, while the fire bombs fell and the ack-ack drummed. *Remember?*"

"Sure," she said. "My husband was alive—then."

He ignored that human dating of the occasion. "I went because, by God, I'm an *editor.* Because I knew what the papers reported was the truth. Because I thought an editor, an American editor, was obligated to help the American people *face facts*. I *still* think so!"

"Even, Coley, if it means you commit newspaper suicide?"

He rocked forward in his chair and began, delicately, to straighten and align the objects which comprised his desk set: clock, calendar, pens, pencils, inkstand, paper cutter, memo pad, the engraved paperweight given him by the YMCA Newsboys Club.

He said, "Sure. Even if it marches me off the stage."

"You think it's *right?*"

"I think *anything* else is wrong. Dead wrong. And almost everybody is wrong. I was on the edge of that conclusion a long while back. Weeks. I reached it when good old Hank Conner came in tonight. Besides"—he turned and smiled at the big woman—"who knows? Minerva Sloan has brains. Lots of brains. The arguments in that editorial make plain common sense. She won't *listen* to them; she won't read them in the places where they're appearing. In her own paper, though, she'll *have* to read them!"

"You think you can change the mind of Minerva?"

"Stranger things have been accomplished."

"I better get to my typewriter."

He watched her go—the magnificence of her hair—the absurdity of her make-up—the splendor of her bosom and hips— the fantastic smallness of her high-heeled shoes. His blood stirred and he half rose.

"Old ass," he said of himself, aloud.

Just before daybreak, remembering he'd had no dinner, he went down to Court Avenue and Fenwick and had pumpkin pie and coffee at the Baltimore Lunch. Some raggedy women, charwomen from the tall buildings, were sliding trays along the vast cafeteria's silver rails. A man—perhaps a once-respectable man—a bum now. One of his own reporters. A young girl in a yellow evening dress, a too-young girl, for the hour, with a disheveled college boy, slightly drunk. The white-dressed people behind the glass counters and steam tables looked sleepy.

He went back up in the lonely elevator and watched dawn invest the cities.

Life returned to the great building, where it had not quite perished in the long night. The presses, underground, shook it a little. Doors slammed. Elevators hummed at intervals. It didn't sleep, quite. And as the light increased, the tower became a tympanum that vibrated in tempo with the increasing traffic down below.

When the sun cut deep into the man-made canyons, throwing aside the rectilinear shadows of the buildings, shining on windshields, bus tops, palisades of glass windows, he knew Minerva would be awake. She would be ringing for her maid. Getting coffee and a folded copy of the morning paper which she owned. Making phone calls to executives who would try, by alert rejoinders, to pretend they, also, greeted every daybreak with all snoring put aside, eyes open and a message-to Garcia avidity for the new day's commands. Coley knew.

His phone rang. "Lo?"

"This is Minerva Sloan."

" 'Morning, Minerva. How——"

"You're fired, Coley."

He put on his hat and coat when he went out that time.

3

Gossip can have good uses. It is deplored because its uses are so often opposite. They depend on who does the gossiping; through idle talk, the well-disposed sometimes find out about the hidden sufferings of others and go to their aid—or they learn the degree of temptation that resulted in a sin and so forgive the sinner. Without gossip, indeed, life would be dull and much of its subtle business would remain unfinished. It has, however, a poor reputation amongst conscientious people; they usually inhibit impulse if the material in their minds seems of a gossipy nature.

Silence can be unfortunate. If, before Chuck's departure for the base in Texas, his father had let drop the fact that Beau Bailey had asked him for a loan of five thousand, Beau's life might have been changed. For Chuck might then have reported noticing Beau, slugged and furtive, as he emerged from a shady building in The Block. Those two facts, if they had by chance come out at the dinner table, might have led Mrs. Conner to express certain observations and opinions she had kept to herself. They were, first, that Charles had returned to service in a concealed but very deep depression, second, that the newspapers had published a picture of Lenore and Kit Sloan and that Lenore didn't seem very happy in the photograph, and third, that Beau was drinking more than ever while Netta, surprisingly, was going around like a cat with the canary well down and the feathers lapped clear. Nora, then confessing her innocent eavesdropping, could have confirmed what Charles had not disclosed and her mother only suspected: Lenore and Kit were, indeed, resuming an interest.

Such, at any rate, were the facts and observations at the collective disposal of the family. Had they been pooled, through gossip, they would certainly have led the Conners to the conclusion that Beau was in worse financial trouble than usual, that he had possibly done something desperate or illegal to try to scramble from his perennial difficulties, that

Netta was "throwing Lenore at Kit Sloan's head"—with some success, and in the transparent hope of establishing a state of permanent family solvency—that Lenore had finally told Chuck their affection was impracticable and that their unexpressed "understanding" no longer existed, and that the neighbor girl was not pleased with the exploitation of her beauty.

If they had clearly realized all this, the Connors, being kindhearted, would have acted. They would have acted out of generosity, even if the lifelong love of their older son and their deep fondness for Lenore hadn't been involved. Hank would have offered Beau the five thousand, selling a mortgage he'd taken for a friend, or cashing in some war bonds, or borrowing on his insurance or, perhaps, just asking for a loan from Mr. Morse, the owner of the hardware stores. But since, by and large, the Conners didn't gossip, the bits and tabs of information which would have made clear a whole only hazily suspected were never assembled.

Beau's "moral fiber," such as it was, consisted of conflicts amongst fears. His capacity to be afraid, however, was considerable. A man who was a physical coward, and nothing else, would have capitulated if possible to the warning Jake had emphasized by having Toledo "slug him a couple." But Beau was more afraid of prison than of blows; could he have served a term under an assumed name, he would have dreaded prison far less than social ostracism. He feared his wife next most of all persons, Minerva Sloan most.

Hence it was not until the last week in October that Beau, made desperate by a series of ever-more-menacing (and constantly harder-to-explain) phone calls, decided to act. Jake, and Toledo, had taken to phoning him at the bank and their voices were not the sort Beau wanted to have the operator hear. Like many who commit crime, however, Beau was brought to the actual deed by idle opportunity as much as by resolve.

It was a period of pre-Christmas inventory.

From the vaults, methodically, with armed guards watching, a number of "portfolios" were fetched for checking. These were, of course, not cardboard "folios" but metal boxes containing lists, account books, receipts, letters, orders, and sheaves of certificates.

And it was while this routine checking was in progress late one afternoon that Miss Tully's mother got a sudden appendicitis, called the doctor, was whisked to the Jenkins Memorial Hospital which, like the Presbyterian Church and some of the city's finest residences, was situated on the shore of Crystal Lake. The hospital promptly informed Miss Tully an emergency operation was imminent; that distracted woman, who had served the bank for twenty-seven years (with a total absence of but eleven days), appealed to Beau. He was not very nice about it, but he let her go.

It left him with her work to be "shouldered" in addition to his own. He happened that day to have nothing whatever left to do. It was three fifteen, a rainy, raw afternoon, and the main floor, with cages all around and stand-up desks in rows in the center, was already empty of customers. The doors were closed and Bill Maine, the front-door guard, was reading a copy of the *Saturday Evening Post* in a shaft of insufficent light that fell from the outer gloom through a high, barred window.

The bank was comparatively quiet. Business machines made more noise than voices. No clerk, of course, could hear the hard rain, for the roof was twenty-odd stories overhead and the rain fell straight. When Miss Tully departed, in still-damp, evil-smelling accouterments for foul weather, Beau was left in his office with three large deposit boxes and Miss

Ames, his secretary, a niece of a vice-president, a recent business-school graduate, suffering now from a head cold.

He set himself to do the checking which had engaged Miss Tully, leafing in a desultory way through the amassed holdings of one John M. Jessup, of Larkimer County, a livestock dealer. If Beau remembered rightly, Jessup was about seven feet tall, had a sparrow's voice, wore two pairs of glasses, had cleaned up on beeves in the First World War, and hadn't been in at the bank since Truman left office. Beau always remembered people. But even those facts did not move Beau to wider ratiocination. What moved him was the observation, in his hands, of ten one-thousand-dollar bonds, issued by Hobart Metal Products when they had expanded the works on the west side of town.

Just half those, Beau thought, would get me out of all my worries. Only *then* did he recall the rarity of Mr. Jessup's visits. And only after that did he glance at the sonorous Miss Ames. "How would you like," he said, "to go across to Sherman's and get me—*us*—some coffee?"

She took the slight falter in his voice for an employer weakness. "Not much. It's raining."

"You go underground. There's a passage. One of the girls down in the stenographic pool will show you." Beau made up, that time, for his prior lack of assurance.

The girl said, "Oke," stuck her gum on the under edge of her desk, rose, and began to make up: there might be boys in the passageway.

When she had departed, Beau studied the opaque glass walls of his cubicle and decided they were, indeed, opaque. Then he looked briefly from the door, at an empty corridor. After that he tried to remember the present market value of Hobart Metal bonds. He thought it was par, but wasn't sure. If he were going to borrow five, he might as well be certain and take six. He folded them on their creases and tucked them carefully into an inside breast pocket. Only then did he remember his exposure in the window. He whirled with horror and stared up at the stacked panes across the street. Lights shown in every one and rain poured between. There were faces and people moving, but no one seemed to be interested in him, in anything in his direction which—when you considered—probably looked like nothing but a lot of teeming rain.

He took the inventory list and correctly reduced the number of listed bonds from ten to four. He then made out, in a disguised writing, a receipt for six bonds and signed it with an indecipherable scrawl, using a bank pen and bank ink. He pulled out the nib afterward, put in a new one, and pocketed the old. Nobody, he thought, could prove who had written the receipt or show with what it had been signed. Not even experts. And, anyway, the absence of the bonds would go unsuspected.

It took two more days to complete the transaction and set his mind at rest. Or momentarily at rest.

The following morning was still rainy. Taking Netta somewhat into his confidence, he explained it would be "useful" if she alibied him with a slight cold. She did not enquire more deeply. She called the bank and talked about "a couple of degrees temperature" and "doctor's orders."

It happened, owing to Country Club contacts, that Beau knew an officer in the Ferndale Branch of the Owen National Bank of Commerce, who was a "good man to go to in a tight spot." His name was Wesley Martinson. Beau had cultivated the man, played a few rounds of golf with him, come to call him "Wes"—probably because his subconscious mind invariably noted down the fact that a fellow useful in a tight spot might someday be handy to him. Beau had that kind of foresight—quantities of it.

Wes greeted him without surprise, ushered him into a private room in the branch bank, sat, performed smoking amenities and said, "Well, Beau, what can we do for you?"

Beau had pretty much taken the measure of his man, through the medium of a hundred off-color stories retailed by Wes with almost writhing relish. Beau therefore chuckled and said, "Frankly, I want you to help me perform a small robbery."

Wes chortled. "Son, that's what banks are for. And you've come to the right banker."

Beau took the bonds from a very old and battered big envelope which bore his name and in which for years he had kept unpaid bills. It looked exactly like something that had lain in a vault a long while, holding bonds. He threw the parchment-stiff, aging paper on Wesley Martinson's desk. "Want to borrow on these."

Wes picked them up, studied them and said, "They don't *look* counterfeit."

Beau chuckled. "Nope. Something I stashed before the tax rate knifed us. Trouble is, I don't want the little woman to realize I'm borrowing on them."

The other man frowned. "I see."

"The hell you do see! However, I'll let you in on the sight, one of these days. She has"—Beau made curves with his hands. "All blonde, and when I say all, I mean *all.*"

Wes unconsciously ran his tongue along the underside of his long top lip. "Isn't that kind of skidding around, for the cashier of Sloan?"

"With her you don't skid, son. She's safely married."

As Beau knew, the invention suited his own need for cover

as well as the other man's mind. Wes chuckled. "I guess Owen
National can help you maintain your little relationship. Security's okay. You know the rates."

"I should!" Beau said and took the proffered pen.

Not that evening, but the next, Beau made his way to
The Block. He was determined, having obtained the needed
money, and a few hundreds extra, for private use when and
if and as needed, to expose himself to no further risks. So he
approached by bus, then taxi, and then a second taxi and at
last on foot.

Jake was there, in his littered office. He took the five one-
thousand-dollar bills without comment. He dug in a greasy file
for some time, produced Beau's I.O.U.'s, handed them over,
and then looked across his cigar stub. "Where'd you get the
dough?"

"Borrowed it," Beau answered cheerfully.

"Off who?"

"Friend."

"What friend?"

"I can't say. It was—a woman." Beau was suddenly very
nervous. He had entered the gambling place confidently,
whistling a little. He had thought that all Jake wanted was the
money. He realized, in a new way, that he was in the windowless back room of a stone building which once had been
a house and was now empty, pretty much. At least the big
downstairs room, with the wheels and dice tables under
dusty canvas, was empty and had been for months—since
the latest police cleanup.

"What woman?" Jake said.

"I told you . . . Look! I paid. We're square. So what?"

Jake didn't have a mean face, a vicious face, even a very
Italian face. He looked like every other man who stands in
a dirty white apron beside a green-grocery stall in an open

market. He hardly lifted his voice. "Toledo," he called, and Toledo, who did have a vicious face, came in from the dark hall.

It was not necessary to say anything to Beau about the meaning of Toledo's summons. Toledo had, a month before, landed three crashing blows on Beau's face, flooding him with agony, weakening his knees, almost making him throw up.

"I just want to know," Jake said, "if this is hot money. I don't *care* whether it's hot or not. I take it, either way. I just want to know. Ask him, Toledo."

Before Beau could cry, "No!" the first blow knocked him off his feet and halfway across the dirty, worn carpet. He got up. He got out a handkerchief. Shaking like a rabbit in a snake's mouth, he said gaspingly, "Okay. I had to borrow a couple of bonds from a dead account at the bank. You guys won't wait. The bank can."

"Whose account?"

"I forget," Beau said.

"Ask him whose account, Toledo."

Beau managed to stave it off this time by darting to the farthest corner as he said, "John Jessup."

Jake nodded thoughtfully. "So okay. What are you hanging around here for?"

Beau ran out of the room, ran down the stairs, tripped, almost fell, and found the gloomy sanctuary of night. He hadn't gone many blocks before he realized, clearly, rather than in a horror-strewn corner of his brain, that now—and forever—Jake really had him by the short hair.

Sweat broke out over him; for several blocks he couldn't remember which street led back to Market.

Beau was one of the luckless. . . .

Two weeks after the termination of his dealings with Jake, two weeks of blessed relief after an at least temporary termination, Beau walked across the marble floor of the bank, on the way to lunch. He had decided, as usual—after a struggle, as usual—that he'd have two Manhattans and pork chops: weather was really cold now.

His eye detected a singular customer amongst the hurrying, queued scores, the dozens writing and blotting at the desk.

It was a very, very tall man, wearing two pairs of glasses, waiting in line at one of the "Trust Funds" windows.

It was John Jessup.

X-Day Minus Thirty

1

Some undistinguished men are heroes; some distinguished heroes are not men at all in the good sense of the name; and such a person was Kit Sloan. He was unaware of the defect as are thousands.

From his ancestors, he had taken his lithe, big body and the resilient "constitution" that went with it. From a forgotten forebear, probably a carefully forgotten one, he'd come by the "Sloan darkness," the coloring of eyes and hair and skin which had suggested to Nora Conner a Latin actor. Some said the Sloans had Italian blood, others said gypsy, and some, of course, hit upon the truth—commonplace in the west: an Indian squaw had participated in combining the Sloan genes.

No one who had lived a long life in either of the Sister Cities would deny that the Sloans had brains; any native of vintage age could add, often from harsh experience, that Minerva brought to the family an additional measure of shrewdness and force besides. Kittridge Sloan, in whom these

elements presumably reposed, conceived of himself as so imbued and endowed with every needful quality as to make
demonstration unnecessary save when he chose. He did not
often choose. To be sure, he was obliged to do a certain
amount of work to graduate from Princeton, where he'd been
sent at nineteen. He enjoyed sports, however, and was so pro-
ficient at them that professors who might otherwise have
failed him were possibly persuaded not to do so by anxious
coaches. Besides, Kit invariably elected the easiest courses:
he had a definite knack for finding paths of least resistance.
Whether he could have exhibited, under pressure, the acumen
of his parents remained unknown; he chose not to try, deem-
ing it unnecessary.

He interrupted his undergraduate career for military service. His mother preferred the Navy, but Kit, for once opposing
her wishes, went into the Air Force. Athletes have an affinity
for flying, often, and Kit, who'd ridden the fastest horses and
driven the fastest cars (with several mishaps in the Sister
Cities which had been expensive to his family and more than
bruising to his fellow citizens), took easily to flying.

He found himself in actual combat, as an interceptor pilot
in the Eighth Air Force, over England, before he thought to
regret the whole thing. Until he was shot at, he had kept his
mind closed to that aspect of his temporary trade. But when,
high in the British air, he felt and saw German bullets entering the delicate tissues of his plane, Kit went into funk. He
dived clear of attack, leaving two wing mates exposed to a
fate which both met soon and heroically. On the ground, he
found a plausible explanation for his "lucky" escape. The attack upon six Nazi scouting fighters had not been observed
by anybody save those engaged. It was a cloudy day.

Kit knew, however, that in some very present mission he
would be obliged again to engage the foe and he knew he

would, again, turn tail. He spent two febrile days trying to figure a way out of a situation which, until then, he had regarded as an exhilarating sport and which, to his horror, had become deadly dangerous. Then, on what he sweatily felt was the eve of his disgrace, he and his fighter group were reassigned to another field and a different activity. Buzz bombs had appeared over Britain and it was the task of Kit to intercept these, if possible.

Attacking buzz bombs was dangerous and demanded skill. Ram-jet engines drove the miniature planes at terrific speed, for that era. It was necessary to wait high above, spot one (or learn of an approach by radio) and dive down toward it, using the acceleration of the plunge to overtake the missile. When these bombs were shot at, they usually exploded in the air and the plane that did the shooting was often unable to evade the blast. Thus, some attacking planes, in the early days, blew up themselves to save London's citizens; others on the same dedicated mission were torn to bits as they streaked into flying fragments. Soon, however, it was discovered that the slipstream of an overshooting fighter could be used to knock down a buzz bomb, tipping it over, causing it to crash prematurely in the open countryside rather than on the intended city.

This feat was a matter of technique and daring. And the V1's had a negative characteristic which perfectly suited Kit's personality: they did not shoot back. A cool and skillful pilot with very fast reflexes, Kit became one of the most celebrated assailants of the buzz bombs and so a hero. Where he would have failed altogether in the purpose for which he had been trained, this substitute endeavor matched his inadequate specifications. No one ever doubted, not even the men in his own squadron, that his "nerve" was anything but consummate. It was, so long as the risks he took involved only decisions made by himself. The appearance of any factor he could not control, such as hostile fire, alone unmanned him. He had cut close to pedestrians and other cars—and clipped a few—all his life: diving on a ton of HE carried by a zombie aircraft was no different. It could not hurt *him* so long as he made no blunders at the controls. That was his psychology and he came home to U.S.A., went back to Princeton, cloaked in a wreath of medals, Sister City awe and maternal ecstasy.

By that time, so long as the issue did not rise in fact, Kit had completely repressed his short-term awareness of any combat defect. He could talk air slaughter on even terms with any ace.

On a cold, gray day, shortly before Thanksgiving, feeling at loose ends and noting (on the bathroom scales, after rising and showering) that he had gained five unwanted pounds, Kit made two decisions which he regarded as important. He would skip lunch for a week. And he would get more exercise.

At breakfast he told his mother, with the urgent solemnity of a businessman who had decided to open a new branch, or a surgeon, to open a peritoneum. They were sitting in the upstairs breakfast room of the Sloan mansion, looking out over their landscaped acres on Pearson Square which, in Victoria's time (or Garfield's or Grover Cleveland's), had been the center of River City bon ton but now, save where Minerva held the fort, was much like the decayed area a mile or so on the other side of Market Street: a run-down neighborhood in which the big houses were compartmented for roomers, or hung with signs denoting piano and voice instruction, furniture repair, spiritualist readings, philately and whatnot, or torn down and replaced by already shabby row houses, which in some instances had yielded again to supermarkets and filling stations.

"Five pounds," Kit said with a shake of his handsome head.

Minerva shook hers in sympathy. "But why not eat a small breakfast and a small lunch?"

"It's a problem, I admit. If I don't eat lunch at all, I'll get hellishly hungry. That means, I'll have to do something pretty interesting in the afternoon, to stave off the old pangs. So I thought I'd drive the Jag out to the airport and fly first. Then back to town and the A.C. for squash. The fellows wanted me to play for the club and I was too lazy. But I'll change my mind. A rubdown up on the roof solarium, maybe a cabinet bath, perhaps even a few fast rounds with Percy Wigman, on days when there's time—and home again. All reduced. Or, if it's an evening out, home and change and scram."

"I wish you wouldn't fly."

"I know, Muzz. Silly of you."

He went at the matter of losing five pounds, and diverting his mind from hunger's pangs meanwhile, with great intensity. His heredity had, after all, geared him for large enterprise and since he'd eschewed them he was obliged to undertake small things in a big way. His red Jaguar roared north from Pearson Square and west the five miles on Elk Drive to Gordon Field, the civil airport. He'd phoned ahead; his fast, small plane was ready. He took off, ignoring rule and law, in the manner of hot Soviet pilots, retracting his landing gear to become air-borne.

High above the vast panoply of the two cities, he stunted. People on the ground watched with fascination. Old hands at the airport, even if they'd missed the take-off, identified the pilot by his performance in the air.

After half an hour, Kit tired of using the gray sky for a trampolin and came down closer to the cities, separated by a leaden river, which soon would freeze and bear a burden of dirty snow on its ice. He cut south and on the way came close to earth. Using the deserted Gordon Stadium as a kind of inverted hurdle, he made several passes into it at an altitude lower than its cement circle of seats, its press stand and TV stalls. The maneuver, also illegal, reminded him of faster and trickier antics over Britain. That thought sent him farther south and west to Hink Field, the military airport, where, keeping to the letter of the law, he annoyed several junior officers in Flight Control by circling the area at the closest permissible approach and shooting past nervous young men in trainers.

Swinging, then, on an arc of several miles, he bethought himself of Lenore Bailey. It was easy, at five thousand feet, to sight the metal glint of Crystal Lake. He came in over it low, circling its banks, unmindful of wincing patients in the Jenkins Memorial Hospital, and, zooming, twisting, he sorted from the residences below the intersection of Walnut and Bigelow. On the northwest corner, the Bailey house sent up chimney smoke. Kit dived fast, pulled out hard, and blew the smoke into the yard. He climbed at full power and came down in a series of loops. He took all of Walnut in a roaring run, at the end of which he zoomed and came back—upside down.

These antics attracted a large and almost unanimously indignant audience among which he could not spot Lenore. People ran out of their thunder-stricken houses—mothers with babies in their arms, housewives with sudsy hands, carrying dish towels, waving pans and pots, and irate businessmen who lunched at home, with shaking fists and tucked napkins. Netta Bailey appeared, in a kimona and hair curlers, which the pilot could not discern; Beau was not there. He did not practice the economical but plebian custom of lunching at home. And Lenore was downtown shopping.

When he could not spot the girl, but only her mother, Kit made one last run over the bare treetops of Walnut Street, flying at crop-duster's altitude, and winged back toward the airport. On the way, he dived through the low-hanging drift of yellowish smoke which was being blown by a west wind from the Hobart Metal Products plant across the center of the two downtown regions. He whipped the smoke into satisfying patterns and took a turn above the skyscrapers of Green Prairie and River City. They rose magically out of the factory smoke and stood above them in a single cluster at what seemed the heart of one great metropolis.

His last trick was a pass at the steel stack of the refining plant beyond the metalworks—a tall column topped by a flame which consumed waste gases and sent a horizontal smoke-trail of its own across the city. Not realizing that the blaze was self-illumined, Kit tried to extinguish it with his prop-wash much in the same way he had once diverted buzz bombs from their courses. But after three passes at the flame he gave up and left both the stack and the plant foreman burning.

He drove back to town, played brilliantly for an hour and a half at squash with Freddie Perkman, took assorted baths and then, in a terry-cloth robe, went out in the solarium of the River City A.C. for his massage. The glass-enclosed summit of the skyscraper building furnished a three-hundred-and-sixty-degree view of the cities, obstructed only here and there by the few taller structures. Kit, having just had an even better view from the air, didn't even glance through the enormous windows of the square-sided roof garden. He lay down on a table and submitted to the attentions of the masseur, who had greeted him with, "Glad to see you in the club."

"Had to come back, Taps; getting fat."

"Taps" Flaugherty, accustomed to the truly overweight bodies of River City's well-to-do, grinned at the near-perfect specimen on the table. "Can't see an ounce, Mr. Sloan."

"The scales can," Kit grunted.

An hour and a quarter later, the red Jaguar took him home. At eight, precisely, he sat opposite his mother in the shadowy dining room of the Sloan mansion, gustily spooning soup.

"Have a good day, son?"

"Passable."

"Any plans for the evening?"

"Thought I'd pick up Lenore Bailey . . ."

That suited Mrs. Sloan for an opening. Her eyes fastened briefly on her hungry son and moved thoughtfully into the distances of the formal room where the gold rims of place plates gleamed from china racks, and cabinets of cut glass sparkled dully.

"You've seen a lot of the Bailey girl, lately."

"Yeah."

"Does that mean anything, Kit?"

He smiled at his mother. "Ask Lenore."

She passed that up with a gesture that was partly disdainful and partly indulgent. She thought, with pride, that the Sloan men had always possessed a way with women. She was able to feel pride, not rancor, now that her husband was occupying a plot in Shadyknoll, with a thirty-foot obelisk to mark the grave of a great industrialist, banker and rakehell. Her son's "conquests," as she thought them (though he rarely found himself obliged to use aggression), did not in her opinion belong in the same category as her late husband's "vices." There was the mitigating fact that Kittridge was an "irresistible young man"; her spouse had been an "old fool"; there was a further alleviating circumstance in the fact that morals, amongst smart young people, had changed. In sum, there was (though she did not admit it) the fact that her husband's perennial blonde had driven Minerva half mad with jealous fury, while she found herself taking in her son's amours an almost masculine and quasi-participatory interest.

"You in love with Lenore?"

"Hell, Muzz. I love 'em all—if they're pretty. If they're as pretty as she, I love double."

"She's an interesting girl."

"How do you know?" he inquired with ample suspicion, and he said in the same breath, "This is good soup."

"You better not have any more. There's roast beef—Yorkshire pudding—I knew you'd be famished."

"How do you know so much about Lenore? She belong to some ladies' aid—or something? You don't see her in church much. She doesn't go."

"The girls that interest you, Kit, naturally interest me." She sighed lightly. "I'm getting older every year . . ."

"Young and pretty and sexy!" He always said that when she said she was aging. It always pleased her.

"Nonsense! Homely as a Missouri mule and twice the size! No, Lenore isn't someone I've seen lately. I do recall she used to attend St. Stephen's when she was an awkward, adolescent girl. I've inquired. It's very easy. After all, her father's in the bank."

"So he is! Never thought of it, really. So he is. Old—what's it?—old Buzz—no! Beau Bailey. He's cashier, or something . . ."

"That's correct." Mrs. Sloan tinkled a coronation hand bell and the soup was removed. A huge roast was carried in. Both mother and son helped themselves not to one, but three thick slices. "The girl's not merely pretty as a movie star. She's bright. Did some really good work in college. Science, I believe. I like a scientific-minded woman. Sticks to facts. Realist. No folderol."

Kit grinned agreeingly. "She's high up in the brains department. You want to know why water expands when it freezes, or all about hydrogen bombs—Lenore can tell you. Who wants to know, though?" He helped himself to pan-roasted potatoes.

"And quite good at athletics," Minerva said.

"What *is* this? You're talking about the woman I love—at the moment—as if she were something entered in a state fair."

"She wouldn't make a bad entry. And that's what I *mean*, in a way."

"Not the old Kit-your-duty-is-grandchildren-supply, is it, Muzz?" He glanced up keenly. "By God, it is!"

Minerva took a long look, a sad look, this time, at the Rhineland castles imbedded vaguely in panels of crimson wallpaper. "You," she said, "are the greatest triumph of my life. But my sorrow is—I have you alone, Kit. *Just* you. I desperately longed for a big family. We needed children. Our holdings—the businesses——"

This, as her son suspected, was not wholly true. A large number of offspring would have provided stewards for the Sloan interprises; but Minerva, after painfully bearing one child, had taken counsel with half a dozen obstetricians and gynecologists to make sure nothing so agonizing and humiliating as childbirth would happen to her again. "I am determined," his mother went on, "that you shall make a suitable marriage and provide me with grandchildren to replace the little brothers and sisters I was never able to supply for you, Kit."

"I *know!* But——"

"A day," his mother said firmly, "is surely coming when you cannot temporize. You're well over thirty, Kit, and I'm aging . . ." She looked away a third time, her large face working a little. "Besides——"

"Besides?" If there was to be a new element in this old discussion he wanted to know it.

"Do you know, Kit, the Adams girl tried to get money from me, again?"

"Lord! I wish I'd never *seen* that babe!"

"You did, though. A bit too much of her. If you had been *married*, Kit, she wouldn't have had the gall—or the public sympathy—"

He laughed. "Isn't that a shade unethical, Muzz? To advocate marriage as a cover for carnal sin?"

"Unethical?" She tasted the word as if it were foreign. Her large eyes glinted. "Possibly. But dam' practical."

"Have you ever thought that if I did marry—Lenore, say— and I'll honestly confess I've done some thinking about it— maybe she'd dislike being a mere brood mare plus a convenient dodge?"

"Lenore," said his mother, "can be handled."

"That's just what she can't be. Since you seem so sure, I'll tell you this much more. I don't believe she'd accept me."

"No?"

"No."

"Have you asked her?"

"More or less—and in a way."

"That sounds," his mother answered, "like one hell of a halfhearted proposal!"

"Wasn't a proposal. Just an inquiry. I said a few days back, maybe a couple of weeks, what if I asked her to marry me?"

"And she said?"

He gave a loud laugh. "She said, 'Drive me home!' "

Mrs. Sloan's eyes were briefly amused. "That all?"

"Not quite. She said if I were the last man on earth, why then, maybe, for the sake of the species, she'd consent."

"Spirit."

"Plenty. Maybe too much. If you want to know, Muzz, I'm fairly crazy about that girl, and she is totally uncrazy about me. I've tried all the tricks, and first base in still the other side of the moon."

Mrs. Sloan considered that for a full minute. "Do you think you would marry her, if she did assent?"

"Search me. Maybe."

"Suppose I added a mother's urging?"

"You can't hit women on the head with a club and drag them home any more. That's just an old *New Yorker* joke."

"An odd thing has happened at the bank," she said, her tone altered.

Kit instantly understood the slight change; it showed in her physical bearing. There was tension, now almost visible— a bringing together of her features, a tightening of muscles in her big shoulders, a slight narrowing of eye. If cats allowed themselves to become gross with fat, such cats, seeing prey or suspecting some distant motion betokened it, would gather themselves that way.

The fact was, Kit understood more of what had been happening in this dinner hour than he showed his mother or even let himself know. He had resisted her efforts to marry him to suitable girls for numerous years. The effort had involved a variety of females in different places—Manhattan debs and Long Island finishing-school graduates, suitable young women from Los Angeles, San Francisco, St. Louis, Kansas City and Chicago. Girls of good or prominent or rich family, met on transatlantic liners and at watering places abroad. A lovely countess who was only nineteen, in Paris; the daughter of a Knight, in London. He knew this constant matchmaking activity was born of her indomitable desire to see her wealth managed by grandchildren bred, presumably under her aegis, for the job; and he could infer from the number of girls and young women presented to him that his mother did not feel love needed to be involved in a match. Perhaps his father's derelictions were responsible for his mother's feelings or lack of feelings. Perhaps she had grown to believe that woman as Wife was more institution than individual, owing to her own almost lifelong acceptance in that way.

The effect on Kit had been to make him contemptuous of the other sex; he usually thought and acted as if women were a dime a hundred. His mother's constant production of them, his own incessant petty affairs with them, had also convinced him that the coin of good looks, wealth, a glamorous background and a reputation as a hero—attributes he possessed, or appeared to possess, in plentitude—was the coinage which bought women. The person behind did not matter, women apparently felt. That, in its turn, damaged the remnants of his ego.

For his ego, however large and confident it seemed to the world, was undermined, though he had repressed the fact that by the standards of other men he was a coward. He affected the casual, the debonair, the slangy and insouciant attitude he had seen amongst rich young men in many lands. But Kit's was not the real posture of witty worldliness; that requires erudition and humor. He had neither. His efforts to be offhand, to understate, to be trivial where large issues were involved and so to exhibit wisdom by hiding its evidence, never came off. An uncured adolescence, a chronic infantilism, crept into his words. And the

"Park Avenue accent," the "Harvardese" which he had endeavored to learn at Princeton and to polish in Britain, was an unstable asset: it deteriorated under emotional pressure to the flat, nasal intonation of his background.

He knew someday he would have to marry; he had long been indifferent to the female object of that necessity. He had put off the date, not to search for a mate he himself desired—that being plainly irrelevant to the question—but merely because his deepest wish was to avoid responsibility. He did not want now, any more than he had wanted at eighteen, to be tied down with a home, a woman, children, things he had to do. Life was "happy" for him only when he could, at will, jump into a Jaguar, or into a plane, or aboard a fast boat, and be gone. He knew he was mother-dominated and usually he thought that was for the best. But he also knew that within his mother was a tremendous "strength"—he never saw it as invidious, as selfish, as masochistic and sadistic—which (if he deliberately or even inadvertently offended her in some fashion she could not brook or would not) might cause her to renounce him, the apple of her eye. And that renouncement, he knew, would be absolute. He would be cut off without a penny—not in her will, but the day she renounced him. His next month's allowance simply wouldn't be deposited and that would be that.

Kit had two frequent fantasies related to such matters. He imagined himself the victim of his mother's fury, and could only see as his way out taking up his plane for a last nose dive into the ground. If she managed to get the plane grounded before he could reach it, there were cars—even rental cars. He had often noted a buttonwood tree that stood on a sharp curve on Elk Drive, about halfway to the airport. He could hit that at a hundred or so. His other fantasy concerned the sudden, unexpected death of his mother and his inheritance of everything that bore the name of Sloan. It was his most frequent daydream.

Looking at his mother now, Kit realized that she had, as so often, mustered some fresh, intangible force to abet her will. Part of her strategy had appeared: he had never before thought that being married would serve a useful purpose in relation to his conduct with the whole world of women. He could see that point. And he could see farther: if he failed to acknowledge it, his mother might, that being her nature and her method, make certain some young lady in the future behaved in such a fashion as to make the point unforgettable. Minerva Sloan was not above allying herself with another against her son, when the allegiance was designed to accomplish some ultimately "good" end.

She had said, "Suppose I add a mother's urging?"

It might have been a warm suggestion, sentimental, kindly.

It was not, as he knew by her abrupt tenseness. "Mother . . ." he began.

The deliberations were interrupted by the butler, who came in carrying a telephone on a jack.

Jeffrey Fahlstead had served the Sloans for more than thirty years. For twenty, they had called him "Jeff." An Irishman, he was, like Willis the chauffeur, unbent by age, stiffened, rather. "It's Washington, D.C., ma'am," he said.

Minerva took the phone, spoke her name, and soon shot a quick annoyed glance at her son.

From the conversation which developed, Kit gathered guiltily that his afternoon flight was dimly viewed by various persons who wanted him grounded, or relieved of his license, put in jail, or given a lunacy test. Complaints had already gone to high Federal authorities. Into this dilemma his mother barged serenely, however. She could have used the "friendly tip" from an important Washington official to have him grounded; and Minera didn't like the risks her son took by flying. But she wanted, that evening, something else from Kit.

Listening to one side of the talk, Kit realized that his mother, coming forcefully to his aid, was going to fix, grease and appease everything and everybody. His mother, he reflected, was completely indispensable to him. The least he could do was to please her in this matter of marriage.

When she hung up, she didn't even make it a long lecture. "Take me weeks to get the thing straightened out," she said, concluding it, "and don't ever fly like that again! But, Kit, I want to go back to our previous talk." She nodded the butler out of the room. "As I said, an odd thing has happened at the bank."

"Really? What, Muzz?"

"You know John Jessup?"

He shook his head.

"You should remember him from childhood. An old horse thief—and one of the smartest men in Larkimer County! Made millions, in cattle mostly. He was one of your father's cronies, years back. It's not important. The thing that's important is this: the bank takes care of his holdings. He doesn't even look things over for long periods. Trusts us, of course, and leaves us free to make certain kinds of changes, so his holdings are open always and we have a limited power of attorney."

"Somebody cleaned him out!" Kit guessed.

Minerva's eyes acknowledged the guess. "Not cleaned him out. Just took six thousand, in bonds."

"Who?" And, of course, he knew. "Beau Bailey! But he's been with you forever, Muzz!"

Mrs. Sloan was looking at her china rail—seeing, now, the expensive plates it supported. "There is no proof, as yet, and Beau denies it, of course. As a matter of fact, the theft of the bonds was a good thing for the bank, showed us an old-fashioned, inadequate method of keeping track that made it easy for certain people to purloin things. We've stopped that system. Jessup came in today, missed the certificates himself, reported. They could have been taken any time in the past several years. Though the ink on the receipt appears quite fresh. However, I suspected Beau instantly——"

"Why Beau, particularly?"

She smiled. "There shouldn't be any little secrets between mother and son, should there? I suspected him, Kit, because I almost *hoped* it would be Beau. I needed, for reasons I trust are now clear, a better hold on Beau even than the power to fire him. He could get a good job in several banks, not only because he's adequate, but because he knows so much about the operations and activities of Sloan Trust. I must say, the moment I thought of Beau and checked to make sure he'd had the opportunity, I did realize that I knew—heaven knows how! Gossip, I suppose—that Beau had always stage-managed a forty-thousand-dollar-a-year way of life on a seventeen-thousand-five-hundred salary."

"They do sort of put on dog, in a small, cheesy way. Like a modernized housefront and barbecue pits, and Netta Bailey—a harridan if I ever saw one—goes for clothes."

"Of course," Minerva went on, "I then really did some digging. I've spent the day at it, largely. Most absorbing. Beau's run up bills just everywhere. He belongs to seven clubs that require stiff dues, stiff for him. They've sent that girl through college lavishly. But what I finally learned— after all, a bank has to have connections with all sorts of people—is that Beau's been betting the horses for some time. And losing."

"So? What's it got to do with Lenore? She never struck me as lacking in guts. If her dad's disgraced, I can imagine she'd bear it. Get a job. She's had some dandy offers for everything from modeling in New York, and a Hollywood screen test, to working in labs at Hobart Metal."

Minerva chuckled. "Be ironic, wouldn't it? Beau took Hobart bonds."

"I don't see——"

"I've decided it's past time for you to marry, Kit. I merely felt I should make sure, by a heart-to-heart talk with you, that you really liked Lenore Bailey. She's quite suitable, and any suitable girl would satisfy me, as I've said a thousand times, if I've said it once."

"Would the daughter of a bank thief be suitable?"

"As far as her father's concerned, he isn't what people generally mean by a thief. He's merely ambitious; he's got more ambition than moral strength. He probably found himself in a situation he thought desperate—it was inevitable he would, sooner or later, with his living standards—and sold his soul for a miserable six thousand dollars in bonds. I've seen brighter men do it for less."

"What's the pitch?"

"The bank, of course, made instant restitution to Jessup. I ordered the matter kept in strict confidence. I haven't proved it against Beau, but I know now I could, by asking certain people the right questions in the right way."

"Meaning a certain big-shot bookie?"

"How right! I could readily, through Netta—I see a good deal of her, one way or another—she's one of a number of social bootlickers who see to it they stay in my good graces—I could easily have a talk with her. I could ask her to get a note from Beau admitting the defalcation. I could then arrange to recover the bonds—he must have borrowed cash on them somewhere in Green Prairie or River City—and that, also, could be learned. Netta could and would see to it, afterward, that any little wish of mine, or yours, was met, Kit."

"Very nice little shotgun wedding—with both barrels pointed not at the groom, but the bride's papa."

"I said, Kit, that I wanted to know how you felt about Lenore. And then I wanted you to *act*—not fiddle years away."

It was all there, he thought, laid on the table, on the damask, right in front of the centerpiece, the bowl of flowers. His last ideas concerning demurrer came to him, and were unvoiced. He did not mention the early background of Netta Bailey. He did not need to. The Sloan name would compensate, socially, for nearly any background stain. And, suddenly, a brand-new vision had come into his mind. He could see himself married to Lenore, no longer engaged in a struggle with her, but holding a lifelong whip over her. If they married because she had to, because she'd done it to save her father from prison, probably she'd go on saving him all her life. Kit could come and go as he pleased, do as he pleased, be as free as he pleased, and she'd have to take it because of a signed confession his mother had somewhere.

This opportunity, to become a husband and remain what he thought of as a "man," appealed to him greatly. Lenore, he had intuitively known, was emotionally far stronger than he. She would have managed him and bossed him. Now, it would be another kettle of fish. He was aware that Minerva had gone through the same thought process, come to the same conclusion and was prepared to explain it if necessary.

He got up, walked around the table, kissed her fervently. "All right, Mother. I don't know if it'll help my cause. But it might. She's about as headstrong and independent a wench as I ever met. I'd *need* a way to handle her!"

"I think," his mother answered, "we've discovered a way."

2

The vast airfield shook with motor noise in the gray, windy afternoon. A dozen huge bombers had left the hardstands and roared out on the runways to take off on a regular training flight. Each one had six propellers. Each prop sent back a wash of air and dust and din, adding it to the boring Texas wind.

Chuck Conner, Lieutenant Conner, closed the door of the office with difficulty. The building behind him, long, low, caked from its corrugated roof to its foundations with dirt, was like fifty buildings parallel to and behind it and fifty more, barracks, on the opposite side of the field. Chuck hunched in his coat, took a better grip on the brief case under his arm and looked for a jeep. There wasn't any in the vast, concrete environ. Just cement and wind and stinging dust, cold, and the planes moving like things from Mars, far out on the flat, tremendous field.

He walked.

Another day, another job, he thought.

A jeep buzzed behind him and he got aboard. Riding was colder. The sky was a yellowish-gray, the color of old laundry soap. The clouds must be moving fast, he thought, but they were without definition, so you couldn't tell.

The jeep stopped at a less dusty building, less dusty, less caked by the wind, because GI's cleaned it with water every day. Chuck went through a storm door and a second door and performed the military amenities with the officer of the day. He went to the colonel's conference room, turned over his brief case to Sergeant Lee, saluted. There were four men in the room: Colonel Eames, the Commanding Officer, Major Wroncke, Major Taylor and Captain Pierce. They looked more serious than usual. Usually nobody took the weekly Intelligence meeting with any seriousness at all.

The colonel, sitting at the head of a worn conference table, returned Charles's salute. Charles sat down and unlocked the brief case. He was acting for Major Blayert, the Staff Intelligence Officer at the base. As assistant, Charles was not always even present at these Staff Intelligence meetings. But the major had been detached, temporarily, to duty at the new briefing school in Flagstaff.

"We have," the colonel said, "some new, secret orders. From Washington." Eames looked at the officers. "They are pretty elaborate and they mean plenty of work here at the base."

Nobody appeared to be overjoyed at that news.

"As you know, contrails have been spotted for years, over Alaska, over Canada."

"And we're ordered to go up and erase 'em?"

Captain Pierce said that. It was like him. He was an anything-but-dour New Englander, a man with a wisecrack for every situation. Everybody liked Captain Pierce. But the colonel, at this moment, was not amused.

"In other words," he went on, ignoring the remark, "we've known for a long time the Russkis have reconnoitered our northern defense perimeter. Lately"— He tapped his own brief case—"they have moved in over the United States."

"Is that positive?" Major Wroncke asked sharply. "Rumors——"

"I know." The colonel hesitated. "Civilian spotting has fallen down badly. And with the last appropriations cut by Congress, the radar defense has had to be reduced." He glanced unconsciously at his shoulder, at the eagle on his right shoulder.

The men at the table knew, with sympathy, what the glance meant. With the long effort at "budget balancing," with the many steps in reduction of Federal expenditures for military affairs, the armed forces had diminished in numbers. That meant, to officers like Colonel Eames, no promotion. As CO of the base he ought to have been at least a brigadier general. He remained a colonel just as the numbers of bombers at the base remained inadequate for the purposes envisaged in the event of war.

"What have they got on it?" Major Taylor asked. He was a fussy man who constantly tried to "move things ahead"—equipment, people, plans, conversations.

"Plenty," Colonel Eames answered. "And not Flying Saucer material, either! Contrails over Nebraska, Iowa, Ohio and all the states down here in the Southwest. Definitely not our own."

"Any contacts?" Major Taylor asked.

"None. Radar blips, though."

"Plane types?"

The colonel frowned faintly at his impatient staff officer. "I'll boil it down to this. GHQ is satisfied that there have been, for some months, numbers of Red planes over this country, flying very fast at very high altitude—probably turbo-prop types—probably photography recon. None of our interceptors has so far gotten up to one fast enough to take a good look. We do have a few rather definite photographs, taken at long ranges with telephoto lenses from our own planes."

"That's pretty definite," Captain Pierce murmured.

Eames nodded. "Very definite. With commercial stuff getting higher every year, of course, and moving faster, GHQ was pretty unwilling to accept the evidence at first. Besides, since the peace efforts are apparently on the verge of success, they didn't believe the Reds would be foolish enough to push their northern recon planes over our states and cities. In fact, they took it for granted all last year that such stuff was being suspended."

"We've felt *them* out," Major Wroncke stated.

"And gotten burned for it," Major Taylor said crisply.

"What's the interpretation?" Captain Pierce asked.

Colonel Eames turned away and frowned. "None. Yet. The point is, we're being ordered to put on a big show. For the next six weeks there are going to be 'air exercises.' That's what the public, and the world at large, will be told. We'll get everything in the air we can, as high as we can, with cameras and arms, also." He tapped the brief case. "Orders here for a new friend-or-foe recognition pattern. Using that, we are expected to keep open eyes, to photograph anything unidentified we see, to fire on it when and if we can overtake it. Bombers are to do the job, not interceptors. The bombers can go up, stay, and cruise."

Major Wroncke whistled.

Colonel Eames smiled without pleasure. "In a nutshell," he said, acknowledging the whistle. "At this base, it means a lot of partly trained crews are going to have to fly some of the latest equipment. It means a logistic problem, just to keep what we've got up and on patrol. Six weeks is a long time. We aren't supplied for it, so we have to get supplied, fast. It means we've got to expand the intelligence side; an Intelligence officer is supposed to fly in every plane."

Captain Pierce laughed. "That's going to chop up the Lieutenant, here, mighty fine."

Charles also laughed a little, but his face was serious. "Excuse me, sir," he said to the colonel, "but did Major Blayert show you the fabric at the last meeting?"

"Fabric?" the colonel repeated.

"That the rancher brought in, sir?"

They were looking at him. Eames said, "I'm afraid I don't get it, Lieutenant. Blayert certainly didn't bring 'fabric' of any kind to the Intelligence meetings, if that's what you mean."

Charles had felt it his duty to explain. But now he flushed. His superior officer hadn't mentioned the shred of old cloth. By mentioning it now, in the major's absence, Charles would be doing his superior officer a disfavor. But it was too late to stop. He explained briefly:

"A few days ago, about ten, an old rancher-prospector came to the base, here, in his Ford. He had found, somewhere up in the Sawbuck Mountains, a piece of fabric, greenish, with some letters stamped on it in white ink. Stuff had been outdoors quite a while; it was faded. Looked like denim, about that weight. The point was, the lettering was Russian, the man thought."

"Was it?" Eames asked sharply.

"Yes, sir. Numbers and initial letters."

"Where is it?"

"In the office safe, I think, sir. Or a security cabinet. Major Blayert thought it of no importance. That is"—Charles felt further embarrassment—"he thought it could have been part of some war trophy or souvenir somebody had brought back from Europe, years ago, after the Second World War.

Some piece of Russian equipment. A pillow cover, maybe. Or wrapping from a box that held something."

"What did you think, Lieutenant?" the colonel asked.

"It occurred to me, sir, that it could have come from a plane. Accident aloft. Explosive decompression might have ripped out some seat covering. Lining. Something."

"But the major didn't agree?"

"No, sir."

Eames considered. "I'd like to see it. Maybe send it to the Pentagon. It could be more evidence of this sort of business." He drew a studied breath and went on. "Anyway, appropriate orders for all of you here are being made out, as of now. We're going, ostensibly, to hold air games. Actually the entire continent is to be scouted by the Air Force, at high altitude, for the next six weeks. During that time, incidentally, there's to be a change in alerts. Condition Yellow will be confidential, as it used to be years ago."

"Isn't that risky?" Major Taylor snapped.

"GHQ thinks not. They've got good information lines into Russia, China, the satellite states. No sign of activity. No mobilization. No evidence, from any channel, of large air preparations. Attack is therefore regarded as out of the question. The point is, if Condition Yellow stood as at present, every tenth civilian sky watcher and every other Filter Center would constantly be reporting our own flights: they won't be announced. Our own planes, then, would touch off hundreds of false alerts; Condition Yellow would flash into every city time and again. The only way to prevent that is to return to the confidential basis."

Charles said impulsively, "If the enemy knew, it would make a good opportunity for . . . !"

The colonel grinned. "It would, if the 'enemy,' as you call

him, showed any signs now of preparation. But he doesn't. So
the Pentagon feels the plan is safe. The official opinion is
that this business of reconnaissance is one more stupid action, one more mere crude breach of ordinary international
etiquette. They spar for peace, but they can't resist the improved chance it gives them to sneak a few photographs."

"Sounds like them," Major Taylor grunted.

"Still," Charles said, "if they wanted to get our planes up,
foul our warning system——"

The colonel nodded. "Orders," he said. "Any more questions, gentlemen?"

There were none. The meeting ended. Colonel Eames
walked across his office with Charles. "Bring back the fabric."

"Yes, sir."

"And don't worry, Lieutenant, about the air games and
your 'enemy.' "

"No, sir."

"I did myself, Chuck, at first. Went through exactly your
train of thought. We have to rely on our own Intelligence."

It was the first time the colonel had ever used Charles's
nickname, even his first name. Charles was unaware that his
commanding officer even knew his whole name. He felt flat-
tered. But he also perceived that the slight familiarity involved a skillful act. Things at the base were about to tighten
up. Half-trained men were going to undertake the work
of trained crews. Ships, inevitably, would crash. People would
be hurt, and killed. The colonel, almost instinctively, had
began to behave with that increased intimacy which danger
and morale required.

All Charles replied was, "Yes, sir."

But the colonel stayed beside him, walking toward the
door. "I even called Washington myself, before the meeting,"
he said. "I suggested restoring Condition Blue to the alert

system, just in case. They thought I was crazy. And I guess I was." He opened the door because Charles couldn't, so long as the colonel talked. "I'll put you in a staff car," he said. "Long way back to your quarters, and a real cold day."

Charles thanked him. He saluted and started for one of the cars.

The colonel called, "And about that—material. Appreciate your mentioning it. Proper, under the circumstances."

A damned good officer, Charles thought, as a sergeant drove him swiftly along the edge of the big field.

3

The Mildred Tatum Infirmary for Colored was a large, brick building on the corner of St. Anne and James streets in River City. Its location, four blocks north of the heart of "Niggertown," was due to a number of factors, none of which was related to the convenience of the patients or the requirements of therapy. Emmet Sloan had always liked colored people in a genuine, if somewhat patronizing, way. His grandfather, coming to River City from Illinois after the Civil War, had been an abolitionist and for a time had run an "underground railroad station" on the bloody road that led slaves from the South to freedom.

Like other Americans of large affairs, Emmet Sloan had welcomed the tide of working immigrants—the "Micks, Wops, Latwicks, Polacks, Hunkies" and others, who had poured into River City at the end of the nineteenth and the start of the twentieth centuries. They worked hard and cheap at mill jobs and in foundries and they thus furnished much of the muscle that was essential to make America great—as well as to make men like Emmet Sloan rich. These people settled near the river, east of Market Street, on the mile-long, parallel stretches of Mechanic and Water streets, for the most part, and on the close-in cross streets. Land there was cheap. In summer it boiled with heat and damp from the river, as well as with mosquitoes. In winter it was raw and cold and gloomy. There were, furthermore, several then-small factories in the district as well as the C.K. and T.T. yards and roundhouse. It was a smoky, clangorous neighborhood.

Gradually, however, the Irish and Italians and Slavs pushed north into the St. Anne, St. Paul and Mary streets area, which came to be known as the "Catholic Section." The Negroes, displaced for a generation to outlying districts, often to mere tin shacks along the municipal dump, poured back in town and filled the slummy vacuum left by the economically ascending "foreigners." These, by the early twenties, were second- and third-generation Americans and controlled much of River City's politics as well as most of its organized vice and its rackets.

Emmet Sloan, perhaps because his occasional patronage of The Block kept him in sensory touch with the dismal living conditions of the Negroes, determined to do something for them. Their direst need was a hospital. And when, in 1937, he foreclosed on a rayon knitting mill on James Street, he rebuilt it into an "infirmary." At first, the inhabitants of the "Catholic" area had violently and actively resented the resulting enlargement of Negro "territory." There had been street brawls. The windows of the Infirmary had been smashed the night before its dedication. But Sloan, a determined man, finally established his gift for its intended recipients, by the costly but very effective means of constructing a much better hospital for the "foreign" population on a site which thitherto had been the territory of "white" people—native sons, one hundred per cent Americans, his "own" group. This in turn caused litigation. However, the "old families" of River City along with its citizens were beginning to move to the suburbs. Looking at maps, thinking of the temper of people, considering the future population and the probable developments of technology, Emmet Sloan decided the migration to suburbs in the thirties and forties was the start of a future landslide. Hence he invested in real estate on River City's edges and was among the first to finance the removal into suburban communities of branches of big department stores. His grandfather had seen what railroads meant to the farm and the city; his father had seen what automobiles would do to make cities grow; now Emmet perceived the automotive vehicle was about to strangle cities. All three had acted on their views with phenomenal financial success.

Minerva had never been much interested in colored people. While her husband lived, she had dutifully inspected the Infirmary from time to time and irregularly dropped in on Wednesday afternoons, when a group of white Episcopal ladies—"meddlesome gossips and prying shrews," Minerva called them—came to the Infirmary to sew. One of Minerva's countless, small sensations of relief, at the time of Emmet's funeral, had been the realization that he would no longer "dragoon" her to those charitable Wednesdays.

In that, to her astonishment, Minerva found she had erred.

Shortly before his death, Emmet had signed a contract employing as the new head of the Infirmary one Alice Groves, an expert in hospital management, with a varied postgraduate background and a doctorate in philosophy from Columbia University. Minerva had paid little attention at the time and remembered only her husband's delighted remark that he and the hospital board had "bribed the woman away from Kansas City." She understood the joys of successful bribery.

After Emmet was decently interred, Minerva had herself

driven by Willis, in the Rolls, to what she thought of as a "last" Wednesday meeting. She was very much discountenanced to find that the new head of the Infirmary, Alice Groves, was *herself a Negress*. A mulatto, Minerva decided on sight. Not only that, but Alice Groves was beautiful, gracious, young and, of course, exceedingly well educated. She spoke English with "a better Eastern accent than my son, Kit," Minerva told certain outraged ladies.

She was warm and kind with Minerva, who made the sourest and most critical inspection in the history of the Infirmary, even though she found little enough to criticize, the facilities considered. After the tour of the hospital, to Minerva's intense amazement, reporters from her own papers, accompanied by cameramen, took pictures of her with Alice and a dozen white-uniformed, dark-skinned nurses. These were duly printed, with captions noting how Mrs. Sloan was "carrying on the traditional family charities." There was much editorial talk about the Infirmary being her late husband's "favorite" charity and about her "nobility" in visiting it while her "bereavement was so recent."

Minerva knew, of course, that it was a put-up job. Alice Groves was well aware her patronage was essential to the running of the hospital. So Alice Groves meant to keep Minerva's interest. She was evidently publicity wise and had used publicity to gain her ends: Minerva could not repudiate a vast amount of printed praise. She came for a few Wednesdays and signed the annual check.

Just when she thought she could let the duty wither on the vine, she learned of a movement to rename the Infirmary. Mildred Tatum had been the first free slave to settle in River City. The colored population had apparently decided that, since they were no longer slaves, their hospital should have a different name. And "school children [Minerva again noted in her own newspapers] had voted by hundreds," in a contest, to call it the "Minerva Sloan Infirmary."

That move Minerva partly checked. She had no wish to be immortalized over the doorway—not to mention on the bedpans and diapers—of a "darkie infirmary." But even as she graciously declined the offer and the vote of children, she found herself that much more enmeshed in Alice Groves's toils. Her very refusal of the use of her name had wedded her *person* to the charity, which was what the administrator had wanted.

Their relations thenceforward were cordial but, on Minerva's part, guarded. No white woman in River city or Green Prairie had ever managed to "take" her against her will, so thoroughly. . . .

On a Wednesday, as usual, Willis drove across town to the Infirmary punctually at three. Alice Groves, as usual, stood at the head of the stairs within the dingy building. She was dressed in powder blue, which, Minerva noted, became her. Behind Alice were the usual starched bevies of nurses, drawn up like a company for inspection.

Minerva made panting, reluctant rounds—baby wards and the new operating room (which was a sickening display of shiny things best not thought about, Minerva felt). She drew the line at visiting the adult wards, and there were no private rooms.

"Right after Christmas," Alice Groves said pleasantly, as they finished the tour and started toward the bright, chintz-draped room where the "Wednesday ladies" sewed, "we're going to start a drive among our own people for fifty thousand dollars."

"Good heavens! Can you raise anything like that?"

"Perhaps not. It's the amount we need to buy a little building in the country, for chronics. There are so many!"

Minerva, headed for the white ladies, was beginning to think other thoughts. "That's really very enterprising and wonderful——"

"I'm delighted you approve. I was sure you would. In fact, I've told the press——"

"*What* have you told the press?"

"That you approved. In fact, I said it was your idea."

"No harm in that," Minerva murmured.

"You're always so kind, Mrs. Sloan!"

Minerva thought grimly that beyond doubt this "chronic home" drive would cost her the uncontributed balance of its quota. She had to admit Alice Groves was a good operator. It might, she thought, pay to take Alice into her camp. Then she saw the hat—the sprouted fright—that Netta Bailey was wearing, and she went through the chatting, peanut-eating, one-day seamstresses with a booming, "Afternoon, everybody! Afternoon, Netta! So glad you're here. I wanted to have a private chat with you—*church matters*—before you left."

It was recognition that both delighted and alarmed Netta. Minerva seldom did more than nod to her, at a distance.

The two women were ideally suited to the "little talk" that took place in the "visitors' powder room," some half hour later. They were suited in the sense that each knew what she wanted and what the other wanted and each knew what she had of value to the other. It wasn't even a very long talk, considering that it proposed to settle the lives of a son and a daughter.

Minerva explained her position, rapidly. "You see," she wound up, "my boy loves Lenore. Crazy about her. Charming girl. I'm crazy about her myself. So *unfortunate,* dear, old

Beau would make a slip at such a time! I have *no sympathy* with crookedness, Mrs. Bailey . . ."

"Of *course* not!"

Minerva squinted, but she could not prove irony in the response. She made a thin, tight mouth, a formidable mouth, and then let it relax into a smile. "However, it was only a slip, a *little* slip, and his first. It must, of course, be his last. I can hardly send my son's future father-in-law packing off to prison——"

"God forbid!" There was, at least, no irony in that.

"On the other hand," Minerva went on, changing her tone to one of intimacy, intimacy tinged with potential regret and the potential withdrawal of intimacy, "we mothers understand things our children don't. Kit tells me Lenore doesn't seem to reciprocate his feelings . . ."

"Oh! I'm *sure* she does!" Netta was alarmed, but not as much as she appeared to be.

"I can understand it. Kit's rather a—shall we say, *frightening* young man, from the standpoint of an innocent young thing."

"Innocent as driven snow," Mrs. Bailey murmured.

"Kit's peremptory, bullheaded, reckless and foolish. I wouldn't have it any other way," Mrs. Sloan said sharply. "But you know and I know how love grows in marriage——"

"Indeed, I do!"

"——so I feel, a word from you, Mrs. Bailey—I *must* call you Netta, and you must call me Minerva—the *right* word . . ."

"I understand perfectly," Netta gulped. "Minerva."

"I'm *sure* you do!"

As soon as she decently could, Netta left the Infirmary and drove home at rocket speed. The first thing she had to do was to sober up Beau, who'd been drinking like a fish since coming home from the bank. Lenore could be tackled after that.

Beau would sober up fast enough when she got through the
fog with the news of reprieve. Lenore would be a more difficult subject.

But Minerva stayed on quite a while, even sewed a little.
When Willis drove her away, she waved from the window of
the Rolls to a contented, gracious Alice Groves on the Infirmary steps.

4

Henry Conner was in jail.

He could hardly believe it.

Two uniformed cops had escorted him up the steps and
taken him into a room and closed a door. The door had been
locked and Henry saw bars on the windows. They hadn't let
him talk, and they'd ignored his shout, "Call Lawyer
Balcomb!"

Presently, as he paced in the room, the door was unlocked
and different officers, men he knew only by sight, said, "This
way."

Then he faced Lieutenant Lacey, who had his feet on his
desk and was grinning. "Evening, Hank."

Henry Conner had not sworn much in years. He now
turned the lieutenant's office blue. "Just *what*," he finally
managed to ask, "is the idea of picking me up and hauling me
into the hoosegow?"

"Don't get riled, Henry. You'll be home in time for a good
night's sleep."

"*You* won't sleep, by God, Lacey, unless you can explain
what in the name of jumped-up . . . !" The square, homely
face was brick-red and the gray hair frizzed in sweat. Righteous wrath exploded in Henry's every syllable.

"Things," Lacey answered, his Irish grin undisturbed, "were really in a mess here, Henry, a few minutes ago. A call came in from a right upset person, known to us, a Mrs. Agnes Fleer, of twenty-six twenty-eight Pine Street——"

"What the hell has that busybody of an Aggie Fleer got to do with *me being grabbed by cops?*"

"——saying that a dead body had fallen out of the rear end of a car. She got the car's number. We radioed. They picked you up."

Henry said, *"Oh."* He sat down. "A dead body, eh? Fell out of my car, eh?" His voice rose, *"Did that old cheese-butt examine the body?"*

"Not closely. She said it was lying in the gutter, hideously disfigured, face bloody, an arm sawed off——"

"She *did,* eh?" Henry's voice was tense.

"She did. And naturally we sent out a red flash for the car with the number she gave us. We told her not to touch the body," Lacey said earnestly. "What the hell *was* it, Henry? When Jones and Billings came in here and said they'd picked you up, I knew——"

"It was Minnie," Henry answered in a peculiar tone.

"Minnie?" Lacey shook his head. "Anyone we know?"

Henry took a deep breath. He stood up. "Look, Lacey," he explained with control. "Minnie is a dummy, one of six the department-store people contributed to Civil Defense. Minnie was made up months since, over at Jenkins Hospital by some imaginative young interns, to look like an atom-bomb casualty."

"I *thought* it was something of the sort!"

"Thanks," Henry said. "And *good night!* And the next time you want me for murder, don't send a couple of prowl cops after me. They might get hurt."

"Just a sec."

Henry kept on going.

He had ample appreciation of the humorousness of his predicament. But he was anxious to finish his evening's duties. The dummy that had led to his arrest was realistic. But they'd used realistic dummies in Civil Defense drills all over the country for years. The tizzie which the mere sight of it had started in Aggie Fleer was evidence of how the general public would react. There ought, he thought, to be more such "wounded" dummies for the public to see. Nowadays Americans whisked out of sight, in ambulances, every injury, every accident case. They hastily wiped up blood when it was spilled. Only doctors and nurses knew, any more, what wounds were. God alone could guess how half a million Aggie Fleers would act if real bombs started bursting over American streets. Take one look at the casualties and blow their tops, he felt sure. He'd have to emphasize the point in future CD meetings. *Do* something about it.

Lacey called, "Just a sec."

Henry spoke his thoughts. "Never did realize how much *education* folks need. Matter of fact, *I* hide those dummies *myself.* Wonder if I should? Maybe there ought to be a permanent display in a downtown department-store window, so people wouldn't faint if the real thing ever came along. *Fat chance* of getting a display!" He started through the door.

"I've got more to say."

Henry stopped and looked back gloweringly. Lacey said, "I told you, your 'Minnie' fell out of your car——"

"Damn it, I was on the way to a rescue drill. I keep Minnie, and two others, in my garage."

"Yeah. Well, when Billings radioed in they had you, without knowing at the moment who you were, I got *another* call."

Henry groaned. "What'd Minnie do? Grave-walk?"

"Some kids found her. And about fifteen minutes ago, Albert Higgley answered his doorbell and saw something in his barberry bushes. He switched on his porch light and took a good look and fell down six steps. They think his collarbone's broken."

"Too bad," Henry said.

"You don't feel any—liability in the matter? A judge might think differently."

"I said, by cracking godalmighty, it's *Civil Defense business!* Some of us *still* stick to duty. If a couple of boys played a prank with poor old Minnie, get the boys."

"We did. One was *your* boy. Ted."

He considered. He chuckled slightly. "Ted, eh?"

"They're bringing him here."

"Ted never did care much for Albert Higgley," Henry mused. "The old squirt owns a vacant lot near our place, has grape arbors on it. Nobody picks the grapes, unless kids like Ted do. One year—oh—maybe seven . . . eight years back—my boy Ted and a couple of other nippers were having grapes. Old Higgley ambushed 'em. Swung with a heavy cane, no warning, just whammed out of the bushes. Broke Ted's nose first crack. He wasn't more'n eight—nine, maybe . . ."

Lacey rubbed his chin. "I see. You didn't charge him?"

"Heck, no! Everybody has one or two mean neighbors."

"He's charging *you*. His *wife* is anyhow. Lewd and obscene exhibition——"

"*What?*"

Lacey nodded. "That store dummy was pretty realistic, wasn't it?"

"Was," Henry said. "And is. The interns went to some trouble to make it more so. Hair, and like that. Point is, if you're going to have personnel trained to stand the shock of human beings burned and hurt, you gotta train them with something that looks human."

"I suppose you do." Lacey gazed at the ceiling. "*Point* is, there's a city ordinance about lewd exhibition. That dummy was female—*and* naked——"

"Dam' *right!* So would *bomb casualties* be! Clothes burned off 'em, and naked as the day they were born, *and* burned—like Minnie."

"Guess I can let you go, Hank. I'll talk to your kid—scare him good—and let him go, too. But I think you may have to answer in court, someday soon—if Higgley's collarbone is really broken—for this 'lewd' business."

In alternations of rage and laughter, Henry told Beth. When he finished, like most excited persons, he went back to the beginning. "There I was, tooling along to CD headquarters to drill the rescue gang! *Wham!* There they came, sirens yowling. 'Pull over!' they hollered, and so help me God, when I got out, they had drawn their guns!"

He slapped his thigh and chortled.

His wife smiled, but not with his hilarity.

"It's funny," she said quietly, "but I don't recall ever seeing Minnie."

He shot her a quick glance, his smile gone. "Minnie's an ugly sight," he replied. "Kept her in that locked closet, with the others. Didn't see any call to show you our chamber of horrors."

"Why, Henry?"

"Well . . ."

"Isn't that what they're *for?*"

"Sure. I suppose, though—that is, I always figured, why upset Beth. She can stand what she *has* to. A lot of people passed out or puked the first time we used those things—and not all women, by any means."

"I think I ought to look."

Henry's amusement, as well as his indignation, were gone, now. "Hell, Mom!" he protested.

She beckoned with her head.

They went to the garage. Henry switched on the light. He unlocked a closet. Inside, standing, leaning against the walls, were two figures of human beings—a man and a child—horribly mutilated. Beth Conner touched the back of her hand to her mouth. She said, almost in a whisper, "All right, Hank. Shut the door."

He followed her, around the Oldsmobile and into the yard, wondering what she was thinking. She whispered something finally, and he thought she said, "The beasts!" He guessed, presently, she had said that, referring to the Reds, maybe, or maybe to scientists, or maybe just to humanity at large. But when she faced him she was calm and she took his arm by its crook. "Hank," she murmured, "don't you *ever* quit Civil Defense!"

5

Lenore said, "I won't!"

Netta ate another pecan. The Applebys had sent them from Florida—too late for Thanksgiving but too early for Christmas. The Applebys had never before sent a gift to the Baileys. The Applebys lived on Crystal Lake and went to Miami every year. Word, Netta thought, must be seeping around, the way it always does, ahead of the fact. The pecans were therefore a delicious token of a bounteous flood to come.

"I think you will," Netta said, "simply because I know you haven't lost your mind."

"Nevertheless, I will not marry Kit."

"Why?"

"How'd you *like* it?"

"I've had worse," Netta said, and then catching herself, she added, "all my life."

Lenore's eyes were savage. *"You've* had worse all your life! Poor *Dad!"*

"It's so plain it hurts," Netta said. "You refuse Kit. Okay. Your father's in jail—five to ten years. Kill him sure."

"Maybe it would—what's *left* of Dad!"

"The house goes. Both cars. All the furniture. Probably even our clothes, forced sales and repossession. Then we have nothing."

"But self-respect."

Netta said quietly, "You've never been poor. Flat. Stony. Broke. Without a friend or a dime—unless you hustle a friend and he gives you a dime. Maybe even a few dollars."

Lenore thought that over. "I doubt it. People would tide you and me over——"

"Who?"

Lenore looked through a window. "The Conners."

"The Conners—the Conners!—the *Conners!* I've heard it all my life. I'm sick to death of it. Who are the Conners? An accountant, that's who! And a crazy young kid who thinks he'll be an architect in maybe ten years when you've got bags under your eyes and a bridge."

Lenore took a pecan. She looked at it, halved it, threw the paper-thin middle husk onto the hearth and shook her head. She felt frightened, cold, sick. She was trapped and she knew it as well as her mother. If it were just disgrace, as such, and poverty, that would be thinkable. But she couldn't face the image of her father in prison, marching in a line to eat, going out on the roads in stripes, cold and miserable and rejected. She knew he was weak. But she knew, also, that he was kind.

Kind and rather gentle and, in his way, loving. Which her mother was not, unless, in some twisted way, she too cared for Beau.

Lenore was intelligent. She was realistic. Her bent toward science had showed it and her studies of science had developed the quality. She had been brought up to like and enjoy "nice" things and to want and to know how to use far more of them than her father could ever supply.

At this moment, however, she realized how very little "nice things" meant in relation to the whole of human life. Her very realism had showed her, long ago, that life was closing in on her. The sweetheart of her childhood had not turned into the dream prince of maturity. He was far away now, doing some sort of menial chore for the Air Force. Desk work. He'd grow up at a desk, drawing buildings that probably would never be constructed, because Chuck didn't seem to have even as much drive as his father. All Chuck's drive was in his head, his imagination. It never came out, never produced.

Long ago she'd begun saying to herself, Wise up, Lenore. He isn't for you. Find yourself another boy.

Well. Her mother had found one. If it wasn't to be Chuck, did it matter so greatly who it was?

Lenore could anticipate the turnings of her mother's mind. She anticipated now, as her mother began, "After all, Lenore, in time . . ."

"I know. Divorce. With alimony. Abundant alimony."

Netta got ahead of her then. "Why not? People like the Sloans expect it." Netta was aware that Minerva had no such idea in mind, but she went on confidently, "I'm sure his mother feels that even an unsuccessful marriage would be good for him. Start him on the way. And, Lenore, have you thought? Suppose you were married a few years? Suppose you came—out—well the way you would. Comfortably off? Even

wealthy? *Then* you might be in a position to give Charles
Conner financial aid till he got on his feet in architecture. You
could get married and be happy, with a settlement from the
Sloan family in your bank account! I mean, if it's *really* love
you feel for Charles, what could you do that would help *more?*
Have you thought of *that?*"

Lenore ate another nut, tossed a hull, twisted her dark hair.
"Thought of whoring for the man I love? No. I haven't. I suppose it's been done, though. By plenty of women."

"Then you'll . . . ?"

"I haven't said," Lenore answered. "I painted myself into
this corner with my own little hand. If Dad isn't to go to the
pen right off, I suppose I've got to get engaged, at least, or
have an 'understanding' with the ape. You've got me in a spot
where either I do that, or Dad's jailed."

"I always knew my daughter . . ." Netta began rapturously, and rapturously she rose from her chair to bestow an
embrace.

Lenore sat perfectly still. "Sit down, Netta," she said icily.
"Let's have no manure in this."

"Minerva will want to know!" Mrs. Bailey breathed, discomfited only momentarily.

"You call her and the deal's off. I'll tell Kit in my own time
and my own way, and the terms won't be—practicing matri-
mony from the moment he slips on the diamond either! Sit
still, Mother! I swear to God, if you put the needle in anywhere, one more time, I'll take a job in New York and be
damned to you and Dad both!"

Mrs. Bailey was slightly disappointed, but not very. She
had always been a main-chance gambler.

X-Day

1

Charles had come home for Christmas. His mother had answered the phone when he called from Texas with the good news. Something wonderful, she had thought, almost always happens around Christmastime.

But the pleasure of having Charles at home again, so soon, had been alloyed. He didn't seem the same. He was thinner. He was preoccupied. Twice, in the first four days after his homecoming, he'd put on his uniform, borrowed the family car and driven to Hink Field, the military base, "on business." Restricted business, confidential business, business that upset him, Beth thought.

On Friday, the Friday before the Monday which would be Christmas, Beth was in the kitchen, working and thinking. It was late afternoon, getting dark, threatening to snow again. A gray light softened the already white world outside. Across the shoveled snowbanks along the drive, across the children-tracked yards, through the kitchen windows, the yellow lights of the Bailey house made a picture post card. The summer shrubs were covered, like igloos: it looked cozy beneath their snow roofs and fluffy sides; the gazebo had a fringe of icicles that shone golden in the light.

Beth was "going over things" in her mind. Yuletide lists. The turkey would be delivered in the morning. The presents were all wrapped and hidden in the bedroom closet. Nora, she was sure, had inspected them thoroughly; it was possible that even Ted had taken a peek: sometimes he was still more like a child than a man. The holly and mistletoe had arrived from Beth's aunt in North Carolina, as usual. As usual, they were going to the Williamses' for a pre-Christmas dinner.

The gifts for the Williams children were already wrapped, too, heaped in a clothesbasket in the front hall.

Mr. Nesbit had sent the tree over from the grocery store that afternoon. If they got back in time from the Williamses' and from seeing Santa Claus in the park, they could trim the tree on Saturday. If they were too tired, Sunday would do. Maybe Lenore would come over and help: Charles would like that.

Old snow slid down the roof, cascaded into the yard.

She opened the kitchen door, hardly knowing why, and looked at the roped-up tree. Seven feet and symmetrical. She could see it in the front room, decorated—see, back through the years, all the Christmas trees of her children and all her own Christmas trees, spangled, shining, redolent, the big magic of childhood: gifts and excitement, seasonal aroma, Santa Claus and love.

Henry drove in, racing the car before switching it off, beating his feet on the frozen doormat, blowing as he entered the kitchen, helping her shut the door. "Beauty," he said of the tree. "How you coming?"

"All right." She picked up a big spoon, stirred the cranberries on the stove. "Do you think we could leave my sister's in time to see Santa *and* do a little shopping?"

He kissed her on the back of her neck, grinned. "Why not? Matter of fact, I have a couple of things to get, myself, still." His look of innocence was absurd.

My present, she thought. He hasn't bought mine yet. And she reminded herself for the hundredth time to phone Mr. Salten at the men's shop and tell him she'd decided to take the dressing gown for her husband and would he please deliver it, rush.

"Maybe," he said, breaking and buttering a hot cinnamon roll, "we could skip Santa this year. Kids are pretty grown-up——"

"Nora would be scandalized!"

"I suppose so." He ate a mouthful. "Mighty good!"

"Don't spoil your appetite!"

"Fat chance," he chuckled. "Hungry as a bear! Truth is, I'd miss Santa, myself. Saw him the first year they put him up and every year since."

In Simmons Park, annually, the stores erected a giant mechanical Santa Claus whose arms moved to hand gifts to children, who talked over a loud-speaker in his midriff and who even sang carols in a sonorous voice. He was the yuletide deity and big wonder of Green Prairie; a child who missed him was unfortunate indeed.

Beth looked at the roast. Her mind moved even faster than her dinner-getting hands. "I've got to find something yet for the minister's wife. Every year I promise myself I'll give her a Christmas present, and every year I put it off or forget!" She handed him a spoon. "Hold this—over the sink!" She took the lid from a pot, looked, popped it back. "And don't let me forget to take the ice cream along tomorrow. It's in the deep freeze. Ruth couldn't afford it this year."

"Where's everybody?"

"They'll be in soon. Nora's over with the Crandon youngsters. I don't know where Ted is. And Charles is shopping."

Henry eyed another roll and restrained himself. "If Chuck's downtown, he'll be late. Never saw such crowds."

"I'm worried about him," she said.

Henry looked at her thoughtfully. "Me, too. It's"——He nodded toward the window, the snow, the gleaming house where the Baileys lived, where Lenore had always lived.

"I think he got his leave to try to see what he could do about it," Beth said. "I'm perfectly sure he's aware what's afoot . . ."

"You should be," Henry answered with mild disapproval. "You wrote him, phoned him——"

She defended herself. "I thought he had a right to know."

"That's the trouble with love. People think it involves rights."

"Doesn't it?"

He laughed and put a sturdy arm over her shoulder, rocking her slightly. "Only when it's returned, Beth. Lenore's kind of drifted away from our boy."

"I don't believe it. It's all Netta's doing! *My!* I wish I could talk some sense in her head!"

"Still?" He chuckled. "After twenty-odd years of trying?"

"Netta's Netta. Too ambitious. Not so bad other ways." Beth sighed a little and tried the boiling potatoes with a fork.

"Ready?" he asked eagerly.

"Heavens no! Half hour till supper, and you know it. They have to be mashed and quick-baked, still. He's worried about something that has to do with the Air Force, too."

Henry followed the transition without difficulty. "Chuck's in Intelligence now, Mother. Guess he knows quite a few worrisome things. He has responsibility—with all these air exercises going on."

"Shake the plaster off the attic someday, those jet planes will. Charles takes things slowly the way you do, Henry." She paused, thought, amended. "The way you do—*sometimes*. He's going to be a real long while getting used to the fact that Lenore Bailey is marrying Kit Sloan, not Charles Conner."

"Is she? You sure?"

"I'm afraid so."

"Won't be the merriest Christmas we ever had," he said quietly. He peered out the window at the prettily lighted snowscape, sniffed the steaming home smell of the kitchen, shook his grizzled head. "Take *me* awhile to get used to the idea of not having Lenore for a daughter-in-law. Always saw those kids together"—he gave a stifled chuckle—"since that day we *found* 'em together! Cute little thing, she was. Didn't blame Chuck a bit."

"Henry!"

He slapped her bottom gently. "Don't be hypocritical, Mother!"

Nora came in.

That is, the front door burst open and stayed open long enough to send a few bushels of arctic air down the hall into the kitchen. Then the door slammed. Galoshes thudded as they were kicked into the hall closet. Then that door slammed. There was a long indrawn sniffle followed by a sneeze. Followed, in turn, by a *sotto voce* "Dammit!"

"Nora?"

"Yes, Mom. Not burglars and not the Fuller Brush man. Not the Realsilk Hosiery man or any *other* secret lover you were expecting." The words sounded nasal. She came into the kitchen, saw her father. "Hi, Pop."

"Nora, let me see your throat," Beth said.

"I'm all right!"

"You sound as if you were catching cold."

"I'm not." Nora coughed defensively. "I feel fine."

"Say ah-h-h-h-h."

Nora stood under the center light, lifted her winter-rouged face, said the word.

"Look at this, Henry. She's getting a very red throat."

"It's not a bit sore," Nora asserted urgently.

Mrs. Conner suddenly sat down. "That's about the last straw!"

"Oh, *Mother.* Just because I've got a little red in the throat."

"It could be measles," Mrs. Conner went on aggravatedly. "They're going 'round."

"I haven't been exposed."

"How do you know? Henry, I just can't take her over to Ruth's if she's catching a cold. The new baby—the other children——"

"I knew it!" Nora said in a low, dismal tone. "I knew it all along. Like a prophecy! This Christmas was going to be utterly totally wrecked for me."

"It isn't Christmas tomorrow; it's the Saturday before," Beth answered. "And it isn't being wrecked at all. You'll have to stay in tomorrow and not go to Aunt Ruth's dinner, so as to be perfectly all right again by Christmas!"

"But we *always* go!"

"I mean you, Nora. The rest of us will go, of course. I'll have to find somebody to look after you tomorrow."

Nora threatened tears. "I'll miss the dinner we *always* have. I'll miss *Santa* Claus."

"Charles, or your father, can take you Sunday."

"Sure," Henry said. He felt unhappy; he seemed to share Nora's distress over the possibility of missing the yearly, pre-

Christmas dinner at Ferndale; he appeared to feel that the matter of not exposing his nieces and nephews to a slight touch of sore throat, even a faint risk of measles, was being over-stressed. "Sure, Beth. I mean—if you really think Nora has to stay away . . . ?"

"I definitely do! The baby's delicate. Ruth was talking about it only the other day. And I know how mad I got when they came here, years ago, and left our Ted with mumps!"

Nora's face contracted.

"You're a big girl, now," her mother admonished. "Don't cry. I'll phone the Crandons."

"They're having a family dinner, too—in River City."

"Well, somebody. You can stay with Netta, I'm sure. She's having a cleaning woman in."

"She's totally despicable! I abhor staying there!"

"She's minded your brothers, often. She's usually a pretty good neighbor when these problems come up."

Nora said, "Phooie! Vixen. Shrew. Termignant."

Henry snorted.

"Termagant," Beth corrected, absently. "She is not. You can stay with her tomorrow if you've still got a raw throat. I'll give you medicine. My, I hope it isn't measles." She moved toward the kitchen phone and presently began to make arrangements for the custody. "We'll shop and hurry home, Netta, so you won't have her on your hands later than, say, four . . ."

Nora was folding and unfolding a cloth pot holder. Queenie, the tomcat, at that moment decided to move from the kitchen to the front rooms. Nora flung the pot holder and hit the cat. Queenie stopped, looked to see who had done him the dirty deed, shrugged and departed. Beth had hung up.

"Go gargle," she said, and she added, "Mercy! The beans!"

Nora stood, regarded her parents balefully, and left the room. From upstairs, shortly, came a sound suggesting bad drains, excepting for the fact that, to an acute listener, it would have become evident that the burbling monody was trying to be a song. This was the case: Nora was gargling, "Aloha Ohe."

The front door opened again and Chuck came to the kitchen, his arms heavy with packages. "Unload me, somebody," he cried. "Boy! What a day! Downtown, it's like a Cecil B. de Mille mob scene. So many people, you'd think they were giving everything away, not selling it."

"Be worse, tomorrow," Henry said, helping his son. "Shop early, they tell you. Serves me right."

Unloaded, still coated, Chuck heard the sound from above. "What's *that?*" He identified the theme and went to the foot of the stairs to add a falsetto alto.

The bathroom door slammed—all but shattered.

2

It was a beautiful morning—and that was the hell of it.

So Nora thought when she opened her eyes.

She dressed lugubriously. Lugubriously, she went downstairs for breakfast. Ted was there. Charles was still asleep. Her father was downtown doing a few "last-minute" things, Beth said.

Nora ate two eggs, three pieces of toast with apple jelly, some bacon, a bowl of Wheaties, a glass and a half of milk and a few prunes. She didn't say a word but consumed the food with the glowering look of a condemned and unrepentant criminal. She watched with an aloof, almost disdainful eye, as her mother cleaned up, as Ted washed the dishes, as Charles came down in his blue suit and best tie and her father returned from town, merry as Santa Claus himself, laden with packages, and reporting the place "crowded as an oyster bed."

It didn't concern Nora.

She looked out the front window for a while. The Jarvis kids went by: Alf and Penny and Kate. All three pulled sleds. The runners squeaked on the dry, hard snow and rang when they bumped over the frozen slush in Walnut Street. They were evidently going over to slide down terraces and out onto the ice at Crystal Lake.

Nora, however, was sure she was going to have to help Mrs. Bailey houseclean. Probably, she thought, old blood-eye Bailey would make her stand on a stepladder and dust chandeliers and poke at cobwebs all day. Probably the stepladder would fall and she'd break her back. Maybe she'd be told to scrub. Nora had read, once, of a farm woman who decided to clean out the gurry imbedded between some floorboards in an old house. She'd come down with diphtheria, the germs of which had survived in the dirt for twenty-six years. It had been the Black Diphtheria, and the woman had died.

Nora felt her mother and father might easily be damned good and sorry they'd deserted her that day.

In what seemed like no time at all, her mother stood there, in her pretty new gray suit and her fox fur saying, "We're just about ready! Get your hat and coat and scarf, Nora."

"Just to go next door?"

"And your arctics. You tell Netta I said you could play outdoors awhile, after lunch. And we'll come right back from Ruth's dinner, so expect us around three. Four, at the latest."

"Can't I go with you?"

"No, Nora, you can't. And I want you to show Netta what a fine cleaning woman you are, too!"

Looking at the old, spotty, brown dress she'd been ordered to wear, Nora felt the Cinderella legend applied to her—backward. Her last hope died. Solemnly, thinking of the Williams home, of tables heaped with goodies, of the fun of riding all the way to Ferndale, of cousins to play with, Nora put on her scarf, her winter hat, her winter coat, her red galoshes.

"Now," her mother said, "run on over."

Nora's run, Chuck said, was "the most halfhearted in the history of feet."

The Conner family, mufflered to the eyes, climbed into the Oldsmobile and drove away.

Nora saw them go as she looked through the Bailey front window and listened while Netta scoldingly instructed the colored woman.

Netta, her face covered with a greenish substance called Chloropack and her hair in curlers, as usual, turned to the child. "Upstairs," she said, "in the linen closet, are stacks and stacks of papers. The first thing I want you to do, dear, is to carry them down cellar. Pile them beside the ash cans."

Nora went up. The sloppy Baileys had simply tossed what looked like about twenty years' supply of papers and magazines in the closet. Nora figured it would take a person a thousand years to cart it all to the cellar. She put her mind on the problem. Downstairs, the vacuum was going. The colored cleaning woman, briefly interesting to Nora because she was named Harmony, was now in the kitchen, scrubbing.

She went into the front bedroom and looked out sorrowfully at her own yard. The Bailey cellar door was on that side, which gave Nora her idea. She opened a window. Icy air gushed in from the deceptively sunny outdoors.

Nora carried an armful of magazines down the hall. She pushed them over the window sill. They fell with a satisfying flurry. She brought another. In due time, she had amazingly depleted the stocks of printed matter in the closet. From downstairs came a voice, "What's that cold draft?" The vacuum stopped and feet pounded. Mrs. Bailey raced into the bedroom. "Good heavens, you idiot! Don't you know how much it costs to heat a house!"

"I wasn't going to keep it open any longer. Much. And I can drop the magazines again, into the cellar."

"Don't talk back! You've chilled the entire upstairs, you lazy thing!"

Netta Bailey was not in a good mood. Cleaning house was far from her favorite task. The new hired woman was proving incompetent. And having Nora about was a liability. The imp had cooled off the hall and bedroom, spread magazines over half the yard, and left a trail of papers from the closet to the window. Furthermore, Mrs. Bailey now realized, having the child in the house made it practically impossible for her to relax, now and again during this hectic day, with a highball. Nora would unquestionably report the practice as extreme alcoholism.

Nora, on her part, was not in a much better mood. "I'm not talking back," she said calmly. "I'm explaining. What I'm doing is efficient. If you want me to slave around here for you all morning——"

"Shut up," Mrs. Bailey said. "Pick up everything in the hall. Then put your things on and go out there in the yard. You'll have to stack the stuff on the back porch, now. Beau hasn't been able to get those cellar doors open for *two years*."

Fuming silently, Nora obeyed.

She was appalled at the amount of snow-covered lawn upon which the falling periodicals had been distributed. She began to pick them up in a desultory way.

A theory she had often entertained in the past now absorbed her: people picked on her. There was something about her— maybe she was a genius, and people cannot tolerate superiority—that caused everybody to want to hurt her feelings, make things difficult for her, scold her, measure out a full and acrid—whatever that was—dose of injustice.

Old lady Bailey was on her high horse, too. Nora thought that probably by the time her family got back, old lady Bailey would have locked her in a closet. Things seemed to work out that way for Nora. Her own home was right there, a couple of hundred feet away, and she couldn't even get in. *Probably.* She stopped collecting magazines and listened. The vacuum was droning.

She ran across the yard and checked. Front door, back door, cellar, garage. All locked. Locked against their only daughter.

The Lindner kids, also headed for Crystal Lake, though with only one Flexible Flyer, passed by.

"Whatcha doin', Nora?"

Nora stared across the Bailey yard, the snow-capped evergreens, the brown wrecks of last summer's annuals. "Blowing soap bubbles."

Annabelle laughed. "Where'd all those magazines come from?"

"Fell out of a Flying Saucer," Nora answered. "They're all printed in Martian."

Tim Lindner said, "Aw—you're crazy."

The sled banged and squeaked down Walnut Street.

Six big airplanes went by. They were above the clouds. There hadn't been a cloud in the sky, earlier. Ted had said so. Ted was always looking aloft at the weather.

Old needle-face, curler-durler Bailey stuck her pickle puss out the door and whoo-whooed. "*Nora!* Hurry with those magazines! I want you to pull rugs while Harmony and I lift things."

And you couldn't pull them *exactly* where she wanted them,

Nora calculated, if you measured with a solid gold ruler.
They'd be lifting and straining and getting red faces—old
snoodle-snozzle Bailey would—did colored people get redder?—
while she tried to get the Orientals the way they wanted
them. Tried and tried and tried and tried.

Nora didn't so much run away as drift away.

She didn't so much desert her assignment as take time out.

She didn't even expect to go as far as Crystal Lake, where
the kids in the neighborhood would be coasting. Though it
wasn't much, as coasting went, since her own father had said
it was hardly fifty vertical feet from the street to the lake.
Green Prairie wasn't noteworthy for hills.

Nora walked, rather rapidly and looking back frequently,
down Walnut, across Sedmon to River Avenue. Crystal Lake
lay beyond, quite a distance, beyond Arkansas and Dumond
and Lake View; and a block south besides. Nora thought she
better not go that far. Moreover, she had eighteen cents, and
there were stores on River Avenue. Not many and not big,
but stores, including the Greek's.

She turned north on River Avenue.

Harry and Everett, the two boys who lived over Schneider's
Delicatessen, and went to parochial school, were standing on
the corner, at Maple Street. A police car had just gone by,
its siren loud, and now another was screaming in the distance.
Nora stood at the corner to watch the second cruise car approach, pass and vanish. Only then was she recognized. Harry
said, "Hi, Nora."

" 'Lo."

"Musta been a robbery, or somethin'!"

"Probably just going out to get beers."

Both boys looked doubtful. "Sure were tearing," Everett
said.

"I know a man—he goes with Lenore Bailey—that has a Jaguar and he goes about three times as fast as any old cops. That's a hundred and fifty miles an hour, I guess."

"You got any money on you?" Harry asked.

"Eighteen cents."

"Want to pitch?"

Nora looked south on River Avenue, toward parallel rows of frame houses, and north toward a patch of "business" district, of small shops and service stations—a tailor and a florist, the Greek candy store and a used-car lot on which the autos stood in solid ranks with six-inch snow roofs. "I'm supposed to be slaving for old lady Bailey," she said. "If she misses me, she'll probably come out like a posse."

"We could go down to the alley," Harry suggested. "There's some swept brick walk. And we'll watch out for the old fizoo."

To her surprise, Nora had increased her assets by nine cents when she saw the Bailey car come around the corner. Mrs. Bailey, a coat on and a scarf over her head, the Chloropack wiped away, was driving with one hand and leaning out to peer every which way, yelling, "Nora! Nora Conner!"

Harry grabbed the two pennies on the brick pavement. "*Brother! Is she ever mad!*"

Everett merely took an appalled look and ran.

The swift defection gave Nora a somewhat exaggerated idea of her predicament. If she had thought the matter over, she would have realized that Mrs. Bailey was—to be sure—annoyed at having her charge vanish. But Mrs. Bailey would not rend her limb from limb. Nora would, at worst, have suffered a severe scolding and perhaps certain deprivations at lunch.

But the sound of Mrs. Bailey's calling and the sight of her driving one-handed, together with her own sense of guilt, plus the unnerving effect of the flight of her companions, set Nora in motion. She darted from store front to store front on River Avenue. The car approached, inexorably.

Then, just as Nora felt sure she would be overtaken, the car pulled up. Mrs. Bailey went into the fruit store. For Mrs. Bailey was combining two tasks: hunting for her escaped ward and running an errand she had planned for later in the day. Mrs. Bailey was not much concerned about Nora, in fact merely vexed. For when Netta herself had been eleven years old, the streets were her home.

In something like panic, Nora fled across the Pine Street intersection and saw, beyond, a possible refuge. It was one she had seen under construction in the summer and investigated, with several nervous schoolmates, in the fall. She had not known it was still accessible.

What she saw was an open manhole, protected by portable iron guardrails and marked with red flags and a red lantern. The manhole was an entrance to the nearly finished, but not yet used sewer under River Avenue. Watching while great sections of concrete pipe were lowered into the trench had been one of Nora's occasional occupations on the way home from school. No longer ago than Columbus Day, with five other sixth-graders, Nora had taken advantage of the absence of the laborers and descended the ladder.

They had found a vast, endless tunnel stretching ahead, with gray light seeping in, at Spruce Street and Oak, at Plum and Hickory and presumably at West Broad. The sepulchral echo of their voices had soon caused all but Bill Fennley to scramble back up the ladder. Bill, however, had actually walked through, clear to Hickory. It was generally conceded to be the most remarkable example of daring in the school year.

Nora went down the ladder like a shot.

Underground, it didn't seem quite so cold. Traffic on the

broad thoroughfare rumbled oddly. The great, whitish tunnel led away to infinity, with blurs of light in the distance, just as it had been on Columbus Day. There was a little water in the very bottom of the huge pipe, now, but not much. Old lady Bailey, Nora realized, would never find her now.

The fact restored some of the girl's aplomb. If she wanted to, she thought, she could stay right there until her family came home. It would be a long wait and she didn't have a watch but maybe she could tell by the sun, though the sun, she realized, was beginning to get weaker as the clouds thickened.

Another idea occurred to Nora.

She had heard much talk about this new sewer. She had even read about it, accidentally, in the *Transcript*. It was costing zillions of dollars. It was going to be opened next summer. A new disposal plant was being built for it, on the river, above the bluff, beside the Swan Island Bridge. An "absolutely pure effluent" would be dumped into the Green Prairie River from the plant, though the river was already so muddy and dirty, most of the time, that Nora felt it foolish to clean up the sewage. The line had been completed all the way from Decatur Road to Jefferson, in the heart of the downtown area, and the existing lines would be hooked up with the main sewer in the spring, diverting them from the over-taxed sewer under Arkansas Avenue.

The idea that came to Nora took into account her knowledge of the sewer, Bill Fennley's safe passage from Maple to Hickory and, in particular, the plain fact that the line furnished an enclosed, secret, presumably direct and simple passageway to Jefferson. True, the way was pretty dark, but there were no hazards along it. One could walk easily, even run, if a person didn't mind a little splashing, in the darkish stretches between the manholes and the light they shed into the dim tunnel. Jefferson Avenue went straight past Simmons Park, where the giant mechanical Santa Claus gave out presents to children who drew lucky numbers, and every child could draw, free.

It occurred to Nora that, if she had the nerve, she could progress unobserved and securely from where she stood, clear to Jefferson, where she could emerge, cross the seasonally thronged shopping area, and see the big, red-coated, jolly figure. Maybe even win a prize. She could come back the usual way, on sidewalks, because if she once managed to see the Simmons Park Santa, thus thwarting her parents and evading the worst part of her punishment, it wouldn't matter to Nora what happened.

Resolutely, she marched away from the brightness that fell from the round hole in the street, toward gloom and a distant ray of light. By the time she had passed beneath the Oak Street intersection, she was a veteran trespasser of sewers and already beginning to wonder if there was any way by which she could assure herself of drawing a lucky number. When you did, the big Santa moved his immense arm and held out a wrapped package to you—candy, mostly—and a mechanical voice said through a loud-speaker inside him behind his moving beard, "Merry Christmas!" He was forty-three feet tall, so making him "work" was an unforgettable marvel. In between, he played music.

She hurried, calm now, intent, full of a delicious excitement.

3

At the Jim Williams home in Ferndale, Beth and Ruth, in the kitchen, were busy preparing the feast. A table, groaning already under stacks of plates, side dishes, preserves, jellies, mats for the hot dishes, silver, napery and favors, waited the onslaught of two hungry families. The silver-headed new baby, Irma, was watching the process of a big family dinner for the first time in her life, round-eyed, lying in a baby pen that had plainly contained other infants and also fended them from the world. Irma seemed pleased with the activity, for she smiled often, burped often, and occasionally shook her rattle.

Ted Conner was upstairs helping Bert fix his radio.

The three men, Jim, Henry and Chuck, sat in the living room minding the baby and such other young Williamses as streamed fretfully through the place. They were killing time, talking about the Sister Cities' biggest Christmas boom in history.

When the phone rang, Ruth pushed open the swinging door. "Get it, Jim, will you? We're making gravy."

Jim went into the front hall and soon returned. He looked unhappy. "For you, Hank. Man who sounds upset."

Henry Conner lumbered into the hall and said cheerfully, half playfully, "Merry Christmas. This is Henry."

A very shaky voice came to his ears. "Henry Conner?"

"That's right. Who is it? What's the——"

"Been trying to reach you for half an hour! This is head-quarters. Brock speaking. Condition Yellow."

Henry felt as if he'd been hit with a forty-five slug. His knees wobbled and he sat down hard on the hall chair. Then he realized it must be either a gag or some crazy test. If it was a test, it was a terrible time for one. Next, he realized that this sort of situation had been envisaged, and a code designed to cover it, so that only those who knew the code could check back on the announcement. For a moment, the proper words were swept out of his mind. He cudgeled his brain and said, in a voice that was nothing like his own, "How many sacks of potatoes?"

"Maine potatoes," the voice replied. "And Idahos. I've got to break off."

That was the question. That was the answer. It wasn't a grim practical joke. It wasn't a test.

It was Condition Yellow. *Real.*

So many things happened in his mind that he was astonished by the mere capacity to think of them all.

He would have to leave and so would Ted. Chuck could stay—no—Chuck was "military personnel" and entitled to the information.

It was going to ruin the pre-Christmas party.

And—*What in God's name am I thinking about a party, for?* flashed in his head.

"Condition Yellow," in its latest construction, meant that enemy airplanes had been recognized over continental U.S.A. It was an alert, currently confidential, which was intended to reach and mobilize all Civil Defense people, police, firemen and other city employees, as well as "key" technicians in industry. For years, for many tedious years of drill, the inhabitants of big cities had planned for Condition Yellow. Henry thought, in the tumbling, muscle-weakening scramble of his mind, that all over America, men like himself, and women, would be reacting the same way to the identical two words. *Condition Yellow.*

At the time they'd dreamed up a code to check alerts, Henry had thought the idea absurd. He was glad now they'd done it. Green Prairie people like himself could at least be sure that CD headquarters—and that meant the military—believed the risk was great enough to warrant the shock and disturbance of a complete but quiet official turnout, on the Saturday before Christmas.

Next Henry thought of the Air Force "exercises" which had been going on for a month. The probabilities were a hundred to one that some flight of our own bombers, off course somewhere, over California or New York or Alaska—anywhere—had been mistaken for enemy planes. It was a thought that immediately, or soon, flashed through the minds of some millions of city dwellers who picked up telephones all over U.S.A. and heard the two words:

Condition Yellow.

With the skies above the continent crossed and crisscrossed by American flights, how could they be sure? Why wouldn't spotters be liable to error? After all, there hadn't been any sign of hostility whatever on the enemy's part.

Even men at the top of military and Government intelligence agencies—men "cleared" to know all the known facts—hesitated. There had been nothing from behind the Iron Curtain to indicate the assembly of long-range planes, the gassing up, the bombing up, the vast number of activities required to launch a "surprise" attack. If this was "it," the experts thought almost as one man, the Soviets had outdone the Japs in their surprise onslaught on Pearl.

The experts, however, reacted dutifully. Others did not.

In cities on the West Coast, the East Coast, and in the South and the Middle West, hundreds of thousands of ordinary persons, men and women, ready for Christmas, thinking the world on the verge of assured and eternal peace, decided for themselves. They were not as well indoctrinated in the meaning of duty as the professionals. It *had* to be an error, these myriads thought—and went back to lunch, to the TV set, to mowing the lawn in Miami and shoveling snow in Detroit.

Not Henry.

When his brother-in-law came into the hall and said, "Something wrong? You're ghost-white!" Henry smiled and nodded.

"Maybe, Jim. *Look.* Don't say anything to the women. Ask Chuck to step in, willya?"

Charles came. *"Lord,* Dad! What's *wrong?"*

Henry motioned. Charles shut the hall door. His father said, "Just reached me from CD. Condition Yellow, Chuck."

The soldier, in the dark blue suit, lost color also. Fear jumped into his eyes and was mastered. His pale lips moved. "That's—what—I've been scared of."

"You think it could be the McCoy? Or some *error . . . ?"*

Chuck strode to the phone, snatched it up, thought a moment and dialed. He waited, then set the phone down. "I called Hink Field—on a special number. Busy. So I can't say. But we can't take chances now."

"On the other hand, I'd hate like the devil to scare Beth and Ruth and the kids half to death—and find it was a bloomer."

"That's true. Suppose you take our car, and Ted—he's due to report, isn't he?—and go. I'll try the phone awhile. We can tell the folks it's a practice—for the moment. I'll come along— on Willowgrove, to keep clear of the Christmas crowds— right after dinner."

"That'll do," Henry decided. He bellowed up the stairs, "Hey, Ted! Hurry down! The fools have called a practice alert and you and I have to make tracks!"

The door from the hall into the kitchen flew open. Two indignant women stood there.

"Henry," Beth said, firmly, "this is *really* too much!"

"Of all the idiotic ideas, on a Saturday, at dinnertime!" Ruth added.

Jim Williams came through the living-room door. "You two stay right here, Hank. This damn fool defense thing has gone too far."

"Long as I'm in it, I have no choice." Henry was shrugging

into his coat, the blue one with the velvet collar. He threw a meaningful glance at his older son. "I'll rely on you, Chuck, for everything. Come on, Ted; get cracking."

4

Below West Broad Street, the mammoth tile in which Nora walked became steadily darker. She had grown accustomed to the short spaces of darkness between the streets; each one, though inky enough to hide her feet from her own view, showed ahead the ever-brightening illumination from the next street. As she walked on from Broad, however, she remembered what a long distance it was to the Washington Avenue intersection. She couldn't see any light at all. Yet she went ahead, believing the darkness would yield in the next few steps to at least the dim evidence of light from the manhole at Broad.

No such thing happened. The curved walls closed over her head, at a point about half again as high as she was. The darkness thickened, deepened, and the echoing sound of her arctic-shod feet came back in a muffled fashion from the distances. She looked back. The light from Broad was dim and far behind. A sense of compression, and with it a gnawing anxiousness, began to replace her eager determination. Still she went on, and steadily she lost the confidence that her progress had established.

Suppose, she thought, it suddenly *drops*.

She went ahead cautiously after that notion, feeling with her foot before she stepped.

Traffic bumbled and shook the place. She put a hand out, touched the damp side of the tube, moved slower, slower. The tunnel was curving now, but the curve was so gradual that she could not discern it in the dark. She did not notice any change until she looked back—for the wan comfort of the distant light—and saw it had vanished.

Panic touched her for the first time.

Yet it was not absolute panic. Had it been, she would have turned, fled whence she had come, screaming, perhaps. Instead, she stopped, shivered, and listened to her own hard breathing. By an act of will, of self-scolding, she brought back a measure of composure. Surely, she thought, it would be shorter to go ahead than the long way back to Broad Street. She admitted she was scared, which helped. And she determined to come out at the very next manhole. No more sewer-walking for her.

She had gone perhaps another hundred feet when two things happened simultaneously. She became conscious of light, dim and somehow different, up ahead. It showed the tubular walls faintly. The bend was also disclosed, and Nora realized why she had lost the Broad Street light to view. But, at the same time, the geography of the city below Broad leaped into her mind: River Avenue slanted straight through Restland Cemetery before it reached Washington and she, presumably, was *under* the graveyard right here! The thought caused her flesh to prickle and a sprinkling sweat to burst out on her body. She felt too weak to move, too scared to scream, and yet unwilling to slide down into the trickling water that marked the exact bottom of the great pipe.

But she felt the dead all around her, not reckoning that the sewer had curved for the very purpose of avoiding the graveyard. She also saw the light ahead was not the white glaze of day, but yellowish, and it seemed to *flicker*.

Then, as her horror mounted, she heard voices.

Nora screamed.

She screamed repeatedly and the voices were still. She, also, listened, and screamed again. For she heard ghostly feet running and the yellowish glow began to waver.

The dead, disturbed, *were coming for her.*

5

Civil Defense headquarters for Green Prairie had been originally located in the midtown area, near City Hall. Its transference to an old high school building, on the east side of town, had followed the gradual realization that, if Civil Defense were taken earnestly, it followed that the midtown area was no place for headquarters: it would constitute the target area of any enemy attack. The present headquarters, unused by pupils after the construction of East High School, was a yellow brick structure set back from the intersection of Willowgrove and Adams.

Henry drove around the corner and into the parking yard on chattering tires. Other cars were ahead, others behind, and cars were waiting in line for space.

"Why don't I drive on home and get my set going?" Ted asked.

"You're too young to . . ." Henry grunted and turned from the line. "Take it home, son," he said gently. "And go easy, because if the cops pick you up, we won't have any communications at all. I'll hitch a ride from here to the South School to assemble my section. If you can, lemme know when the folks get home."

Henry said that over his shoulder. Men were running, like himself, into the school building. A few spoke his name. One or two called, "Know anything?"

Then they were in the lobby, at the place where they'd

learned in the many drills that sector wardens were to report, if possible in person, otherwise by proxy, in emergency.

Douglas McVeigh was standing at the top of the steps on something—a table, maybe. Men and women ran in, saw him and either ran on to their posts because they belonged in H.Q., or stopped for orders.

That plan was working, Henry observed. Thirty or forty volunteers had gathered where McVeigh stood above them in as many, or as few, seconds.

"All personnel to their posts," McVeigh was saying as Henry rushed in and was recognized. "Hi, there, Hank."

"How"—Hank struggled to phrase the burning question in every mind—"how *authentic* is it, Doug?" He realized, as he spoke, he needn't have doubted any longer. Doug McVeigh was stone grim, for all the ease with which he spoke, waved, nodded. He was using every ounce of his Scotch steel to hold himself that way: easy-seeming.

McVeigh glanced around, waited for a half-dozen new arrivals. "This is *it*, folks. A very large flight of long-range bombers is somewhere over Canada, right now."

A woman began to cry audibly.

"No time for *that!*" McVeigh said shortly. "Get going, everybody!"

"Thank God we're only a Class-Two Target Area," a man beside Henry said.

Henry raised his voice. "Who's for South School? Henry Conner here. Need fast transportation!"

"Come on, Hank." Luke Walters ran through the growing crowd in the lobby. "Mollie and I were notified at the store."

Hank was driven from the school yard toward Willowgrove at breakneck speed, in spite of Mrs. Walters's angry protests, by the excited owner of Green Prairie's largest stationery store.

"What about your clerks?" Henry asked.

"Eh?" Luke was somewhat deaf.

"In your store? The clerks? They okay?"

"Man—I *left* 'em! Didn't say a *word*. Condition Yellow means we gotta streak. But *not* a *general* alert. *Right?*"

"Yeah. You fix up the store cellar, the way we recommended?"

Luke hated to have his driving interfered with by talk. And it was difficult driving: Willowgrove seemed to be filled, suddenly, with people who were trying to lose their lives—people going too fast, in both directions.

They made it safely, somewhat to Hank's surprise, to his sector H.Q. Cars were assembling there, too, and people, moving quickly, were streaming into the building like ants, taking the places they had learned to take through the years.

Hank went to the principal's office, shucked off his coat as he began giving orders, skimmed his hat at the rack and sat down. He rang a special number and reported himself at his post, his checkers at work, his people arriving in good numbers.

At the Walnut Street house, Ted drew up, his heart hammering and his ears crimson from the cold. It had been some drive, the way everyone was traveling. Looked as if quite a few were already making for the country. So it was evident that "security" about Condition Yellow was being partly violated.

He parked the car face out, in the drive, as it should be in a time of emergency. He was panting a little as he bounded up the porch steps: he'd never driven a car that far before, or anywhere near that fast—sixty, on one stretch.

Then he remembered that nobody had thought to give him a key. He couldn't get in without breaking something.

He chose a front window because it was handiest. The glass shattered; he reached in . . . the lock turned.

He ran up both flights of stairs, threw himself into the broken swivel chair at his work table, clapped phones on his head and started to pull switches, turn dials.

Presently a hysterical and varied chatter began to pour into his astounded ears.

"It's real," he whispered to himself. "It's—*it*."

Anyone looking at the teen-ager in that transfixed moment would have thought that "it" was the most wonderful thing that the young man could have hoped for. It wasn't, exactly; but nobody could top it for pure, raging excitement.

In Ferndale, Chuck got through at last to Hink Field. Dinner was spoiled. His mother and his aunt were indignant; Ruth was, in fact, weeping with disappointment and rage. He could hear her say, over and over, "The fools! Oh, the *fools!* They're little *boys*, really. It's all a big game and they *love* it."

Grimly, Chuck hoped that she would go on forever thinking it was just a "big game."

The baby started to cry, as if she, too, realized the party was over, spoiled, done for.

That was when he dialed for the twentieth time and got through.

"Captain Parker here," a voice said.

"Jeff? This is Chuck Conner——"

"Chuck? Report out here as soon as possible, hunh?"

"Know anything?"

There was a minute pause—as if the captain had looked over his shoulder. Then his voice came, tense, low and fast. "*Yeah!* Only a Yellow alert, so far. First wave sneaked in low, somewhere above Great Slave Lake. Spread out and cruised slowly. They're split in pieces now and under attack. Thing is—thing that gets *everybody!*—a wave is coming *from the south!*" The voice became flat again: "Okay, Conner. Report, Hink, instanter."

At that moment, Charles Conner had perhaps the most accurate information of any person within the main confines of the Sister Cities.

He walked back into the distraught living room and said, casually almost, "Mother, I've got to report to Hink, myself. Guess I should take you home now; we'll have to use the buses."

"Take my car," Jim said.

Chuck looked at him. "Wouldn't you rather keep it, under the circumstances?"

Jim was sitting in his easy chair now, his face puckered with indignation and a glass of beer in his hand. *"Hell.* This phoney-baloney? Take the car, boy."

"It may not be—phoney . . ." Chuck didn't want to frighten his uncle, merely to warn him. And he didn't want to violate his own trust. He was cleared to know the thing he now knew. Unauthorized civilians in this region, so far, were not supposed to know anything at all.

Jim Williams stood up, his expression sardonic. "You complete your call?"

Chuck nodded.

"The Hink Field soldiers take it straight?"

Chuck nodded.

"Bunch of idiots! I tell you—even if this spreads all over the country—it's fake. Some lousy Government idea of a test run. Making the civilian population knuckle to the military. Damned fraud, I say. Watch my vote next time! *Brother!*"

"Just the same," Chuck said, bringing his own and his

mother's coats, aware of his mother's eyes, "if you hear the air-raid siren, get down in your cellar with all the kids—and *stay* there."

Jim was grinning. "That's a hot one! Notice what the man said, Ruth? *'If* we hear the sirens!' Son, there aren't six sirens in all River City and the nearest one to Ferndale is audible in a strong wind only about to the reservoir."

Chuck had forgotten the great difference between the defense preparations of the two cities. He said, "Promise this. Keep the radio on."

"Believe me, I will. Should be a circus—everybody running like headless chickens!"

"Keep the radio on. If you hear a Condition Red, get in the cellar and get there fast and stay there!"

"Sure. *If* we hear a Condition Red. Fat chance!"

Chuck gave a worried glance at the Williams kids, saw that Ruth was still merely scornful, and opened the door. "Promise?"

"Sure," Jim said negligently. *"Gosh!* I never realized I had such spooky, damned fool relatives."

In the Williams car, Beth said, "It's real, isn't it, Charles?"

"Damned real."

"You were told—more than you can tell us?"

He turned into Willowgrove, avoided a speeding truck, and started south. "This is for you, Mother—and only you. Dad will get it shortly beyond doubt. The whole area, I guess. There are two . . . three waves of bombers on the way and one's coming from the south—God knows why or how."

She didn't answer. He looked around. His mother had bowed her head and shut her eyes and he realized, at first with a sense of shock and then with a sense of its fitness, that she was crying.

6

It wasn't the dead, Nora realized as she looked in fixed horror. The dead didn't wear hip boots. It was just some sewer men carrying lanterns. Her relief was overwhelming.

Almost any adult who had passed through such a series of ideas and corresponding nervous and visceral shocks would have folded up quietly on the curved cement. But Nora, relieved of the infernal terrors, now faced terrors common to persons of her age: the terrors of angered adults.

"What the hell! A *kid!*"

Nora called timidly, "Hello."

The men held up lanterns. There were three of them. "What in God's name you doing here?"

Nora perceived in the man's voice more astonishment than wrath. The men behind also seemed amazed. Astonishment in adults offered, not peril, but opportunity.

"I'm lost," Nora said. "I was running away from—people— and I saw a ladder in a hole. I went down—and slid—and I guess I hit kind of hard and when I came to my senses I was wandering in this place. Where is it?"

"Issa bout Washanan an' da riva," a man with a mustache said. "Da poor leetle keed."

"They were boys I was running away from," Nora went on hurriedly. "Big boys. Men, almost. They asked me to do— terrible things." A woman in distress, Nora felt, one who was trying to get sympathy, should be in distress for a more suitable reason than pursuit by Mrs. Bailey.

"Be goddam!" said the Italian.

The man who'd spoken first said, "What's the name, sister?"

"Nora Conner."

"You sure you didn't come in here a-purpose?"

"I don't even know where it is—or what, exactly."

"I'm Ken Smith and don't tell any more dam' lies. Come on, Nora, we'll get you out."

"Where?"

"Washington Avenue." The man held the lantern up but could not read her face. "That suit you?"

"Anything," she said dramatically, "to get out."

She almost told them that she'd thought they were the dead from the cemetery. She realized in time, being Nora, that the confidence, true and horrific though it might be, would reveal the good knowledge she'd had of her whereabouts.

They walked along with Nora second in the file. "What were *you* doing here?" she asked.

"Trying to stop a leak in a joint."

"Are you the superintendent?"

Ken Smith grunted, "Foreman." Light showed ahead and soon a ladder and a round, white eye above. Ken boosted her. "Scraggle out, kid," he said. "And don't come in here any more. They got *rats* in this sewer as big as you."

Nora climbed. She thought Mr. Ken Smith was about half a nice person and half not very nice. There was no such thing as a rat as big as she. The higher she got and the closer to the light, the surer she felt of that. In a moment, she was outdoors.

The light hurt her eyes for a while.

When the hurt stopped, she started over Washington.

All around, now, were the big buildings, the skyscrapers, and the shops. The sidewalks, though broad, couldn't hold the people. They tramped in the snow, packing it down, and they bulged out in the street, off the curb, and cars honked at them. Cars piled up at every cross street; people going over in big bunches sometimes made the cars wait over an entire green light, honking in fury, but helpless.

There were all kinds of people and thousands of kids. There was everything on earth in the store windows—mannequins in silk dresses and men's silk dressing gowns, cameras and Kodak film and wonderful, enormous snapshots in the window of Eller's Photo Store. There were toys and windows full of candies and huge boxes in Slater's, wrapped in silver paper and tied with silver ribbons with imitation holly berries as big as apples and probably a lot of nothing, Nora thought, in the boxes. On every corner, there was a Santa Claus ringing a dinnerbell and holding out a box for money and down Central Avenue the Salvation Army was playing carols, but she decided it would take too long to push her way up and watch the lassies with trombones, though she wanted to.

She got across Central finally, after waiting two lights, and she decided every soul in the county must be doing their last-minute shopping. She noticed, too, that people were in kind of a bad temper—doubtless because they were shopping so late and the things they wanted were all shopworn by now or sold out and they had to take second choice. The carillon in St. Mark's suddenly began to play "Silent Night" and a few large flakes of snow came past Nora's nose, making her look aloft at the weather. She saw it was completely cloudy, and she expected it would soon snow hard, giving them a white Christmas in the Sister Cities three times over, counting the snow on the street.

The press of people—intent, hurrying, pouring into stores and pouring out, people for the most part bigger and stronger than Nora—became worrisome. The prospect of hard snow also offered problems. Simmons Park began to seem quite far away, though it was actually only a few very long blocks, less than a mile, from Central. A mile was usually as nothing to a determined Nora. But a mile in a mob, with the threat of snow—and no lunch—was something else.

When she got across Central, she began to wonder whom she could find to help her. If her father had been at work, in the Phillips Building, everything would be simple; but he wasn't; he was in Ferndale, stuffing himself with roast pork and potatoes.

She peered in the Morgan-Fenwick Department Store windows. And she thought of Mr. Bailey. The Sloan Bank, after all, was only a short way farther downtown and she'd heard Netta say Beau was working because they'd kept open a few "cages" for Christmas-rush deposits, and Beau felt he should be there.

She walked down Central, the biggest street, the most important.

The falling snow and the snow on the wide sidewalk made peoples' voices whispery. It muffled auto horns; even the metronome clank of a loose tire chain sounded fuzzy. Iron bells in St. Mark's played "Oh, Little Town of Bethlehem," and the Santa Clauses rang shrill bells; people put money in pots that hung on tripods, and the Salvation Army blared out "It Came Upon the Midnight Clear."

Bemused by these matters, Nora inadvertently walked past the vaulted entrance of the Sloan Bank and found herself looking in the window of the White Elephant Restaurant, just beyond. At the sight of people eating, she swallowed several times. She pushed her nose against the cold glass and wondered if twenty-seven cents was enough to give her entry. She considered going in, anyway, and ordering, and then telephoning Mr. Bailey or somebody. They could come and pay the bill. Once before, though, Nora had tried that, and the people in the other restaurant had asked to see her money before serving her. So she'd run out, vastly humiliated. It had even made her father sore.

Still, Nora didn't want to risk such ignominy.

Four very pretty women, not very old women, were eating their lunch right under Nora's nose. Her magnetized gaze traveled from syrup-dripping waffles to chicken salad. One of the women started watching Nora and soon said something to the others; all of a sudden she jumped up and came out the revolving door to the street, in the snow, without her coat or hat and said to Nora, "You hungry, honey?"

"Yes, ma'am."

"Haven't you got any money or any folks around here?"

"I was Christmas shopping," Nora explained readily. "And I ran out of funds. I thought my daddy was in his office, but he's gone home already."

"What's your name, dear?"

"Nora Conner and I live out on Walnut Street. That's near Crystal Lake."

"My name's Alice Groves and I'm having lunch with three nurses. Would you like to eat with us? I'll buy the lunch."

Nora hardly bothered to consider the fact that Alice Groves was colored and so were the other three women she said were nurses. She had a vague feeling that perhaps some people would not approve if they saw her eating in the White Elephant window with four colored ladies, but Nora privately thought the majority of colored adults were a good deal more interesting than nearly any grown white people. She accepted.

They introduced themselves. It seemed they were all trained nurses at the Mildred Tatum Infirmary, which Nora knew about, and Miss Groves was head of the whole thing. They were off duty, Christmas shopping, and having lunch here at the White Elephant.

"Order anything you like, dear," Miss Groves urged.

Studying the menu, Nora thought that colored people got lower wages, so she skipped the blue plates and main dishes. "Would it be all right if I had two sardine sandwiches and then waffles?" That came to ninety-five cents, a good deal.

One of the nurses—her name was Rebecca—laughed quite hard.

Alice Groves said, "It would be perfectly all right."

Besides that, they gave her the best seat. There was one seat from which you could watch a man across the street on the flagpole on the top edge of the building which, Nora determined by counting the windows, was only a paltry fifteen stories high.

He was interesting to watch because he was more like a bug up there than a person. And while they had lunch, he came down, riding a kind of horizontal ladder on ropes. As he crossed the sidewalk to a small truck he had parked there, she could see he was lame. On the truck was painted, not in real lettering but just homemade letters, "Steeplejack Sam—Your High Repair Man."

There were the crowds to watch also, and Steeplejack Sam, as long as he was up high on the fancy stonework around the top of the building, though she lost sight of him on the street, right away. There was a lot to hear—the different kinds of music, including the Muzak in the restaurant, and what the nurses said. When Nora finished eating, they asked her if she would like ice cream, but she said not, politely. Then they told her they were going to Toyland in Marker's store and she could accompany them and they would put her on a bus for home later.

On the way to Marker's, one of the nurses, Evangeline Treely, decided to go into Vance's and send her mother some fancy stationery, so they went there, and it took over an hour to push through the customers and find what Evangeline wanted and locate a clerk and pay and get change. Then they did start for Toyland.

Nora had forgotten all about the giant automaton Santa Claus in Simmons Park. The nurses were wonderful people to be with, she thought, and there wasn't any great hurry about getting home because the clouds had lifted a little and the snow had stopped, and if her family came home and worried about her any, it would serve them right for leaving her behind.

7

Ted Conner was alone on Walnut Street. He was in the attic. A little snow was falling, but the paper had said it would probably clear in the late afternoon. He hoped so. Reception would be better if it cleared up.

At first he had wished someone was there. The news was tearing in—the unbelievable news which he'd been trained to handle. Its effect on most of the older people in Green Prairie, or any other city, would have been horrifying in the extreme. Some of them, after hearing the broken bits of conversation and the news from the neighboring states, wouldn't have been able to go on listening. You couldn't exactly tell what was happening from the reports, direct and relayed, that Ted tuned in on. But you could guess.

Denver had said somebody farther west had said they couldn't raise anybody in San Francisco. Or Los Angeles either.

A guy he had often talked with in Omaha, an old gaffer named Butts, who had a sender with plenty of oomph, came in laconically. "Hello, Green Prairie. . . . Hi, Ted, son! . . . Seen anything?"

"Not here, not yet. Over."

"You will—and maybe we will, looks like. Dallas got it."

"Big Eddie? Over."

The Omaha voice, venerable, quavering with age rather than alarm, came dryly across the winter-swept plains: "Big Eddie among other things."

"Big Eddie" was the term CD ham operators in the region had come to use for "atom bomb."

Mr. Butts went on. "That, we're sure of here. Otherwise, conditions normal. Yellow, of course. Evidently nothing headed this way—yet anyhow." The old man actually sounded disappointed.

Ted cut back one time more: "Is that all you have on Dallas?"

"That's all, son. Station W5CED reported. He's outside the city some twenty miles. The blast wave bent his aerial, he claimed. One big flame is all he can actually see. Where Dallas is. Or was. As the case may be."

At that point Ted wished the family was at home. It was an awful thing, he thought, to be sitting up there alone in the kind of dim attic room, with tubes glowing and word of practically the end of the world pouring in. But nobody to tell it to.

He considered running over to the Baileys' and getting Nora. She was darn good company at a time like this, and she would sure like to take the extra headset and listen with him. However, Nora would be an unauthorized person. That observation reminded him of duty. In Condition Yellow, he was supposed to get on the CD network with other locals and stand by for orders and relays.

He sighed heavily and tuned according to regulations.

The whole air around Green Prairie and River City was on fire with communication, all right. Somebody at headquarters—Al Tully, it turned out—soon was saying, "Station W Double Zero CDJ. Come in, Ted Conner. Over."

Ted's hands moved swiftly. His voice said in a business-like way, "Conner, here. W Double Zero TKC. Come in, please."

"Where the hell you been?"

"On the way. Driving myself—alone—in Dad's car!"

That any person should still be able to get a thrill from so minor a matter seemed to stun Albert Tully. "Nothing from your district at all. *Why?*" he asked.

"Dunno." At that moment, at Ted's side, an illegal phone, which he had installed himself and plugged in as he sat down, began to ring. "Here it is! Stand by . . ."

He grabbed the instrument, thanking his stars he'd violated the law, for otherwise he would probably make about a thousand trips up- and downstairs in the hours ahead. To his surprise, he heard his father's voice. "That you, son?"

"Yes, Dad. Say! *Dallas* was hit! Frisco and LA don't answer."

"Good God!" Henry Conner was shocked to brief silence. His son, listening in on a ham radio set, *knew*. All Henry knew, in the principal's office in South High, was what came from State CD. Not much, nothing as appalling as the information Ted had tersely stated. "Mother home yet?" he finally asked, and Ted heard him swallow, it was so loud.

"Nope. Not yet. Nobody here."

Henry's voice was tighter, more brusque. "Okay. It's just as we figured. Phone lines swamped downtown. Can't raise H.Q. We ought to have paid for a direct line, like I said, and the phone company's supposed to put us through. Try and do it. The whole thing's a mess."

"I got H.Q. here," Ted answered. "They want your report."

"Good kid! Tell 'em—in general—we're doing all right. We're about forty-five per cent mustered, at a guess. I'd say the doctors and surgeons are worst. Not reporting they've followed the plan and gone outside town, most of them. But we're quietly getting all movable people out of Jenkins Hospital, into the homes around, with the homeowners mad as spit, even though they volunteered for it."

"Why," Ted passionately asked a question that had been burning in his mind, "don't they let go with the *sirens?*"

"You forget!" his father said. "Condition Red is only for the direct attack. Planes actually *headed toward us.*"

"I don't forget," Ted answered. "I just suspect planes are headed for *everybody!*" He heard the slam of the front door and stood up, looking out a window. "I guess Mom just came in," he said. "I see Chuck in Uncle Jim's car."

Henry said, "Thank God! Shoot in the report, son—and I'll send you a runner soon, if I can't get a wire."

When Charles Conner approached Hink Field he brought and received an assortment of impressions:

On the streets and the open highway, he had passed, and even been passed by, thirty or forty vehicles, mostly private cars, bearing families, outward bound and going like hell's chased bats. These obviously were people who reacted to the confidential news about Condition Yellow by packing up and getting out of town. Or they were people who had been told by somebody who ought not to have told them. Perhaps they'd had short-wave receivers of their own and begun to pick up news from police channels and the like. Anyhow, they were getting away from the city.

Like his father and brother, Chuck had skirted the busiest section of the two cities, following Willowgrove clear to Walnut. Willowgrove was residential for the most part, wide, and

it had fewer traffic lights than the north-south streets closer
in. But even at that distance from the center of the Sister
Cities, a distance at which the proud skylines of both merged,
he'd seen enough to realize that Condition Yellow had not
fazed most people. Certainly the mob downtown didn't know
of it yet, or the people would have started home and Willowgrove itself would have been a bumper-to-bumper proposition. He had made home easily, changed, and gone on.

Beyond the tan fence and gates of Hink Field, a crescendo
of noise told Chuck that the base, at least, was reacting. As
he approached, accelerator on the floor, six jet planes came
in low, cut around, and climbed at full power. His pass put
him through the gates and he parked in the section reserved
for junior officers. He went into Flight Operations, not because that was where hastily assembling servicemen were
expected to report, but because he had already officially visited
the Hink Field command and his orders were special.

Nobody stopped him or questioned him, which was unusual. The WAAF secretaries and stenographers, the sergeants
and corporals, seemed just to be sitting around the big rooms,
rather stiffly. Hardly a typewriter was going. Outside, beyond the windows, a jet took off, shaking the building. Up
above the building, he knew, the radar antenna was circling,
the sock was flying in a moderate breeze, the anemometer
cups were whirling and the men behind the great blue-glass
windows were vigilant. At the door of Control Ops, he was
stopped by two soldiers with rifles in their hands and bayonets
on the rifles, which was anything but usual. He wouldn't have
got farther if Lieutenant Colonel Wilson, the general's aide,
hadn't come out to the water cooler while Chuck was arguing with the guard.

"Oh," the lieutenant colonel said, "Connel. It's you."

"Conner, sir." Chuck smiled a little.

"You're the Intelligence they sent over from Eames' outfit?" The Lily cup from which he drank trembled minutely.

"Yes, sir."

"Your colonel's notion was sure solid! Might as well come in and watch the shambles."

In the Operations room, on the left-hand wall, was a huge map of the United States, Canada and Mexico. On the right wall was a large-scale map of the Hink Field region, showing all of two states and parts of four more. Around the big map, in a cluster, between the American flag on one side and the hat rack on the other, were perhaps forty officers. Two of them were moving colored pins and colored flags on the big map. Another was advising them, according to messages he received from headphones.

The group was absolutely silent. Men smoked. One man even blew his nose. But nobody said anything for a long while. The flags moved toward Chicago, Chuck saw, and Indianapolis, Detroit and Toledo. There were scarlet flags on four cities—all of them, Chuck observed, coastal cities and big ones: San Francisco, Los Angeles, New York and Philadelphia.

Finally General Boyce spoke. Chuck couldn't see him because he was shorter than most of the other officers and stood closest to the map.

"It appears that the assault from the south is a small wave. Note it seems to have broken into three parts. Nothing coming this way. The northern waves, both of them, split east and west. It would seem, gentlemen, that we aren't on the target list."

Those words were followed by a quiet but ubiquitous murmur as the men addressed each other. That gave Charles a chance to say to the lieutenant colonel, who stood beside him, "What are the scarlet flags?"

"H-bombs."

Chuck felt sick. He didn't answer.

Now, to his astonishment, a civilian pushed out from the crowd. Chuck recognized him, though he was ash-pale, almost blue-lipped and his features were screwed up with the torture of his fears and his determination. It was River City's Mayor Clyde. "I repeat, General," he said almost in a shout, "if we are not yet threatened, we must maintain Condition Yellow! You start those sirens and you sign the death warrant of maybe a thousand people. Great God! The whole population and the county around is jammed downtown, and they'd panic!"

The general followed the mayor and the men parted to make a clear path. "I know. I *know*. And decision here depends only on emergency. Nothing has come through from the Second Army. Zinsner!" he called.

The man with the headphones heard and removed them. "Yes, sir?"

"Anything from Colorado Springs?"

Zinsner spoke, inaudibly, into a mouthpiece he held in his hand, waited—while the room waited—and shook his head. "No word, sir."

"But you have contact?"

"Certainly, sir. That is—we *still* do."

General Boyce, Major General Boyce, paced in front of a desk, on the thick carpeting. Mayor Clyde followed him for a little while, gave up, leaned against the desk and wiped his face with a big linen handkerchief. He got out a cigar and lit it. The general faced the room abruptly. "What's your opinion, Berdich?"

A man wearing eagles, a man with a thin face, very white skin, pale gray eyes and an Adam's apple that traveled up and down above his collar when he talked, said, "Can we properly call this an emergency? Our radar has a range of better than two hundred miles. So far, we have accounted for every blip——"

General Boyce lost his patience. "Good *God,* Berdich, I don't want a *résumé!* Just, 'Yes' or 'No.' "

"No," Colonel Berdich said.

The mayor looked at him in a gratified but still-frantic fashion.

"Tetley?" asked the general.

A tall, dark man, who looked more like a college professor than a soldier, stepped forward through the group. He was a major. He said, "I say Yes."

"Why?"

"From what we can gather, the little coming in, I suspect some of the attacks are by guided missiles, homing on the cities, launched from the air. Range could easily outreach our radar and the speed would be supersonic. Even two hundred miles might not give us a Red Condition time of even ten minutes."

"Ten minutes is still ten minutes," the mayor muttered.

Boyce whirled. "Ever try to empty a thirty-story building in ten minutes?" He began to pace again. "Trouble is, there's no official operational plan for *precisely* this situation!"

Another officer said, in a remarkably calm tone, "We've got the area ringed with search. No report. That gives us about *five hundred* miles."

"We'll wait," the general finally said.

As if that were a command, the men clustered around the map again, watching to see what changes were made according to reports relayed in a near-whisper by Zinsner to the men who moved the pins and flags.

The difficulty at Hink Field was the difficulty experienced in those same hours at many other military installations. Stations that should have given reports had vanished. Cities close to command areas, like Denver, had been hit and the news had not yet reached the right information centers: what had happened in Colorado's capital was unknown for seventy-six minutes at the military communications heart in Colorado Springs. The knowledge then arrived—as a rumor. Some command centers had, themselves, been stricken and posts dependent upon them waited vainly for orders. Beyond that, some Air Force bases so concentrated upon defense activity that it was impossible to find wires for a steady alert service to near-by cities.

Here and there, over the entire continent, the sky was peopled with dying young Americans and their dying enemy. Many older officers, on the ground, followed the pattern of their training and decided that it was of greater import to attack the swiftly materializing foe than to keep the civil centers posted at the cost of time, energy, communications and frantically needed personnel.

It is always so. The beleaguerment is foreseen, on paper, and acted out in drills and games of war. The curve of crises, the links of possible catastrophe, are known ahead of time. They are "possibilities." Within their limits, a military effort is made to account for every circumstance. Friendly officers play the part of the "enemy" and plan every conceivable attack. "X-Day" plans are drawn up, studied from every angle, stamped "Top Secret" and filed away. To be sure, chains-of-command are notified concerning them; communications and alternate communications are established; and whatever else seems required for every emergency is fashioned and stockpiled, or learned by troops, or kept on hand—or, if the appropriations do not meet the dire extremes of military vision, at least exists on paper.

Surprise assault has rarely found the adversary ready. At Pearl Harbor, the radar worked, the in-flying enemy was seen in ample time to change that masterpiece of ruin, but a weak military link in the chain cut off fact from command. The nation then being attacked, the United States, believed many wrong things: that their planes were far superior; that the Japs had a congenital defect of eyesight which incapacitated them as pilots. Those Americans who thereupon died like flies before the guns of Zeroes had only a moment in which to see how mistaken they and their countrymen had been. The inferiorities then—as in this later case—and the defects, too, were American.

Faced by that ultimate martial calamity, inconceivable and majestic—invasion with atomic arms—most military men reverted (as their long discipline had made sure they should) to conventional means and ends. This was war; this, therefore, was not the affair of civilians. Their duty was to defend and defense spelled attack. Their ideology, their often logical position was this: that it mattered more in the flickering instants to bring down a grievously armed enemy plane than to keep any given city, only potentially menaced, in step-by-step contact with events which occurred so fast in any case that the best-informed staffs were soon far behind.

Much, of course, that was needed now and in a certain place was stored elsewhere, or existed in insufficient quantity, or could not be got ready in time, or it existed only in prototype, or on order—or merely in blueprints, as a dream might exist.

Much was expended in error. The rockets that ringed Detroit went up, after mistaken recognition signals, and de-

stroyed seven American bombers two hours before the single
Soviet plane launched its missile onto Detroit from a position
far to the north, far beyond the range of the improved Nike,
in Canada.

Of all the blunders, the most serious was that which derived
not from military judgment (or any lack of it) but from the
philosophy of domestic politics. Civil Defense had always
been considered a matter for states to organize and administer.
The Federal Government had advised, urged, supplied research and data—and left most practical decisions to the
states. So the fact that any day, on the briefest notice, every
city might go to war had been considered as each city's own
business, or as the business of the state in which it happened
to be.

Some states had responded relatively well; others, as might
be expected, where politics was the measure, hardly at all.
Much had been done in Green Prairie for that reason; little,
in its Sister City across the river. What had not been clearly
observed in the Pentagon, or by any other branch of authority,
was this: that in any "next" war, while the armed forces went
forth to fight as one, the states and cities would be obliged to
defend themselves as variously as a hundred different medieval principalities besieged by a single adversary.

In every other fashion, these cities were bound together,
interdependent, and dependent upon the nation as well. Under atomic assault, they were obliged to react separately and
according to the diverse provisions of the separate states.
The situation, from the military point of view, was all but
hopeless. There was no way to standardize procedure. What
Maryland was ready to do, Ohio had not yet even thought of.
When, in the space of a dozen hours, the actual onslaught
took place, this disorganized, decentralized, variable whole
soon lost every tenuous relationship. Wires went, tunnels blew,

power stations became vapor in the sky, nothing worked that should have; the people at Pearl were paragons of preparedness by comparison.

The analogue—raised to some nth power—went further. For the enemy not only struck on a great shopping day, and during generally poor weather, but in a period of imminent holiday when the military itself, bone-cut by tightened budgets, was cut again by holiday leaves. In many areas, the blow fell before a commanding general got back on duty, before enough technical sergeants were at their proper posts. Pearl Harbor on Sunday was far readier than U.S.A., in that moment of hope concerning peace, that Christmas holiday.

Such thoughts passed through the mind of Charles Conner in the ensuing hour. They were characteristic of his sort of mind. For he had been one of the few who had seen beyond the pacifistic, international horizon and noted that the stepped-up reconnaissance of U.S.A. by the Soviet might be designed to cause clouds of search planes to take the air, filling it, confounding the imperfect radar screen, mixing up signals, and thereby facilitating attack. His imagination had such sweep, along with the constant ability to discount what other men were saying and what they believed.

He was, of course, like every sentient American that day, aghast and unable to weigh emotion. But unlike most, he could set emotion aside, in a single area of his mind, and use the rest for reason.

He thought, toward the middle of the afternoon, that the Sister Cities would probably escape. Many other city areas of equal size stood unscathed, unmenaced. The enemy planes had flown far; they'd been in the air a long while; they had faced every form of interception America could muster. It was considerable. And pilots of jets, after the first few quarter hours, did not bother to press the triggers of their guns and rocket-releases. Wherever they saw the Red Star on alien wings, they plunged headlong. As they died, they knew they had struck a target which no man, with but his one life, could afford to miss.

In the general's Operations office, there was no true awareness of passing time.

Outdoors, planes came in, refueled, took off. The cups on the wind gauge kept turning, the sock streamed and the radar antenna swung in its interminable circle. The snow stopped; the clouds lifted but did not dissipate. And then, in the gilded brightness of a winter day, in the rise of light that so often is the first admonition of the day's shortness and the imminent twilight, certain pins on the great map turned from their coursing far below, to the south. They turned in a direction that made the room so still Chuck heard breathing, and nothing else.

8

Lenore sat under the drier at Aubrey's Beauty Salon, on the eleventh floor of the Manhattan Department Store. She could see a line of other Christmas-primping women, chic women, for Aubrey's was the smart hairdresser of the Sister Cities, and she could see the magazine in her lap, *Harper's Bazaar* for January. She could reflect, if she wanted to, on why she had been handed the latest issue of one of the most modish magazines. In years past, they'd given her an old copy of the *Bazaar* or *Vogue* to read under the drier. But the mixture of gossip and dynasty is potent and Aubrey's was a center of both. The fact that Lenore was probably soon to be the bride of Kit Sloan gave her a high priority for everything, even magazines. Only Minerva herself, along with half a dozen other dowagers, a movie star who had married a River City tycoon, and three or four rather pushing career women, could have pre-empted the new copy of *Harper's Bazaar*.

Amongst all persons and concerning all things, however trivial, there are pecking orders—showing how little good has been done mankind so far by reason and logic, by democracy and humanism, by liberty or faith or any other ideal. In all the main things, ants and dogs, jackals and people are still much closer together than any of them imagine.

Lenore, however, did not want to look at the priority magazine. She did not want to look at the overweight (or, rarely, underweight) wives of the Sister Cities' socially elite. There they were, with Aubrey's pastel kimonos covering underthings picked up in Paris, with their hair wet and nasty, with creams on their faces, with shampoo girls and manicurists working over them like operating-room nurses, with tongues a-clatter in a persistent effort to abet their own status at the expense of other reputations, with cigarette smoke curling through their jewel-weary fingers, with Aubrey's special recordings playing an interminable litany of baritone mush and Aubrey's special perfume making the air like a brothel or perhaps a harem.

Lenore wanted to look beyond it all, out the windows. She could do it by scrunching lower than the attendant liked and by rolling her eyes up toward her forehead. She could see, then, the blue sky patches and a big, unopened snow-bag moving in overhead, against which rose the sides and tops of half a dozen of the nearest skyscrapers—a winter vignette of the Green Prairie sky line. It was the blue, diminishing bits of sky she wanted to see. For they, somewhat like her own freedom and self-respect, were being closed up and eradicated; overcast, was the word. Yet she had a sense, haunting, unhappy, hypnagogic as the drier's hum, that everything was happening because she willed it so, that by some different magic of her own mind she could break the dark spell of her days, perhaps even push back the invading snow clouds.

The drier was a head noise like, she thought, things people hear on the verge of nervous breakdown. The sound, she knew, was steady but it seemed to have changing cadences and various volumes; it was her head, her hearing, her own nerves that perceived unevenly. Low on the horizon, between buildings, the remaining blue sky looked moonstone pale; high up, it was cobalt, like a bluebird's back. This, she thought, was a true distinction and not fancied.

"Francine," she called, wondering what Lizzie, what Edna or Dot had been francophized for the sake of swank, "my nails are dry enough for the last coat. And I'm in a hurry."

Francine came obediently, sat down docilely.

The new cocktail frock had come up from the Grand Salon de Couture on the second floor. Lenore's mink coat would conceal it while she finished shopping and until, at five thirty or thereabouts, she drove under the canopy of the Ritz-Hadley for Thelma Emerson's party. Everybody would be there. Kit would be there. Nobody would be there.

She fidgeted in the chair. She had a headache. It would grow worse, she knew, in the floors below and the stores beyond, while she jousted with people-onslaught around the counters, in the aisles. Then, worse still, over at the Hadley, under the lush dim lights, where the women would look at the women to see what they'd done to themselves this time and the men would look at the women just to see. They'd dance in too-crowded places, there and elsewhere. One martini, two martinis, three martinis away from now the headache would not be a pain but merely a sense of stiff places in the brain, waiting for tomorrow morning. She'd have lost a glove and a handkerchief, borrowed Kit's after using up her Kleenexes, had her lipstick mistletoe-smeared by anybody, and got her shoes wet somewhere between car and curb: a glamour girl in a Christmas-scented night eroded by the exigencies of her good time.

She almost wanted to cry and she wouldn't have wept in Aubrey's for the million dollars she would soon doubtless have, many times over. She wouldn't have wept *anywhere*. Wasn't she, *right here*, making the bed, *herself*, that she would lie in?

The feelings of confusion, the sense of trapped helplessness, that came over her every day were girlish feelings, maidenly sensations, no doubt. She almost regretted that she did not have her mother's acceptance of the flesh, her mother's near-welcome of love's lesser uses. Then Kit, and all Kit meant—to Lenore, to Lenore's family—would never seem a Galahad, of course; but Galahad would seem instead just another man, no different from the Beast that woke up Beauty, or a clown. To Netta, males were like that: commodities; humanity-in-pants. But to Lenore, one male remained stubbornly other.

Chuck, she thought, oh, *Chuck!*

The words were warm within her, stirred within her. The buzzing drier sang them for a little while. Chuck, oh, Chuck. Her eyes, on the disappearing blueness, grew bright; her breasts lifted up and her lips came apart; she breathed faster as if the machine's rhythm had set tingling inside her some other beat, some amorous cadence of the blood.

She was startled when Francine stopped painting lacquer on her nails, framed words, called thinly, "Lucky, *lucky* you!" The girl squeezed her arm passionately and reflected in her own eyes Lenore's expression. Looking at the common prettiness of the manicurist, Lenore could not keep herself from thinking: this is Kit's kind of girl; they talk the same language. But Lenore had a decency of her own. She smiled gently. She said, exhaling, "Aren't I lucky, Francine?" If she bit her tongue afterward, the girl couldn't see that.

The drier went off suddenly, unexpectedly. For a split second, Lenore could hear the other machines and the overriding noise of woman-talk. Then the effeminate voice of "Aubrey" came from behind her chair: "A call for you, Miss Bailey. I'm very sorry. I tried, personally, to explain you couldn't answer right now. I said you'd call back. I offered to take the name and number. They were extremely rude, whoever they were. They insisted you be told it was your sector calling about some yellow goods, an emergency matter."

Lenore said, *"Wha-a-a-at?* It doesn't even make *sense! Wait!"* For it did make sense. She ducked out from beneath the drier, feeling her hair, and ran toward the phones.

"Yes? Lenore Bailey speaking."

"My God." The voice was flat, secretarial. "Have *we* been playing tag to reach *you!* This is Beatrice Jaffrey, Lenore. There's a"—her voice fell to a whisper—"Condition Yellow out. Has been, quite a while."

Lenore's answer was faltering. "Today? Good heavens, they can't *expect* us—unless it's—*serious?"*

"It's so serious," Beatrice replied, "I can't wait for your double-take. Make tracks, honey!" There was a click.

Lenore hung up. For half a minute, she merely stood beside the high shelf of the half-enclosed booth, her hand resting lightly on the mauve telephone. *She was going to miss Thelma Emerson's party.* The fact gave her such a sense of elation that all other facts and all other assumptions were crowded out of her mind. She was possessed by a kind of happiness, a surge of joy, something she had not felt for a long time.

I hate him that much, she thought with astonishment.

Certainly it's too much hatred for a bride. If I didn't know before, she thought, I know now. Dad and Mom will hate *me*.

In the ensuing seconds, other parts of her brain meshed. Her good mind and the good education which had disciplined it took charge of her thoughts. Thoughts that plunged, climbed, curved in the dizzying pattern of cars sluicing over the track-maze of a roller coaster. Cars as seen against the summer skies on Swan Island. Her belly felt that way, besides: roller coaster.

All these people, she thought, staring at the people in the perfume, the peignoirs, the soft-sexy drape of music.

They haven't been told. They aren't supposed to know. It's the latest, newest change in the orders.

It must be *genuine,* she thought.

Somewhere planes must have come over the borders, had a dog fight maybe. Maybe the air exercises started it. Maybe our bombers ran into something foreign scouting us.

Only then did she think, maybe it's *it*. *Blitz*.

Condition Yellow.

Confidential to CD personnel. Assemble with equipment. Was there a Phase Two, any more? Or not? Would the people in the store get a warning, during Yellow, if things grew more serious than however things were? Or would they have to wait for the Red, the sirens? She couldn't recall. The codes and schemes and plans had changed and changed again; her struggling mind could bring to consciousness only a succession of Federal directives, state directives, local directives. Among them, she couldn't isolate the last set. Orders in effect.

Should she *tell* anybody? Absolutely not! That essence of the directives remained unchanged. Might panic the store. For nothing.

Be hard, she thought, to make a fast trip home, now.

She walked back, half a minute after hanging up.

Aubrey was nervous. He would have said "distrait." He was passing the fingers of his left hand, delicately, back and forth over the palm of his right.

"Darling," he said, "you're pale! It *was* important, after all! A shock?"

"I'm not sure," she answered. "But I've got to go at once."

"You're not dry yet," he said. "Not combed out."

"Your left hand," Francine added anxiously. "Not finished."

Lenore began taking off the kimono. She picked up a comb. She raked and tugged; pins fell around her. Aubrey protested, tried to seize the comb. Women began to lean out to watch, their eyes alert and fascinated, the driers like big, cockeyed, silver crowns suspended over them. Francine was trying to help. But Aubrey curtly rejected, had stamped away to pout.

"I'll put my suit back on," Lenore said. "You can send my dress to the house."

Francine replied anxiously, "But I'm not sure we can get a messenger this late! And it's *Saturday*. And Monday's Christmas. You'll want it before Tuesday!"

Lenore had a thought, at once weird and charitable, shattering and kind. She ran to the dressing room, pursued by the manicurist. She picked up her handbag, fumbled, produced a five-dollar bill. "You live out toward Edgeplains, isn't that what you said?"

"Yes. But I won't get off for two hours."

Lenore pressed the bill in her hand. "I'll speak to Aubrey. He'll let you bring it out—early, perhaps. And then go on home."

Francine showed delight. "I could help do our tree!"

Lenore was head-deep in her skirt. "Sure," she said. She

thought that Francine could do what Francines did, now. Now and forever. Kit could have her if he wanted, the Kits of the world. Francine could revel in the little bought pleasures of life, the pleasures she longed for so intently that all wisdom was excluded by desire. It was the only thing you could accomplish for some people: comdemn them to their bliss and its going price, big or little.

She presented Aubrey with a twenty-dollar bill: *"Merry Christmas!"* Lenore's dark, dark hair rode her neck like a mane; her dark blue eyes were excited; her long fingers shook: "Look! Let Francine off now and let her take my dress to my house, please!"

He rolled his eyes at his customers. "I'm short a manicurist as it is."

"A special favor! I have to have it! I'm dining tomorrow with Minerva——"

"I *couldn't,* Miss Bailey. I . . . ! But . . ."

But he was adding the bill to others in his pocket.

The street wind and the bell-jingle hit Lenore. She raised the mink collar around her cheeks. The shock of the weather changed the pitch of her thoughts. Concerning the impulse which had caused her to bribe Francine's early way home, she said to herself wryly, First reaction: pure melodrama! Calm yourself, moron!

She calmed herself.

Twenty-five dollars, you idiot! she said to herself.

She said, winding through the crowd on Central Avenue, It would be a small price for a life, though. And she said, Who on earth would have believed Aubrey would accept the money!

She said, What on earth has gotten into me that makes me feel positively elated?

She said, Chuck.

At the parking garage, where the Baileys always kept their cars downtown, at least fifty women and half that many men were stamping on the frigid concrete waiting for the boys to bring their coups, convertibles, and sedans down the ramp. Lenore was appalled. It would take twenty or thirty minutes for her Ford to appear. And they'd been trying to reach her for a "long time."

How long? They hadn't said. Condition Yellow was how old? Of what significance? They hadn't said. She wondered if she should find the manager, ask him for special service. If she mentioned Civil Defense, it would be a violation of rules. And nothing else would faze him, probably, for doubtless half the people standing and stamping there had tried other ruses and bribes.

She glanced out at the street. Cabs were hard to get also. Just about impossible.

Suddenly, she worried.

Looking down the side street, looking toward Central and across it, looking at the ocean of December-muffled humanity, she was scared. For the first time, she wondered where Chuck was, her father; her mother was at home cleaning. As if in further answer, she saw, or thought she saw, in the distance, Nora Conner walking along beside a colored woman. It was only the briefest glimpse. Lenore had an urge to race after the child, take her home. The urge died: Lenore's primary concern was different. She turned back to the ticket booth, a square of pasteboard in her hand. Then she saw Mr. and Mrs. Ellinsen getting into their car. If they were on their way home, at Ash and Arkansas, it would do. She ran up to them.

Merry Christmas, Lenore, and sure, we're going home. Crowds tuckered us out!

Mr. Ellinsen was definitely not an expert driver and

Lenore began to sense, as they first tried Court and then River to make their way south in the heavy traffic, that there was something vaguely wrong in the traffic itself. Every once in a while, a private car would take a wild chance to make a small, extra gain in the procession. Every once in a while, a lone driver would clamp down on his horn and shoot past everybody, like a cop. That in turn (evidence, she knew, of Civil Defense people on the way toward their sectors) irritated all other drivers.

"People have gone absolutely crazy today," Mrs. Ellinsen observed. "I've personally seen three collisions—minor, though. If it gets much worse, it simply won't be possible to *live* in cities any more!"

Lenore didn't reply to that.

She saw another thing. An entire fire company, sirens roaring, bells jangling, ground and tore, braked and ricocheted—south, through the jam-packed streets.

"Wonder where the fire is?" Mr. Ellinsen asked. And he tried, without much success, to gain a block or two in the swathe opened by the red-painted trucks.

Lenore did not reply to that either. She thought there was probably no fire. She thought that, following regular Condition Yellow procedure, the Green Prairie fire-fighting equipment would all be heading out of town—all save a few stand-by pieces. When the emergency was over, they'd come back. Or else, of course, when the need turned cataclysmic. Doctors, she thought, would, or should, be heading out of town for the same reason. Nurses, also. Certain engineers and technicians. Various Red Cross people and their equipment.

At Arkansas and Walnut Street they let her out. She thanked them and hurried. A car or two went by, fast, on Walnut; otherwise the residential area seemed deserted. She began to run. There didn't seem to be anyone at home in the Conner house, she thought; then she saw, bright against the dulling afternoon, a light in the front attic window. She smiled. Ted Conner would be there, at his radio. Her steps slowed and she almost went in, went up, talked to Ted for a moment. She felt Ted would be able to tell her a lot about this alarm. And Ted might know where Chuck was at this point.

Reluctantly, she went on. She'd been summoned and that meant a beeline, not stops made out of curiosity, certainly not stops for inquiry about people, even people you loved.

She swung open her own front door. "Mom!"

"I'm in here!" Netta was reclining on the divan. She had a magazine, a highball, a box of candy, a fire going in the grate, a radio on, and she talked in a barrage as Lenore stripped off her coat, gloves, galoshes. "What a day! What a *hellish* day! The new maid's *impossible!* I'm not through with cleaning. You'll have to do your own room, yourself, tomorrow. Why didn't you go straight to the Ritz? That Conner brat ran away on me!"

"I thought I saw her downtown."

Mrs. Bailey sat up a little. "*Well!* On her way to see Santa, I bet! Beth said she had a cold. *I* didn't see any signs. Saddled me with the child, and the child skipped. I even went racing down to River Avenue looking for her. Somebody said that she saw me coming and popped into a manhole. *Imagine!*"

"Manhole!"

"The kids do. School kids. There are ladders. That's what they said in the fruit store. Young *hellion!* You can go blocks underground in the new sewer. Down to the cemetery—and beyond. If you're that much of a fool. Me, I wouldn't walk in one for a fortune. Where's your new dress?"

Lenore decided not to tell her mother anything about her

major decision. There wasn't time. And it no longer mattered to Lenore what her mother thought. She knew what her mother would say and try to do. That didn't matter either. She answered, "Mother, I got yanked away from Aubrey's by Civil Defense."

"What?" Mrs. Bailey didn't understand; she was so completely baffled she could not even react.

"Now, Mother, take this calmly. I got an alert. It means nothing probably. Perhaps just a special drill—to see how we respond when we don't in the least expect it. But it meant going through the routine. Coming home. Getting into my clothes. Going over to the school—all such. I'm in a *hurry*."

By then, Netta understood. She understood and was calm. "You simply haven't time for it," she said. "I didn't think you could be so flighty! If your new frock wasn't ready, you'll have to wear your indigo. It looks well on you. Your hair needs more fixing. You'll have plenty of time to get to the Ritz-Hadley—*plenty!* You can even lie down for an hour, if you're tired. You *look* a bit fagged!"

"Mother. I'm going to the school!"

"My dear, Kit would be furious."

"Call a cab for me," Lenore said. "If you can't get one here in twenty minutes, see if a neighbor would drive me over. Anybody."

"See here, Lenore. I've been patient about this Civil Defense business for long enough. I know you did it just to annoy me, anyhow. But you are *not* going to cut an important party and break a date with Kit, just because some fool rehearsal has been ordered. Get that perfectly straight."

"Get this perfectly straight," Lenore answered. "It's an alert. Official. I was summoned. As soon as I can change, I'm going. If you try to stop me, I'll—I'd even call the police!" She went.

Netta Bailey thought that over; her hands shook as she raised her highball, swallowed deeply. She knew that when Lenore was in that mood, nobody could do anything with her. She went to the phone. She called the Sloane house. Neither Minerva nor Kit was there. She told the butler that Lenore had come home with a sick headache and gone to bed quite ill, but nothing serious. The butler said he would "inform" Minerva and Kit. Netta then phoned Thelma Emerson and told her the same thing. It would never do to let Kit, or people like the Emersons, think that a mere girl-scout duty like Civil Defense had caused Lenore to break a date, to miss a social event.

As an afterthought, Netta called a cab company. She was told there would be a long wait. So she tried the Davises. Jimmie said he'd knock off shoveling the yard under the clothes line, gladly, to drive Lenore anywhere she wanted to go.

Lenore came downstairs, dressed in her bulky yellow decontamination suit, carrying her radiation counter. Netta regarded her with bitterness, but silently. She was silent because she didn't trust herself to say anything. She was afraid of a quarrel now: things had gone too far, too well. She had no way of guessing that things had also gone—from her viewpoint—to smithereens. She stonily eyed the beautiful young woman's head, strange above the cumbersome garment.

Jimmie Davis's feet pounded four times to make the steps, to cross the porch. Freckle-faced, wearing heavy gloves, a wool cap, a sweater under his jacket, high school personified, he reached to ring the bell. Lenore opened the door hastily. He said, seeing her, *"What the . . . ?"*

"Civil Defense stuff," she replied. "Take me over to the South High, Jimmie, will you? And thanks a million!"

He was gallant: "Who *wouldn't* leave off shoveling his

mother's drying yard to take the world's top beauty for a tour?"

Lenore laughed at him and turned to Netta. "Take care of yourself," she said.

Netta grunted.

It didn't have the appearance of a parting.

Conscious of the slick chick at his side, proud of his driving skill, Jimmie Davis made time. It had started to snow; it was slippery; but he made time, anyhow.

"You're *very* good," Lenore said. It was all she said the whole way. For Jimmie, it was sufficient.

He didn't notice anything special as they stopped at the curb near the school. "Big turnout!" he said. No more.

She nodded, waved her thanks.

But she had noticed.

The parking yard was filled. People were going swiftly through the school doors. Various teams and squads were assembling. Things were being done without any special haste, it appeared. But it was all so *quiet.*

As she walked along the wire fence around the play yard, she observed the quiet.

Nobody yelled neighborly greetings to new arrivals.

Nobody blew a car horn for the hell of it.

Nobody was telling a boisterous joke to a knot of male volunteers.

Everybody was Sunday-solemn. She also saw, as she swung through the gate and started for the gymnasium doors, where the radiation people had their station, that everyone was pale.

So she knew, before anybody told her anything, it was *it.*

And like them, she turned pale.

9

Minerva Sloan found that morning, and to her vast annoyance, four names on the lost leaf of her Christmas list which could not be ignored. That meant, in spite of the Saturday crowd, which would also be a last-minute crowd, she would have to go into the middle of the melee again and make four purchases. The items would be mailed, and they would probably be delivered late, but the postmark would show her correct intentions.

It was Willis, her venerable chauffeur, who bore the brunt of the hardship, of course, driving in tortuous traffic, finding a place to double-park (no police disturbed Minerva's car) and waiting in the tedious cold. Minerva decided, since she was obliged to go out, that she would shop in Green Prairie rather than River City. It was farther, but she could stop in at the bank and save herself another trip on the following Tuesday.

Her errands, to her annoyance, took double the time she had generously allowed. The clerks were tired and rude, the gifts in the shops had been mauled, and traffic moved not at all, for long periods. She put off the bank expedition until afternoon and had Willis edge through Front Street (where the big tractor trucks backed up at warehouses made the way a zigzag, but where the very adroitness of their drivers kept some motion in the long lines of vehicles). Thence, by other streets, she went to Wickley Heights Boulevard where two policemen and a gaudy doorman kept things moving along the elegant, curved façade of the Ritz-Hadley.

Even that usually serene hostelry was crowded. Minerva had intended to refresh herself in the Aztec Room, a euphemism for the bar. It was jammed. A hundred kids, minors, college students home on vacation, were dancing to an abominably loud jazz band. Dancing and illegally drinking, too.

Minerva backed out of the hot room and had her cocktails on the Palm Terrace, a wide hallway which looked out, through twenty-foot-high glass windows, on the landscaped hotel lawns, the eight-lane parkway, the river—and the slums on the opposite shore. Georges, the headwaiter in the Empire Room, brought a menu to the Terrace. Minerva ordered. She was notified when the meal was ready and dined sedately at an east-facing window, a window hung with wine-colored draperies that gave a view of the putting grounds, the winter-empty swimming pool and the Broadmere beyond.

She was considerably mollified by the time she returned, wrapped in her silver-blue mink cloak, to the outside canopy. The tall, mannerly doorman summoned her car. She was still amiably aglow, still pleasantly aburp, when she entered the bank, let in by Bill Maine who rattled nervous bolts when he saw her car.

The moment she entered, she knew things were wrong, very wrong. Too many clerks were rushing about; and they were rushing too hurriedly; besides, they were carrying too many things. She caught sight of Beau Bailey, looking white, trotting in the nether distance. She bawled, "Beau!"

He turned and hurried up. She stared at him as he drew near. The man, she thought, is *mortally frightened*.

"What the devil is the to-do about?"

Beau trotted even faster to close the gap. "Minerva! Get home immediately! Condition Yellow—been in effect for hours! Don't you *know*?"

"Know *what*? What on *earth* are you talking about?"

He clapped a fat hand to his forehead. "It's all over! The rumors, anyway! Air-raid alert! The radio and TV aren't saying, but people keep *calling*. The most *terrific* rumors. Enemy planes everywhere! Many cities hit! Condition Yellow here, though, *still* . . . ! Thank God."

"Beau, *listen*. I don't know what you mean."

"Russian bombers," his voice answered, with a thin, squealing overtone, "are said to be attacking our cities. The CD people have given the bank its special alert! *Hours* ago!"

"Are you *mad?"* Minerva peered at the man. "I just had lunch at the Ritz. There was absolutely no *sign* of such a thing!"

"I *know*. That's what I'm trying to *tell* you! The radio is going on, and the TV, as per usual. Only, no announcer *sounds* right or *looks* quite right, any more. Evidently *they've* heard more than they're permitted to tell! But Condition Yellow is *official*."

"What in the world *is* this yellow condition?"

"The first air-raid alert. That's why"—he looked over his shoulder, along the polished marble floor, toward the closed tellers' windows—"that's why everybody's rushing around! Condition Yellow means we have to get all important papers —bonds, stock, cash, records—down in the deep vault."

"See here, Beau," Minerva said solidly, "I don't know what's panicked you. But I do know nothing of the sort is happening."

"You *do?"* He seemed on the verge of inexpressible relief.

"I know it *morally*. I would have been notified! It may be that those incalculable damned fools have started some sort of a crazy air-alert *practice* again. They did it before, you'll remember. It could even be a real foul-up—an alert the military started, because they made some *error*. *That* has happened. But——"

Beau's hope was perishing before her eyes. "If you'd step into Mr. Pavley's office, where there's a TV set . . ."

"I will," Minerva said. "I *will*. Because, believe me, this hysteria has got to stop!"

Her first, creepy inkling came when she saw the live show in progress at the local station. The actors were saying their rather stupid lines, but merely saying them. Their gestures were somewhat alien to their words. And their eyes kept straying from the business in hand, as if they were watching something or somebody in the studio, rather than playing to each other. It was not, as Beau had said, normal.

Minerva picked up a phone. She dialed a number. It was busy, so she tried another. She gave that up because she got the busy signal with the first digit: the automatic switching station was busy as a whole. *"Something's* happening," she admitted.

She went out on the floor of the bank. Her eyes roved over the place slowly, from the vaulted windows to the huge light fixtures that hung down on chains from the remote ceiling; she looked at the balcony that ran around three sides and at the figures moving there hurriedly. She gazed at the spread of gleaming marble, big as a skating rink, usually peopled by hurrying depositors, people making withdrawals, people doing business—with her. From nowhere, unwonted, a line came into her mind: *This, too, shall pass away.*

It annoyed her greatly. But it alarmed her slightly, too.

Another thought entered her busy brain. Suppose, right now, the sirens let go? Whether in earnest or in some crazed drill, they would catch her here. Right here. In the middle of town, in the bank. At best, she'd be delayed for hours, getting home. At worst! But the worst was preposterous.

She turned to Beau, who had accompanied her, agitated, wringing his hands frequently. "I don't know what this is all about, but I think I'll go and find out. I'll phone you."

She left the bank, quite quickly.

After she had departed, Beau went back to his office. He put on his muffler, his rubbers, his coat and his hat. He went out on the mezzanine and down the stairs. Nobody saw him, nobody who had importance enough to question his going. He pushed through the crowds to the Kyle Parking Garage and waited an endless forty minutes for his car to come down the ramp. He drove east, to the Wickley Heights section and so, circuitously, toward his home.

Traffic was bad and constantly getting worse and it was nervous traffic. He saw fenders banged twice, but the drivers didn't even get out to argue. They just went on.

He thought three things, mostly:

He wasn't required in the bank on *any* Saturday.

Under the Sloan skyscraper were the best air-raid shelters in the center of town, the vaults. If anything did happen, the employees he had left there would be the best off of anyone in the area.

A man's place, in a crisis, was at home.

His car radio played dance and Christmas music. The regular programs were no longer on the air. Just records, as if somebody in authority had ordered the change.

10

Things had been happening to Nora, inexplicable things. In the middle of the fun at Toyland, when she'd been waiting in line with a million other kids to try the slide that ran for two whole stories beside the escalators, some colored girl in a yellow uniform and a thin coat had come up to Alice Groves. They had talked a minute. Alice had then yanked Nora out of line and said, "That was one of my probationers. They heard me say I'd be here in Toyland. She came for me. I've got to go back."

"Why?"

"There's been an emergency."

"Can't I just take my slide? It'll be my turn, soon."

Alice said, "No."

So they were outside again, on the street in the mobs and hurrying. The nurses with them followed, as reluctantly as Nora. "You'll have to tag along with us," Alice had said, "and we'll telephone your people from the Infirmary. I haven't time to wait to get you on a bus." And she added, "I should never have come over to Green Prairie on a day like this!"

"Why?"

"Because now there's an emergency, and heaven alone knows how long it'll take us to get the Ferndale bus. If I could find a taxi . . ."

They were still looking for an empty taxi when they passed the Sloan Bank on the way to the bus terminal. Minerva Sloan was just coming out and Alice spoke to her.

At first, Minerva barely bowed her recognition and swept on toward her car, but Alice made her stop. Nora didn't hear what Alice said because there was one of those tie-ups on Central Avenue just then, which set all the car horns blowing. But Mrs. Sloan, whom Nora recognized, nodded, though she looked mad. Nora, the three nurses and Alice Groves all got into the limousine.

Two nurses sat outdoors with the chauffeur. The car went to Central Avenue Bridge and over it and turned east and finally reached the Mildred Tatum Infirmary.

"I'll take the child to my home," Minerva said.

Nora thanked the colored girls deeply and sank back on the cushions. "This is very kind of you, Mrs. Sloan," she said in a pious tone.

She was surprised to see that Mrs. Sloan didn't even hear her, hardly knew she was there at all. Mrs. Sloan's mind, Nora thought, was probably failing.

11

Coley Borden was walking in the Christmas crowd, too. He looked ten years older than he'd looked on the night when he had written the full-page editorial that had ended his newspaper career and was still reverberating in the Sister Cities. But there was the same sardonic humor about him, and a hint somewhere of his subtle human understanding, his love of his fellows. Persons in the throng who bumped him, if they troubled to look at him, also troubled to say, "*Sorry.*" Not because of his age but because he looked like such a nice little guy.

He was on his way to get the only Christmas present he intended to give: something for Mrs. Slant, his housekeeper. What she needed, he reflected, thinking warmly of the good care she gave him, was Covermark for her wine-colored birthmark and a little plastic surgery for her wens. What he was going to get was a wrist watch. She'd said, months before, sighing as she picked up a dust mop and went to work on Coley's study, "I do wish I had one of those newfangled wrist watches. Be so downright handy."

He had remembered.

The best jewelry store was Wesson's and he was going to get the watch at the best store. No diamonds—but a good watch.

It had been a long trolley ride from Edgeplains and it was a long walk across town from the trolley line. On the way, he passed the Court Avenue entrance of the Transcript Tower and he stepped inside it, briefly, full of such recollections that he knew he should hurry on, before one of the boys came by and caught him red-eyed. It was worse than being caught red-handed, Coley thought.

He felt an arm on his shoulder just then and he heard a familiar voice:

"Hello, boss. Somebody tell you?"

Coley smiled and raised his head and there was Payton, the city editor, grinning, but looking odd, too. "Tell me *what?*"

"Thought that was why you'd come down here." Payton glanced apprehensively at the streaming people and lowered his voice: "The whole country's under air blitz, Coley. They're holding it back here, to prevent panic, in the belief this area is not on the target list."

"What *is* this?" Coley asked softly, "April Fool?"

"It's *it,*" Payton answered. *"You* should know!"

Coley stepped back till he felt the firm stones of the skyscraper against his shoulders. "God help us!" he whispered. "God help us all." Then he snapped, "What's the *Transcript* doing about it?"

"Standing by—for the story."

"That maybe it'll never print! Where *you* going?"

"Out to CD headquarters. Vilmer just ordered me there."

"Well, get on, son. Don't waste time with a broken-down old prophet!"

Payton grinned, patted his former boss on the arm, and hurried into the crowds.

Coley stood awhile, without moving. Perhaps he was thinking. Perhaps he was merely summoning the strength to get going again.

He entered the building, finally. He took an elevator to the top. When he stepped out, the smell was familiar, the sounds were remembered and fond; the look of the place was home itself.

12

Where Chuck Conner stood, the news came abruptly, repeated by Zinsner, who had first signaled General Boyce:

"Three planes—four-engined turbo-prop bombers—now diverted from main wing—Green-Prairie–River-City destination probable. Approach in Sector two-oh-nine. Repeat: two-zero-nine. Intercept at distance one hundred fifty miles minimum or combat probably ineffective. Bomb carrier probably equipped to launch medium-range missile. That is all."

General Boyce began giving orders which were swiftly relayed to all fighters aloft. Then he looked at the mayor of River City, but not with bitterness. "Condition Red," the general said quietly, "and God pity them!"

The siren stiffened Henry Conner at his desk. He had put in a telephone call and now somebody—he could not remember who—was saying over and over in a faint voice, "Hello? Hello? What do you want? Hello?"

The great wail of fright went over the city. It rose to a scream. Air raid wardens in Henry's sector tightened their belts, pulled at their helmets, looked up at the still-bright sky and walked on. "Take cover!" they yelled at all other pedestrians. Men in the rescue squads in the high school playgrounds began rechecking equipment. The engines of bulldozers and cranes roared into trial life and were stilled. In the gymnasium, below Henry, the Radiation Safety volunteers anxiously examined their monitoring gauges. At the hospital on Crystal Lake, the last patients who could be moved safely were taken out. The returning ambulances poised themselves in the parking yard. Superintendents and head nurses began unlocking closets stacked to the ceiling with drugs, medicines, bandages.

At the Broad Street Police Station, all but three men had already reported and half had already been assigned by Lacey to street duties. In the near-by firehouse, the men listened incredulously. They knew they were as ready as they could be under existing circumstances—and not ready at all.

Henry knew that. He went on with his work.

In the attic, on Walnut Street, the iron shriek hurt Ted's listening eardrums. "There's she *goes!*" he murmured. "Oh, *boy!*"

His mother came upstairs, again, gray-faced. "I haven't found a trace of Nora," she said, waiting for a lull in the sustained bellow. "Nothing. Netta said she just *went.*"

"She'll be okay," Ted answered, feeling frightened. "Trust old Nora!"

Mrs. Conner sat down on the bed, under the college pennants. Her eyes had tears in them. She held her hands together and didn't move all during the next crescendo of the siren. "It's happening, isn't it?" she said, then. "It really is!"

Ted got up, shucked off his phones, gripped his mother's shoulders and said something, when the siren allowed it, which changed Beth. It was, under the circumstances, the right thing—and a remarkable thing for a sixteen-year-old boy to say. "Just about every other mother in America has a Nora, someplace, right now," he told her.

The woman stood up then, looked intently at her son, nodded slowly. Her answer was blotted out by the siren; but Ted knew approximately what it was: "I'm supposed to go over to the church."

He knew what she meant, because she smiled at him in a loving way and left the room.

He went back to his seat. His damned hands were getting slippery. The old sweat.

The limousine was moving through Pearson Square when the crescendo-diminuendo sound reached its chauffeur. He speeded up, ignoring Minerva's rap on the glass partition. He swung the big car into the driveway. He leaped out nimbly for his age. "We better get in the cellar," he said.

"*Nonsense!*"

"I've kind of fixed it up, ma'am. With the help of Jeff and some other servants and the gardener. It's right comfortable."

Minerva listened to the faint and far-off rise and fall of River City's inadequate warning devices. The sound of a police car, passing in the distance, its own siren going, was much plainer.

Willis was waiting, holding the door, and yet looking away and upward toward the winter lace of treetops and the glimmer of high buildings in the distance.

"If any 'preparations' were made in my cellar," Minerva said, "I should have been told!"

"We thought you might object, ma'am."

"I *would* have! Insane . . . !"

"It was owing to the gardener's brother, mostly. He went through the blitz in the last war. Near London." Willis coughed vaguely. "You see, ma'am, this house is pretty close in toward town, for so fine a place. The big buildings are only a little more than a mile away."

Minerva, scornful but shaken, said, "Very well. Come on, Norma."

"I'm *Nora*. Do you think there'll be an A-bomb?"

"I think," her august guardian replied, "there will be the biggest scandal in the history of this Government! But Willis. thinks otherwise, so we'll go to my cellar."

Beau Bailey had just reached his door, too, when the sirens went. He rushed inside. "Turn off the gas!" he yelled.

Netta, who had run upstairs, shouted back, "The last pamphlet told us to leave it on! Lenore made me read it."

"Where in hell is she?"

"At the high school, naturally."

"At the . . . ? Oh. You mean, she really went—with all that junk?"

"She really did. A long time ago. Come up here, Beau, and help me pack!"

"*Pack?* Ye Gods, woman, there's no time to pack. That's the Red alert! We're going down by the furnace!"

"And leave all my new clothes up here? I should *say not!*"

Beau stood at the foot of the staircase, vacillating. "Where's that cleaning woman?"

"I sent her home an hour ago."

The siren rose and fell, rose and fell. Slowly.

On the radio the music stopped, and Jim Williams frowned. He did not know about *Conelrad,* the radio way of trying to baffle enemy bombers. But he turned dials and tuned in on the emergency wavelength:

"Repeat. This is a CONELRAD Radio Alert. Enemy bombers have attacked the United States. A condition of confidential alert has existed for some hours. *This is not a practice. Not a drill. This is real.* Enemy planes, possibly bearing atomic weapons, are said to be approaching Green Prairie and River City. *Take cover immediately. Everybody. Take cover instantly! Condition Red is in effect!* Sirens are now blowing.

Persons in cars draw to curb and wind up windows and get
on the floor below the window glass. All persons near windows
get below the level of the glass. Take refuge in cellars and base-
ments, if possible. *Instantly*. Repeat——"

Jim switched off the radio. "Hey, Ruth," he called, "you
hear that?"

She came from the kitchen. "Yes, I did. I don't believe it."

"Neither do I," Jim said. "Must be a walloping hoax." He
went to the window in contravention of the radioed orders.
He looked out. "Some cars are stopping, though. Most aren't.
Maybe they haven't got their radios on. Or radios in 'em at
all." He snickered. "Just like that Martian gag!"

Ruth's hands were wet with dishwater. "What a day!"
she said, "What a *crazy* day!"

Jim finished pouring the beer, and drank it rapidly. "All
hell would have broken loose long since if there'd *really* been
an attack, anywhere."

"Not necessarily," his wife argued. "They're not supposed
to give you that Condition Red warning unless planes are
actually heading toward your town."

He lighted a cigarette. "You think maybe we ought to go
out and rally the kids and take 'em down cellar?"

"Let's see what the radio says now." She turned it on.

The siren burst into his brain as Coley stood in the outer
offices on the editorial floor.

The effect was amazing. Everybody—secretaries and rewrite men, copy boys and stenographers, editors and sub-
editors—rose together and rushed at the place where Coley
stood. He flattened himself against the wall. As they streamed
past, he could tell from disjointed phrases, and even better
from the fear on their faces, that they'd been aware for some

time of things unknown by the people on the street, the shoppers, the store clerks. *Trust newspaper folks.*

Some pushed buttons frantically, for elevators. Most started the long, spiral trek down the twenty-seven floors of staircase.

An elevator car came up, and was instantly packed. "No more," the operator yelled, and the siren drowned him, but the door, closing automatically, divided the people between those inside and those left standing.

It was a time, evidently, when being on the top floor was a benefit. Because every car came up there first, and when it left it was full, so full it would not be able to stop for any more passengers on the long way down.

There were some eighty people on the top tower floor. Coley knew. It took about three minutes for them all to go. He just stood there, bewildered by the confusion, unrecognized by persons who were united in one idea: getting to the ground, or under it.

Nobody, he observed glassily, was trampled. Nobody was even hurt much. The newspaper people were, perhaps, better used to crisis than others. But nobody helped anybody either. They just shoved into the elevator cars or stampeded down the stairs, letting the slow ones be last. Their feet sounded loud on the steel and cement steps, whenever the siren went low—mingled with the tramp of other feet getting into the same shaft of endless steps, from floors below.

Coley could imagine what it would be like, on those stairs, farther down, where the numbers of fleeing people became too great for the width of the stairs, for the interminable, rectilinear turns.

By and by, he went through the city room to his old office. There were papers on his successor's desk. There was

copy and proof. There were cigarette stubs, thick in the big
ashtray. There was a phone left off its cradle. Coley put it
back.

The very walls, when the siren rose to its top pitch, seemed
to vibrate. He looked out over his long-time command, the
city room. Blue streams of cigarette smoke rose above
places at the copy desk where, brief moments before, men
had sat. The chairs would still be warm. The smoke flattened
under the hanging, hooded lights and became stratified. The
place seemed vaguely alive, yet it was empty; probably some
of its recent inhabitants were already dead, or dying, down
there below in the terrible stair well.

Coley went back into the managing editor's sanctum. He
walked to its familiar windows. He opened one and leaned
out and looked up. The clouds were high and thin. It was going to be a clear night—clear, and very cold. Here and there
toward the west, blue sky showed through in slits and streaks,
blue tinged with pearly colors. He could only see one airplane
—a jet, from the speed—and it was going away, north and
west, across River City.

A scarf of light fell down every skyscraper. The day was
still bright, but waning; indoors, the twilight effect would be
noticeable everywhere. Coley wondered, as he stared at the
infinitely familiar vista, what was happening elsewhere. He
regretted, momentarily, that he would probably never know.
Then, with the siren penetrating his very skull, he looked
down.

"Great God," he whispered softly.

The cars in Court Avenue and on Madison were packed
solid and standing still. The sidewalks were black with people.
People who hadn't obeyed the shelter signs. People who
wouldn't stay in the jam-packed stores. Coley supposed
others, other tens of thousands, were following the advice of

frantic section managers and floorwalkers disporting sudden air-raid-warden brassards—huddling in fear where the arrows indicated shelter.

But the ones on the street were desperate. The streets themselves were already packed with cars and trucks. The sidewalks wouldn't hold the humanity that gushed from the big buildings. The people, driven by the siren, gripped now by stark terror, rendered of sanity, were trying to make progress *over* the vehicles. They swarmed up like ants— slid off—climbed again—some going toward the river, some toward the south, some east, some west—all merely going, for motion's sake. Thinking, *escape!*

It was like looking down at ants in an anthill calamity. He could see what was happening, both in the mass and to individuals. He saw a woman in purple clothes fall flat and he saw a man use her body, an instant later, as a steppingstone to cross the radiator of a truck.

Then, suddenly, the siren was still. It dropped its brazen voice, rattled death in its own throat and fell silent. But silence did not follow.

From the streets below came the most bloodcurdling sound Coley had ever heard or dreamed of, the sound of thousands upon thousands of people—men and women and children— in absolute panic, in total fear, in headless flight, being trampled, being squeezed to death, having ribs caved in and legs broken, screaming, trying to escape. The combined tumult of that agony came up the building sides, up the concrete cavern walls, to Coley's ears, as one sound.

He could not reckon with it in his mind.

It was so awful he wanted to stop up his ears.

It was such a shriek, wild and incessant, as made him want to end it by some act of mass assassination—or to plunge into it, down the long stories, so as to perish with it, simply to avoid hearing it more. He jerked his eyes away from that in-human scene.

And thus he was one of the few, one of the very few, to see it coming. He would not even have seen it, so tremendous was its speed, had it not approached almost straight toward him, though at a higher level.

There it is, he thought strangely.

It was quite long, dark, but with a flare of fire at the tail end that shone palely against the winter sky. It had a place to go to, he supposed, and it must be near its place. The nose end was thin and very sharp.

Then, where it had been, almost overhead by that time, a Light appeared.

It was a Light of such intensity that Coley could see nothing except its lightness and its expanding dimensions. It swelled over the sky above and burst down toward him. He felt, at the same time, a strange physical sensation—just a brief start of a sensation—as if gravity had vanished and he, too, were a rushing thing, and a prickling through his body, and a heat.

And he was no more.

In a part of a second, he was a gas, incandescent, hotter than the interior of any furnace. In that same part of a second the proud skyline of River City and Green Prairie smoked briefly, steamed a little, and no shadows were thrown any-where in the glare. The façades—stone, concrete, brick—glazed, crinkled, and began to slip as they melted. But the heat penetrated, too. The steel frames commenced to sag and buckle; metal, turned molten, ceased to sustain the floors upon many floors. Peaks of skyscrapers, domes, steeples, square roofs, tilted sideways and would have toppled or crashed down, but gravity was not fast enough, not strong enough; it was only for that part of a second.

The great region, built so slowly, at such cost, by men, for a second liquefied and stood suspended above the ground: it could fall only sixteen feet in that time. Then, in the ensuing portion of a second, the liquid state was terminated. The white in the sky bellied down, growing big and globular, a thousand feet across and more. The liquids gasified: stone and cement, steel and plaster, brick and bronze and aluminum. In the street—if anyone could have seen at all, as no man could in the blind solar whiteness—there were no howling people at all. None.

On the sidewalks, for a part of a second, on sidewalks boiling like forgotten tea, were dark stains that had been people, tens of thousands of people. The Light went over the whole great area, like a thing switched on, and people miles away, hundreds of people looking at it, lost their sight. The air, of a sudden, for a long way became hotter than boiling water, hotter than melted lead, hotter than steel coming white from electric furnaces.

Clothing caught fire, the beggar's rags, the dowager's sables, the baby's diapers, the minister's robe. Paper in the gutter burst into flame. Trees. Clapboards. Outdoor advertising signs. Pastry behind bakery windows. In that second, it burned.

Busses caught fire. Paint caught fire on the sides of trolley cars. Snow vanished and grass burned. Last year's leaves caught, the garbage in open pails, shrubbery, tar-paper roofs, the asphalt in streets and wooden blocks, gasoline being poured from hoses, the paint in hardware stores, and the wires above ten thousand roofs—the TV antennae wires—glowed cherry red, then white, then fell apart while slate beneath melted.

Every wooden house for two miles began smoking. And

tombstones in Restland glowed dully, as if to announce the awakening of those they memorialized. In that second part of a second.

The plutonium fist followed:

It hammered across Front Street, Madison, Adams, Jefferson and Washington, along Central Avenue and rushed forward. The blast extinguished a billion sudden flames and started a million in the debris it stacked in its wake.

Under the intense globe of light, meantime, for a mile in every direction the city disappeared. In the mile beyond, every building was bashed and buffeted. Homes fell by thousands on their inhabitants. Great institutions collapsed.

The fist swung on, weaker now, taking the lighter structures and all the glass, the windows everywhere, hurling them indoors, speed-slung fragments, ten million stabbing daggers, slashing scimitars, slicing guillotines.

Invisible, from the dangling body of light, the rays fell.

Men did not feel them.

But atoms responded, sucking up the particles of energy, storing them greedily to give them forth later, in a blind vengeance of the inanimate upon the yet-alive.

Men felt the fist, the heat, but not the unseeable death that rode in swift consort with the explosion.

River City, from the Cathedral on St. Paul Street to the water, from Swan Island to Willowgrove Road, a mile-sized arc, with all the great skyscrapers it contained, was nothing. A flat place, incandescent.

Green Prairie, from Washington to the river, from Slossen's Run to the tip of Simmons Park, was gone. Forever gone. A vapor in the heavens. Plains restored, strewn with indecipherable rubble, with deadly fractions of nothing.

Beyond that, for a mile, each acre of land underwent such

convulsions, such surges of heat and twisting avalanches of blast, as to leave little man might use.

The belly of the fireball flattened. An uprising dust column, assembled by the vacuum left behind the outracing blast, hoisted the diminishing white horror toward the heavens. It went out, leaving a glow of lavender and orange, ascending, spreading. Two great metropolises lay stricken below, as the mushroom formed and soared.

The heart of the cities was gone. A third of their people were dead or dying or grievously hurt. A million little fires were flickering, anucleating, to form a great holocaust. And this had required the time in which a pensive man might draw a breath, hold it reflectively and exhale.

CENTRAL AREA OF
RIVER CITY
showing certain streets
and landmarks

PRIVATE ESTATES

BALL PARK

Path of Guided Missile

K. & S. R. R.

FERNDALE

FIRES ONLY LOCAL

(ROUTE No. 401 TO KANSAS CITY)

WILLIAMS

JAMES ST.

Mildred Tatum Infirmary

St. AGNES HOSPITAL

ST. PAUL ST.

St. ANNE ST.

MARY ST.

MECHANIC ST.

WILLOWGROVE ROAD

WATER ST.

RAILROAD YARDS

NEGRO DISTRICT

GROUND ZERO

SLUM

RIVER DISTRICT

WAREHOUSE

RAILROAD

Reservoir

"THE BLOCK"

NEW CATHEDRAL (ROMAN CATHOLIC)

MARKET ST.

St. STEPHEN'S EPISCOPAL CHURCH

TWO THOUSAND YARDS FROM GROUND ZERO

DEPOT

RIVER CITY A.C.

BEACH

PRAIRIE

SWAN ISLAND

AMUSEMENT PARK

DRIVE

ELK

OUTER LIMIT FIRES ONLY LOCAL

DETONATION POINT

TWO HUNDRED YARDS FROM

APPROXIMATE

FOUR THOUSAND YARDS

SEVERE DAMAGE

GLEN GLEN COUNTRY CLUB

GOLF COURSE

SUPERMARKET

ALLEY

PEARSON SQUARE PARK

SLOAN ESTATE

HIGHLAND DRIVE

GREEN

RAILROAD

RUINED MILL

FENWICK ST.

HOBART METAL PRODUCTS CORP.

To AIRPORT (GORDON FIELD)

It

1

Even the siren's tearing willawa—the announcement, hooted across the city, that Condition Yellow had become Condition Red—did not entirely convince Henry Conner's inner self of reality. The long years of work were here to meet their meaning. Yet he thought of them as a dream. The committees and conversations, the drills and exercises, even the arguments seemed like neighborly games, pleasant habits. They had gone on and on, in crackling autumns and the sweat of remote Julies. He could not think of their significance, or that they might be of benefit.

It was the Light that changed him.

"Duck, everybody!" he bellowed, forgetting that, with the first siren notes, his trained staff had started automatically towards the school corridors to lie down on the cold floor, feeling, all of them at the same time, a new trepidation and the old, familiar self-consciousness, the incongruity.

"I'll be with you in a minute," he had called, almost

apologetically, as they began to file through the doors. "Just want to finish this phone call. . . . Checking with the Parkway people about the road patrol."

He wasn't supposed to delay after that alarm. Not even he. But he waited. The telephone soon told him the men were out on duty, the cars marked, all the necessary things done, and nearly three quarters of their assigned numbers on hand.

"Good," he said.

His fingers drummed the table, his friendly eyes, narrowed with thought, looked unnoticing from his borrowed office on the top floor of the school.

Then his unseeing eyes were seeing, seeing too well, too much. The Light gushed over the trees. The view turned white; only degrees of whiteness existed anywhere outdoors. His retina beheld a scene like a positive negative lifted up to the naked sun, a scene of trees and roofs and the front of the tall hospital, Crystal Lake and more trees, more snow-clad grounds beyond, white, brilliant, one step from transparency.

"Duck, everybody!" he had bellowed at the empty room.

He shoved back his chair, fell on his face, crawled beneath the desk. The fist struck the building. It lurched. Steel-hard air ripped part of the roof away, went around walls, closed beyond and, driving and sucking, took the windows on one side across the schoolrooms to shatter and cascade along the walls, flung the rest out in the day, horizontally in the velocities, the temperatures, the glare.

Henry got up, looked at a crack through which the sky showed, watched plaster dribble, heard bricks cataract into the yard, stamped on a firebrand that dropped in the room, stared at the unglassed windows, noted by the scene beyond how the last flare of the fireball was vanishing. Still it imbued with livid light a cityscape that seemed disorderly now and heaving, that had begun to show sudden smokes.

He was all right. And people, scared, moving weakly, were coming back from a corridor where every electric bulb had gone out.

"There's a fire downstairs," someone said.

"Two men," someone else said, "are lying in the hall. Under bricks."

"It was worse on the bomb side," somebody murmured. These voices came dimly, through the ringing of his ears. They were looking at him and filing back, more all the time.

"Okay," he heard his voice begin, "Trent and Dawson, see about the fire. The house crew'll probably be on it soon, but check. The house medical's in the gym. Send for them—start picking the bricks off the hurt men. Leete, inspect the other side and report back. Have the runners' information collated downstairs from now on; just bring me the main points."

Someone else said, "Maybe this building is no longer safe!"

Henry felt his lips turn into a grin, and the feeling buttressed him just when he needed support. "So what?" he replied. "It's still here! That's at least something."

People began to move, to do things—slowly, Henry thought. . . .

Ted Conner went under his table. The Light came. The house bucked and screamed as if some cosmic claw hammer were trying to open it. A thud seemed to compress his body on all sides at once. His radio equipment, the precious store of instruments earned by hundreds of mowed lawns, was flung on the floor and smashed. Hundreds of hours of work done on the set by his father, too: smithereens.

He picked himself up. His leg was bruised and bleeding. He drew out a jagged piece of Bakelite.

He went downstairs. The house was battered, but it was a house and their house still. His mother's china cupboard lay on its face; broken cut glass glistened on the carpet. The kitchen was a shambles of crocks and pots and pans.

He went out in the back yard, stupefied. The clapboards on that side of the house were scorched, but nothing was burning. The blast, he thought, had put out the fire. The building looked tilted a little and askew on its foundations.

Queenie came up to him, mewing.

Beau Bailey bolted from his front door and ran, yelling something Ted didn't catch. . . .

Netta had insisted on trying to get her clothes down to the cellar. She argued; Beau, increasingly panicked by the siren, had taken a reluctant armful down and stayed—in the warm company of the furnace.

For him, the Light was a stabbing bar that shot through the dirty coal windows and turned the place to day.

For Netta, still upstairs, it was incomprehensible, an irritant. Her reaction was to run to the window and gaze obliquely north toward the perplexing source. She could not see it, quite. But she did realize it was a phenomenon of some new, fantastic sort and, dimly, she began to feel horror.

The blast brought the window in on her. Her face, her breast, her abdomen were sliced to red meat; she was doll-flung to the opposite wall, mercifully knocked unconscious.

Beau, calling, coming up a step at a time, afterward, found her. He assumed she was dead and watched the pulsing blood for no more than a moment. Then he tiptoed down the suddenly treacherous stairs and entered his living room. "Need a drink," he said quietly to himself.

He found a bottle finally that wasn't broken. He drank from it and with it in his hand, without a coat, he went out-

doors. He had a vague idea that somebody should do something about Netta.

As he left his house, not aware he was running, he kept calling, "Where's a doctor? Where's a doctor?"

Those were the words Ted Conner heard and did not understand—before he went back indoors, checked the gas and
the lighting circuits (there was no power) and got his coat and
hat in preparation for making his scarey way over to the
school to report.

It was what they had always planned he should do if his
radio set was knocked out, or the power failed.

Mrs. Conner was on her way to the Presbyterian Church, a
fairly long walk. She was wearing her old winter coat—glad
she hadn't given it away—and carrying a heavy suitcase.
The suitcase was her own idea and she hadn't told Henry
about it. In it were "odds and ends," assembled by Beth as
she had listened over the years to Civil Defense talk about
what might happen. She had slipped onto her arm the bras-
sard of her volunteer corps: "Emergency Nurse," it said, in
red, white and blue felt letters.

The sirens were warbling like wounded demons and the
only other people on foot were air-raid wardens, here and
there, who hurried toward her to tell her to take cover, then
saw the arm band and grinned and called, usually, "Hello,
Mrs. Conner!" or, "Watch it!"

She answered mildly. She was thinking about Nora. And
she was obliged, besides, to cross carefully at the intersections. There weren't many cars about in this part of town;
but the ones moving were hitting sixty or seventy and taking
corners on two wheels, some headed away from town but most
of them converging on South High where Henry would be.

The Light caught her on Ash Street, near Arkansas Avenue. Henry had told her to get down in the gutter with the curb between herself and the hot whiteness, but she was afraid of the cars. There were, however, small terraces in the Wister's front lawn, where Maud had crocuses because of the southern slope. Beth dropped on her hands and knees, then flattened herself. The blast and the Wister windows and some of the tiles from the roof went over her and she was not hurt.

She got up and trudged on, carrying the suitcase still. When she reached Lake View Road she saw that the windows of the Jenkins Memorial Hospital had been blown away; and the steeple of the Crystal Lake Presbyterian Church, her destination, a hospital itself in the event of emergency, had been broken off at the middle.

In Ferndale, Jim Williams's family assembled while the sirens wailed unheard, and only the ultracalm radio voice gave a warning. Ruth, whoo-whooing, brought the older ones in. Jim hastily put some Coke in a pail—and some beers—and pulled out the screw driver which served as a bolt for the cellar door. The house was heated by oil stoves, so he'd had no occasion to go down to the cellar for some days.

When the door creaked open, he knew by the smell, however.

He switched on the light. Sure enough. Water had seeped in during the thaw, a week back. There was a dark pool of it on the floor.

"Wait up, you!" he called, and went down the cobwebby steps. He found the handle of an old shovel and probed gingerly.

"Water down here," he reported disgustedly. "About a foot deep! We better stay upstairs after all."

Relieved, the entire family went back to the parlor. They sat around uncertainly, the kids, for once, quiet. Ruth, alone, stood. When the Light came, she snatched the baby from its pen, where she'd just put her down. Irma began to sob irritatedly. Ruth patted her, feeling comforted because the little thing was in a mother's arms, where all infants should be in moments of blinding, fearsome Light.

Jim said, or began to say, loudly and to all, but with a still-unconvinced tone, "Maybe we should do like they told us —duck——"

The blast wave struck. The Williams house, more than a thousand yards nearer the place of the fireball than the sturdier Conner home, had its top floor mashed as by a mallet. The windows screamed into the room. And that year they were double; Jim had put on storm windows. Don's hand was amputated. Jim lost much of his face; it became scarlet stew. All the children fell, bleeding. But Irma, the baby, being kissed by her anxious mother, received a pound of glass in her back and lungs; she was torn almost apart.

Ruth was not hurt at all—the baby having shielded her—not hurt at all, physically.

Kit Sloan, on his way home from the River City Athletic Club, was in a temper even before the sirens started. The seasonal parties, dances, balls and festivities had given him an alcoholic nervousness. He'd decided that day to play squash early, get his rubdown, and come home to dress in time to make it over to the Ritz-Hadley for the Emerson cocktail thing.

But his customary opponents hadn't been on hand. There was a rumor going, about an air-raid drill; and the three best players in the club, Green Prairie men, were in Civil Defense. He'd been obliged to bat balls around by himself for an hour, curtly refusing to "give a game" to inferior challengers.

His cabinet bath, plunge and rub after the disappointment had failed to restore his well-being.

So he drove vexedly in the Christmas crowds.

It wasn't far from the club to Pearson Square, but the waits for lights, the bumper-to-bumper pace between lights, made it seem a long way.

When at last he reached the southeast corner of the square, he saw that traffic along the south side was so badly jammed he decided it would be quicker to run the Jaguar beyond the side opposite, cut through an alley, and drive across the interior park itself, on a paved path meant for bikes and baby carriages. He doubted if the cops would bother him; he'd done it before, as a gag, at night. He figured he could blast a hole in the stalled traffic with his horn, thus getting into the Sloan driveway long before the log jam could be broken.

The decision saved him from swift death.

The siren caught him in the alley. He had to wait even there for three huge trucks, unloading behind the supermarket, to disentangle themselves and move down to the square. He followed. By then, a group of teen-age boys, attracted by the red car, were begging him to give them a ride. He ground up his windows in fury.

When the Light came, he didn't think at all. He shot to the floor of the car and covered his head with his arms: whatever it was, it was that kind of thing—a war kind, deadly. His reflexes so interpreted it. The blast followed.

The supermarket behind him disintegrated. The three-story brick houses beside him turned into brick piles. The cars and trucks across the square were pushed, lifted, rolled, skidded, mauled.

He did not see that; bricks roared down upon his car, bricks mounded in front of it, barricading the view; bricks buried his car. He lay in sudden dark and the choking dust of mortar.

People in the winter-locked square felt the heat of the bomb first. Their clothes smoldered, flamed. They screamed and fell. They wallowed and writhed. Yet a worse thing had befallen them in that chip of time: from the fireball which towered and expanded hideously in the near distance, they soaked up neutrons and gamma rays and were dead although to themselves alive-seeming still. The rays pierced every truck, every car, the thick wood, the thin steel, and the men and the women and the children inside, though they should live awhile, were doomed. Many perished then and there of blast and concussion and bashing; the rest, who thought they had escaped, were left with only a little while to live.

Trapped, hardly sensing as a special phenomenon the blast itself, Kit picked at the split glass of a window in his car. Bricks fell in on him but the illumination increased. Frantically, he pulled in more bricks. By and by he had a hole through which he could worm his way, hands first, tossing bricks aside.

Behind, he saw the supermarket. Smoking. Here and there, in the no-man's-land look of it, things moved. He faced around and gazed up. The mushroom cloud, boiling with what seemed cubic miles of colored fires, was spreading out. Its edge was even with the far corner of the square.

The houses near by were shattered, some smashed flat. His own, he could see, across the empty square and the lawns—where trees lay prostrate, their boughs still heaving—was wrecked. Why, he wondered, was the square so empty? Then he looked again and saw the bundles of clothing, the blackened things, the charred people, the dead and the still-moving dead.

His horror mounted. He heard bricks slide and scrambled away from the buried wreck of his car. He decided he would have to walk across the square. *Have* to.

It was hard going. Things—just things—had dropped into the place—and, he soon realized, things were raining from the hot, spreading cloud. Part of a piano fell down and then a dead pooch hit and rolled and something like a stove lid rang on the hot asphalt. He entered the park. People were opening the doors of cars, hanging out, gasping. The ones on the ground were black. Or red. Or both. With holes, meaning mouths.

A woman in what he first thought was a red sweater, vomited, sitting up straight in her car, vomited all over her own windshield. A man got out of a car that was upside down. He fell and didn't rise.

A door in a house opened and another man came out. A short, broad-chested man. He said something like, "Owowow-owowowowowo," and began to run down the sidewalk, toward Kit, who stepped aside. Between the sounds he emitted, the man *clicked* as he ran. Every step, Kit saw, left a blood-gob on the flagstones. He saw the reason. Both the man's feet were gone and he was running on the ends of his shinbones. That was why he seemed so short. He went a good ways, perhaps a quarter of a block, with his arms up and his fists doubled, like a track runner, and then he fell.

Kit thought of not going to his house, of going in the other direction, away from the expanding cloud. It was darkening the sky now. It looked exactly like the Technicolor newsreel shots; a bit darker, perhaps.

He began to trot. He slipped on somebody's blood, recovered and hurried.

A young woman, a pretty young woman with bright blue eyes and blonde hair sat up, right in front of him. He halted, mouth open. "Mister," she said, "will you help me get on my feet?"

He tried to. But when he reached down for where her arm should have been he felt gritty pulp and looked and it was just coming through her coat sleeve. She saw it, too, and screamed; he could hear her screaming all the way to his own lawn.

He went around the house once. It was on fire in several places. There was no sign of life. He wasn't even sure his mother had been at home anyway. She'd said something about having to shop.

To shop.

He spun around. From the heart of the city, a great smoke was rising. Beneath it, lighting its base, was fire. Somewhere he'd read that, in twenty minutes, the fire storm would come. The whole center of the city. You had at least twenty minutes to get clear, but then the temperatures rose with the holocaust. To six thousand degrees.

He thought, desperately, of a car. He rushed to the garage. Its second floor had fallen down and over the four great doors. There'd been a car under the porte-cochere. He ran there. It was burning. Had to get out. Twenty minutes. He must have wasted ten already.

He went fleetly north across the square, through its park, noticing nothing this time, sliding and getting his balance without looking, stepping on stones, boards, bricks, soft things—indiscriminately.

All Nora knew, for sure, when the ground jumped, was that the atomic bomb must have hit.

They'd been in the subcellar, with candles, sitting in old, discarded chairs—Minerva and Willis and three maids and Jeff, the butler, and the gardener. All around them were racks of dusty wine bottles, barrels of wine and cases—the tissue paper around the bottles, mildewed. They couldn't have been sitting there, Nora thought, for more than a minute. Then the whole place jumped and the candles went out and it was like being on the Whipsaw ride at Swan Island, and the maids screamed, but not like amusement-park screaming.

Then—the air full of moldy-smelling dust.

And the maids were hollering their fool heads off.

Minerva, who'd been saying something about, "Going back up, if this absurd situation lasts any length of time . . ." had been shut up by the tremendous heave right there.

Nora's chair slid on the bare earth floor. Barrels fell and bounced and rolled.

Then Willis, his old voice fierce, yelled, "Quiet!"

Peculiarly, Nora thought, the maids became silent.

"Are you all right, ma'am?" Willis asked.

Mrs. Sloan didn't answer.

A match struck. Nora noticed how it shook, how the hands that held a candle wobbled with it. Whoever it was, the gardener, she thought, had trouble sticking it to one of the shelves that held wine bottles. The first thing Nora saw was the maids, hugging each other, pale as death. The next thing she saw was a big wine barrel that wine was gurgling out of. Then she saw Mrs. Sloan, underneath it.

"We'll have to get out of here," Willis said. "And get *her* out."

"Better wait a bit," the gardener answered.

"Wait—the devil! The building above us is probably on fire. Try the door." Willis came over to the chair where Nora was sitting and smiled faintly. "You all right, Miss?"

"Fine," Nora said and she pointed to Mrs. Sloan. "Her legs are pinned under."

Willis nodded.

The maids began to whimper. He stood in front of them. "Stop that, every one of you!" he said. He turned to the butler. "Jeff, tear off a shelf-board and bear a hand! We'll have to prize that hogshead off her. If she's living."

Nora heard the butler yanking in the gloom. One of the maids went back there with him and returned first, carrying a two-by-four. From the door, which he'd opened, the gardener called, "Stairway's kind of blocked and it does smell smoky-like."

Willis was kneeling, listening to Mrs. Sloan's heart.

Her eyes were shut.

Willis said, "Well, clear a way through somehow! There's plenty of cellar exits. But just that one, up from here."

Pretty soon, they had moved the barrel. The butler, whose name was at least Jeff, Nora thought, was looking at Mrs. Sloan's legs, holding another lighted candle and pulling up her skirts in a most casual manner. "Busted—smashed," the butler said. "Have to make a stretcher. Some weight!"

From the door of the wine cellar, the gardener yelled, "We can get around this junk. But hurry! I hear it crackling up there!"

So they dragged Mrs. Sloan. The maids went first, though —they ran. And Nora was next to the gardener, who went last. As she followed the dragged woman, she saw Mrs. Sloan's pocketbook on the floor underneath the place where she'd been lying. Nora took it along and nobody paid any attention.

"Hurry up, kid," the butler said. That was all.

The cellar was half caved in and you could see lines of fire, through cracks overhead. The smoke was awful. Nora ran past the men with their slow-moving burden to the square of outdoor light, and she raced up stone steps, gratefully, for she was at last outdoors. She hoped she was in time to see the mushroom cloud, and she eyed the sky eagerly, ignoring her smoke-induced cough.

She was in time. In plenty of time.

And she saw more. The whole city, to the south, seemed on fire. It was, she told herself, extremely spectacular. It was unforgettable. She took a good look so she would never forget.

Then, and only then, having done her civilized duty, she looked at the house. The great Victorian pile was also burning. Flames surged in the broken guts of the building and curled among the down-hammered slates of the roofs and the many gables. It was all afire. The car that had brought them was on fire.

Willis said, "And the garage is blocked."

Jeff was eying the city. "Do you think . . . ?"

"I hell-sure do! Gotta get out of here."

"She should be in a hospital——"

"Right." Willis glanced at Nora, at the gardener, and said, "Where'd the girls go?"

Nora reported. "Ran. Just ran."

The chauffeur shrugged. "We'll have to put her in a barrow, I guess, Jeff, and get her to the street. Maybe we can catch a lift—or borrow a parked car . . ."

Minerva Sloan overflowed the wheelbarrow, Nora noticed. Her head hung out and her legs hung out, and there was some blood on them but not much. The men had a very hard time pushing her. The ground was soft and there no longer was any snow—to Nora's surprise. In the drive, though, it went easier. The gardener helped, too, taking the longest turn with the wheelbarrow.

It would be dark presently, Nora thought. The light, at the moment, was pinkish, as if a sunset had begun. But it was not a sunset at all and came from the south. It was the start of a fire storm, she knew.

When they reached the street, they stopped.

It was the first time Nora had got a good look at any dead people and now there were so many she could hardly decide which ones to look at first. They were mostly blackish, but some were scarlet and some had faces and bodies that looked exactly the way a steak looked when it caught on fire. And some, she saw, weren't exactly dead, or completely dead. A few in cars were opening and closing their mouths or moving their arms feebly and one girl about Nora's age kept bumping her head back and forth between the front and rear seats in a sedan. Some people in the park were crawling around and you could hear screams and groans, mostly from where some big store was crushed about flat and the brick houses had caved in. It sounded like birds in the distance, the screaming, Nora thought: twittery and as if a big flock made it. Sparrows or starlings.

When they had all looked out over the square for a while and not said anything, the gardener turned around and stared with a peculiar expression at the mushroom cloud and the fire getting brighter underneath it and he just ran. He ran through the park in a zigzag and toward the west where, Nora realized finally, there was a big noise of other people yelling and raging around, though you couldn't see them at that distance: just wreckage.

Jeff the butler, who was a tall man with large cords in his neck, looked at Willis and the chauffeur said, "Lost his head."

"Shock," Jeff answered.

Willis looked across the square as if he, too, would like to run; but then his eyes soon began to move along the row of cars which wasn't exactly a row any more.

It was chilly now and getting dark quite fast. Nora had lost her hat but she never had taken off her woolly coat and she was glad of that. She tried to remember as much as she

could of all she had heard at home, ever since she could remember anything, about atomic bombs. She realized that this
one had gone off quite near, but she also realized she didn't
know how powerful it was or exactly how near. And she had
to admit that, even if she'd known, she could only guess about
the radioactivity.

She did recall, though, that people had put cars close to test
bombs and they'd had their tops squdged down like some of
those on the street, but people had started them right away.
Willis was walking along, looking at the cars that stood on
their wheels and weren't full of broken glass or smoking or
anything. Once in a while, he bent forward and looked inside
—to make sure no person was on the floor in a mess or anything.

At long last Willis got into a car and started it and drove it
slowly down the street, winding around things. He and Jeff
got Mrs. Sloan in the back somehow and she moaned once
but her eyes didn't open. Willis said, "Where to?" in a funny
way and Nora thought probably he had a certain percentage
of "shock," also. Maybe about forty per cent, she thought,
and she thought Jeff had about fifty and she had ten or maybe
twenty per cent at most.

The car started along the street very slowly, going this
way and that, but the lights were smashed and you couldn't
tell exactly what you were running over. They went around
the east side of the square, sometimes going up over the curb,
and past a brick house that was burning inside fiercely. Nora
saw then that sweat was pouring down Willis's face and he
was crying and the butler beside him was looking straight
ahead at absolutely nothing.

She was sitting between them and not being paid any attention to.

When they reached St. Paul Street, they couldn't make a

right turn because of the rubble so they went on north.

Finally Jeff said, "The City Hospital's the other way, Willis." He spoke quietly, as if he didn't want to hurt the chauffeur's feelings.

But Willis wasn't making a mistake. He answered, "Jeff, there won't *be* any city hospital down there."

Jeff said, "Check," and sounded crestfallen. "Where you headed?"

"I thought we might get through farther up here and around east and back to St. Paul on that side. The Infirmary."

"Mrs. Sloan would be highly incensed——"

"I don't know if she'll ever be highly anything."

There was less rubble and there were fewer fires up that way and they began to see a lot of people who weren't hurt at all, just running around. Many were going in and out of houses, carrying things, and some families already had beds and bedding and trunks and suitcases and piles of clothing out on the street. Quite a few had put things in handcarts and even on children's wagons, and they were hurrying along, pushing and pulling and carrying babies. All the windows were broken and all the sidewalks were littered with glass and there were very few parked cars.

Willis noticed that, too. "People that could," he pointed out, "grabbed a car and beat it."

When they crossed Market Street—which changed its name from Central Avenue at the bridge which Nora rightly supposed was now vaporized—they could see hordes of people everywhere, nearly all of them running north with something in their arms or on their backs, and children. But some blocks down, where the big Cathedral was plain to see because it was on fire and half-mashed anyhow, firehoses were shooting up and fire trucks were all around.

"That's what comes," Willis said, "of having all **Harps in** the Fire Department. Save the Catholic church and let the city go."

Jeff said, haughtily, Nora noticed, "I guess it isn't important. Half the fire companies must have been wiped out and the rest couldn't do much. The flood that floated Noah couldn't put this out!" He laughed a little; cackled, Nora called it to herself.

They covered about three miles to go about one straight mile and often they had to back out of streets because they could see they couldn't go through. Sometimes people tried to stop them; and always people begged for rides and once some foreigners yelled a lot of words they couldn't understand and threw stones at them.

When it got quite dark and when they were out of the region where the fires made it possible to see their way, Willis found a bigger car with locked doors and windows. He broke the windows with bricks and he raised the engine hood and fiddled under it and they moved Mrs. Sloan, though it seemed all they could do. Nora took her pocketbook along, carefully. But the car lights helped a great deal when they finally got the other car moving, and some teen-age boys came shooting past them in the car they'd abandoned and hit a fire plug not three blocks away.

Once, when they were on the other side of Market Street, a plane went over, out toward Ferndale. It was flying terribly low and terribly fast and it was a very big plane. But only Nora bothered to wonder what it was doing there. She thought maybe it was a drone, sampling the atomic dust, but she decided there was no way to tell. She realized that Chuck would be at Hink Field in all probability and he could tell her, later, when she got home. If she ever did get home.

By the time they got to where they could see the Infirmary, the fire storm was really going full blast. It made one big blaze right in the middle of the Sister Cities about five miles high and maybe, Nora decided, two miles across. Since she had expected it, she took it for granted exactly as she did all other A-bomb phenomena: it impressed her without unduly astonishing her. But she could observe that Jeff and Willis were simply appalled. Several times, flicking his eyes up at the rising tower of sheer flame, Willis bumped into things with the car.

Pretty soon he stopped.

He stopped because the street ahead was solid with people lined up—or, rather, just there in a solid mass—trying to get to the Infirmary. They were all hurt. Some were bleeding and some were burned and many were both. Some had no faces as such, Nora noticed, and some had bones showing through their flesh and even through their clothes. And the whole mass of them, thousands and thousands, made one loud sound like community singing. A lot of people were already on the ground, unable to move or dead, and nobody paid any attention to them.

"I'll have to get through somehow," Willis said.

"It isn't possible."

"We can't let her wait for her turn here. She'll die, most likely."

Jeff stepped out of the car. His hair started to blow and his coat flickered and Nora realized it was very windy. That would be the air moving in to feed the fire storm and it could reach hurricane force, they had often said, and suck fire engines and even people into its center to burn. The butler took a look at the hurt people, who were all around him now, and a long look at the big torch in the sky, and he just ran, like the panicky maids.

"Smelled 'em, I guess," Willis said.

Nora stepped out. He didn't prevent it. She felt the cold-

ness of the pouring air on one side and the heat of the verita-
ble Mount Everest of fire on the other. It was about the same
altitude, she thought, to its top, where big slices of fire
jumped up independently, in the sky, above the summit. She
drew a breath and she thought Willis was right. They
smelled like hot meat, burning fat, smoking grease and burned
hair.

Then a terrible thing happened.

Willis got out of the sedan, too, and Mrs. Sloan was in it
alone, and Willis suddenly grabbed his shoulder. His face became distorted and he tried to say something, tried to gesture,
but he fell down on the pavement of the street. Nora squatted
down and shook him and said, over and over, "Mr. Willis!
Mr. Willis!" But he didn't say a word so she knew his heart
had failed.

It wasn't surprising, she thought. He was a very eld-
erly man. But more people were coming into the street all
the time, pushing toward the Infirmary in a great stinking,
screaming, sticky mob and soon they would hem her in. If she
didn't want to spend the rest of the night right there, she'd
have to move. She thought she might be able to go up the
street again and around and come into the back or the side of
the Mildred Tatum Infirmary. It was, in fact, not merely
the only way to escape the increasing crowd but the only hope
of getting a doctor for Mrs. Sloan, though she hesitated to try
it, because now she would be all alone.

2

The bomb had gone off nearly an hour ago.

With demented clarity, Kit Sloan realized he had been running this way and that, trying to get distance between him

and the great fire, without making much headway. He had turned his ankle twice and he was still going on it, but it was swelling. Sometimes he covered a block or two and then had to retrace his steps because of a rubble mass or, more often, a jam-packed shambles of human beings filling the street from wall to wall and headed away so slowly that he didn't want to be impeded by them.

Foreigners, mostly.

Their area had not been annihilated, just set on fire here and there, mauled, dumped in its streets. So they were on the move, on the way out of town, Polaks and Hunkies and Latwicks, Yids and Guineas and Micks. Not many Nigs. He even thought, racing past a bleeding family, there was a reason for the dearth of shines in the stampeded mobs: Niggertown was right on Ground Zero.

Up until he reached Elk Drive, a wide concrete boulevard with the parkways between, a kind of insane logic governed his actions. He had to escape. His mother was dead, in the city or in the ruins of their house. So his responsibility was for himself alone. He had nobody else to save. The fire behind, the dead and dying around, the hideous condition of the hurt—these acted as spurs and goads. If he had been like many people, they would have driven him to less violent activity, to crazed stasis, perhaps.

He even knew that Elk Drive had been his first goal. On Elk, he could get a ride of some sort, steal a car, or even run on by himself, using the lawns and adjacent fields, to get out of town. Elk Drive was wide and roomy and the houses were set well back, out through the developments, clear to the open countryside. And Elk Drive led to the municipal airport. He could gas his own plane up, if need be, figure his own chances in the traffic pattern, take off without consulting the control tower, and fly until he found some neighboring city or town

—Omaha, KC, Oklahoma City, even a small place like Kaknee or Dennis or Elvers—where there had been no bomb, where no fire roared as high as the stratosphere, as massive as an Act of God.

Traffic was whizzing on Elk, using both sides of the parkways to go in one direction—away. The people on foot used either the middle strips or lawns, running or walking, and there were thousands. But, still, they moved—every man and woman and child at his own chosen pace. There was room enough.

He stepped into the yard of a house, the Whittaker home, he realized with a kind of infant's pleasure at mere identification. He threw himself down, to pant and rest, watching the fire-struck masses surge west.

Then the plane came.

Fast and low.

In the dark, Kit wouldn't have seen the markings if it hadn't banked so as to catch the raw glare from downtown. That made the red stars plainly discernible on the wings. *My Christ,* he thought, *Soviet.*

A turbo-pro job.

For an instant, vainly, he watched the sky behind it, assuming an American jet had driven the enemy to earth. None came.

What came, soon enough, over the length of Elk Drive, over the people running in scattered thousands, over the whizzing cars and fast-lumbering trucks, was a swift polka-dotting of white in the plane's wake. Parachutes, Kit realized. Little ones.

They opened and began to descend. He watched them drift down, drift his way, in wonderment. Soon, one came quite close overhead. He stood up with the idea of capturing it. Then he heard, above the pandemonium on Elk Drive, a hissing beneath the chute and saw a shining metal canister. Too late, he perceived that a considerable cloud of wind-dispersed vapor was blasting from the canister, under pressure, as an insect bomb spews mist. The vapor from the falling chute surrounded him, dampened him. And at last he knew what it was. Others on the street, caught in the swirls of mist, also guessed.

"Germs!"

"Bacteria!"

"It's disease war!"

A truck, driven by a man who must also have known, braked ferociously to avoid a settling, sizzling missile. Instantly, fifty cars crashed behind it. And the chutes came down over the lot, spraying the dead and the injured along with the unharmed.

Kit knew he had breathed the stuff. He knew he had licked his culture-moistened lips. He knew his clothes were damp with it. So he knew that the thing he had been trying to escape had overtaken him. He spat, vomited, discarded his jacket and trousers, wiped his face with a handkerchief till blood came.

But from then on, he did not have even a demented logic. No one had sanity, on Elk Drive, after the bacteria sprayed them.

3

Ruth Williams still carried her dead baby. Its insides had come through its back, slowly, as she walked, and finally they'd jiggled so loose and slack that she stepped on them now and again. Jim came along behind her, his face clotted up in the cold, his hand on her back—because he couldn't see. Behind Jim, holding onto a length of clothesline, came the rest of the family. People who saw Ruth leading, walking, tripping a little, slipping now and again—for visibility was good in the torchy night—said things and were sick or they screamed, and Ruth always smiled a little at their discomfiture.

Finally, Ruth threw it away.

They went faster, afterward—through Ferndale, down the main street, past the broken windows of all the stores.

4

Beau was lost.

How he got so far downtown he never knew.

He remembered the railroad tracks, beyond Cold Spring. He remembered, because he almost got killed there. A train —mixed and covered with people like flies on flypaper—came around a bend, headlight shining, folks scattering ahead. Some got hit. The train gave a whistle blast and thundered by, out of the city, Beau guessed. Even so, he must have taken the wrong direction on the tracks afterward. It was hard to remember which way you'd faced, after you'd rolled down an embankment.

For a long time he didn't identify the great pyre with direction. He had not tried to reason where the bomb had hit. He'd been in his cellar at the time—and the Light had merely been omnipresent, not directional, down there.

He was somewhere around the Simmons Park area, though, in Wickley Heights, he thought.

He stopped to take bearings.

"Quite a night," he said aloud.

Netta's dead, he thought.

There was a big apartment building, a swanky place, on

this street, he noticed. Nobody around. Nobody at all. The wind was blowing and the street was warm, nonetheless. The building had broken windows, big ones, because the ground floor was for shops. He thought there might be a liquor store. He had lost his whisky bottle when he'd jumped out of the path of that goddamned wildcatting railroad locomotive.

He didn't think it would get very far, going like that, with the rails probably spread here and there and debris on the tracks.

He walked along in front of the fire-illumined building, waded, rather, in deep glass that was slippery. All the street trees had been knocked over in neat rows pointing the same way.

He stopped.

It wasn't a liquor store.

It was a jewelry store.

The big window was just a glass jaw, like a shark's, that a man could step through. The glass counters were conveniently shattered. Inside, things glittered in the firelight, brighter than glass, and different colors.

Beau said dazedly, rather happily, "Well!"

He went in and picked up a bracelet and then a necklace. "Well, *well!*" he murmured. He commenced to stuff his pockets, humming. He hummed, "Happy days are here again . . ."

5

Hook and Ladder Company Number 17 pulled back to Broad Street, according to plan. The sea of fire began at Washington, to the north. Nothing could be done to stop a fire storm. It had to burn itself out, leaving just ash, the Hiroshima effect. The temperature inside it would rise to six thousand degrees or better. Any people alive, under that circle of one flame, would crisp and cremate, or, escaping that in some deep cellar, suffocate. For all the oxygen of the atmosphere near by would be used by the fire. Everything that could be oxidized would burn. The "air" would be CO and CO_2.

They reeled in their hoses and backed and filled until the equipment was turned around, the hook and ladder, the chemical engines, the pumps, the hose wagons, the chief's car. Then they got aboard and went. It was their second major move. The first had been made in Condition Yellow—when they'd rendezvoused in Edgeplains and waited. It was a good tactic: the firehouse had been wrecked.

They thought maybe they could save the Police Station and everything from there south. So they came over from Sunset Parkway again, east, to the station. They noted, on the way, that the CD people were on the job. They'd dynamited clear through from the parkway to River Avenue, where a row of wooden houses had caught. Two bulldozers, sweating it out in the heat, had knocked down a scrabble of advertising signs, a house, and some miscellaneous junk that would otherwise have carried fire deeper into Green Prairie.

The chief, going past, cut his siren and tramped on his horn and waved, and one of the men on a dozer waved back.

When they got to the station, they piled out. There were lights in the windowless building and even the green lights outside were burning again. An auxiliary plant. Over toward Bigelow and Cold Spring, it looked comfortingly dark, though the firemen knew brands and sparks would be raining down there and probably clear to the city limits. The CD people would have to take care of that. The business of Number 17 was the big stuff, like the row of stores blazing on Broad. Fortunately, the wind blew toward the center of town from every compass point, feeding the fire storm; it made peripheral fire-fighting practicable. If it hadn't been for that in-sucked wind, all Green Prairie would have gone.

The trucks fanned out. The growling sirens fell silent. Caps fell from fireplugs, hoses were screwed on, streams of water traversed Broad and crashed into the seething row of stores, sending up inverted spark-rains that could not be seen against the central city, the solid background of flame. Now, it vanished at the top—an unbelievable fire mountain that pierced a downreaching, outspreading pall of smoke. Smoke, with the dust from the bomb, canopied the Sister Cities.

Lieutenant Lacey, looking military neat, came out of the Police Station and pointed at a huge lump of debris in the street—a tangle of metal, half-melted, unrecognizable, and as big as a small house. "It fell," he yelled in the fire chief's ear, "right after the blast. Think your men are safe around it?"

The chief stared. "God knows! Around it is where they gotta be, anyhow, if they're going to keep this fire from spreading."

"I phoned the school," Lacey said, "for one of those radiation people. They haven't got many. And Christ knows we need 'em in a million places!"

The chief nodded. A roof fell across the street and he ran from the station steps to deal with the changed circumstances. This conflagration would have been a three-alarmer, in ordinary times; it was a mere match-sputter now, which the Green Prairie company would have to deal with alone.

The Ford came fast, considering the condition of the streets. Somebody had stuck CD flags on both sides, so Lacey ran down and yanked open the door. "Big gob of metal dropped in the street," he said. "I've kept my men clear of it, but the firemen have to work beside it."

"I'll check."

Lacey stepped back and stared. It was a woman.

She piled out, wearing some sort of plastic thing that made her look like an Arab, and carrying a box with dials and wires. He followed her.

She didn't even glance at the fire engines or the men swarming in the street or the blazing buildings. She went through the puddles, in boots, to the girder or rail mass he'd pointed out. She held a shiny metal rod out at it and began walking slowly around it. Because it was a woman, Lieutenant Lacey went right along with her. He could see, in the heaving firelight, that the dials on her gadget were jumping. But that didn't make her back away from the big slag heap, so he didn't back away.

"It's hot," she said. "Plenty."

"We'll hose it down," he answered.

"I mean—radioactive. Looks like something blasted from a building. Steelwork and wiring. Balled up in the air and hurled out here."

"Is it killing the men?" he asked.

Lenore chuckled and shook her hooded head. "No. They'd be safe even sitting on it, for a matter of a few hours. But I wouldn't want it in my dining room for good."

"Cigarette?" Lacey asked.

Lenore unzipped her transparent face protector. "I'd love one! Heaven knows when I had my last one, and I've got a list of calls to make"—she jerked her head toward her car—"as long as my arm." She threw back her hood, inhaled, and said, "Thanks. You look spic and span, Lieutenant."

Lacey grinned. "This is the third uniform I've had on tonight. First one caught fire. Second one got—bloody . . ."

"Sorry."

He said. "Sorry? The *devil!* Rugged night!"

Lenore took a long look at the seething fire storm. "It is that."

"You're the Bailey girl, aren't you?"

"I am. Why?"

Lacey answered, "Thought you might like to know something. My men have searched from Broad, here, to Ash. Your mother was pretty badly cut up. Or *did* you know?"

Lenore shook her head. "Dad?"

"Nobody else in your house, that we found. Your mother's up at the Crystal Lake Church. She'll live, I guess. Maybe she's on the lawn, though, so no use looking. The church is crammed with the ones worst off."

"I haven't time," Lenore answered. She said, "Poor Mom!"

A man ran up the street toward them. "Hey!" he yelled. "Hey!"

"Another loony," Lacey muttered. He reached out with one arm and stopped the man.

He wasn't out of his mind; he was merely burned badly and having trouble seeing. "I came across Broad on Bigelow from the cemetery," he said, choking. "Place is loaded and the people can't get any farther. Broad's too hot. Look at me!"

"Have to blast a way to 'em," Lacey said. He stared toward the fire chief.

"They're cooking in that graveyard!" the man said. He added, "Cooking alive. Thousands of them. Oh, my God, my face hurts me terrible."

Lacey stared at him. "Go up in the station. Say I sent you. Lacey's the name." He freed the man. He'd need another uniform, now, Lenore thought. And she thought of the cemetery, long and wide and open, back behind the fire that was raging along the north side of Broad. Something stirred in her mind and receded and came to the fore. "Doesn't that new sewer, under River Avenue, cut close to the cemetry?"

"My *Lord!*" Lacy answered.

He left her. He ran to the chief.

Lenore saw them talking briefly, a two-man pantomime against the flames. Then the chief tapped some men, piled into his car, and it turned. Its red eyes glowed as it headed for River Avenue—and a manhole: there were manholes near Restland, too, and emergency exits; if necessary, they could also dynamite a hole.

Lenore stepped carefully on the stub of her cigarette, thought how crazy that was and hurried back to her car, carrying the heavy counter.

Half an hour later, the first of more than three thousand men, women and children began climbing from ladders along River Avenue, from the new sewer where earlier that day Nora had walked. It was the biggest single mass exodus from the fire area.

The people who managed to reach Simmons Park got away easily along Willowgrove. The people who made it to the reservoir, were safe.

Lenore didn't, of course, stay to see the hordes clamber out of manholes. By the time the first of them drew breaths of clean air, she was on the top of an apartment building, over on James Street, not far from the Golf Course.

The CD rescue men were using the roof to get people out of a burning hospital building beyond, a hospital for chronics who could not be moved (until now) and the mentally disturbed. They were coming over on ropes to the apartment; but the roof there, broad and flat, had been covered two inches deep with a curious dust, a fall-out from the bomb-cloud. The men working wanted to know if the dust was—as usual, Lenore thought—"killing them."

It showed only twenty mr's—very weak radiation.

She went down by the freight elevator—with men wearing miners' lights on their hats and CD brassards who were obliged to keep fighting with two women maniacs—down to the ground, out to the yard, into her Ford and on to the next call.

6

Toward eight o'clock they brought food to Henry.

He had not left the room, had scarcely moved from his desk.

He had been aware for some time, subconsciously, of the smell of hot food. In his mind, he had ticked that off as one more thing going according to plan. Plenty was not. But the mobile kitchen, earmarked for his headquarters, had evidently come up; the women volunteers were heating beans in cauldrons, firing up the coffee makers, opening stacks of gallon fruit cans, running bread through the slicer.

The high school's windows had been boarded up with plywood. A large kerosene stove was shedding heat and smoking slightly in the corner. Canvas had been nailed temporarily across the big crack in the roof. An engineer had made his inspection and assured everybody the high school wouldn't collapse. There were plenty of kerosene lamps. For people in other rooms who didn't have heaters, there had been an issue of coats and sweaters, collected from God knew where by God knew whom. A bevy of determined housewives, wearing arm bands and having nothing better to do, had come in with brooms and dustpans, raised a fearful dust, and cleaned out the plaster and loose debris.

At a desk pushed up to face his, Eve Sanders, acting as

secretary, kept typing out notes—summaries of word that came over the walkie-talkies, and from the few ham radio stations still operable; and from runners from all parts of the area: boys on bikes, mostly. But the Motorcycle Club, having cleaned up the preliminary search and police auxiliary work in Henry's sector, was checking in now in numbers, for message work.

On blackboard stands, beyond Mrs. Sanders, three men kept writing and erasing. Henry, just by looking up, could tell where his main crews were working. The Fire Department companies, after a two-hour fumble and an effort to run things their own way, were in direct liaison with him now, and some of the phone company linesmen were already making emergency connections on standing, usable lines that crisscrossed the sector.

Henry felt lucky, fantastically lucky.

Only a small arc of the area of very severe damage intruded his sector. And the fires were being handled. He had plenty of casualties—glass, mainly—burns, next—shock —and miscellaneous. He also had approximately nine thousand very badly hurt people from the area closer in. There had been some panics, at first. They had blockaded Dumond, Arkansas, River, Sedmon, Ames, VanNess, Bigelow and Cold Spring avenues. That had stopped the cars mostly, though an undetermined number of people—"thousands" they said out along Decatur, exaggerating, no doubt—had got beyond the city limits, during the long span of Condition Yellow and later, before they'd set up the blockades.

Where traffic piled up, the loud-speaker trucks had sailed in. Many fugitives, of course, had trudged ahead on foot. But the speakers had brought most of the panicky groups back toward town, toward the high flame, the radioactivity, the horror—by argument, cajolery and threat. There was no guarantee of a way to live in the countryside; but in the city, the loud-speakers bellowed ceaselessly—there was food, shelter, clothing, medical aid, all that people required.

A great many of the doctors and nurses in Henry's sector had followed the plan for Condition Yellow, but many had not. The ones who had packed the prescribed medical and surgical equipment in cars, and driven with their families to outlying areas, were now back in town at work. The doctors and nurses and other "key personnel" who had refused to respond properly to Condition Yellow were now dead, or among the casualties themselves, or trapped behind the irregular rim of fire that circled the fire storm proper.

Thousands of people had been rescued from homes, stores, apartments, factories, lofts, buses, trolleys, other spots suddenly rendered perilous. Thousands remained, even in Henry's area, in distress and danger. But the trained hundreds in his groups, with growing numbers of volunteer helpers from the unhurt, were tearing into every problem as they came to it, dousing fires, removing the injured, streaking them to Crystal Lake. They were carting bulldozers and cranes on flat truckbeds around the perimeter of ruin, smashing fire lanes, crumpling fire hazards, sweeping debris from trunk thoroughfares. They were performing prodigies shoulder to shoulder with the regular firemen. They were standing fire watch on the rickety tops of once-handsome buildings. They were pacing, armed and alert, in every street, looking out for looters. They were sweating with the Water Supply people over emergency means to divert Crystal Lake down its overflow to a hastily dammed gulley above Broad, where the fire hoses could feed. They were commandeering the contents of damaged stores, especially food stores and clothing stores, and bringing truckloads to Hobart Park where a vast "dump" of supplies was accumulating. They were—the women—tending the hurt, the shocked, the frightened, helping the surgeons, assisting the nurses, corralling the hundreds of lost children, making out tickets of identification, making out cards for withdrawals of food, clothes, shoes, whatever was required.

All that and more was happening when the food came for Henry.

He took a big bite of a hot corned beef sandwich. He swigged coffee and picked up a plate of beans.

"Why don't you come over to the other side," one of his assistants said, "and take a look."

Henry surveyed his assistants. They were working efficiently. Things, at the moment, were comparatively quiet. He said, "All right," and carried his plate and his sandwich into the corridor as he went.

From an opposite, unshielded window, he could see.

Between this top-floor vantage point and the fire storm, nothing remained that stood higher.

The single flame of the burning city-heart could not be followed to its summit. It disappeared in smoke, in smoke so thick and dark, so folded and contoured it looked like a range of hills in the sky, upside down, illuminated by fire. The flame itself was yellow-white and solid, a curving wall that slanted in toward the center and could be followed for a thousand feet or more to the place where smoke screened it. Silhouetted against it, for a mile and a half, were the intervening buildings and homes, many burning with separate fires.

The city roared like a volcano and the night shook.

Henry stood still. He stopped eating. It was his city, his life, his boyhood and manhood and it had died and this was its funeral pyre—this tremendous thing.

The heart and significance of the city was gone. Only its people, the majority of its human contents, could be saved. But they had raised it up.

The city, he thought, transfixed by the magnificence of its dying, *was* the people. It was an extension of their bodies.

When they had been primitive men, they had added the hides of beasts to their own insufficient body hair and the protection of caves to that, and then huts, and now a city. The railroads and all the cars and the motors and engines had been added to their muscles. To their ears, telephones, radios, communications. To their eyes, TV. The very pavement of the streets and the traffic it bore were extensions of the bare feet of men.

It was all, Henry thought, just a big human body—all that city of his and the city beyond it. All part of *man*. If his blood did not actually flow through it, his mind did. If his cells did not actually develop the intricacies of it, his brain cells had contrived every bit. It moved and had life and function and meaning and purpose only when, and only because, the nerves of man moved first, commanding his giant self-extension, his city.

It was dying, Henry thought, the huge superbody of man. But *not man*.

"Okay," Henry said. "I've seen it."

He went back.

"The goddamndest thing!" a runner reported breathlessly, as Henry came back, "happened out Bigelow, beyond Decatur. A train, loaded with people, pulled from downtown and got all the way out there before it smacked a freight. The whole shebang went off the rails. And nobody even *noticed* until an hour or so ago! Hardly anyone lived. It was going about ninety when it hit."

Henry merely nodded.

7

Ted Conner was carrying a walkie-talkie with the mixed gang of firemen, cops and CD people who were trying to crash and beat their way back down James Street to Simmons Park. It was outside his father's sector, in K. But the Sector K headquarters had been wrecked, and they were borrowing people from adjacent areas. The Wickley Heights section, near where they worked, had been hit hard. Most of the people, the ones who could move, had got out by way of the Golf Course, even people who ran clear across Simmons Park, farther in. But there were undoubtedly plenty more in the big houses, the luxury hotels, the fancy apartments, who couldn't move, who were there, still—with fires breaking out and a wind that rushed toward the one, municipal flame, tearing loose cornices, ripping off roofs, bringing down walls. You couldn't leave people there.

Besides, if they reached the park in spite of the fact that a corner of it was enveloped in fire storm (Ted knew that, from Hink Field, which already had planes in the air, reconnoitering and reporting back to the field and thence to CD), the men might be able to cut across the far side, go the long block east, on Jefferson, to the curve in the river and reach the two bridges there. They were the first ones standing, the planes said, and both of them were loaded with people, and mobs had backed into River City from these bridges. They seemed trapped—as well as the men in the planes could tell, flying in the heat, the smoke, the suction and draft and the downfall of solids.

In fact, Hink Field relayed, River City's organization had itself collapsed and nobody on that side of the river was doing much officially. The bulk of the population was already on the move, outside town.

The crew on James Street encountered another block: the façade of the Shelley Garden Apartments had slid into the highway. Bulldozers began raging at the mountains of bricks. That meant a wait before the next advance. So Ted walked over to the sidewalk and sat down on the curb.

A bank, with white marble walls, shielded him from the burning sky.

He unshipped his walkie-talkie because the straps were cutting into his thin shoulders. He got out a Hershey bar someone had handed him when they had mobilized for this job. It was limp from the heat but he ate it, wishing he had a drink of water to go with it.

The curb on which he sat trembled with the thunder of the fire. The wind that blew was cold and fresh, though, except for occasional surges of smoke from something left behind, burned and practically out, or safely doused down. Up ahead, dozers charged, bricks avalanched, dynamite let go and men yelled orders. When they had cleaned a lane through the cascaded apartment house they'd move on. Until then, he could rest—unless one of the chiefs or the wardens wanted to send a message. Then they'd start hollering, "Signals!" and he'd have to run up.

Ted took a dirty handkerchief from his hip pocket and wiped sweat out of his eyes.

Because of his job, he knew a great many miscellaneous facts that he had passed on to nobody, for lack of time and owing to the concentration everywhere on the struggle at hand.

The diameter of the main fire was just over two miles. He knew that, from Hink Field.

It took in the whole business district, the shopping area, the skyscrapers and stores, the central half-circles of both cities and all of Swan Island on the east, the warehouse district on the west, nine bridges, the railroad yards, and various other "undetermined areas." For the next mile out, in every direction, damage was severe and fires were numerous but would not, so Hink Field stated, "anucleate with the main fire storm."

There was no estimate of the casualties. Owing to the delay in warning by siren, an "undetermined but vast" number of persons had been caught by the bomb in the downtown area.

He knew things like that, miscellaneous scads of them, which had come deluging over the walkie-talkie, intended for others.

He knew more—most of it, too, from Hink Field.

New York was gone. H-bombed. The whole thing.

So were San Francisco and Los Angeles and Philadelphia.

About twenty-five other cities had been hit by fission bombs like the one which had struck the Sister Cities, "probably a secondary target or target of expediency," they asserted.

Germ war had begun on some of the people around the edge of bombed areas, and elsewhere nerve gas had been used.

Every state had declared martial law.

Two vast waves of bombers had come in across Canada.

Two enemy aircraft carriers, the existence of which had not been known, had made their way into the waters south of the Gulf of Lower California and launched planes equipped with robot missiles which were armed with "unexpectedly powerful" plutonium bombs.

The bomb that had detonated over Green Prairie River was now estimated at approximately one hundred kilotons. The aiming point was thought to have been the Central Avenue-Market Street Bridge, and the actual Ground Zero, a few hundred yards west. The robot bomb had been launched at a distance of more than a hundred miles and apparently guided by TV-radar devices. The launching plane had been brought down, in a suicide dive, by Captain Leo Cohen of Hink Field, only seconds after the discharge of its missile.

Ted knew (if he cared to think about it) that:

An all-out counterattack had been launched.

Moscow and Leningrad were gone.

Several other Soviet cities had been destroyed, the names of which he could not even pronounce, let alone remember.

The Eastern seaboard of U.S.A. was in rout and panic.

The whole state of Florida had been declared a hospital area and casualties from the rest of the nation, which could be transported there, would be accepted.

Texas and the Gulf States also had "hospital reception" areas.

(Who in hell could reach Florida or Texas when we can't even get to River City, Ted thought?)

There was no longer a place that could be called either Washington or the District of Columbia. An H-bomb hurled by submarine had exploded there.

Above all else, Ted learned, fear of new raids drove the millions into the winter, the oncoming dark, the universal chaos.

The radio air was hot with speculation. Obviously, the enemy had used only a small part—so far—of his plutonium bombs. Possibly the enemy had now exhausted his supply of hydrogen weapons. But perhaps a rain of them was scheduled to fall later. More likely, the foe had launched his attack prematurely, in order to keep the United States from taking the little further time needed to build an immense arsenal of H-bombs. This was a Soviet "preventive war," many thought, undertaken with whatever the Russians had—a genocidal, eleventh-hour gamble.

But even if the enemy had managed to prepare only five

H-bombs for their blitz, it was enough to panic those who survived. Planes, scouting cautiously, were beginning to report. . . .

The District of Columbia was a white-hot saucer, deep-hammered in the land. The Potomac, and the tides, rolling back over the depression, were turning into mountain ranges of live steam. Where Philadelphia had been was a similar cauldron. Manhattan Island was gone—demolished, vaporized, pressed beneath the Hudson—and the sea was already cooling over much of Brooklyn, Queens, the Bronx, Staten Island and the Jersey marshes. That half of the "Golden Gate" which had supported San Francisco had also vanished: a peninsula with a city upon it. Los Angeles County was a bowl of white-hot gravel. Conditions like those in Green Prairie and River City prevailed only at a distance from the H-bombed cities, in suburbs and lesser metropolises, on perimeters circling for a hundred and fifty miles around each city.

Ted heard all that, and more—more than the mind could grasp.

The President was dead.

Martial law wasn't working in many states because the National Guardsmen couldn't reach mobilization points, or were too occupied dealing with situations right where they were to go anywhere else or, in some instances, had no mobilization point left to go to.

People, by millions, were streaming in their cars and on foot and by boat and train and rail and ferry and bridge from all the cities of U.S.A. Unhit cities feared that they would be next.

Nothing stopped these people.

Word that no further waves of Red planes had appeared anywhere did nothing to stop them. Even shooting at them as they stampeded did no good. They just piled over the dead and went on.

These items had boiled up out of the babble on the walkie-talkie and out of gossip between parties using it and on the ham set to which Ted had at first been assigned duty. He thought about some of them for a while.

Finally, he got up from the curb, feeling more tired than when he'd sat down. Just around the corner, he saw a drugstore. It was dark inside, of course, not on fire, and without windows. He hurried toward it, licking his lips thirstily. The soda fountain seemed intact, except for broken glass. The water spiggot didn't produce, but the soda spiggot did. He got a wax paper cup and filled it and drank and filled it and drank until he was not thirsty any more.

When he came out, he saw, in the flickering semidark, somebody on the top steps of a red brick residence across the street. He thought it was a woman; he didn't know why. Because she was sitting down, he went over to see. When he got near, he could see well enough, too well.

She must have been knocked out for a long time. But not so she couldn't get up finally, and make it through her front door. Then—her insides must have popped. At least, she was sitting in a great puddle of blood, trying—his gelid eyes saw —to push things back inside her. But what stopped Ted was the fact that her organs seemed to be moving with a convulsive, blood-camouflaged, separate life. She kept pushing them against the rent across her abdomen and all of a sudden the biggest object let out a blat and Ted knew what it was: a baby, unborn—born, rather, right then, when she had stood up to run out—and the woman was trying to get it back within herself—probably it was too soon.

She looked up at him so he could see her eyes in the reflected glare and she sort of smiled as if she were embarrassed and he could tell she was stark, raving crazy. Then she flopped over, but the other thing went on blatting and blatting, its breath catching on every intake.

He was sorry he'd just drunk so much soda.

Back on the corner, they were yelling, "Signals! Signals!"

He hitched into the walkie-talkie and trotted toward the men. "Here I am!"

"For crissake, stay in the main drag, willya? We needya!"

8

It was cold out at Hink Field.

It was a cold, icy-clear night, with stars.

Toward the cities, of course, the stars were obscured. And even directly overhead, they were dimmer. That was owing to the fire. It lit up Hink Field the way a flare from a private gas well lights a farmer's barnyard. It threw an immense pall of smoke across the eastern sky. But the high, steady wind from the northwest blew it away from the airports. And at Hink, by midnight, the thermometer was down to twenty.

They were doing what they could. It wasn't much.

The enemy had stabbed in with four planes. Not three, as the first report had stated. One had carried the bomb. Cohen got it, died with it, too late. One plane had either been strictly reconnaissance or had turned yellow. It had vanished to the west, at any rate, right after the bomb. The other two, going fast, had run around the perimeter of the city, time and again, pursued by fighters that couldn't catch them. They'd taken their time and ultimately dropped parachute-borne aerosol-spray germ bombs. After that, one plane had calmly landed in Gordon Field and the crew had tried to surrender to the airport police. It was found that one of the crew members could speak English, just before a civilian had snatched a Tommy gun from a cop and shot the whole crew.

The other plane had been brought down by Lieutenant Pfeffer, in a jet fighter. Pfeffer had come back from that feat alive.

General Boyce had ordered his Crash Plan into effect.

He had stripped the Base to send food and medical supplies, hospital corpsmen and medical officers into the cities. He had sent all the Base fire-fighting equipment. He had called up every enlisted man and every noncommissioned officer, paymasters, bandmasters, cooks, bakers, dental hygienists—every man in uniform except the regular guard. To these he had added the mixed service personnel who had reported to him, since his was the only military establishment in the region: marines and gobs, naval officers, WACS and even WAVES, many veterans, and all the National Guardsmen who showed up there, when they learned they had no armories left. He broke out every weapon and all the ammo. He started officers organizing rescue and aid squads, emergency military police, technical-assistance squads. He sent all the communications and signal people he could spare to the Green Prairie CD authorities: he couldn't raise anybody in River City who would accept that kind of help.

He put some of his technical staff to work on bomb determinations. He sent out his two helicopters, with special observers to swing around the stricken areas and spot and report rescue needs. He sent light planes in, and two bombers, to reinforce that mission. He prepared parachute bundles of water and food for quick air-drops into the areas where people were trapped by fire and debris—parks and playgrounds, golf courses, reservoirs, playing fields. He got volunteers, three hundred, all he needed—though most were without experience—to jump as required into such beleaguered areas.

He kept Colorado Springs fully informed as to the situation, civilian and military. He knew about the western and the northern stampede of the panic-driven people of River City before the first cars and trucks began to pass Hink. He had a road block set up and the people cared for as fast as they arrived. However, he was aware that two main refugee groups—perhaps a hundred thousand people in each—were following Route 401 which led eventually to Kansas City, and along Elk Drive toward Gordon Field, the civil airport. He sent a heavy guard to the airport to try to stop the stampede there and another, the first members of which were air-dropped, to block Highway 401 if they could.

Straggling, secondary mobs were moving west along the river valley and south from Green Prairie; General Boyce let them go: there was only the empty country ahead, but he hadn't manpower enough to try to protect it.

He did not realize how futile such efforts would be until the account of what happened at Gordon Field came in by military phone. When his motley troops arrived there, several thousand people had already reached the airport and most had gone on past, but hundreds had turned in. They were without control or meaningful plan—fear-maddened men and women and children who rushed indoors, promptly looted the airport concessions, smashed the furniture, insanely demolished the ticket counters, rushed out on the field, entered waiting planes, got themselves hit on runways by service equipment and, in general, turned the airport into headless hell. They were reinforced by persons arriving from the main highway at a rate of a hundred a minute or more.

A naval commander with an ice-cold voice soon requested permission to shoot. General Boyce refused it.

Twenty minutes later, the naval officer phoned again and

reported that his men were being attacked and in some cases wounded or killed by mob members who grabbed away their guns and bayonetted them.

Boyce ordered the shooting.

A cluster of men in a variety of uniforms, backed into a corner of the airport, fired at an advancing, howling horde of citizens, killing and wounding many, including children. They had time for two more volleys before they were over-swarmed by a wave of madmen who yelled, "Gestapo." Their weapons were wrested from them and turned upon them. Most were slaughtered.

On Highway 401 the carnage came sooner because the mar-ine colonel in command ordered shooting at the first signs of a failure of his attempt to halt traffic. The shots stopped cars and big trucks and blocked the road. Cars and trucks behind broke through a farmer's barbed-wire fence and drove around. When they were again shot at, some drivers leaped upon their assailants in pure frenzy. Others drove cars through them. Shortly, the remnant of the colonel's men were in hid-ing, behind a rise of ground, watching the maniacal hordes pour north—the flame, smoke, radiation and hell of River City hot on their backs.

Chuck Conner had not been sent out on any of these patrols because orders for him to stand by had arrived from his home base. Colonel Eames had signed the orders personally, it appeared, and although Chuck protested that he knew River City and Green Prairie better than most of the men sent in to assist, they stuck to protocol, assigning Chuck to the Oper-ations room, pending the availability of transportation which would make it possible to carry out Chuck's orders. So Chuck saw the fire storm from a distance of many miles. But his knowledge of the two burning cities helped in shaping plans for reconnaissance and for air-drops.

He was aware, as the night progressed, that General Boyce held himself to blame—and himself alone—for the local delay in using the sirens. Chuck remembered the discussion in the afternoon, as if he were remembering something that had happened a year or two ago; he knew that the mayor of River City was responsible for the delay, if anyone could be held blameworthy.

"The old man," a captain said to Chuck as they studied the wall map and the incoming reports, "is in poor shape. I never saw him so quiet. He thinks he lost the people in the shopping crowds."

"That's foolish!" Chuck answered, staring at the map, wondering if the K. and C.L. railroad embankment would make a firebreak of any lasting value. "Because, if the sirens had let go, they'd have just traffic-blocked themselves and been penned under Ground Zero all the same!"

"You sound mighty calm about it all, Lieutenant!"

Chuck gave a ghastly smile. "That's the only way I dare be. All my folks are—yonder—in it."

"Oh." The other man tapped with a pencil. "Sorry."

Chuck's smile was steadier. "It's okay."

He merely happened to be coming back from the latrine when he saw the general step out through the door onto the field. It was a peculiar thing for him to do and odd for him to be alone and Chuck stepped out to speak to him. But the general had already walked some distance onto a hardstand and was staring at the fire. He was wearing side arms. Chuck had thought nothing of that.

General Boyce whipped out his forty-five and shot himself through the head so suddenly that Charles couldn't even shout. And before Charles reached his side, three grease monkeys had arrived and were kneeling.

Toward midnight, Charles was assigned a patrol and ordered into River City to do what he could about panic, looting, whatever might be handled. "Only," said the tragic-faced colonel who gave the orders, "don't expose your men to fire unless you have to. Don't try to obstruct any big groups of human beings. We can only let the madness itself burn out of them—and God help whoever they encounter!"

9

By what back streets and alleyways Nora had come, climbing over what masses of brick, past what unspeakable sights, Alice would never know, didn't ask, didn't want to know.

"There's a child in here," one of the nurses had said, as Alice moved out of one blood-washed operating room and started toward the other. "She wants to speak to you."

"Good *heavens!*" The superintendent's annoyance was plain.

"She says you bought her lunch. She says she wants help for Mrs. Sloan. And she has the old dame's pocketbook, with eleven hundred dollars in it."

Alice Groves looked at a curved needle, threaded with a suture, which she held in her hand. She listened to the soughing of the fire wind and watched the jitterbug reflection on the painted wall, felt tremor in the floors and listened intently to the groan that came up from the hot streets. Somehow she ran her mind backward to the cities that were gone, the streets, the skyscrapers, the White Elephant Restaurant. "Oh," she said slowly. "Where is she?"

Nora was brought. Her hair was burned ragged, her eyebrows were gone, her face, on one side, was red and peeling. Her mittens were two big holes through which her fingers showed, raw—from the broken masonry everywhere. Her shoes were slit and her feet bled. Nobody could have recognized her under the dirt; she was hardly identifiable as a child, or even as a person. But her voice was about the same. "Hello, Miss Groves. I left Mrs. Sloan in a big car up the street a few blocks. But it took *so* long to get here!"

Alice Groves thought of all the people between that "car" and the Infirmary. "What's wrong with her?"

"Her legs got mashed and she's unconscious."

"Is her body mashed?"

"Oh, no. She's all right. Her heart's going good. We listened to it."

"We?"

"Jeff, that's her butler. He ran—toward the end. Willis, that's the chauffeur. He had a stroke or something."

"And you came on here?"

"Well, I finally did. I had to go back and around and every whichway—and I climbed in a window that was too little for some men—because they were thinking of climbing in and couldn't." She added, "Colored men. They boosted me."

"I don't know who we could send," Alice Groves murmured. "Could you tell the nurses where her car is and what it looks like?"

"Oh, yes. It's a green Buick sedan and it's just this side of St. Angelica Street, a little on the right."

One of the nurses said, "Let her die there, the old rip!"

Alice Groves shook her head. "She—her husband—built us this place. And she maintained it. And she was coming to us for help."

"She didn't *know* she was coming," Nora said honestly. "She was brought."

Alice smiled. "Miss Elman, see if Dr. Symes will come off a ward and take a bag and try to reach her. He used to play football, and if anybody could get through . . ."

Another doctor, a colored man, in white, white clothes bloodier than any butcher's, leaned from the operating room doorway. "Miss Groves, could you *please!* We've got a *bad* head wound here . . ."

Alice nodded. "In a sec!" She addressed the nurse again. "Have we got a bed anywhere—crib—cradle—mattress . . . ?"

"Yours is still empty . . ."

As the superintendent went back to work, she said, "Take her up. Give her a shot—she's out on her feet."

10

On the phone, Henry Conner said sharply to the Presbyterian minister, "Well, if it's starting to freeze people on the north side of the Lake, move them where they get some warmth!"

"There's no more space on the banks, Henry."

"Great God! Beg your pardon. You mean . . . ?"

"I mean, Henry, we've got the church full and Jenkins Memorial and every house that's safety-inspected and all the terraces around Crystal Lake—you can't walk fast without stepping on a hand! And the thermometer's down to thirty now, and we've run out of blankets!"

"Build fires. Bonfires."

"Where? With what?"

"Good God—beg your pardon—that's Jerome's lookout. Where is he?"

"A side wall fell and killed Jerome, Henry."

The sector chief sat a moment, drumming on his desk. "Look. See about this. There must be five . . . six gas stations above the lake on Windmere. Build your fires by using fences, porches, houses—if you need to. Take the manse apart. And pour on the gasoline. Siphon it down—garden hoses . . . !"

The minister's voice was steady. "Will do, Henry."

11

Kit looked back. You could see the light of the fire still but not the flame itself. He didn't know where he was, just some-place well to the west. He didn't know the make of the car he drove—and recalled only dimly that he'd hit a fellow on the head to get it. He'd done that after seeing the wreck of Gordon Field and giving up the hope of flying. He was about at the end of his rope, he felt; *bushed.* When he hit a stretch where he couldn't see a car ahead, or car lights in his rearview mirror, he watched along the side road and spotted a big, white farmhouse. He turned in the drive, switching his lights off. There were cattle in the barns, he could hear them. There were ducks in the trees, white ducks. And light leaked around the front window blinds, so someone was in the place. He knocked.

The door opened a couple of inches. "I need help," Kit said. "Penicillin," he added, eagerly.

A gruff, not inimical voice replied. "You alone?"

"Yes."

"Come from the city?"

"Yes."

"I'm sorry, mister. We don't dare let no one in. The radio tells us folks out here not to open doors or even show a light."

"I saw your light."

"Not from the road, you didn't! I looked."

"I'm Kit Sloan, maybe you've heard the name. I've got to rest a minute. *Bathe!* Eat something, get a drink of water . . ."

"You mean—old lady—Mrs. Minerva Sloan's son?"

"Yes." Kit shivered. Bubonic, maybe, cholera. Musn't let them know he was infected.

Chain rattled. The door opened.

Kit's red eyes fell first upon a tall, rufous farmer with a shotgun across his arm. In the parlor behind him were four pretty girls and a plump, middle-aged woman who looked something like all four. Only one lamp was lighted and the radio was talking like firecrackers, but turned down low. The girls were young—perhaps twelve to seventeen or eighteen. Kit said, "Thank you, sir," to the farmer.

"Guess it's all right," the man answered. "You ain't armed, even. Couple of fellows stopped by a minute ago—they were. I was kind of nervous, but they tried the door and then beat it. Your mother's bank holds our mortgage, Mr. Sloan."

The smiles of the frightened girls, the sturdy look of their mother, the composed tone of their towering father brought Kit part way back to his senses. He looked down at his clothes, repressing horror. Some Asiatic disease, probably, that the sulfas and antibiotics wouldn't touch.

They all looked.

"Marylou," said the bearded man, "run up and get something from Chet's closet. Mr. Sloan, here, is kind of dirtied up." He set the shotgun in the corner and turned to his unwanted guest. "My name's Simpson. Albert Simpson"—— He jerked his head—"The missus—my daughters, Mr. Sloan. The bank."

Kit said, "This is very kind of you."

"I'll get you something," Mrs. Simpson put a workbasket aside. Kit realized, with a kind of feverish resentment, that she had been listening to everything the radio must have been saying—and darning. "We have fresh milk . . . ?"

"If you have anything stronger . . . ?" he ventured.

"I'm afraid that——"

"There's brandy—in the medicine chest," Mr. Simpson said.

"Brandy would be fine."

"Sarah, go get it."

They stared while he poured all their brandy into a tumbler, which it half filled, and then drank it like water.

"We're prohibitionists here," Mr. Simpson smiled. "More or less. I don't suppose you'd care to say anything about— where you came from?" He saw Kit's immense shudder. "Likely not. What's *that*, now!"

He rose, grabbed the shotgun and went to the door. The sound of a big truck grinding up the driveway grew louder and louder. Then it stopped on shrill brakes and many men's voices filled the night.

The door knocked.

The farmer unlocked it, on the chain. "Who's there?"

They shot him through the head.

The front windows kicked in.

In a trance of horror, Kit watched the men enter. Two— then four or five—then a dozen. They were grinning a little. They were drunk. They were the kind of men who wear caps and work in alleys. They eyed the girls with joy.

On the staircase, Marylou stopped—a clean shirt and washed jeans folded over one arm. She started to back up the stairs.

Her mother and sisters said nothing, nothing at all.

"Come on downstairs, baby!" one of the men called, smirking.

Marylou backed another step. The man aimed a pistol and fired. The railing chipped. Marylou came on down then, still holding her brother Chet's clean clothes.

The women looked hopefully at Kit. He said, in a thin squeal, "You men move on."

"Oh, yeah?"

"This is a private home. You've just done *murder!*"

Kit threw himself on the floor. It was his idea to get out—nothing else. His powerful muscles sent him slithering toward the dark hall. He didn't even try to pick up the shotgun. He heard their shots and vaguely felt referred impact, from the floorboards. He reached the hall. He half stood, unchained the door, ran out.

Somebody bellowed through the smashed windows, "Hey, Red! *Get* that jerk!"

Kit saw the trees against the luminous sky line, the square silhouette of the truck, the palely white porch bannister. Flame squirted from the truck and his body was seared. He fell down the steps and lay without moving on his back.

He wished, seeing the stars as they began to swim and cavort, he'd at least grabbed the shotgun and plugged a couple of them.

In the parlor, the men turned toward the rigid women. "Going to be a nice little party," one said, licking his lips. "Private-like."

Others laughed. One yelled, "Hey—*Red!* Come on in! We found *five* of 'em!"

They moved toward the four girls and their mother.

She said, softly, "Pray, children."

But nobody was listening to prayers that night.

12

Toward morning, but in that part of the hours when it should have been darkest, Henry left his second-in-command at his desk and went out in the night with the police lieutenant, Lacey. Some streets, some avenues, were slots leading arrow-straight to the fire storm, box-ended with flame. Other thoroughfares merely caught the downbeat of illumination. On them, great shadows danced as the grotesque, the monstrous pyre flickered in the sky. Here and there, night infiltrated a row of houses, loomed in a stand of stores or glowered from the windows of a stalled streetcar. Elsewhere, a building or a home burning individually—and as a rule under siege by volunteers—made a big candle for this block or that.

They went farther south. Henry had the lieutenant make their first stop, so he could inspect the injured on the banks of Crystal Lake.

Torches and bonfires glared on the near terraces, glimmered across the ice. Upon the metallic surface of the lake itself, men hurried hither and thither, some pulling children's sleds heaped with clapboards and smashed steps, balustrades, broken ladders, branches, anything combustible. In the once-elegant yards all around other men were chopping. The earth was humanity-covered—a litter of supine men and women and children, blanketed, quilted, dressed like hobgoblins, warming fires spaced between. The snow here had turned to mud. And here the roar of the fire storm was a mumble. The earth quivered only a little.

Here, the night was rent by one single shriek, one voice of a myriad in agony.

Lacey crossed himself when first he heard it, as he stopped his car and switched off its siren.

Henry went closer. His skin pimpled with horror, his feet

felt like freight, he wanted to retch. But the fires sent a drift of woodsmoke over the bloodscape and the burned-meat smell was abruptly overridden. He saw a doctor whom he remembered from the meetings.

"How's it going?" Henry yelled.

"Don't be a *fool*, man! *Oh!* You, eh, Henry?" The physician straightened up. A syringe glinted in his hand. "What can you expect?" he bellowed back. "They're still dying! Blood's run out. Plasma was out for a while—Army got some in. Cold. Some freeze."

"I can't spare any more people right now."

"We've got *people* enough," the doctor answered, bending even as he talked, fishing for an ampule in a case slung over his shoulder. "Unless you have more *medical* people."

"No more medical people." Henry shouted.

The physician stabbed a needle into the arm of a child. Her mouth opened. She was screaming. You couldn't hear it at all, Henry realized. It was lost in the general scream.

"Help from outlying towns——" Henry broke off, said it more loudly because the doctor had cupped his ear, "Help from outside will be coming in by morning."

The doctor just nodded and turned away, looking at the patient-covered earth for the next one.

Because of the red headlights and the siren, they got across on Decatur and came back north to the Country Club, where the brief meeting was to be held. The clubhouse had no windows but it did have electric lights, which astonished Henry until he recalled that he had voted—years before, when he'd still had his membership—to put in a power plant simply to show a little spunk to the electric company. Ambulances were feeding people into the club. It was a better place than the shore of Crystal Lake.

They went into the main room, which seemed a bright

glare after a night of emergency illumination. A few dozen of the scattered easy chairs had been pulled together and faced in one direction. Sighing, not removing his overcoat, because it was cold there, Henry dropped into a chair. Lacey took a seat beside him. Perhaps fifty men were there already. They, like Henry, were just sitting, sitting low in the upholstered chairs, saying nothing.

The CD chief, McVeigh, came down an aisle left between the chairs. He was followed by two women who wore CD brassards. They pulled up a big library table, helped by the men in the front row. Then McVeigh faced the sector leaders and their delegates:

"We've had to pull out of headquarters," he said. "Fire storm making it too difficult to save the place." His face grimaced as if of its own accord: "What was *left* of it, I mean to say. Here's why I asked you to come over or send a delegate. We've got it bad, but River City's far worse. The bulk of their firefighting apparatus lost. Most doctors dead or casualties. Short —almost out entirely—of every class of personnel. The whole city panicked. Nobody's coming down from Kansas City or up from Omaha; nobody who'll do any good, that is. Hundreds of unchecked fires over there, besides their half of the main show. Thousands—tens of thousands of people—still in the city. We don't have to worry, for the moment, about the bulk of them. Because mostly they swarmed out of town. Point is, what can the Green Prairie outfit do to help —if anything?"

Not a man in the room spoke.

McVeigh nodded. "I know how you feel. I do myself. But what are we dealing with? Certainly not local pride. Simply human numbers. If you can save ten here, you let one go there. *Right?* All night I've been getting appeals from Jeffrey Allison—he's *their* chief. I can't decide alone. You'll have to help me. We never figured we'd have to salvage River City. It was their job, that they didn't prepare for. If you sector heads could spare even one person in ten, of every classification, beginning at dawn———?"

A man whom Henry did not know stood up. "I can't spare a man. I can't spare *myself here*. I can use ten more for every man and woman I've got!"

There was a sound of agreement.

McVeigh studied the faces for a moment. "About fifty thousand people," he said slowly, "crowded into the ball park. God knows why. Somebody started it—the rest followed. Maybe a third were kids. They filled the field solid; then the bleachers caught fire and the whole mob stampeded. *They're* up there, what remains of 'em. Not one doctor. *Nothing*. That's how things are all over River City."

Henry stood up. "How can you get people around?"

McVeigh's face cracked with a momentary look of relief. "I've got trucks. The roads in close are almost deserted now. The main swarm's gone far beyond. You tell"—he jerked his head toward the women with arm bands—"these ladies how many men you can spare and at what point they can be picked up—and I'll deliver them across the river. God knows they're needed!"

"We'll tithe," Henry said.

Lieutenant Lacey grabbed his arm: "You *can't* do it, Hank! That doctor just told you—we're short on the medical end———"

"No medical end at all at the ball park."

"You'll be letting Green Prairie people die!"

Henry nodded. His eyes were empty. The room was listening to this private argument. "Sure. Green Prairie people will die. One for ten, didn't he say?"

McVeigh cut in. "That's about the size of it. Much as our

people can do here, they can do ten times as much where there isn't any functioning group at all."

"Okay," Henry said. "We'll get going. I'll have about a hundred and fifty ready in an hour—for your first load."

Henry stalked from the room. Behind him, he could hear other sector chiefs making offers. It didn't hearten him. He felt no pride in having started the ball rolling. He'd never done a tougher thing in his life: he'd condemned some of the provident to save many of the improvident. He wasn't even sure it was just.

"Mr. Conner!" someone called from across the club porch. "Yeah?"

The man ran up. "Thought you ought to know. Your son Ted was running a walkie-talkie down the line. Got buried in a brick slide. They're trying to dig him out now." The man said that and ducked away through the dark. He picked up a rolled stretcher, slung it over his shoulder, trotted toward a waiting ambulance.

Henry took hold of a porch post. He felt Lacey's hand on his arm.

"I know about where that crew was," the police lieutenant said. "Let's go!"

The other man sobbed just once. He took one immense breath. His head shook. "What the hell extra could two of us do? Let's get on."

While Lacey drove, Henry used the car radio. He ordered his subordinates to take one tenth of the personnel—medical, rescue, first aid, decontamination, and so on—off what they were doing. Quietly, firmly he put down frantic protests. He arranged for the assembly of the selected people and said he'd be back as soon as he finished his inspection.

While Henry gave the orders, Lacey kept glancing at him. He looked, shook his head, turned to the business of driving through partially blocked streets, past fire-fighting points, and turned back to stare again at the man beside him, to shake his head slowly. Henry didn't notice.

They went down to the perimeter. That was where things were toughest. All the way around the fire storm's edge. The spot they had chosen was the closest practicable approach, on Bigelow Avenue.

This particular juncture of street and flame occurred at the site of a number of apartment houses built in the latter part of the First World War. They had been vast structures, six stories high, brick on the outside, wood within—built hastily to accommodate white-collar workers in the booming new industries of the Sister Cities.

The atomic bomb had not only collapsed these buildings on their tenants but hurled on top of them, by some freak of blast, the contents of a half-dozen small factories and machine shops, closer in town, along with the scrap and metal stocks in the yards of the plants. From this area, all night, Henry had been besieged with calls for monitors, for medical and aid people, for rescue and decontamination personnel as well as fire fighters. Here, more furiously than anywhere else in his sector, the rescue battle raged. It was conducted against a backdrop of the fire storm which seethed straight into the sky at what seemed no distance at all, down Bigelow Avenue. It was actually some blocks distant, yet near enough so that a man could not stand long exposure to the direct heat of it. For intense heat baked outward from the fire wall in spite of the wind, a near-hurricane draft which bellowed and squealed down the street, tearing loose parts of roofs and sucking them in, whipping the clothing of the rescuers with painful force, even knocking down men and women who tripped or were careless. The wind fed oxygen to the titanic, fiery wall.

There was no water pressure in the mains here. They had

been shattered. The fire companies had long since abandoned the scene. All that stood was a great moraine of debris which had been apartments the day before—a miscellaneous mountain that furnished a barricade against the fire-head, a flame-lee, but no windbreak.

Into it, during the night, spelling one another, men had tunneled their way. Wherever they had holed through to rooms, halls or their crushed remains, they had found the living and living-dead——these last because masses of metals in the machining area were close to the fireball; they had been violently irradiated and were giving back that deadliness now. Some of the tunneled corridors in the debris were entirely safe; many were passable to people who did not stay too long: but some were contaminated beyond a radiation level that permitted any exposure, however brief. And the farther the rescuers fought their way into the fantastic scramble of the apartment houses, the more deadly the ray dosages became.

Henry had come to this place with a view to ordering his crews back farther. The proximity of the fire storm constantly threatened the rubble mass with burning, in which case it would become a mere addition to the central torrent of heat and flame. The general outdoor radiation level, high at many points near the fire storm, was endangering everyone who worked in this area for too many hours. South of the apartment buildings, furthermore, was a wide, empty space in the process of conversion from a near-slum to a new development. It had been bulldozed bare and would serve, even if the crushed apartments caught, to prevent further local spread of the great, central blaze. This fire, in any case and most providentially, had only a minor tendency to eat its way outward: the hurricane force of in-sucked winds controlled and delimited the fire storm: it could not be put out by any human device, or by any number of human beings and machines; but it would burn out.

Shielding their faces from the hot wall of light, the two men approached a group of rescuers at work on the mountain of debris. One of them stepped forward, a man so black with soot and white with plaster as to be unrecognizable. He bellowed above the drum roll of the fire, "Hi, Henry! Ed Pratt."

Henry nodded. "What's the situation now?" Ed, who had a house-painting business, was in charge of this team.

"About like our last talk. We got out over a hundred people, but we've only dug in about halfway." He gestured toward some men hauling, tug-of-war fashion, on ropes. "We're trying to deepen a passage now." The ropes disappeared in a hole in the mass.

Henry went closer, followed by Lacey. "How hot is it?" He was not aware that he was shouting. The fire storm here was like near, continual thunder. But it was necessary to converse in shouts almost everywhere that night.

Ed waved at the blaze. "Gettin' warmer in there all the time. Awful-looking thing, ain't it?"

Henry hardly glanced at the intimidating fire wall. "I mean, *radiation* hot?"

"Oh! This new tunnel we're making—I dunno. Got a monitor in there now, measuring!"

The rope-pullers shouted in unison, heaved together, and from the ragged entrance of their "tunnel" they drew forth a huge fragment of floor and ceiling lumber. Henry could see that the opening ran for at least a hundred feet into the wreckage. He shuddered and asked loudly. "How do you know that cave will hold up?"

He couldn't see Ed Pratt's expression but he could guess it from the man's voice: "We *don't* know! Matter of fact, a few hours back one tunnel roof fell. We were trying to work the fire side of this mess then. Lost five of my people—and one of your radiation monitors. Couldn't get back to 'em. A whole hunk of apartment came down between them and us."

"You mean—they're *still* in there?"

"If they weren't crushed, they maybe are. But it's pretty hot on that side now. They're probably cooked up by this time."

A figure—then another—showed in the tunnel. Behind trudged a third and a fourth. They carried flashlights. The broken, snaglike intrusions in the tunnel made their approach slow. The first one, Henry saw, was wearing the yellow, plastic garments of a monitor and carrying a counter. This was the one who addressed Ed Pratt and, until he bent close, he didn't realize it was a woman. Even then he did not recognize Lenore.

"It's too high a level," she reported. "We got to a lot of metal and kind of a big cave beyond, but it's too hot to stick around. You can't send your people any deeper, Mr. Pratt. In minutes they'd get enough radiation to be sick—maybe die."

The men who had made the perilous trek with her stood by, panting a little, opening and shutting hands that were raw from pulling on timbers, throwing brick, moving heavy bits of building. Other rescue workers gathered around and passed the report along. One of the three who'd gone into the tunnel with Lenore said, "Pity. Beyond that opening she talked about, you could hear kids calling."

Henry looked with fear and horror at the demolished building, at the frightening flame. He looked at the rescue people, and they were eying him. "This whole crew," he yelled out, "will get in touch with my headquarters for another assignment!" He jerked his head. "Abandon this! You've done what you can."

That was that. Men nodded. One or two women cried. But people began throwing picks, shovels, crowbars, a block-and-tackle, other gear into a metal truck. A bulldozer came alive and moved off in the street. Joe Dennison was driving it.

That was that—until Henry heard a shout near the tunnel mouth and saw two men rush in.

"They shouldn't!" The woman with the radiation counter exclaimed.

Henry recognized her then. "Great God Almighty," he whispered. He reached out and gripped her arm. Her teeth showed white in a kind of smile. Her face was black as a miner's.

"How about your family?" Lenore asked. She was hoarse from much shouted talk.

Henry felt the pain again. "I don't know, dear! I don't know!" He held his head close to reduce the need for bellowing every word. "Ted's under a brick slide . . ."

"I'm sorry."

"Mother's up at the First Aid. Nora—search me! Chuck reported yesterday at Hink Field."

She nodded. She looked, briefly but in a special way, at the fire storm. Henry knew what she was thinking: Chuck was not in there; he hadn't been caught downtown as she'd feared. But she didn't mention her feelings. "Gotta get cracking," she said and left.

He looked, now, at the tunnel. That was where she'd been. In that hole through hell. There, where the roof might fall, where there could be a gas explosion, where she might be burned alive or slowly baked alive, suffocated, smothered, crushed, even drowned, pinned in some spot where a pipe leaked.

The crew was clearing out in cars and trucks, going someplace unknown to Henry. He hadn't asked where. There were more assignments than people. And his people, he reflected grimly, were being reduced in numbers now to aid River City.

"Shall we get along?" Lacey asked.

"*Wait.*" Henry approached the tunnel, followed by the lieutenant.

"You recognize your neighbor? The Bailey girl?"

"Yes."

"Guts."

Henry didn't reply. He just nodded and bent to peer into the dark dreadfulness of the hole the rescuers had made and abandoned, the hole into which two men, against orders, had plunged. For what seemed a long time nothing happened.

It wasn't, Henry thought, actually long, but merely long by the standards of that night: ten minutes, perhaps, or maybe less. Then he saw a wink of lights and shadows moving. One man made his way to the tunnel mouth and put down the thing in his arms. It was a baby and it cried.

The man turned back.

"Got a torch?" Henry asked the policeman.

"*You* can't go in!" Lacey yelled back. "Too risky for *you!*"

"Got a torch?"

Lacey went to the squad car and returned. He followed Henry into the tunnel.

Far down, they encountered the other man, helping along two children, who wept and shivered. Lacey, on Henry's orders, led them back.

It was quiet in there. One of the men said to Henry, "You

stay here, sir. Beyond this point, the radiation's bad. There's only one more kid and Sam's getting her free. No use exposing yourself. We've already had the full dose and he won't need help."

The man left. He was gone awhile. Henry stood still, more frightened than he'd known he could be.

He could see, in the light of a lantern left by the tunnel-makers, what had happened. A weight of machinery and sheet metal had cut through the collapsing building and piled up, just ahead; that was the point of peak radioactivity, he was sure. Beyond, apparently with another lantern in it, he saw a kind of opening, room-sized; a girder or some other structural member had held up the debris. Beyond that was a doorway with a smashed-off door. Behind it, somewhere in the darkness, they'd found the children.

The second man came, with a form on his shoulder. A little girl, unconscious. As he passed the metal mass, he turned his back and put the inert girl in front of him, shielding her body with his own. Henry appreciated that what these two men had done might succeed, for the children. They might survive. But the men had quite likely received ultimately fatal doses of radiation when they tore a path around the intrusion of scrap metal. Some of the rescue squad, too, had probably been marked for sickness, at least, by working there, before Lenore arrived to measure.

Henry said nothing then. The man indicated the lantern with his toe. Henry picked it up, following. Soon they were outdoors in the light of the fire storm—in the strange night, where a cold wind blew on their faces and their backs were seared by heat. Lacey had loaded the other children.

The man carried the unconscious girl to the car and put her in, too. His brave companion was just standing by the fender, a smile of satisfaction on his face.

"I'll send a car back for you two," Henry said. "We'll do everything we can—over at the Country Club. Got good doctors there. They may be able to . . ."

One man said, "Thank you."

Henry gazed at them. "That was the finest thing I ever saw. Who *are* you two guys?"

The nearer one, a rather slight man, who was dabbing at the blood from a cut on his arm, laughed and answered, "I'm Jerome Taggert, minister of the Bigelow Street Baptist Church, and Sam is Father Flaugherty of St. Bonaventure's Roman Catholic . . ."

Henry said, "Oh," and kept looking back at them as Lacey drove away.

13

Six men rode in the weapons carrier. Chuck was in command.

A sailor drove. They cruised street after street of the severe damage area. But there was not much left to do. Where they heard screams, they investigated, helped if they could. They didn't search buildings and houses: it was too dangerous and there were too many such structures ready to fall, falling occasionally with an alarming roar, on fire, smoking. Here and there in River City they encountered individuals or groups at work—police, a few CD volunteers, firemen. These few who had stood fast were trying to concentrate on such measures as would save the little that remained.

They had thrown a guard around St. Agnes Hospital, east of Market, and prevented the mob from stopping all useful work inside. They had kept the fringe fires from eating their way to the Mildred Tatum Infirmary. They had checked the reservoir for dangerous radioactivity and taken the dead bodies out of it. They had collected most of the wandering children, hurt or not, and sent them in cars outside River City to a big orphanage. These and other things the citizens of River City had done in the long night. But their training had been near nil, their numbers were pitifully inadequate, and for every saving effort they made, they had to watch helplessly while many times the number were lost.

Chuck realized, as they drove through the empty streets, that it was getting light. He gazed toward the fire storm, but that was not the source. The flame, in fact, was lessening in width and density. The light came from the sky again, from the east, where the sun would soon rise.

The sergeant in charge of the two-way radio began to speak, saying a number of "Yes, sirs" into the mike. He signed off.

"That was Hink Field, Lieutenant. All squads not engaged now in vital action are to rendezvous at the field. There's to be breakfast. Dispersion afterward to try to check panic in the outlying areas." The sergeant spat from the vehicle. "That ought really to be an assignment. The base said that about twenty towns around here have been taken over——"

"Taken over?" Chuck repeated.

"By the mobs. River City people, mostly. But they said it was nothing to what was happening up toward KC. People from here, in cars, have piled up against people from Kansas City, also in cars and trucks, headed this way—and all roads are blocked—and they're hungry and freezing and fanning out, burning barns and houses just to keep warm, cleaning out every little town, smashing all grocery stores and super-markets, all jewelry stores. Women are being advised to take to the woods, all over the nation. *Boy!* If *that* isn't something!"

"Let's go," Chuck said to the sailor-chauffeur.

As the weapons carrier rushed toward the new "front,"

Chuck thought of the conversations he'd had, over the years, with his father.

Here it was. Here was all that the experts said could never happen. Here was gigantic panic, uncontrolled and hideous.

To tens of thousands of River City people, this was the pay-off. It wrecked such small hopes as they'd cherished, destroyed their trivial but hard-won possessions. In so doing, it broke their link with the rest of the nation, with humanity itself. In reaction, they were turning on humanity, on each other, with a final, mindless venting of their stored-up resentments, their hates, their disappointments.

Here was the infectious breakdown of the "average mind," the total collapse of man in the presence of that which he had not been willing to face. This was the lurid countenance of something unknown because he refused to know.

Here, too, Chuck could see, was that other fear—the horror of a bomb survived, raised to excruciating horror by the terror of another. *Get out of the city:* it was all they could think of. *Get out now while you still have unburned meat to move your unbroken bones.* That simple.

People in all cities, apparently—even where no bomb yet had fallen—were going out in the same way, for the same reason and with the same violence of fear, which would reach astronomical scope as soon as they found the countryside no refuge but a place of hostility, of unwelcome, of battle, of different but equally terrible peril.

Since these human effects were like his father's predictions, like them, yet even more formidable, Chuck thought that beyond doubt his father's further fear was sound. His dad knew people. His dad had felt that perhaps, just perhaps, the great cities would not only vomit themselves into the countryside, but that the self-expelled people would not go back to any city, now, or soon, or ever, in some cases. To tens of millions the only image of a city would be, for months, for years even, the image of what they'd seen happen to people in their own city or of what they'd heard had happened in many cities.

And who would set the pace for this flood of depopulation? Who but the worst elements, frightened beyond caring, doing what had thitherto been only fantasy, having a last fling —criminal, psychopathic—in the presence of the end of the world?

Green Prairie had tried to brace itself even against that; Chuck prayed they were succeeding.

River City had not even tried.

The vehicle surged over a hill. Across the prairie was the village of Harmondale. It had stood there as long as Chuck could remember, like a post-card village, like a Grant Wood painting, neat and crisp, stores and steeples, white houses and red barns—a pretty cluster of orderly habitation.

Now, even across intervening miles, it had changed. Flames licked up the church spires; smoke rose over Main Street. And all around the village was a multitude, with its trucks and cars and luggage and duffel—a dark smear of humanity closing in on the hamlet, scores of attackers for every defender. Harmondale was fighting, still, for whatever remained of its life. As Chuck's driver slowed, they could hear a constant fusillade of guns in the town.

But what could his men do against that human amoeba? The village would be sacked and abandoned. The amoeba would go on, hungrily.

14

Beth Conner trudged home. She had waited awhile in line, for a ride, with other women being relieved. But many of them lived farther away; and some didn't even have homes of their own to rest in any longer. She decided to walk and she moved along in the smoky streets, still carrying her suitcase, breathing whitely in the frigid air.

It was Christmas morning, she thought dazedly.

When she saw the house, she stood for a long time, with tears in her eyes that did not fall.

It didn't sit quite right any more. A chunk of the roof was gone, up over the boys' room in the attic. The front yard was a pile of debris—some from the house, but most of it tree limbs shoved aside by bulldozers going down Walnut Street. The windows weren't there any more. She walked around in back. The paint on the rear wall was scorched and the boards were blackened here and there. The blast had quickly blown out the fire started by the heat. Lots of people had been lucky that way. The metal garage was all right.

She went back around to the front and glanced over at the Bailey house. It was about the same, except that the modernized façade had peeled off and you could see beams and studs and lath and plaster clear across the face of the house. The people across Walnut were better off. There was a slight dip in the land, behind the Conner and the Bailey house; the bomb blast had rushed up to it; and the houses across the street had been given some protection by those on the Conners' side.

She went up on her front porch. The steps were loose under her feet and there was a big white, printed sign nailed on the door. "Inspected," the sign said. "Safe for occupancy.

Use extreme caution. Beware of fire." Underneath that, was written in red pencil, "Radiation level okay. Am okay, too. Love. Lenore."

"Bless her," Beth whispered.

She went in and put down the bag tiredly. She'd had three or four hours of sleep, all told.

She looked out the kitchen window. A great smoke towered over the north view, but there was no visible fire. The kitchen was a shambles, but she had expected that. Women coming and going from the vast hospital area at Crystal Lake had described just such messes already. She tried the gas stove; it didn't work. She went back to the hall and opened the suitcase. There was a Sterno stove in it, six cans of pink fuel, powdered coffee, sugar, tinned milk—amongst many other items. She took the things for coffee, and a flashlight, and went back to the kitchen and tried the water but that didn't run either.

Downstairs, in the air-raid shelter Henry had fixed up years before, were the five-gallon bottles of distilled water he made her change every six months. She was too exhausted to lug one up but she found a pan on the floor—silently thanking Lenore, because she otherwise would not have used any metal objects. She went down in the cellar. Light penetrated it from numerous places; she could see how the house had moved on its foundations. She poured water and went into the jelly closet, discovering that most of the canned things were still on the shelves where she'd placed them, labeled and tidy, all summer long and all during the fruit season in the fall. They could eat, then, without drawing from the Green Prairie food stocks.

She went up with the water, unfolded the little stove, lit the solidified alcohol and put on the water. Someone knocked at the front door, frightening her. She ran to it.

"Hi, Mrs. Conner! Henry home yet?" It was Jed Emmings, from Spruce Street.

"Not yet."

"You all right?"

"Yes, thanks. Are you?"

"You bet—and thank God. So are my folks. I just came by, to let you know your Ted's okay, too."

"Ted?" She stared at him perplexedly. He was filthy dirty, like almost everybody. "I didn't know," she said finally, "Ted was hurt."

"Hurt bad, Mrs. Conner. But he's over in the Green Prairie Country Club, getting real good care. I was on duty there. I talked to him."

"What *happened?*"

"Got buried in a brick slide. Broke both legs."

"But . . . ?"

Jed Emmings smiled because he understood. "Absolutely okay, Mrs. Conner—or I'd have said so. No head injuries worth worrying about and nothing internal. Chipper and full of beans already. In traction, of course."

She said, "Thank you, Jed."

He nodded. "Glad to tell you. Glad to bring *some* good news to *one* door, anyhow!"

He went down the walk.

She noticed that the sun was shining. She hadn't really noticed that before. She felt almost surprised that the sun was still there in the sky in its place.

When she went back to the kitchen, the water was close to a boil. She found an unbroken cup, rinsed it, put in some hot water and a spoonful of powdered coffee, started to take sugar and refrained, sat down on the seat of an armless chair to sip the hot fluid.

A little later, she heard car brakes.

I got home just in time, she thought. More visitors.

The car went on before she reached the hall and what she heard, she did not believe. It was Nora's voice calling, "Mummie! *Mummie!* Aren't you *home?*"

There she was, running up the walk, the way she always did, and Mrs. Conner felt things start to go black because she did not, could not believe. But there was a car, going away, a colored girl at the wheel, and it wasn't quite the same Nora, coming up the steps on her spidery legs. She wore a different coat, too small for her, and a dress Beth didn't recognize. Her hat was missing and one side of her long bob had been chopped off short. There was a big pad of bandage on her right cheek. Mrs. Conner still wasn't absolutely sure, until she felt Nora in her arms.

"We thought——" she started to say.

Nora leaned back and looked up. "I had one *hell* of a time, I *really* did!" Nora said.

Henry didn't get home till evening.

15

Outside of the place where Washington had been—far outside—in a big house that had belonged to a famous eighteenth-Century American, some fifty men held a meeting in the lamp-lit drawing room. The men came there by automobile, mostly; but three or four walked, and one arrived as the original householder often had, riding on a horse. Some of the men wore bandages, two were brought on stretchers, and all of them had to go through a considerable process of identification at check points around the estate. Bayoneted rifles and even cannon bristled on every hand.

When they had assembled, when they had waited for an

hour beyond the agreed time—and greeted a few additional arrivals with quiet joy—a man who wore the white garments of a doctor, and around whose neck a stethoscope hung, said to a man in slacks and a tweed jacket, "Mr. President . . ."

The man shook his head. "I haven't taken the oath yet."

The doctor shrugged. "Mr. Gates, then. I think you ought to have the meeting soon, if possible. The Secretary of State is slipping fast."

The man in tweeds, in slacks—"Mr. Gates"—walked to the middle of the handsome drawing room and stood at the head of a carved mahogany table. A young man handed him a gavel and he rapped. Talk stopped. Every person present turned toward Mr. Gates.

"The meeting," he said, "will come to order."

Chairs moved. Attendants brought stretchers close.

Harry Jackson Gates was sworn in as President of the United States. It was done quickly, in low tones. The only Justice they could find gravely administered the oath. When it was over, all but the new President sat down. He returned to the head of the long, gleaming table. On it, there was only the gavel and a Bible.

"Our group," he began, in a somber voice, "constitutes, as you all know, all the high-echelon members of the Government who could be assembled, this frightful Christmas Day." He looked at a notebook which he took from a jacket pocket. "Three members of the late President's Cabinet are here." He named them. "Supreme Court Justice Willard. Seventeen members of the United States Senate. Thirty-eight members of the House of Representatives. In an adjacent room, General Faversham and some other high military officers are waiting and I shall ask them in—with your consent. All in favor?"

There were grave "Ayes."

"Opposed?"

Silence.

The new President nodded to the guards at a far door and it swung back. The military men came in quietly, took chairs.

The President spoke their names, gave their rank, and continued:

"I shall be brief. As you know, panic reigns from coast to coast. Four great cities were totally obliterated by hydrogen bombs in the afternoon and early evening of the twenty-third. Washington met the same fate later. Twenty-five cities have been struck by plutonium bombs of exceptionally high power. Some twenty millions of us were killed or injured in the attack. Untold numbers, hundreds of thousands, are dying in the progressively worsening riots. It is the judgment of the military"—he paused, looked at the officers—"that weeks, if not months, will be required to restore order, and an indeterminate interval, many more months, to bring the nation back to a state of production and communication which will support the survivors at a survival level. I am sure you are, in general, familiar with those ghastly facts."

There were murmurs of assent.

"Three possibilities face the United States of America. The first is—surrender."

A heart-rending *"No!"* was wreathed in low-toned murmurs of rejection.

"The enemy," the President went on grimly, "has offered terms."

That, too, stirred the audience.

"We have learned the terms by radio, through neutrals. They are quite simple. We are to surrender all atomic weapons, to dismantle all atomic plants and works, to allow enough of the enemy free access within this nation to ensure that the status is permanent. There will be no occupation, no tribute."

His eyes went over the room. Some of the haggard faces were stony. But some glowed with hope.

"A great predecessor of mine, in an hour of trial, once called an example of wanton assault 'a day that will live in infamy.' No phrase, in any language, can be made to speak the evil now done to this nation. I shall not try to give you any condemnatory words. But, let me point out, the offered terms *seem* reasonable. It is *only* a seeming. If we grant those terms, nothing—ever afterward—can prevent the enemy from working upon us whatever his further will may be. We know his philosophy. We bleed now under his treachery. Disarmed, we shall surely soon be enslaved. But surrender *is* one possibility.

"Another—is to continue the assault we are making. I assure you, the foe is suffering grievously. But his cities are so few, his dispersion of populace is so great, that our gallant Air Force cannot readily drive his people into the general panic that has uprooted this nation and destroyed its social organization. In time our effort might be equally effective. We must inquire if we have the time. The bombs, the planes, the determined men to fly them, we do have. But let us suppose the effort took thirty days. Meanwhile, other assaults would probably be launched against us. Our citizens would continue to battle one another, freeze, soon die of hunger, go mad. In the end, there might remain in both nations that utter wreckage of civilization which the few predicted for so long, and the many refused to believe. But that is a *second* possibility."

"The third?" a woman's voice called. "What's the third?"

For a moment, the new President reverted to his old habit as Speaker of the House. "The lady from Massachusetts asks the third. I'll explain as best I am able. I am not a scientist. The military will amplify."

He frowned, cleared his throat. "First, I must state that

my late, great predecessor, though he worked hopefully for peace, somewhat feared a situation like this. He feared, as did his Chiefs of Staff, the very danger we have encountered. He, with them, prepared a threat of their own—of our own —a dreadful threat, intended only for use as a menace. You are familiar with the *Nautilus* . . ."

The silence in the old room was absolute.

". . . the first of the atomic-powered submarines. As the 'peace' negotiations reached a high degree of intensity, it was felt in the—the"—he stumbled—"White House that the enemy was probably sincere. But the possibility remained that such negotiations might be the immediate precursor to the disaster that now is fact. Or to the threat of it. Consequently the *Nautilus* was drydocked and secretly reconverted. She is still a ship, still a submarine, still atomically driven, but she is also a bomb. She contains, now, the largest hydrogen bomb ever assembled, and around it and in her sides, replacing armor, and in her keel, for ballast, is the element cobalt with other readily radioactivated elements. She stands, this day, in the North Sea, awaiting orders. She could be sent swiftly into the Baltic. She could approach the ways to the enemy, dive to bottom, and explode herself."

"The crew . . . ?" someone interrupted.

Gates said nothing. His long, thin face turned toward the questioner and his hazel eyes burned into the man. Then, at last, he spoke again.

"This is one of the greater-than-super weapons mentioned at least as far back as the Truman Administration. Its exact effect is not known and cannot be calculated. A few scientists fear its detonation at sea bottom might actually set up the planetary chain reaction. Most say not. I believe the latter. It would, however, unquestionably devastate the enemy's nation, obliterate perhaps two-thirds of his people and leave hundreds upon hundreds of thousands of square miles of enemy land radioactive, deadly even to vegetation. It might, according to the uncertain vicissitudes of weather, of high-altitude winds, of the so-called jet of air which waveringly girdles our planet, transport a large amount of this lethal material across the Pacific and conceivably leave here a lesser but real train of death and sickness, sterility, misery and additional fear. That is an indeterminate risk involved in the weapon's use. It is our third possibility—the only alternative I can offer to a surrender that would surely become unconditional with passing time, or to a continuation of the existing holocaust with present weapons. I shall have a few of the military men and scientists speak to you . . ."

An hour and a quarter later, it was voted to order the *Nautilus* to proceed—and to demolish herself, and the foe.

16

They could have seen it from the planets.

On Mars, if there are naked eyes, they could have seen it without other aid.

On that Christmas night, the Baltic Sea erupted. There was no warning. The faint signals the *Nautilus* received were not intercepted by the beleaguered but seemingly victorious Reds.

She penetrated the Gulf of Finland, dove to bottom and her skipper, summoning the men, prayed, flashed a last word, and touched a small button installed some hours before on the table directly below the periscope. The rays, the temperatures, vaporized Finland's Gulf in a split part of an instant. The sea's bottom was melted. The Light reached out into the Universe.

Finland was not. Lithuania, Latvia, Esthonia, they were not. Kronstadt melted, Leningrad. The blast kicked up the ashes that once had been Moscow, collected the burning environs and pulverized them and hurled their dust at the Urals.

In the ensuing dark, a Thing swelled above the western edge of Russia, alight, alive, of a size to bulge beyond the last particles of earth's air. On the wind currents it came forward, forward across the north-sloping plains, a thick dust that widened to a hundred miles, and then five hundred, moving, spreading, descending, blanketing the land that night, and the day after, and the next. It thinned, over Siberia, thinned and spread until it was no longer blinding, till men could no longer see it or smell it or taste it. But still, where it rolled, day or night, they died.

The farther it surged from the reshaped Finnish Gulf, where the sea had come sparkling back, the longer men took to perish. But they perished. The radiation-emitting particles filled their lungs, they contaminated their food, they polluted their water and could not be filtered out. Men swallowed, ate, breathed, sickened and perished in a day, a week, two weeks —men and women and children, all of them, dogs and cats and cattle and sheep, all of them. Wherever they took refuge, men still perished. On the high Urals in the terrible cold. In the deepest mines, the steam-spitting darkness. There was no refuge from the death; it took them all, the birds of arctic winter, the persistent insects which had survived geological ages, the bacteria—all.

Surrender of those who survived, the southern dwellers of the nation, was delayed because they could not find who should make the offer; they did not care how abject the terms might be. But days passed. A week. Two weeks. And the message winged from Tiflis. It was over.

The last war was finished.

The last great obstacle to freedom had been removed from the human path.

17

On a sunny afternoon, just before June became July, during a Midwestern heat wave, a young man pushed a hand mower back and forth over a Walnut Street lawn in the city of Green Prairie. He looked to be twenty-two or -three years old though, actually, Ted Conner was not yet nineteen. He had grown big, like his Oakley grandsire, the blacksmith, bigger than his father, a good deal bigger than his older brother. In addition, there was something about his face (besides the scar on the forehead) which suggested more years than the teens. He limped, too. It was noticeable when he walked over to a shady spot behind the ferns and picked up a glass jug of water. His right leg was slightly shorter than his left.

He took a bandanna handkerchief from the belt that held up his shorts; he wiped his mouth, then his brow. After that he returned to work. But before he started the mower's clattering monody he looked at the house for a moment.

Two and a half years had passed, since the Bomb.

But only the attic windows were boarded up. Glass was still rationed—along with a hundred other things—but householders had enough, now, to take care of two floors per family. It was the necessary new construction, as much as replacement, which had caused the shortage to last so long.

The Conner house needed paint. Every house did, these days. But paint was short, also, though not rationed. They hadn't bothered yet to try to get the house back exactly on its foundations. Men had come, that first winter, with powerful

jacks and pushed the frame building as near to its proper position as they could. Joe Dennison had helped with his bulldozer. And Ed Pratt had followed with bricks and cement,
bringing out "temporary" foundations to support overhang-
ing sills and to close in the basement. A power pole, sawed on
a diagonal at the top, leaned across the drive from a concrete
base on the ground to the eaves, a brace against winter wind.

Have to paint that pole, Ted thought; wouldn't want it to
rot.

He moved again, drowning out the cicadas in the trees with
a not dissimilar sound.

His father had boarded up all the windows that first winter,
when there was no window glass and when he had been in
the hospital. At the Country Club, that was—with many
other people. He was among the lucky. Plenty of them hadn't
left that place alive. They'd died of about everything you
could think of, injuries and burns, shock and even of radiation, like that Catholic priest and the Baptist minister. So
many people . . . !

For a moment, the fear of those days returned to him. No
one had been sure of anything. Everything was short—food,
blankets, bandages, medicine. Nobody knew whether the war
was over or not; they knew only that the Soviet planes didn't
come back. Mobs were ravaging the countryside; for weeks
it seemed the armed forces couldn't stop them, couldn't restore order, couldn't prevent the looting and the murdering
and everything else. Everybody was scared, scared the bombers might return, scared the mobs might come back to the
cities or to what was left of cities.

That time passed.

Peace came. Then, for more weeks, the burying. It was
still going on when he could sit up in bed and look out the
window. They made a new cemetery of the Green Prairie

Country Club golf course, the last nine holes. Digging and blasting all through February and March, burying people, or whatever they found that had been a person. Later that spring, in common with other bombed cities, they designed their Cenotaph and it stood now above the graves—a monument to the ninety-some thousand known dead of Green Prairie. There was one in River City, also—for a hundred and twenty thousand. At what had been the ball park.

Ted mowed down the edge of the sidewalk.

It must have been—when?—around June, around this time, two years back, that they'd stopped all the mobs. What a job! *Still* a job! Some of the towns and villages that city dwellers had overrun were almost as bad off, afterward, as the bombed areas. Nobody knew, exactly, how many people had been killed by the crazed fugitives or how many people had been killed in self-defense and killed by the soldiers and the police. The total was thought to be more than a million. More than two million people had been hurt that way, besides, and as many more driven mad.

But things were getting better everywhere, and fast, now.

When he finished the edge of the walk, he went around the house, limping a little, for a bushel basket. His mother had set one out on the back porch. Before he picked it up, however, he stood on the porch, looking north.

Nora had been right: you could just see the top of the new Farm Industries Building that was being erected near the devastated area—Green Prairie's fourth huge postwar structure. It wasn't going to be a skyscraper, just an immense, horizontal building, with parking zones around it. Not that there were too many cars to park, as yet, Ted thought; or that there was much gasoline to run them.

The bushel basket, when he picked it up, seemed odd. It wasn't made the regular way and it didn't appear to be the right size. He saw faded stencil marks and read: *Produit de France*. The good old Frogs! he thought. In the "Aftertime," they'd kicked through—the French and, of course, the English, the Italians and Belgians and Dutch and the Latin-Americans and about everybody else except the Russians—who almost didn't exist—and the satellite countries.

With America bathed in blood, martyred, crucified, a flood of aid began. In that first dreadful winter, unreckoned millions of Ted's fellow citizens were saved by European bounty. He even recalled foreign labels on some of the medicine bottles at his bedside, when he'd been smashed up.

Now, the basket was another example. Everybody in U.S.A. owed something tangible to lots of people abroad. He chuckled a little, thinking what hell that had raised with the old "isolationists."

Then he went around in front of the dilapidated house, raked up a green mound of fresh-cut grass and carried it, in the French hamper, to the chicken yard. The Conners now had more than sixty chickens and five pigs. Henry was even angling for a cow; some of the Crystal Lake people had offered grazing room on their estates.

His mother came down the street, walking slowly because of the heat and because of her mood. But when she saw the mowed grass, saw her tall, broad-shouldered son mopping his sweaty light-brown hair, she moved faster and she smiled.

Ted knew where she had been. He didn't ask any questions—just said, "Hello! Been expecting you. Haven't we got company coming for supper?"

"A lot of people! The lawn looks lovely, Ted!"

"It would—if we had a matching house."

She laughed. Her eyes moved to the even more tatterdemalion house in which the Baileys had lived. "I think our place looks fine! Call it *quaint*." Her tone changed. "I believe Ruth is getting better, Ted! The doctors over at the Home think so, too!"

"No *fooling!*"

She nodded. "I'll bring you some iced coffee."

"Dandy!"

He was in the back yard when she brought coffee. He went indoors and washed before sitting down with her on the kitchen steps.

"You know," she said slowly to her son, "Ruth's never been able to say—what did happen."

"I know."

"She's *told!* The doctors a few days ago. And me just now!"

The young man gazed over the sun-yellowed green of the lawn to the cool blue-green of its shady places. "Bad, hunh?"

"Too awful to think about . . . !"

He drank the cold coffee, tinkled ice, refilled the glass from a pitcher. His mother's weekly visits to her sister, in the asylum they referred to as the "Home," invariably depressed her. Today, however, she seemed in a different frame of mind: hopeful, but frightened. Ted knew—most people in these days knew—a great deal about such attitudes. "Better tell me," he said. "Right now. And get it over with."

His mother glanced at him lovingly and nodded to herself. "I—I guess it isn't *really* any different from—thousands of stories like it. Only, when it's your own sister . . . ! Your own nieces and nephews . . . !"

"Sure," he said.

She sighed and her eyes looked far away. "They got the warning on the radio," she finally began, "the red signal. They started for the cellar, but it had a foot of water in it. Jim, the fool, decided not to take cover. The windows blew in on them, including new storm windows, she said. It—killed the baby, Irma—but . . ." She halted.

Ted murmured, "But what?"

"You see—Ruth was holding the baby and the baby's body saved her face. It ripped up Jim's face and chest. They— just decamped—ran away—like so many people. Ruth in the lead—the others following—holding a rope. Some teen- age boys, in a car, saw them—saw young Marie, that is. The boys stopped and talked. They soon got out and took Marie, and nobody's heard any more about her. She was only a little older than Nora."

Beth hesitated. Tears welled in her eyes.

"And then?"

She averted her face, but reached for his hand. Her voice continued evenly. "Ruth got them to the ball park. People were pouring into it. Ruth thought it was probably some kind of shelter or aid station. I suppose everybody on the outside got that idea. Inside, it was dreadful—packed. Jim had to lie down—he'd bled so badly, all that way. And—she'd— *dropped* the baby somewhere. It was dead. Anyhow, brands kept falling from the sky and finally the bleachers caught fire so badly no one could put them out. That was when peo- ple stampeded. Besides, there was a rumor going around that Russian planes would drop germ bombs on every large crowd. They did, too—where they found crowds! That whole mass of hurt grownups and kids started for the exits at once. Ruth rolled Jim under some steel seats—he was nearly unconscious —and she tried to save the youngsters."

"*Save* them?"

"Yes. From the mob. It was like a river of people, she said, like trying to protect them from a rising flood. And the kids were hysterical, sure they'd be burned to death, trying to get out. Don broke away with Tom, finally, and got sepa- rated from Ruth. Trampled. And a man actually yanked Sarah away from Ruth—because they were in his path—and hurled her to the ground. That was what happened." She wept sound-lessly.

"You mean—they *all* . . . ?"

"Most of the children in that ball park were trampled to death. It's—inhuman, isn't it? But that's what people do. Ruth lost the youngsters then and there. But, somehow, the crowd carried her out of the park without killing her. She was nearly suffocated by the pressure. Her feet didn't touch the ground for minutes at a time. She had ribs broken. But she was pushed and driven through a gate. When she could, she went back. She found Jim again and he was unconscious. So she stayed there. She thinks she was there—with thou-sands of others—for two days. Some of our people finally got to her and brought her out—and she doesn't remember much, after that, for a long time. You see, Jim had gone into a fever the day after, and died of it, or loss of blood, of un-treated infection—shock—all that. Her family was wiped out before her eyes—and she lived—and it's no *wonder* she—lost her reason!"

Ted turned his mother around and forced her head onto his shoulder. She wept quietly there and he held her. Because she was weeping, he felt relieved. If she hadn't cried, he would have worried. It was almost always the ones who didn't weep, didn't show emotion, didn't speak, who were liable to crack up later. Pretty much everybody knew that.

He knew, also, that she would soon do just about what she did.

She pulled herself away, blew her nose on a clean hand-kerchief with holes in it, and said, "Imagine a tough old charac-ter like me! But I just *couldn't* break up, in front of Ruth. I *had* to take it evenly. Ted! I really hope, now, she'll recover!"

"I wouldn't be surprised," he answered. "Not a bit. She could come home here."

"Do you think Henry would mind, if I tried having her here when the doctors say it's possible?"

Ted looked into his glass, empty again. "Sometimes, I think the old man doesn't mind anything this side of hell. He's got more guts than grizzly bears."

Mrs. Conner sniffled in a manner reminiscent of the younger Nora. "I know. And I'm glad I cried this out in front of you, Ted. Because now, I can tell *him* straight, without a whimper—if you promise not to tell on me, for being feeble-headed?"

He winked at her.

She bustled to her feet. "Here it is nearly four o'clock and I've got twenty-odd guests to feed!"

"Ye gods! I thought it was just us and the Laceys."

"I asked both families that have moved in the Bailey place." She glanced across. "They're new, and they don't know a soul in this part of town. I thought we'd get them acquainted. Their names are Brown and Frazetti."

"I know. Already met the Frazetti kids. Twins."

She nodded. "What about the Brown girl? Have you seen her?"

"Didn't know there was one."

"She's sixteen," his mother smiled. "Blue eyes and the prettiest red hair I ever saw. If you aren't in love with her by nine o'clock tonight, I'll lose a bet."

"Phooie," he said.

"Wait till you see her! Name's Rachel."

Ted looked, also, at the neighboring house. For a year and a half after X-day, it had been occupied by people billeted by town authorities. Then it had been roughly remodeled inside as a double house and occupied by two families. After one winter, they had moved again. The present occupants had arrived recently.

"I wonder what happened to Beau," he said.

She stopped in the screen door, holding the coffee pitcher and the glasses. "I doubt if we ever find out now!" She thought of her visit with her sister. "Though you can't tell, can you?"

"Nope."

It was the way it was in those days.

Lenore's mother had been sent to Florida and she was still there, undergoing plastic surgery. But Lenore's father had vanished.

Weeks had passed, months, and now two years and a half —with no word. The bureau set up by the Federal Government to trace people hadn't located him. Or any sign of him. Netta knew only that he'd been in the cellar when the Bomb burst. After that, he walked into the silences. He was one of the anonymous dead. Or one of the unidentified mad. Or one of the unfound bodies. Or someone who had a new name and a new life somewhere else—because he'd come to unable to remember, ever again, who he was, where he lived, what his name had been——or because he had wanted to forget.

Nora came home on her bike.

Since he had been thinking about the already-remote "Aftertime," Ted saw Nora in a new light. She was fourteen now and trying to behave like eighteen. Occasionally, for minutes at a time, the effort was fairly convincing. She'd changed in two years and half. She was hardly a kid now. There was something very precise and well-cut about her profile which (wonder of wonders, he thought) had an almost *sweet* look. Her nose didn't turn up so much. Her hair, light like his, was not lank like his any more; it was wavy, like their mother's. And her clear blue eyes were getting slanty—exactly, he thought, as Nora would prefer it: slanty-eyed women got the dangerous men, she claimed.

At this instant, however, she behaved on the kid side. "Mom!" she yelled through the kitchen screen, "Mr. Nesbit didn't have enough hamburger to make fifty patties. I got sixty hot dogs instead."

"That'll be fine, dear. And don't bellow."

She yodeled briefly, put away her bike, came around the house and approached her brother who was clipping edges. She then assumed her pseudo maturity. "Good afternoon, *beast.*"

"Greetings, afreet. How's things?"

"Ted. Will you give me an answer to a serious inquiry?"

"Sure. Any old answer. What's your problem?"

"I'm not kidding. Do you think it's *inevitably,* in *any* case, a mistake for a fourteen-year-old girl to be engaged?"

He concealed his grin by great attention to the grass. "Is she deeply in love?"

"Very," said Nora in a deeply-in-love tone.

"Well"—he rose on his knees, thought somberly—"is the boy able to support her?"

"He will be someday. He's extremely intellectual. He intends to become an anthropologist."

"Be all right," he said, nodding in self-agreement. "That is, if the girl's going to have a child."

"Oh! You *meanie!* You evil thing!"

"If they're going to have a child," he asserted in an offended tone, "I *really* think they *owe* it to the little stranger to marry."

"There are times," Nora said, "when you ought to be afraid the earth would open and swallow you up! I'm talking about the sacred kind of love, not the profane kind!"

"They're so interchangeable," Ted murmured. "You start out on the profane tack—and lo!—you're full of nice sentiments, just when you could do without them. *And* vice versa."

"*You!*" she said. "What do *you* know about it?" Idly, she raked up grass with her fingers and threw it on him. "A girl in my class," she said, "is leaving school this summer to take a job. I don't think it's sensible for a girl to abandon her education——"

"Maybe she's a moron."

"She's merely an orphan," Nora replied. "I wish school didn't last all summer, now. I bet I have to go clear through high school, this way. Just because so many schools got wrecked. I wish I could go to Europe on a student tour. Do you think Dad would ever let me?"

"Dad might, in a few more years. But would your fiancé?"

"Scum!" she said. "What's Queenie doing?"

"I dunno. I haven't asked him. Every pretty female in the block, doubtless."

"I mean—over by the Baileys'—by the old summerhouse?"

Ted peered through the hedge and across the sunlit lawns. "Search me!" The cat was staring in the gazebo, through the lattice, standing on his hind legs. "A peeping Tom cat, I guess."

"What a *lowlife*," she murmured fastidiously—and she went away, to see what Queenie was doing.

She came back in less than a minute, running. "Ted! Ted! Oh, Mom! Ted, you were right! The Crandons' angora is having kittens in there! His kittens, Queenie's, I bet!"

"*Sans doute*," he replied and rose, limping more than usual, as he followed her.

Even Mrs. Conner came out and looked. There were three kittens on a forgotten pillow—three, thus far. The Crandons' angora looked proud; Queenie looked appropriately suspicious, pleased, defiant and generally paternal.

"How dreamy!" Nora kept saying. "How perfectly dreamy!"

"Profane love," her brother suggested, with a wise nod of the head.

"It is *not!* Cats don't . . ."

"What on earth," Mrs. Conner asked, "are you two fighting about?"

"Nora's life interest of the moment," Ted said, beating her to the reply, leaving his sister open-mouthed. "Something people for years have been calling sex."

Beth chuckled. "You better get dressed. Your father will be along soon. And you still have to bathe, Ted."

Henry Conner signed his mail, said good night to his secretary and went down two flights of stairs to the ground floor of the West Side store of J. Morse and Company. The main building and the warehouses had, of course, vanished with the Bomb. They were using the West Side branch for business offices now and would go on doing so until the new Morse Building was finished. At present, it was a set of blueprints, the work of Charles Conner. Under the Emergency Building Code, they wouldn't even lay the cornerstone for nearly another year.

He walked along the sales aisles, enjoying, as always, the sights and smells of a hardware store—glitter of chrome, glass and steel—geometrical array of hand tools, garden tools, ornaments, plumbing fixtures, the splashes of color in the kitchenware section, the aroma of tar and rope and metal and machine oil.

The Oldsmobile was parked behind the store, near the loading area. It gave him an almost sentimental feeling: it would be good for quite a few more years. The old buggy had taken quite a beating, though. He looked in the trunk, to check, and drove away in the hot sunshine, aware that its hotness was diminishing, that there was a breeze. He was scheduled to pick up Charles first, then Pad Towson and Berry Black, then Lenore. Next week the car pool would be Towson's lot.

Charles wasn't waiting at their meeting place.

Henry was glad. He parked the Olds and got out. He looked for a while at the building where his elder son worked. The Green Prairie Professional Building had been the first one erected according to the new plan and the first one to invade the "total destruction" area. It wasn't high, not a skyscraper, only four stories. But it was as tremendous as the Pentagon-that-was, in Washington-that-used-to-be. It was something like a ranch house, but blocks long, with many "L's" and "courtyards" between them, with gardens, patios, glassed-in restaurants, even a skating rink in the courtyards.

Someday Green Prairie and River City would have a hundred such buildings all around the circle of ruins, and inside it, and here and there out to the suburbs besides. "Semidecentralized," they called it, and "horizontal expansion." It replaced the vertical growth of the skyscraper age which had let fumed air, heat and darkness and slums accumulate in its canyons.

These buildings took more room, but as architects like Charles had argued—why not? There was plenty of room for them in the prairies. They *left* plenty of room, too, room for broad streets with underpasses at intersections, room for vast parking areas, room for gardens, for parks, for picnic grounds right in the center of the city, room for swimming pools and dance floors and everything else that added to life's enjoyment.

It had not been so difficult as many had expected to "sell"

the once-crowded city dwellers on the new pattern for living. Most people had detested many aspects of urban living. And even those who clung to old ideas habitually were shaken in their conservatism. For nobody who had lived in a bombed city wanted to spend another hour, if he or she could help it, in such a deathtrap. To be sure, there was no menace, any longer, of bombs. But the memory that haunted millions slowly pervaded the whole population. Hence the new, "wide-open" cities satisfied unconscious fears, even in people who otherwise would have clung to the traditional-style city: to the narrow streets, the picket-fence skyline, the congestion, suffocation, gloom and noise.

Indeed, by this time, unhit cities were considered "obsolete." Those that had been bombed provided people with a surge of exhilaration, for the bombing had proved an ultimate blessing by furnishing a brand-new chance to build a world brand-new—and infinitely better.

So Henry gazed at the structure where his son worked. Then he faced around, walked to a fence, and drank in the scene opposite.

The rough circularity of the destroyed area could be perceived from where he stood, though a man in the middle of that desolation could see the circle more plainly. Such a man could pivot three hundred and sixty degrees: everywhere the earth would sweep away, bare and comparatively flat, to standing buildings (or ruins) approximately equidistant from his position.

Now, looking across from one edge, Henry drew a big breath and expelled it with force. He never could get it through his head that something his living room could easily contain had removed the familiar cityscape, left it as nude as this. And all in a night, consuming in hours what had taken men generations to put there.

Now, in summer, weeds were growing out there. The red-brown nothing was relieved by sprawls of green. And the arid circle was bisected by the river. Its blue water could be seen, darker where the afternoon breeze ruffed it. On Swan Island, there was a tangled mound, a pimple on the earthen face, where the tracks of the roller coaster had been vaporized, leaving, nevertheless, sundry heaps and embankments that had supported other rides and contained the chute-the-chutes pond. That earth had not been boiled away, or wholly flattened.

Near the perimeters, in the river, he could see the rusting, rectilinear tops of collapsed bridges. These hadn't been pulled clear yet, hadn't been sent back to the smelters. And everywhere, making a din, sending up dust, machines worked. Like men on Mars, they lumbered in this desert, disinterring and reburying, with mammoth indifference to all meaning. If one watched a particular dozer or earth-mover, one would see the substance of archaeology, the potsherds of recent twentieth-century Americans. A refrigerator would be turned up, or a bathtub, or a kitchen stove or, perhaps, stone foundations, a brick wall. These would be pushed into shallows, crushed flat, covered again—to make a firm base for the coming metropolis.

It had been going on for a long time.

The fumbling engines had labored there in winter, scarring the snowfalls, making dark tracks and darker scars in the white circle. They had sloshed there during the past spring when heavy rains had turned the area into a land of small lakes and of uncharted streams that backed up, overflowed and ran on until they finally found the route to the river and added their colored muds. Someday the engines would finish. Paving machines would follow, planting machines—the masons, carpenters, roofers, electricians, plumbers—all of them.

Someday, where he looked at dusty nothing, a new city would rise.

By and by, no one would remain even to miss the old one. When all the mourners had died, Henry thought.

Then the Bomb would be no catastrophe at all, but pure benefit. "End of an era," they would say. "Good thing, too," they'd add. "Can't imagine how they stood those old cities," they'd assert. "Barbaric." "Positively medieval."

It seemed incredible to Henry, for a moment. But he was a shrewd if humble student of his fellow man, so he knew it to be true. Nobody rued a billion buried Egyptians or sorrowed for gone Romans. A few marveled or rejoiced at what they, in their crushed past, had contributed to the present; but not one grieved over the cruelty of time's heel. Even Pompeii was viewed as an excitement. Henry could not recall one touring neighbor who had brought home from its ashes a sense of melancholy. So it would be here. So it should be.

He felt Chuck's hand on his shoulder. "A penny," Chuck said. He didn't wait for the thought he'd bargained for. "Great day, Dad! Old Minerva Sloan finally accepted our drawings—mine, that is—for the new bank building! May mean a partnership! But, *brother!* Is that crippled old dame a sourball!"

Henry said, "Peachy!" He held his hand out, gravely.

They walked together to the car.

Henry carried his thought along one more step. Everywhere catastrophe had struck, something other than rank weeds grew in the ash, the crumpled walls: opportunity. Opportunity for young men like his son who were able to dream and able to put the dreams on paper so other men could turn them into substance.

They picked up Pad Towson and Berry Black and, finally,

Lenore. The men were just two businessmen coming home from work, tired, looking forward to whatever home meant: a hot soak in a tub, slippers, a highball, a meal.

But Lenore was different. Excited. Privately excited, for she slipped into the front seat between Charles and her father-in-law and silently took her husband's hand, keeping her eyes on him.

They delivered their passengers before she began to tell, talking to Charles but permitting Henry to hear. "I've got *news*."

"I can see that!" Charles smiled and kept back his own "news."

"Good news. I *think* it is."

Henry sensed the tenseness in his son's voice. "Are you going to *tell* it?"

"I'm pregnant."

Henry heard his own faint breath-catch. He slowed down, jostled, as Chuck wrapped his arms around her. "I thought . . ." Chuck broke off.

After they had kissed, she said, "So did I! So did Dr. Mandy, at first! I got so *much* radiation! Now we know different! I'm *not* sterile."

Charles whispered, "That's just too wonderful to believe."

She said, matter-of-factly, being Lenore, "It's actually only seventy-five per cent wonderful."

"Which is enough miracle for these days!"

Henry butted in, perplexedly. "I don't get . . . ?" He checked himself. "Oh," he said.

Lenore turned to him then, and took his arm too, hugged him also. "About a quarter of the babies, Dr. Mandy said, are born dead—or not in their right minds—if their mothers were rayed."

Chuck murmured, with the extra poignancy of the still-new

husband, "That's a *terrible* thing to face, I know! But *Lenore, dear . . .* !"

She said, "Not *too* terrible. Just means I might have to have four, for every three we keep. So what? Can't you imagine how *I* feel, to know I can *have* them? And does this country need babies *now!*"

Henry let go of the wheel with his right hand. He reached out, touched her dark hair, moved his hand under it, found her neck, squeezed it lightly and went back to driving. He didn't say anything more than the touch said. But she looked toward him fondly as she snuggled against Charles. It would be, she felt, the finest thing on earth to have a father like Charles. But, certainly, it would be *almost* as fine to have such a grandfather as Henry Conner would make a boy—or a girl.

At the house, they could see smoke from the fire in the barbecue pit, and the assembled next-door neighbors, along with the Laceys and their children. Two strangers besides.

Henry went around and opened the car trunk. Al had put the keg in at five. It was wet with its own coldness. A whole keg of beer, and a bung-starter with it—beside the tire tools.

"Gimme a hand," he called.

But Chuck was already streaking through the hedge. "What do you think?" he called. "Lenore's going to have a baby! I'm going to be the father of a child!"

Mrs. Conner's eyes blurred with happiness.

Nora Conner's did not. "That's *nothing!*" she said. "Queenie's just *been* the father—of five."

Henry came up. "Somebody help me with the beer. . . ."

Beth reached out, caught his sleeve and whispered, "A couple of professors here, Henry. They're making a survey of the region to find out why things went so badly in River City and so well, comparatively, over here. I hope you don't mind. I asked them to stay for supper."

Henry looked across the lawn and again spotted the men. "Hell," he said. "Time we quit talking about it! Only difference was, some of us tried to swap freedom for security; the rest of us went on *fighting* for freedom, as usual."

"Tell them that," Beth said. "They'll never find a better answer, no matter how smart they are, or how long they ask."

Henry's eyes moved, stopped again. "Who's that redhead Ted's mawking at?"

"Lives next door," Beth replied. "She's mighty sweet."

Henry stared at the girl a moment longer. Then his twinkling affectionate gaze traveled on to the Bailey house. "Kind of where we came in, isn't it, Mother?"

"People don't change very much or very fast," she smiled.

Henry nodded and walked over to meet the professors and his new neighbors.

The sun went down and left the lawn in gilded light.

Queenie yawned—and touched his mouth delicately.